ABOUT THE AUTHOR

DR. ROBERT T. CROWLEY could write this excit-
ing story about a surgeon because he has travelled
the same road himself. It is rare for a surgeon of Dr.
Crowley's distinction to turn his hand to novels.
Robert Crowley has not only reached the top of the
medical tree (he has served on the staff at Bellevue
and Lenox Hill Hospitals in New York, the Alfred
Jennings Hospital in Detroit, and now runs his own
clinic in Kinsman, Ohio), he has also published one
highly successful suspense novel, COFFER OF
SATURNO and a series of medical novels.

SOME WITH STEEL

by Robert T. Crowley, M.D.

*"Some physicians
try to cure with herbs,
and draughts, and simples.
And some with steel
cut at the dying flesh."*

—GREEK FRAGMENT

POPULAR LIBRARY • NEW YORK

DEDICATED—To the Professor and all he taught

Mortuus Adhuc Loquitur
(Though Dead He Still Speaks On)

1

The Charity Hospital sprawls at one of the crossroads of the city's badlands. It is a massive architectural abortion of brick, limestone, and more brick, with the general look of a mausoleum. Its size, and grimness, like its cost to the taxpayers, are monumental. The vaultlike main entrance is on St. Marks Street. Glowering across from it, in a kind of sinister rivalry, is the Criminal Courts building. There a heroic bronze figure of Justice, sworded, blindfolded, and scales-bearing, broods on a pedestal between granite columns.

Behind the Charity is Hastings Hill. Hastings is hardly a hill, but a low, wide slope, smoky and noisome. On it a jam of factories belch soot, smells, and metal products to the railroad and the river below. East of the Charity is Velle Street. Velle is the extremity of the city's down-at-the-heel business section. Cheap, dubious, and cut-rate enterprises fight losing battles against bankruptcy along it. Pawnbrokers, bail bonders, and loan sharks have addresses there. It is bum-infested by day and whore-haunted at night. The Frivolity Burlesque Theater is on Velle and so is the Asterion Cafe. Mercer is the Charity's west-bounding street. Most of Mercer Street is taken up by the Public Market. What is left of it is a jumble of small and mostly legitimate business concerns. These form a semi-respectable buffer between the Charity and the maze of ramshackle tenements and dead falls lying beyond.

From this strategic position below the city's navel, the Charity functions as a cloacal organ. It receives, filters, and excretes the swarming masses of human molecules around it. Like any cloaca the Charity is ugly, dirty, and necessary. Along with this it has some peculiar distinctions. One of them is that, from time to time, it probably shelters as much diseased human protoplasm per cubic foot as any lazar house in the world. By reason of this, the Charity is unexcelled in its opportunity for the observation of sickness and death. Sickness and death are the particular province of physicians and a lot of physicians have learned about them there.

Much of that learning is acquired in the clammy precinct of the Charity morgue. Here a large part of the constant current of disease and death flowing through the Charity's wards and operating rooms ends on the autopsy table. The dead protoplasm composing that current is systematically dissected, examined, and the findings recorded. Whatever ailed it during life is thereby usually determined. In any case, all diagnoses made there are officially final and the individual body becomes another number in an endless file. The Charity's morgue is thus its ultimate clearing house, and like most clearing houses, it is in continuous operation. One or more of its porcelain-topped tables is likely to be in use at any hour of the day or night with varying spectators. The autopsy surgeon and his assistant are always there of course, and at one time or another so are the undertakers. Most of the time there is a small delegation of interns and residents of the Charity staff. And very frequently there is a representation from the police. This is because the Charity and the law have a long-standing and intimate relationship. All accident cases, mayhem and assault injuries, attempted murder and suicide, dead or alive, are brought to the Charity, along with the line of duty cases from the police force itself. It is not unusual to find policemen at a Charity post-mortem at any time, particularly from the Homicide Bureau located in the Criminal Courts building across the street. . . .

That afternoon the audience in the morgue was larger and a good deal more impressive than usual. The interest of the Homicide Bureau was apparent from the presence of Inspector Rybecki himself, and a retinue of two subordinate sleuths. The inspector, very sharply attired in a new green suit with matching shirt, tie, and handkerchief, sat in one of the front-tier seats. He flashed his gold teeth elegantly in a smile as Roy came in. Beside the inspector, Capshaw of the press sat lethargically. Capshaw, still unwashed and sleepless from a session at night court, picked his nose reflectively as he scribbled on a pad. Next to him was that familiar exponent of the mortician's art Mr. Mario Lopardi, guiding genius and owner of the Elite Funeral Parlours (Funerals of Distinction). Obviously Mr. Lopardi regarded the occasion as important. He had come in person this time instead of dispatching an assistant to collect and bear away the remains. More than that he had sneaked away early from another and probably cheaper funeral to do it. This was apparent from his courtly dress. His skinny body was encased in a cutaway and striped trousers only somewhat threadbare and oversize. These, the rusty derby, winged collar, and Ascot tie gave Lopardi a tarnished, old-world look something like a Balkan diplomat. There was also the usual representation from the Charity staff, a few residents and interns lounging in the back-tier chairs.

Roy returned the inspector's nod, gave a cold eye to Lopardi, and went to the locker rack. He took the cigarettes and matches out of his tunic and put on the long rubber apron. He had powdered his hands and was getting on his gloves when Lopardi rose uneasily from his seat.

"Dr. Maines . . ." There was an earnest unction in Lopardi's voice.

"Yeah, Lopardi, what is it?"

"I was wondering about what time I could have the body."

"Same time as always. When we get through with it."

"Before five o'clock?"

"I said when we're through with it."

Lopardi mused for a moment. He looked at Roy sorrowfully.

"Couldn't you be a little cooperative, Dr. Maines? I'm asking because the family's anxious about the time of the funeral. I've got to tell them when—"

Roy turned on him irritably. "Listen, Lopardi, this goes on every time there's an autopsy when you're in on the body. You're one of the few undertakers who's always sniffing around and making a Goddamn nuisance of himself. Go on back and sit down, will you?"

"I'm only considering the family, Doctor. They want the funeral as soon as possible. You see—"

"Who do you think you're kidding, Lopardi? 'Only considering the family,' my ass. Only considering yourself you mean. You buck-hungry little guinea bastard. You don't want to hang around that trap of yours doing a late embalming job. That's it and I know it, see? So don't give me any of that pious horseshit about the family. I'm sick of it. You've probably got this funeral figured for one of your bigger clips—a thousand dollars or something. Go on back to that Goddamn charnel house of yours and wait. You'll be called the minute we're through."

"But I promised the family there could be a viewing—"

"To hell with what you promised the family. This is a medical examiner's case and you know it. It's got to be a complete autopsy, including the head, and we're going to take our time."

"I was told—"

"I don't give a damn what you were told."

"You always want my cooperation," Lopardi said. Roy cut him short. "The Pathology Department of the Charity always wants the cooperation of all undertakers about autopsies. The trouble is we don't get it. Particularly from you. Anytime we want a post-mortem on a case you have the undertaking job on we have a hell of a time getting it. If you talk to the family first we almost never do."

Lopardi spread his bony hands.

"But I don't have anything to do with that Dr. Maines. It's up to the family about that. I ain't the family. I can't give consent."

Roy looked at him contemptuously. He had his gloves on and a cigarette lit. As soon as Sam Lohman came to help, he was ready to work.

"Look, Lopardi, let's not have any more crap about this shall we? I'm tired and I've got a lot on my mind. But while we're at it let me tell you something. I've been an intern on pathology for quite a while now so I know a lot of undertakers and I know you.

"Here's what happens almost always. We want the autopsy because we want to know the cause of death, so we try like hell to get an autopsy. We ask for it from whoever's responsible in the family. The family's pretty upset with the death and the rest of it. They don't know whether to say yes or no, so they ask the advice of a couple of people. Usually the priest and the undertaker. If they both say yes, we get it. If either one says no, we don't. The family's never keen on having their dead cut anyway. The funny thing is that the priest almost always says yes to the family. But not you. You always try to talk them out of it. You tell them it will ruin the body and all that. I can give you about a dozen instances where you've done it, and don't deny it." Just then Sam Lohman, the pathology technician, came in the door.

"Hello, Doc," Sam said. "Sorry, I'm late."

Sam looked at Roy and then at Lopardi. The situation was apparent at a glance. Lopardi's gesthsemanes about autopsied bodies were no novelty to Sam. They had happened too frequently. Sam had a sense of humor and no reverence—

"What's the matter?" Sam said. "The guinea vulture upset because he can't heist the meat home right away?"

"Yeah," Roy said. "Stricken with grief about the bereft family. He deeply shares their sorrow."

Sam hurriedly began getting on his apron and gloves.

"Maybe you forgot, Doc. Mr. Lopardi has grave responsibilities to the public. Very conscientious, too, especially when there's a buck in the wind. Only looking out for the welfare of the dead aren't you, signor?"

Sam grinned at Lopardi.

Lopardi ignored Sam.

"May I ask just one favor, Dr. Maines?"

"Go ahead," Roy said, "as if I didn't know."

"Would you please remember to tie off the big vessels so I can embalm the face right? The last time they weren't tied and—"

"I'll tie them," Roy said. "Why don't you go to a graveyard somewhere and forget about it? Go die somewhere so you can tell the customers what it feels like. But for Christ's sake stop bothering me."

Lopardi shook his head dejectedly and sat down.

"Let's get started, Sam," Roy said.

They turned to the body on the glistening expanse of white enamel. Sam cut away the coarse cotton cloth of its swathing while Roy looked at the accompanying chart. The official medical examiner's form clipped to it gave the usual terse details. "Di Genova, Guido Francesco, male, white, 50 years, etc." Roy studied it briefly, picked up a knife, and turned to the body.

What was left of Guido Di Genova was a stiff, waxen effigy of a man in middle life. The heavy arms, now wooden in their rigidity, were attached to a barrel chest. Both chest and arms were profusely tattooed. The thickly muscled neck supported a square jut of jaw. The rest of the face was strangely well molded and benign. The most arresting features of the body was neither its face, development, nor tattooing, but the four black holes through the front of the chest and upper abdomen. These holes were obviously the cause of Di Genova's body being on the slab. The gun had apparently been fired at extremely close range and the black holes explained the attention his remains were getting from the professions of medicine, law, press, and the trade of undertaking.

Roy made the conventionally shaped incision, extending from the ends of the collarbones to the center of the chest and down the midline of the belly. Inspector Rybecki rose casually, lit a cigarette, and came to the table. He looked meditatively at the corpse and the work upon it.

"Got it good, didn't he, Doc?"

Roy nodded, rapidly turning back the skin flaps formed by the incision.

"You know," Rybecki went on reflectively, "this one was a real bad son-of-a-bitch, but pretty smart at that. We had the bastard in the line-up so much he practically ran it himself. Twenty-four arrests and only two convictions with light sentences. We been trying to hang it on him good for a long time and never really could. What time did he finally go out, Doc?"

"Don't know exactly," Roy said. "Take a look at the chart will you, Sam?"

Sam wiped his hands on a dry sponge and thumbed the clip of papers.

"Says here admitted 2 A.M., expired 8:02 A.M."

The inspector nodded. "The son-of-a-bitch lived six hours with all them slugs in him. Tough boy, eh Doc?"

"Must have been."

"Any idea what he got it for?" Sam said.

The inspector sucked his gold teeth thoughtfully. "Yeah, we got a pretty good idea what for, but not who did it. This hood was a farily big dope pusher. H and C both. He hung around over on Velle Street mostly. We knew what he was doing and like I said we had him in the line-up damned near every session, but we could never get him right. Too smart to carry it on him, used drops and blinds all the time to pass it. It went along good for him quite awhile and then something happened. It's hard to say exactly what. Usually when this happens to a junk pusher he's started cutting his stuff too much, yapping around too loud, or threatening to sing on somebody."

"That doesn't sound big," Sam said. "Why a big deal about him? How come the big law and the press over here just for him?"

"The thing that figures here," Rybecki said, "is the tip we got. A while back one of our best stoolies said he was about ready to sing on somebody big. I think that's what he got hit for—to shut him up. I think maybe I even got some idea who, but not enough yet. If we could prove it we'd really have a hot thing going. It'd be plastered in every paper in the country. That's why Capshaw's over here smelling around—right, Cappy?"

The inspector jerked his head around to Capshaw, still abstractedly picking his nose and writing.

"What's that, officer?" Capshaw looked up.

"I said you owned controlling interest in Stasia Kondoleon's whorehouse—the cheap one on Peake Street."

"Right," Capshaw said, "come in anytime. Inspectors can get it on credit."

Capshaw began writing again; the inspector turned back grinning.

"That Capshaw's a Goddamn card," he said.

Roy cut the breast bone and ribs and began sponging the bloody fluid out of the open chest.

Lopardi watched this procedure apprehensively, leaning forward in his seat. Finally he got up and came over.

"Mr. Lopardi, the mortician, to see you, Doctor," Sam said. Roy glanced up at Lopardi in annoyance.

"Now what, Lopardi?"

"I just wanted to remind you to tie off the big vessels. You see—"

Roy compressed his lips and straightened up from the table.

"Goddamn it, Lopardi, one more peep out of you about this post and you're going to be thrown out of here right on your skinny ass. Now sit down and shut up or else."

Lopardi retired sorrowfully. He pulled his coattails up carefully as he sat down again.

"The guinea meat specialist giving you a bad time, Doc?" The inspector's teeth glinted in amusement.

"He's been grousing around all morning about this post," Roy said.

"Dr. Maines has become callous," Sam said. "He is blind to the concern of a true artisan about his work."

"This is liable to be a very big thing for Lopardi," the inspector said. "He don't get a funeral like this every day in the week. This Di Genova was supposed to have a lot of scratch stashed away. He got away selling the stuff for a long time and kept what he got for it. Lopardi figures the widow Di Genova will want to give him quite a send-off. She's taking it pretty big. A full-course guinea funeral is some family tombola."

"I've never seen one," Sam said.

"Well, you ought to," Rybecki said. "Don't miss one if you get the chance. It's the Goddamndest whoop-te-do you've ever seen. An Irish wake ain't nothing beside it. You Jews," he nodded to Sam, "ain't got nothing much either by comparison. All you do is wind the guy up on a sheet, slap him between a couple of boards like a hamburger, and plant him before he's really cool. Then you stand around at the grave and yowl and start ripping your clothes apart. According to the guineas that ain't the way to say 'aw revoor' to the deceased. When one of them flips they really make a federal case out of it if the family's got any dough at all to do it with. That right, Lopardi?"

"I'm sorry, Inspector," Lopardi said. "I didn't quite hear what you were saying."

"I said all undertakers are pimps on the side when business is bad."

Lopardi did not answer.

"No sense of humor," Rybecki said.

"Mr. Lopardi is sensitive," Sam said. "His professional duties make him moody."

Working methodically, Roy tied off the great vessels in the chest and removed the heart.

"Yeah, like I was saying," the inspector went on, "the guineas really lay it out for the deceased. Nothing too good for the defunct. If they ain't got the dough on hand to do it with, they go borrow it. The departed gets the full treatment —first-class embalming job so he looks healthier than he did before he cooled, fancy casket with eight handles, couple of truckloads of flowers, and a band."

"A band?" Sam said.

"Hell, yes, a band, big or little, but a band. Usually a couple of trumpets, trombone, one of those big, mooing, fart horns, whatever you call them, and a flute or two, but a band anyway. They get the guy all decked in the hearse, under the flowers, in his bronze casket and in a soup and fish suit. The band tunes up and they fall in and take off around the block. The broads are all in black and so is everyone else in the parade. They get to blubbering and moaning and crying more and more at every step, even people around who didn't even know the guy, so by the time it winds up you can hardly hear the music. Then after it's all over everybody gets swilled on guinea redeye and goes home still crying. It's a great show but expensive. Don't miss going to one—Jesus!" —the inspector suddenly interrupted his own disquisition— "take it easy, will you, Doc? This here's a brand-new suit!"

Roy had taken out the heart and lungs and dropped them with a splatter on the drainage table in front of the foot tank.

"Sorry, Inspector," Roy said. He picked up another sharp tool and began making long, regularly spaced cuts through the tissue. The knife grated on hardness.

"Here's one of them," Roy said, picking something out of the last incision.

"That one of the slugs?"

Roy nodded and passed it to Sam, who washed it in the drainage tank and put it on the side table.

"Lower lobe of the left lung," Roy said.

The knife grated again. Roy passed another one of the deformed pellets to Sam.

"Lower part of left upper lobe."

".38's," the inspector said authoritatively. "Don't lose any of them will you, Doc? I got to mark 'em all and take them over to ballistics for checking. Hey, Manny."

He turned to one of the lethargic subordinates behind him.

"Manny, get on the phone and see if those late pick-up guns are .38's, .38 automatics."

Manny nodded, rose heavily, and went over to the desk phone. Roy examined the lungs closely and then went back to the body and searched the opening in the chest.

"Here's number three imbedded in the thoracic vertebra —looks like it nicked the vein. That's where most of the bleeding in the chest was coming from."

Roy dug the bullet out with a pick chisel and handed it over to Sam. He dipped his gloved hands in the foot tank, dried them on gauze, and lit a cigarette before opening the abdomen. He looked toward the back of the room where Ransahoff, the resident on emergency, was smoking and talking with a couple of interns.

"Hey, Ransahoff and you guys come here."

Ransahoff and the boys detached themselves from their seats and came over.

"What you got there, Roy?" Ransahoff asked, supporting his thin, stooping body by his elbows on the foot tank.

"You wanted to see the chest cavity when I got it cleaned out. Here it is."

Ransahoff craned foward a little.

"Does he have a cut intercostal, Roy? He had a hell of a lot of blood in the chest when he came in. I thought the slugs probably got one of them."

"The intercostals are all right but one of them nicked the hemiazygos vein. That's probably where most of his chest hemorrhage was coming from. Here, look here."

Roy stuck a probe in place in the vertebra where he had dug out the third bullet.

"Jesus," Ransahoff agreed, "right through the side of it. No wonder he never really got out of shock. All the blood and plasma we poured into him down in the emergency room went right out that hole."

Ransahoff shook his head sadly.

"Think of all that plasma and blood we wasted—2000 c.c.'s of blood and 2000 c.c.'s of plasma."

"If you guys in admitting had been on the ball this guy would probably have made it," Roy jeered, winking at Sam.

"Why, you bastard, you, Maines," Ransahoff said. "We did everything but suckle him at our own breasts down in emergency. The surgeons killed him."

"Like hell, you were probably over at the Greek's having a hamburger. To hear you admitting-room guys tell it, if you'd had a pint of plasma and a couple of c.c.'s of adrenalin you could have fixed Christ up after the crucifixion."

"There's something to that," Ransahoff agreed gravely. "By the way, are you going to open up the abdomen now, or stand around with your finger up?"

The inspector, who had been following the conversation with amused interest, turned to Ransahoff. "Did you take care of him when he was first brought in, Doc?"

"Yeah, I was on last night."

"Listen, tell me something. Did he talk at all? Mention any names that you heard? Anything like that? Like who done it?"

"No, not that I heard. Hell, he was in too bad shape then to do any talking. Deep shock—no pulse and no blood pressure. I heard he came around a little bit though after we got him up to the ward."

Rybecki nodded. "Yeah, I saw him right after that. He was conscious then when they brought his wife in. He wouldn't say a Goddamn thing. I had a stenog from headquarters over to take any statement. Didn't get a Goddamn thing though. Bastards like this never talk."

Roy had the abdomen open now and was methodically exploring the pale, glistening bowel that rose above the bloody fluid.

Capshaw finished writing, stuffed the pad and pencil stub in the side pocket of his shapeless topcoat, yawned, and sauntered over.

"Operation a success, Doctor?" Capshaw inquired casually.

Roy glanced up briefly.

"You don't hear any complaints from the patient, do you Cappy?"

"That's because the anesthesia's good."

"The best there is," Roy said.

"Any more dope on this?" Capshaw turned to Rybecki.

"You got all we got, Cappy. Wait a minute. Hey, Manny."

Manny moved ponderously at the desk where he had finished telephoning and was sitting tilted back in the chair with his feet up, looking blankly at nothing.

"Ballistics got a couple of .38's over there picked off of guys in the line-up. That's all, Inspector."

"That's a startling development," Capshaw said. "That all?"

"What the hell do you want, Cappy?" Rybecki said, "the killer for questioning and the trial record already? This Goddamn thing just broke at two this morning."

"The press expects very rapid disclosures in this instance because that astute nemesis of crime, Inspector Stanislaus Rybecki, is on the case," Capshaw said.

"Balls to you. Don't start biting the hand that feeds you. Anything we get that can be released you'll get. Ain't I always been right with you?"

"An inexhaustible source of oracular information, Inspector. Incidentally, did the bereaved Madame Di Genova make any comment?"

"Nothing so far. Probably don't know much. We had her over at headquarters right after her boy here flipped. She ain't bad—quite a dish in fact. Charlie went right on the make for her didn't you, Charlie? Charlie here is hell with the women."

The inspector's other thickset henchman grunted unappreciatively. Capshaw, like the rest of them, had been watching Roy complete the final stages of systematic carnage on the body. He looked at his watch and yawned widely.

"Anything unusual about all this, Doc? Any unexpected findings?"

Roy looked up.

"Just what you see, Cappy. Multiple gunshot wounds. Death due to shock and hemorrhage. That's all, Cappy. Any one of those bullets could have killed him."

"Thanks, Doc." Capshaw scratched his chin and addressed the rest of them collectively. "Any of you gentlemen care to join me in a drink? Inspector? Anybody?"

The inspector shook his head. "Got to get back to the shop, Cappy. Next time."

There were no takers. Capshaw pulled his hat down and was about to start for the door. At this point it opened and the Old Man came in.

"It's the Old Man," Sam said to Roy under his breath.

Roy straightened at once as he came over to the table. The Old Man's eyes swept the body and the group at the table.

"Good afternoon, gentlemen," the Old Man said. There was a chorus of respectful replies.

"Almost done, Maines?"

"Yes, sir, just about—all there is now is the sew up and the dictation."

The Old Man looked fixedly at the body for a moment.

"Death due to hemorrhage?"

"Yes, sir."

"Why didn't they operate him?"

"He never got out of shock, sir," Roy said.

The Old Man nodded to the group again and went out.

"The big boy," the inspector said, looking after him.

"That's right," Sam said.

"I hear there's nothing he can't do in the line of cutting. I also hear he's as tough as they come."

"That's right too," Roy said.

"Well, I hope he's around when I get mine. Maybe he'll cheat you guys out of another job like this."

"There's nobody better," Roy said.

"Old Lopardi gets the meat early after all," the inspector said, grinning. "Say, Doc, would you mind cleaning off them slugs real good? And dry them good. I don't want to get any crap on this here suit."

"Sam, get an envelope out of the desk and put them in it for him, will you?"

"Never mind that," Rybecki said. "Just dry 'em good and I'll put them in my pocket."

Sam dipped the pellets several times in the clean water of the foot tank, dried them on a swatch of gauze, and dropped them in the inspector's hand.

"They're all marked the same, Inspector."

Rybecki turned toward his inert henchmen. "O.K. boys, off your asses and let's get back to the shop."

He lingered for a minute curiously watching the whipped inverting stitch Roy was making to close the incision.

"Well, that's one more lousy no-good son-of-a-bitch I can scratch," he said.

"*De mortuis nihil nisi bonum,*" Sam said.

The inspector arched his eyebrows at Sam. "What's that?"

"*De mortuis nihil nisi bonum,* it's Latin," Sam said.

"Hell, I know it's Latin or some kind of fancy subjunctive talk you scientists use," Rybecki said. "What's it mean?"

"Concerning the dead, speak only good," Sam said, translating literally.

"I'll let Lopardi take care of that department. He'll speak good of him if he gets paid for the funeral. Hear that, Lopardi? Talk nice about this bastard. So long, boys . . . Doc."
Followed by his deputies, Rybecki went out the door.

The closure was done now and Roy dipped his gloved hands in the head tank and began washing the sponges. Sam brought the stiff hands together across the chest and tied the thumbs together with a strip of gauze.

"O.K., all yours, Lopardi," Roy said. "Where's your wagon?"

"It's out at the back ramp, Dr. Maines," Lopardi said, getting up quickly. "We'll move it right out." Lopardi departed, followed by Ransahoff and the others.

Roy pulled the neck strings loose on his apron and took it off, then he removed his gloves and sat down at the desk. He pulled the rubberized cover from the battered portable dictaphone, checked the disc, and picked up the mouthpiece, pressing the release button at the side. The disc began revolving slowly. Roy lit another crumpled cigarette and began the dictation.

"Autopsy Number 383. Medical Examiner's Case. Performed 4:30 P.M., October 17. Dr. Roy Maines for the Medical Ex. Six copies, two to Homicide Bureau."

He paused, released the button, and began again.

"The body is that of a well-developed, well-nourished adult white male, five feet ten and one-half inches in height and weighing an estimated one hundred and seventy pounds . . ."

The recording disc ground on to the rapid monotony of his voice. Sam finished cleaning the table and the tools. This done he took off his gloves and apron. At this point the door swung back to admit Lopardi and his assistant with the dead basket and the stretcher on which they wheeled it. They transferred the body from the table to the basket and latched it. Then Lopardi came over to the desk. Lopardi's tone was conciliatory.

"I'd like to thank you, Dr. Maines, for tying off the vessels. It makes things a lot easier for us."

"O.K., Lopardi."

Lopardi stood hesitantly looking at him.

"Dr. Maines, I just wanted to say I hope there's no hard feelings. I'd appreciate it if you'd go over to the Asterion and have a drink on me. Just tell Chris it's on me"—he nodded to Sam—"you and your assistant, that is."

"Skip it, Lopardi. Just remember next time we want a post, don't job it up for us with the family."

"But, Dr. Maines—"

"Never mind all that. I'm busy."

He pressed the release button on the mouthpiece again. Lopardi shrugged and shook his head. They watched him and his assistant maneuver the stretcher and the basket expertly through the door.

"How about going over to Chris's for a little coffee or a beer, maybe, Doc?" Sam said.

"Can't, Sam," Roy said. "I've got an appointment with the Old Man in about a half hour and I better not have any booze on my breath. I might drop over later."

Sam's eyebrows arched.

"The Old Man huh? You're not in any kind of a jam are you, Doc?"

"Jesus, I hope not," Roy said. "Not with him. I don't know what this is about. He just said he wanted to see me at five-thirty today, that's all I know about it. I don't want to be late either."

"Never keep the king waiting, eh Doc?"

"That's right. Kings maybe, but never chiefs of surgery, not this one anyway."

"I wonder what it feels like to be right up there next to God the way he is? Do you think he can walk on water the way he walks on everybody's necks around here? Jesus, I've never seen anything like it. One word from him can turn this Goddamn joint or anyone in it inside out—"

"That's how it is when you're the *Herr Geheimrat* professor," Roy said.

"Must be great. Well, good luck Doc. See you later maybe."

Roy sat for an instant watching Sam's shabby figure move out the door. He checked the key of the dictaphone again.

"The external markings of the body are remarkable in that the upper extremities (both) are extensively tattooed about the flexor and extensor surfaces. Beside these there are on the anterior surface of the chest four separate and distinct penetrating wounds . . ."

The rest of it took twenty minutes. By then it was almost time for his appointment with the Old Man.

2

In the library of the Charity Hospital there is a portrait of Amos Abelard Hand, M.D. It shows the Old Man three-quarters length and life size. The picture makes him an erect, lean, and ducal figure in a long, immaculately white coat. He is noble of brow, keen of eye, and his hands are predominantly featured. In one of them he is holding a book. The other rests on a table with more books and some medical paraphernalia on it. The hands are long with sensitive-looking fingers. The over-all impression given by the picture is that the subject is an academic aristocrat. It also implies that he is alert, incisive, meticulous, and handsome. It makes him look the way a layman thinks a surgeon ought to look and wants him to look. It was done by a famous and expensive artist but not a great one. It is in a heavy gilt frame with a plate beneath. The plate says, "Amos Abelard Hand, M.D., Chief of the Surgical Service of the Charity Hospital."

On the whole it is an arresting and impressive picture. It should be remembered, too, for it bears absolutely no true resemblance whatever to the Old Man as he really was. Actually the Old Man looked like an itinerant livestock judge or a small-town hardware merchant. His bearing was neither erect nor aristocratic. It is true that he was tall enough, but any impression of regal carriage was negated by his habitual stoop. His brow was certainly not noble. He was merely bald with enough hair so that he did not look completely so. It would be difficult on casual acquaintance for anyone to note his keenness of eye, because they were rarely wide open. His usual expression was one of half-lidded sleepiness. But on this point there is some truth in the picture, for when his eyes were fully open they were a hard and colorless blue. His hands, made much of in the picture, were neither long, nor artistic, nor sensitive. They were only big, and the knuckles were knobby and the fingertips spatulate. He was not meticulous in his dress. He habitually wore cheap clothes and they fit him badly. His white coats, when he wore them, were seldom clean. In the whole picture there is only one true implication about him. This was the books the artist had painted in as suggestive background. These imply learning, curiosity, and skill. Amos Hand had great learning. More than that he had a high and particular wisdom. He also had the stubbornness of a mule. He ran the Surgical Service of the Charity Hospital with a steely and despotic hand. To his face he was called "Sir," or "Dr. Hand." Otherwise it was the "Old Man," and not infrequently "the old son-of-a-bitch." The Old Man was seated before an immensely littered desk when his secretary ushered Roy in.

"Well, Maines," he said, "sit down."

He picked up a sheet from the confusion of papers on the desk, looked at it, and then at Roy.

"A while back you put in an application to come on the Surgical Service. I didn't have an opening then. I do now. Do you still want it?"

Roy had not foreseen anything like this. Ordinarily the Old Man didn't even consider any applicants for residency on the Surgical Service until they had had at least one full year in the Pathology Department doing autopsies, handling gross surgical specimens, going over the microscopic slides, and the rest of it. This was four months early, which meant he'd get started on the long grind that much sooner and done with it that much faster. He was a little sick of the routine on pathology by now, too, after eight hard months of it—of the endless gutting of the dead, the endless staring sessions over the microscope, and the endless dictation about both. But more than that it meant that the Old Man had picked him for use out of a long line waiting for the chance at the surgical residency and the distinction of being one of the Old Man's "boys." It meant that the period of sweating out being passed over for it was done with. It meant that he could forget the other alternatives he'd thought about if the Old Man didn't take him on—like resigning himself to being a general practitioner, marrying Katy, and going out to some town somewhere to make a start. Katy was all for that anyway. But now he had it. This was it. He could forget about anything else. There was only one answer.

"Yes, sir, I certainly do. I want it very much. I hoped—"

"Good," the Old Man cut him off. "You'll be taking Blinn's place. Sorry to lose him, but his father's just had his second coronary. Blinn's going back home to take over his practice. He won't be back."

Roy felt a moment's sympathy for Blinn and an instant passing remorse at his own jubilation. He knew Blinn and liked him—a hard worker, and a good guy, smart too, smart enough to know the chance he was giving up.

"So," the Old Man went on, "that leaves the vacancy and you can begin at once. I'll see that you get released with credit from pathology tomorrow so the record's straight. Blinn doesn't leave until day after tomorrow so that we'll give you the day off tomorrow. We'll start you officially day after tomorrow morning. You can use some of the time going over Blinn's patients and learning the ropes from him. Blinn's on K ward, that's on Dr. Santry's side of the service, so you will report directly to him when you come on—"

"Goddamn it," Roy thought, "Smiler Santry. That's the only lousy part of this. I'm going to start under that son-of-a-bitch, the Smiler. That's not so good. I wish to Christ I were going to start under Wilder or Wortle instead."

"Yes, sir," he heard himself saying automatically.

One of the phones on the Old Man's desk buzzed briefly, and the Old Man twanged into it, "Yes?"

Roy could catch some of the metallic inflections of the Old

Man's secretary at the other end, delivering a spate of words.

"Who? No, I will not talk with them now. In about an hour. Why are you bothering me with this?"

There was another short exchange and a faint click on the other end. The Old Man hung up and turned back to Roy.

"Now, Maines, let's get the rest of this settled. The first thing is that you will stay on the service with me until I think you're ready to go out on your own. You understand that and you plan on it—is that right?"

"Yes, sir, I understand."

"All right, you're willing to spend the time. Now the next thing. Your application says that you're not married. Do you anticipate getting married any time before you're finished with me?"

"No, sir. I haven't anything like that in mind."

"Good, I strongly advise you against it. I don't like having married surgical residents. When they are, it means that my surgical service or their wives are neglected. And it is never my surgical service. They can either be husbands or surgeons. If they want to be husbands they can stay with their wives. If they want to learn surgery they will spend their time with me."

The Old Man ruminated for a moment. "Now there's just one more thing. You cannot learn honest surgery or honest anything else if you are not honest yourself. And by honest I mean honesty of the mind—intellectual honesty. That means that you either know a thing or you don't know it. When you know it, the answer to any question is 'yes' or 'no.' When you don't the answer is 'I don't know.' Do you know what I mean?"

"Yes, sir," Roy said. "I know what you mean."

"All right, Maines," the Old Man said. "I guess that's all."

Still numb with the surprise of it, Roy got up.

"I'm certainly very grateful for the chance, Dr. Hand. I—"

The Old Man cut him short with a nod and a motion of the hand. On the way out Roy got a last glimpse of him slouched over the desk staring off into space.

"Well, I've done it, by God," he thought as he walked down the hall. "Signed up with the Old Man for a good long stretch in this pesthouse. A lot of them want it but I got it and early at that. Working under that bastard Santry even for a while won't be any cinch but I'm going to have to do it. And Katy. I wonder if she'll stand still for sticking it out with me? I've got to tell her and I might as well make it tonight. Off tonight and tomorrow. I'll make it tonight. I'll have a couple of drinks and call her and get it over with. But I've made it one way or another—I am now officially one of the Old Man's serfs."

Serfdom was not a bad synonym for the Old Man's surgical residency. His service at the Charity was distinctly feudal in character. It was organized in the form of a pyramid, with the Old Man at the apex wielding absolute and undisputed rule over any and all of its parts. Its base was the hundred-odd beds holding the sick and dying for which he was ultimately responsible. And in between, like a feudal vassalage under the king, were the physicians of the surgical staff who held well-defined authority and rank. Immediately under him and responsible only to him were his three attending surgeons, Wilder, Santry, and Wortle. These were certified and all long senior in age and experience to the struggling rank of learning novices, the resident surgeons beneath. Attending surgeons were in a manner of speaking the dukes of the Charity's surgical peerage. To make that high and ghostly station and the kudos that automatically went with it (among oter things the title of associate professor of surgery) required talent, tenacity, and long apprenticeship. The prestige and prospects, once attained, were considerable. Particularly the prospects, because if and when the Old Man retired or died, his successor would be inevitably appointed (by the Charity's Board of Regents) from the seniors of his surgical staff. And this was the ultimate, the end of the road, the ne plus ultra so to speak. To become the chief of the Surgical Service of the Charity Hospital left nothing more. A man could rest on his laurels, for he was almost automatically famous. The quotations in medical journals, his honorary degrees, the clamor for his consultations and services by the rich and publicized made him so. At least that was the way it had been with the Old Man. And no doubt it would be that way with whoever came after him. So far, though, there had been no signs of waning in the Old Man. He was at the moment as tough, productive, and competent as he had been when he became chief twenty years before. There was no telling how long the Old Man might go on. During his years of tenure he had done so much to establish the Charity as a recognized seat of surgical learning, by his work and his writing, that they might let him continue indefinitely. The Old Man was sixty years old.

These considerations had no doubt crossed the minds of his

possible successors many times. They were of no concern to Roy Maines, though, as he left the Old Man's office and went down the hall toward the Charity's main entrance. He was beginning the Old Man's Service in its lowest echelon as a first-year resident. His main concerns, then, were to celebrate and in the process to tell Katy what had happened. That he dreaded, because it would certainly not be easy. But first with a day off ahead of him he was going to get pleasantly drunk, at the Asterion. Then he'd get to the business with Katy. Katy was a hell of a good one (a tiger in bed too). He would explain it to her after a couple of drinks and she would understand about it and go along with him as she always had. She was a real rare one, Katy.

He went down the stairs and shouldered his way through the Charity's lobby, jammed with the waiting for evening visiting hours. Outside on Velle Street it was getting dark now and the jumble of neon signs were lit. He waited for the green of the traffic light and crossed the street before the shadowed line of halted cars on his way toward the Asterion Cafe.

The Asterion (meaning "little star" in Greek) Cafe had become, over a period of some years, a kind of unofficial annex of the Charity and the Criminal Courts building. It was also very frequently a haunt of elements of the working press, notably reporter Capshaw. Its popularity with all of these arose from three basic factors. One was its location. It was a short walk from the Charity, the Criminal Courts building, and the offices of the *Daily Record*. Another was its hours of operation. The Asterion kept open all night as well as all day seven days a week. Third, and most important, was the proprietor and certain of his liberal policies regarding regular clientele.

Christophoros Demos Notopoulos, owner and operator of the Asterion, was a Greek and therefore no fool. He was not without a certain personal charm that stemmed somewhat from an inherently generous Hellenic heart and partly from an instinctive understanding of the respectable poor. He fed and slaked his customers at prices they could afford to pay. He did this with profit to himself along with their satisfaction. It was his policy in line with this to extend an understanding credit for food and drink, but not too far. On very rare occasions he even might lend money, though never in breath-taking amounts. He was perceptive, and on this account he took, gave, and enjoyed a large amount of personal and usually good natured abuse, particularly from his Charity contingent.

He genuinely liked them, and, as far as a layman could, understood them. He also understood their continual insults well enough to give them endless opportunities for them. He knew that they were tired enough, insecure enough, and sentimental enough to enjoy it. Being Greek, he relished it on occasion himself. Chris had his favourites in this, and otherwise—as in the extension of credit beyond a usual margin, and the lending of money. Those favored were well aware of this and pushed their preference with him to the limit. Like all saloon-keepers Chris was a sort of parasite existing on the good will of his heterogeneous clients. But he was an honest, amiable, and welcome one.

Chris was in the true tradition of all Greek bar and restaurant entrepreneurs. And he had all of the characteristics. His love of his establishment, like his love of money, was a deep and touching thing. He gave it the same doting devotion that he gave American currency of any denomination. He was seldom out of the place. To Chris the Asterion represented a frightening investment in refinement. It was his, all his, and it now conformed precisely with his ideas of taste and elegance. Chris's pride of possession in the Asterion was particularly understandable considering its humble beginnings. In the early days of his tenure, the Asterion had been one of the lousier Greek joints along Velle Street where drunks, bums, and inexpensive whores went to get in out of the rain and drink unbelievably bad whiskey. The transformation of the Asterion into a rendezvous of luxury with a cultivated clientele from the Charity and the Police Department was inordinately sudden. It had, Chris felt at times, been engineered by fate. It had begun with what appeared at first to Chris, when he sobered up, as a wild gesture of profligacy. The fact was that, while expansively drunk on his own whiskey, a commendably rare occurrence, Chris had gone to an auction. Possibly he had done this out of a certain curious sympathy, for it was actually a sale of the effects of a bankrupt Levantine colleague, another saloonkeeper. In any case, with his Hellenic love of bargains, and with the whiskey coursing wildly in his veins, he had bid on, and acquired, an imposing property. This was a bar forty-two feet long. And a thing of arresting magnificence.

Sober, Chris viewed it with justified alarm. He was a man with a white elephant. It was too late to stop the check he had written for it. He was now faced with a weighty decision. He could try to sell it to another drunken Greek, a highly unlikely possibility. He could put it in storage—throwing away money for nothing. Or he could, at assassinating expense, install it in the Asterion. At a cost which wrung his heart, Chris cleared an entire wall and installed it. It had stayed there for some time—as the *piéce de résistance* of the establishment and a solid emblem of Chris's growing prosperity.

This bar was a truly regal item. It was a grand thing of imitation red marble that stretched away toward the kitchen in the rear with an opulence of golden faucets, spigots, and taps. Behind it was a long, fluted-glass mirror. This made an opulent bas relief for a spate of imperial-looking bottles, Araq, Uzo, Metaxis, and other fiery and exotic beverages of the Levant. There was also a solid representation of the cheaper brands of American whiskey. As a special artistic touch, gilding the lily so to speak, Chris had an arrangement of tasteful chromo prints contributed by sundry liquor salesmen. These, without exception, were likenesses of unusual young ladies. There was considerable variation in position, but each held out provocatively a plainly labeled bottle. The flower of these houris was the Metaxis advertisement which covered the central panel.

This was a picture, larger than the rest, of a darkly roseate maiden. She was of obvious Circassian origin, liquid of eye, draped in a leopard skin, and wearing golden sandals. To the Western mind, perhaps she might have seemed somewhat heavy in the hocks, but otherwise there was no doubt of her ideal proportions. She sat pulsating with suggested seduction on a golden couch, holding a bottle of Metaxis clasped like a phallus in her sprangled fingers. Chris looked at her not infrequently and was wont to wonder why there were never any women like her except on liquor advertisements. As a regular cash-paying customer of Stasia Kondoleon's whorehouse he had opportunities of making disconcerting comparisons between art and life. There had never been any women even remotely approaching his vivid Metaxis queen. Chris often reflected on this and sighed.

Chris's installation of the bar had started a chain reaction of wastrelsy with his assets. It was impossible for so princely a possession not to reduce to squalor the rest of the Asterion's interior. This discrepancy was apparent even to Chris. It was also instantly noted by Chris's more sophisticated clientele, including Inspector Rybecki. Examining it for the first time, the inspector's critique on it was loud and eloquent. It fell on Chris's ear with more impact then Rybecki imagined.

"This here bar," the inspector had pounded it with his ham-like fist for emphasis, "is damned fancy merchandise, Chris. It's a great piece of furniture. But," he looked at the scarred tables and chairs clustered humbly around it, "it's like a diamond in a goat's ass. You get a bar like this, you got to fix up the rest of the joint to go with it. See what I mean? This crap," he made a broad gesture toward the whole interior of the Asterion, "has got to go. You got the makings of a real class layout here. A regular rendayvoo-type joint. Look at the rest of this stuff by comparison—a dog wouldn't piss on it."

The inspector downed his third free bourbon.

"You got to go whole hog now. You got to really fix the place up. It'll cost some dough sure. But what the hell's dough to a guy like you? You got a feeling for real high-class stuff or you wouldn't have got this in the first place. Now you got to make the rest of the layout go with it. You wouldn't put the Venus de Milo, that there great Greek statue, in a nickel toilet, would you? Hell no!"

Chris had listened to this pragmatic wisdom, pensive and impressed. He had done it, too. He went to the bank and got money. He secured a third-rate interior decorator. When they were done, the new decor of the Asterion generally conformed to the nobility of its bar. There was imitation parquet flooring. The lighting was indirect and subdued. This discreet form of illumination lent an air of intimacy but allowed customers enough vision to find their mouths with bottles and glasses easily. The scar-stricken teetering chairs and tables vanished. They were succeeded by a phalanx of confidential-looking booths, rich in mahogany veneer, and red plastic almost like leather. There were mural panels too, along the newly refurbished walls. These panels were a special touch of the homosexual decorator Chris had hired. They depicted pastoral or court scenes from the more decadent French kings. Limp-looking youth in lace lay around with lutes before limper-looking ladies, who looked like men. They were in gilded frames. Another considerable addition was the new juke box. The juke box even rivaled the bar in magnificence. It was a mechanical marvel of metal and bubbling light. Its repertoire had no less than one hundred selections. Chris had much respect for it besides its beautiful sounds. It was cheatproof: it rejected slugs. In short, the Asterion was transfigured into a milieu of elegance the equal of Stasia Kondoleon's reception room. Chris's pride in it was consummate and touching to behold. When he looked upon it, his eyes were suffused with a mystic satisfaction. This real class place was his. This belonged to him, Christophoros Demos Notopoulos. And at those times he was reminded of his vast progress since the long gone days when he was a dock walloper in Piraeus. He had been young then, young and hungry, and wholly unaware of this glory to come.

Chris was at his usual station between the bar and the cash register when Roy came in. At the moment Ransahoff and a junior intern, Kilroe, were the Asterion's only customers. They were in one of the front booths, a string of empty Szabo's Bohemian Beer bottles on the table before them. Chris momentarily stopped the reflective paring of his nails and nodded.

"Good evening, Doctor."

"Hello, Chris," Roy said.

He went to the booth and sat down facing Ransahoff.

"All right, Euripides," Ransahoff waved to Chris, "let's have three more."

He turned to Roy. "You finally get all done violating the dead, you Goddamned ghoul?"

"All done," Roy said. "Soul to God, body to Lopardi, and reports to the file."

"That pathology is certainly a crude specialty. Even worse than surgery. All blood and dead guts and no finesse at all. Only an insensitive bastard like you could do it. Look at you—just finished ripping the bowels out of that poor dead son-of-a-bitch and now you're over here drinking."

"It's an honest speciality though," Roy said. "Not like yours. You have to have larceny in you to be in internal medicine. All internal medicine is bullshit and different colored pills. You get a patient, bullshit him till he thinks you know what's wrong, then you give him a white pill. Nothing happens. More talk and another pill, red this time. You keep this up till he either gets well or dies on his own hook. If he gets well you take the credit—he dies, nothing could save him."

"Listen to the cynical bastard," Ransahoff said. "By the way where were you? We looked around for you after the autopsy."

"I had to go over and see the Old Man," Roy said. He tried to make it sound casual.

"Jesus, the Old Man? What for?"

"I'm taking Blinn's place on surgery, starting under Santry."

"Well, I'll be Goddamned," Ransahoff said. "You really are, huh?"

Roy nodded.

"Well," Ransahoff said, "congratulations, Roy. Every man to his own poison. Personally I couldn't take it, particularly with Santry for openers. I'm getting the hell out into practice after this year. I'm Goddamn sick of being poor in order to get smart at being a doctor. This chronic insufficiency of funds being a resident gets to be quite a pain in the ass. A piano player in a whorehouse makes more in a day than I do in a month. I've got it figured though. The thing for me to do is get out in practice. Or better than that, marry a lot of money and then I can sit back on my ass and practice medicine like a gentleman."

"Yeah. Exactly. Like Dr. Ward. He's got the right idea. Ever met Ward, Kilroe? Well, you will sooner or later. You haven't been around the Charity long enough yet. When you do, look well. Ward is a valuable example to neophytes like you. Should be carefully studied. Ward, Roy, and myself are contemporaries. Same intern class. But look at the gulf between us now. Here Roy and I are, doing more time in the Charity so we can learn a little more about doctoring— a couple of out at the ass residents—a little better than interns like you. And what is Ward? Ward is a gentleman doctor. He interned with Roy and me and he was a piss-poor intern. Right, Roy? Right. But now he lives in Crosse Parke, eats high off the hog, and drives a Cadillac longer than Lopardi's hearse. Why this big discrepancy between guys like Roy and me and the eminent Dr. Ward?"

Ransahoff emptied his glass and signaled Chris.

"I'll tell you why. Did he piss away his time like Roy and me have trying to learn more? He did not. He's smart. He saved time and effort. He married a broad with a lot of dough instead."

"Nancy Lyons Crane," Roy said.

"That's right," Ransahoff said. "How the hell did you know what her name was?"

"I was at the wedding," Roy said.

"By God, that's right. I'd forgotten. The Cranes had the temerity to invite the whole Charity staff. It's a gesture aristocrats make with peasants sometimes. We taught them a lesson though. We made a shambles out of Snotwood, or what-

ever it is they call that Grand Central Station of a house of
theirs. That's when they had the reception. It was great. One
of our boys threw up on the dance floor and everything. That
was Dr. Palmer, a brother intern of ours, wasn't it Roy? Too
bad it had to happen. Up until then Palmer looked like he was
doing all right with the new Madame Ward's sister. That sister was a pretty sexy tomato. Don't you think so, Roy?"

"I didn't get much of a look at her," Roy said. "I got there
late. I was busy with the champagne and buffet."

"Well, she was," Ransahoff said. "She's an actress in New
York. Radio and television. I forget what the hell her stage
name is. Aline something or other. She's an extremely well-set-
up young lady. A real sex boat. It's a good thing I'm not lech-
erous or those knockers of hers would haunt my dreams till
I'm eighty."

Ransahoff pointed a finger at the central panel of the bar
mirror where the Metaxis queen gazed limpidly down at
them.

"Looks a good deal like Our Lady of Lourdes over there.
In fact there's quite a resemblance. Her equipment is very
similar. The point is that Madame Ward's sister is quite a dish.
Rich, famous, beautiful, and, I guess, single at the moment.
Great opportunity there for some young, dashing, handsome,
son-of-a-bitch like you, Roy."

"Sure," Roy said.

"But not if you're going to stumble around on the Old Man's
Surgical Service for the next ten years. It'll be too late then.
This broad will have been through a couple of husbands by
then and probably be in Timbuktu."

Ransahoff flagged Chris for three more beers, and went on.

"I'll have to give the Old Man credit though. He's got the
best service in the house. When you get through with him,
you'll be first class with a knife. The son-of-a-bitch is an ogre,
but you'll know your surgery all right. The trouble is when
he's through with you, you'll be so tired and beat up from his
service you won't be worth a damn. You'll be ready for
a wheel chair."

Chris brought three open, dripping bottles and set them on
the table.

"On the house," Chris said.

"Well, by God, thank you, Menelaus. It's about time
though—incidentally," Ransahoff fumbled in his pocket, "as
a mark of gratitude I'm going to let you cash a check for me."

Chris's eyes narrowed slightly. They always did this when money was mentioned.

"How much, Doctor?"

"Don't get spastic, my Athenian tycoon. My niggardly salary. Just fifty bucks. O.K.?"

"You owe $16.85 not including today. I take it out?"

"Oh yes, indeed. Certainly, by all means. Who wants to owe a Greek money?"

He signed the check and handed it over. Chris peeled some bills from a thick roll and counted out some silver. Ransahoff pocketed all but a nickel. This he pushed toward Chris.

"Change not right, Doctor?"

"Very," Ransahoff said. "That is a gratuity for you, my myrmidon. Money is nothing to me."

Chris bowed and picked up the nickel.

"I give it to the orchestra. For this they play all night."

Chris went to the juke box and dropped in the nickel. Melody began to throb out of it in a melancholy cadence, muted trumpet and subdued piano. The instrumental harmony faded down and a low, husky female voice began to mourn out the words:

It's part of the game with a dame
When you're under her lure and just can't be sure
That her heart and her words are the same
It's part of the game with a dame.

She loves you and leaves you
Breaks your heart and deceives you
To nurse your pride and your shame
That's part of the game with a dame.

So you go with a sigh and a tear in your eye
She's turned you and spurned you
And you walk a little bit lame
That's part of the game with a dame.

But forget all the heartache and blame
Till another comes by and you make a new try
Just remember they're still all the same
It's part of the game with a dame.

The music ebbed to its finale in a series of dejected minor chords.

"God, what feeling, what sentiment. Reminds me I've got a very big deal going tonight," Ransahoff said.

Up front the phone rang. Chris answered it. It was the hospital for Kilroe. Kilroe went to the phone.

"Very big," Ransahoff said. "You know the redhead up on J ward? The willowy one with the big tits? No? Well, next time take a good look. I've had her out a couple of times. Made quite an investment in fact. She hits that bourbon bottle like it had insulted her mother. Last time it cost me damned near ten bucks. So far no payoff. But the chips are down tonight, Roy boy. Her roommate has gone away for the weekend. I figure the odds now are on my side, all the way."

Ransahoff looked at his watch.

"Jesus, Roy, it's getting late. We'll have one more then I've got to get out of here. I don't want to keep Moonflower waiting. Not tonight."

The beer came. Ransahoff drained his and stood up.

"Good luck," Roy said.

"Right," Ransahoff said. "Listen, just one thing. I didn't mean to be offhand about your getting the job with the Old Man on the surgical service. I know there isn't anyone around the Charity who wouldn't give his Goddamned teeth to have been picked for it, even when they have to start with an utter son-of-a-bitch like Smiler Santry. You know, I think it's great, and you're just the kid who can do it. Congratulations. Forget about the beer, it's on me. See you later."

Ransahoff made an indecent gesture at Chris as he went out, and Kilroe came back from the phone to finish his beer.

"That Goddamn switchboard. They never get anything straight even with the schedule posted right up there in front of them. Just called me for the emergency room and I'm not even on tonight."

Roy looked at him thoughtfully.

"You're on surgery, aren't you, Kilroe? On Smiler Santry's end of the service? How is it?"

"You know the Smiler, don't you?" Kilroe said.

"No," Roy said, "only what I've heard. Before I went on pathology I put in my time on surgery with Wilder and a little while with Wild Will Wortle. So I really don't know."

"You were lucky, Doctor. Jesus, I've got another month with that son-of-a-bitch and I guess I can stand it. But I can hardly wait to get out from under him."

"Blinn was his resident—how did he make out with him?"

"I'm sure sorry to see old Blinn leave," Kilroe said. "Jesus, I don't know how he took it like he did from that bastard. I can hardly stand it myself."

"That bad, huh?" Roy said. "I'm taking Blinn's place you know."

"It's pretty bad," Kilroe said. "I don't envy you."

"Tell me about it." Roy signaled Chris for two more beers.

"Well, I'll tell you, Maines," Kilroe poured and drank, "I had the idea that I might want to go on in surgery when I took the internship here. That was one of the reasons why I took it—to learn it from scratch and with somebody real great, like Dr. Hand. I don't feel that way now. Maybe if I had been with Wilder or on Wortle's end of the Old Man's service I still might. But I draw Smiler Santry and I don't feel that way about it any more. All that I can think of right now is finishing under him before I get fired so that I can tell that insufferable, scheming, arrogant, megalomaniac tyrant to kiss my ass for good. I know I may sound a little paranoid but I've gotten that way working under him. 'Yes, sir. No, sir. Wipe your ass, sir?' I've taken it too. But I couldn't go on taking it. I can do it for a while longer though. He's just having his last whack at me before I get my certificate for my time here. Anyway I'm not so keen on surgery now. I'll do some general practice first."

There was a buzzing in the region of the phone booth in the rear. It was for Kilroe.

"Kilroe's is on me," Roy said to Chris.

"Thanks, Doctor," Kilroe said on his way out.

Roy sat alone slowly finishing what was left in his glass after Kilroe had gone.

"Chris, let me have a double shot of bourbon."

Chris's thick eyebrows elevated a little.

"Whiskey now, Doctor? Not beer?"

"Yes, whiskey," Roy said irritably. "What's the matter, don't you sell whiskey?"

Chris shrugged and brought a bottle and a glass. The raw cheap burn of it gradually subsided into a comfortable glow in his belly. He had another on which he almost gagged. Then he went to the phone booth and dialed Katy's number. He began to get a queer tight feeling in his stomach even through the liquor the moment her voice came on.

"I'm down at the Greek's," he said. "How about meeting me here? I've got tonight off."

"But Roy, you're calling so late. I hadn't planned . . ." then followed the familiar feminine gambit of dubious hesitation, and, after more conversation, consent. Roy went back from the telephone booth and sat down to wait. He waved at Chris. Chris brought the bourbon bottle again.

"You better have a little coffee or something too, Doc," Chris eyed him judiciously. Chris was right. Just now he was comfortably drunk, but if he kept on. . . . Chris brought the coffee. Almost an hour went by before Katy came in.

She stood just inside the doorway for an instant looking around before she saw Roy wave at her from his booth across from the bar. Then she caught sight of him. The knot in his stomach suddenly began to tighten again as he watched her slender figure move toward him.

Katy Winter was not beautiful but she had that sensuous quality about her face and body that made men look at her as if she were. This was the first thing that had struck Roy about her when they had met almost a year ago, and he had never ceased to be aware of it. Sometimes when he looked at her, his loins ached. The most arresting feature of her narrow oval face were her eyes and a wide red mouth. The eyes were full and dark. They gave an impression of obliquity that was not actual because of the artificial slant of the brows above them, and her low hairline. She had a lot of very dark hair worn severely back from her forehead. Roy watched her face as she walked toward him, but he was, as always, conscious of her body. She had the body of a bacchante and she, consciously or not, moved it like one.

Roy got up and helped her with her coat. She sat down across from him. Her eyes caught the half-gone whiskey in the glass and the coffee, and her brows went up a little.

"Why, Roy, straight whiskey? You're a beer boy. What's the matter with you?"

Roy felt himself grinning sickly. "Medicine for my stomach. Come on, have some."

He nodded to Chris. "Rum and soda for my grandmother here."

"I'll get a few of them down her first," he thought. "That way it ought to go a lot better."

"You didn't tell me you were going to be off tonight, so I was going to the shower for Lucille Cameron. She's one of the girls at the office. She's getting married the twenty-eighth."

"Jesus," Roy thought, "that's going to make what I've got to say sound just fine. It's got her thinking in the wrong direction before I start."

Katy took off her gloves. Chris brought her drink and she sipped it thoughtfully. "That reminded me about us. It hardly seems possible that you're just about through at the hospital. It's been so long, hasn't it, for both of us? And do you know what I've been thinking? I thought we might just as well make it as quiet and as soon as possible. How does that sound to you? In two weeks even if you want to?"

Her face had a bright expectant smile on it now as she looked at him that almost made him groan out loud. "I've decided it would be foolish to have any big to-do about it. Just a few of your and my friends to stand up with us. It would be foolish of us to do anything else. We'll need that money to get you started in practice. Don't you think that's right?"

"Oh, my God," Roy thought miserably. "This is it. Here goes . . ." His voice went suddenly strained and thick. "Listen, Katy—Chris, another couple of drinks—listen, Katy. Now just listen to me and don't be upset. You see it's this way. You know the Old . . . I mean, Dr. Hand, Amos Hand, the chief of surgery at the hospital? Sure you do. You've heard me speak of him a lot of times. He's the greatest there is, remember I told you that? It's a great break for anybody to train under him. It's the best you can get. The very best. Well, today, listen what—"

The bright smile on Katy Winter's mouth instantly perished and something baleful took its place. She stared at him fixedly. Her dark eyes became a little teary-looking and her lips compressed. Her voice sounded small, strange, and suddenly tired.

"No, you listen. I don't have to listen. I know exactly what you're going to tell me. I know exactly what's happened. You've signed on for the residency in surgery over there at that damned hospital. And that's another four or five years. You told me that once a long time ago and you laughed and said you wouldn't think of it because it was all sweat and no money till you got through. And you said that anyone who did it was a damned fool because he couldn't do anything besides that. He couldn't get married or anything because he'd be married to the Surgical Service and the Old Man. Dr. Hand, the chief, whatever it is you call him. That's what you said. And now you've done it, you've done it. Anyway . . . haven't you?" There were big tears in her eyes, big tears getting ready to drop.

"Listen, please, Katy, listen—"

"No, you listen. I'm not through yet. And now you're going to ask me to go right on waiting. Doing just what I have been this long. Not seeing anyone else, waiting for you to call, listening to your excuses when you're late and when you don't show up. All that. Sitting around with you when you do because there's no money to do anything else. Sneaking into and out of bed with you anytime there's a chance of not being caught. All that. And you want me to do it like I have been and go right on doing it for the next four or five years?"

The tears were flowing freely but there was a change in her mouth. The wide red lips had set themselves in a way he had never seen before. This was a taut straight line.

"What you want is a mistress. Not me—not a wife."

"But Katy, listen to me. I love you. Maybe later—"

Her voice came now very levelly and with a surprising timbre of finality in it:

"Well, you can start looking for one as of now, right now, Doctor. Secretly I guess I always knew this would happen. I've been a good deal of a fool but this is the end of it."

She stood up suddenly. She was crying again, this time audibly.

"Good-by, Roy, and good luck. I think you're going to need it."

Roy tried to get to his feet. It was a small space in the booth between the table and the seat. The liquor and the way he was feeling had made his legs a little rubbery. He struggled awkwardly.

"Katy, wait! Wait a minute, Katy!"

She was almost running toward the door. It opened the instant she got to it and she collided with someone just coming in. That was Capshaw. By the time Roy got out of the booth she was gone.

Capshaw stood a moment staring after her, then he looked over at Chris in his usual stance between the cash register and the bar.

"Jesus," Capshaw said, "what's with that dame?"

Chris gave him a barely perceptible, warning shake of the head and arched his eyes toward the booth where Roy had sat down again, chin in his hand and elbows on the table.

Drunk or sober, Capshaw had the instantly triggered curiosity of all good newspaper reporters. At the moment, he was, as usual, neither drunk nor sober. He immediately sensed a situation of some kind involving something of interest. In spite of Chris's covert gesture he could not resist it. Doc Maines was a good one, and a good doctor. Maybe there was something . . . He had to find out what it was anyway. Chris silently shook his head "No" at Capshaw. Capshaw ignored him and went over to the booth where Roy was staring absently down at the table. Capshaw's eyes caught it too, all of it, and the unfinished drink across from Roy. Capshaw smiled faintly. So that was it.

"Hello, Doc. Mind if I sit down?"

Roy looked up.

"Oh, hello, Cappy," he said listlessly. "How are you? Sit down."

"What are you drinking, Doc?"

"Bourbon."

Capshaw waved two fingers at Chris. Chris came over with it and poured out two.

"Just leave the bottle, Christopher, my boy," Capshaw said. Chris set the bottle down and went back to the bar.

"Come on, Doc," Capshaw said, "drink it up. Whatever it is, it's not bad enough to come between a man and his whiskey."

Roy nodded and took the glass at a gulp.

"That's a boy," Capshaw said and poured two more.

"What's the matter, Doc, broad trouble?"

Roy looked at Capshaw and was suddenly very glad to see him. He liked Capshaw, but anyone who came then would have come at the right time. Someone to drink with, someone to talk to.

"That's right, Cappy. She just walked out on me for good."

"I know how you feel, Doc. It's happened to me—happens to everybody. But you'll get another chance. Here, let's have another drink."

"No, I won't," Roy said, "I won't at all. I never will. She means it."

"They all mean it when they say it. But they get over it. They'll tell you to go to hell, but they get over it. Give her time to cool off. She'll be around when you want her."

"No, not this one." Roy knew that the liquor was making his tongue loose. He knew he was going to talk. But at this point he didn't give a good Goddamn. "Hell, I was going to marry her as soon as I could."

Capshaw grinned.

"Pretty serious, huh, Doc? How long has it been going on?"

"A year, almost."

Capshaw poured two more out of the bourbon bottle.

"Look, this is none of my business, and you can tell me to go to hell if you want to. But what was the matter? Mind if I ask?"

Roy considered this, licking his bourbon-burned lips reflectively. He felt better now. "She didn't want to wait any more. I can't blame her, Cappy. That's what I was going to ask her to do, was wait, quite awhile maybe. Four or five years even."

"That's a long time, Doc. For what?"

"Till I get through surgery with the Old Man. Dr. Hand, that is, you probably know who he is—"

"I know all about him. I've been a police reporter almost as long as he's been honorary police surgeon. Come on, we're empty."

The bottle clinked on the glasses again.

"I get it, Doc. I get the picture. She doesn't want to wait till you get through doing what you got to do so that you can do what you really want to do. Right?"

"Right," Roy said.

"Well, let me tell you something Doc. I don't know much about women, but I know a hell of a lot more than you do. I've been a newspaperman a long time now and I've wined them, dined them, laid them, watched them, and written about them for just about that long." Capshaw paused. "You don't mind if I pontificate on this subject do you?"

"No," Roy said, "go ahead and pontificate before I get too drunk and can't hear you. Go on pontificate about women for me."

Capshaw poured himself another drink and sat turning the glass in his fingers.

"You feel real guilty about this dame, don't you, Doc?"

"Yes. That's right. That's part of it," Roy said.

"Well, let me tell you why you shouldn't," Capshaw said. "I could write a book about this. But I won't. I guess I'll never write a book about anything. So I won't write a book about women. I'll tell you, you poor lovelorn son-of-a-bitch about them instead."

Capshaw half drained his glass, looked at the grubby hand

that held it, at the frayed shirt cuff and the worn sleeve of his jacket about it, and sniffed.

"The standard general concept that women are inferior to men is a misbegotten untruth. Always remember that for openers."

He pulled his worn coat sleeve down over the frayed shirt cuff and went on reflectively.

"The fact is that in most respects they are considerably superior. This is true for the physical. Pound for pound they are not as strong as the male but they are a lot more durable—witness the fact they live longer. More male infants are born in the ratio of two or three to one but fifty years later the ratio is reversed—there are more old ladies than old men. They survive longer because they are physically tougher. They are also shrewder, braver, and far more practical. There are more shrewd women than there are shrewd men, and turn for turn a shrewd woman will take a shrewd man every time. Women are braver and more practical than men because they are realists. They see things as they are and as they themselves relate to those things. Women are not given to the curious age-old male failing of clouding fundamental issues with egotistical, romantic, melodramatic claptrap. It is too bad that all the wars are not fought by women. They would be bloodier, but a damned sight shorter. A woman in a serious fight has no regard for any code. She uses any and every weapon she can and no holds barred and no quarter asked or given because she knows the main issue is to win. . . ."

As he listened to this in a gathering fog of bourbon, Roy found himself wondering about Capshaw. It was apparent that Capshaw was serious about what he was saying. And he was saying it earnestly and with an undeniable conviction. He really did know, Roy felt, about women and he was saying what he knew very well. Capshaw could really talk as well as write. This surprised Roy a little, for it was the first time that he had ever heard him let go on and on about an idea. Most of the times before that they had sat together over a drink at the Asterion, there had been only the bantering superficialities of drinking conversation. But now he was hearing Capshaw talk seriously from his worldly, case-hardened wisdom. What he was saying about women was searching, cynical, and with a good deal of truth in it. It was very unusual to hear women talked about that way. But, it was not surprising coming from Capshaw, because Capshaw was pretty unusual himself.

Hugh Martin Capshaw was a man misplaced from birth. He should have been anything but what he was. That was a hack reporter on the *Daily Record*. Granted he was an outstanding hack, by reason of the copy he wrote. But still he was a hack writer on a newspaper at the age of forty-five when he could have been something other and certainly more solvent than what he was. Capshaw's inherent gifts were considerable. He had a trenchant and inquiring mind. He had originality of thought. He had an almost surgical ability to cut away nonessentials and get to the heart of matters. He had along with it a good deal of formal and miscellaneous learning too. He had graduated *magna cum laude* from an eastern college having quite a measure of prestige. The habit of omnivorous reading that he had acquired there had stayed with him. He still read omnivorously. And this he recorded and filed in his lean, elongated head almost automatically. He was one of those rare individuals with what is called a photographic memory. He could, for example, read and retain an endless volume of print, such books and newspapers, and remember it almost verbatim for days, weeks, months, and in some cases, years later. He never consulted the morgue of the *Daily Record* as most of the others did. He did not have to because much if not all of it was somewhere in his head to be called out when he needed it. But Capshaw had much more than this phenomenal factual memory. He had a good deal of feeling for the people about whom he wrote. These were ordinarily the misshapen, the moonstruck, and the damned who appeared in the police court, which was his regular beat. He had a particular and almost encyclopedic knowledge of crime and criminals historic and contemporary, and no small acquaintance with the latter. It was probably on this account he had an amused kind of contempt for much of the law, and for many of those who enforced it, including the police—particularly the police. But he was an eminently good reporter of the doings of both. In this, the *Daily Record* had quite an asset in Capshaw. This was universally recognized in the *Record's* higher echelons so that a great many of Capshaw's inherent delinquencies were overlooked. His hard drinking, loud and ribald criticisms, refusal to conform to editorial policy, and episodic fits of undependability could have gotten him fired many times over. But they did not because of this recognition. Capshaw was well aware of this and took a good deal of satisfaction in exploiting it. Nothing was sacred to Capshaw, not even his own security, and he frequently twisted the sensitive tails of his editor and his publisher to the last turn of the screw. In fact he had a positive gift for stopping just short of an irrevocable decision to boot him out for good.

This unique status of Capshaw's on the *Record* staff had been established over a period of some fifteen years. He had come there looking for a job after his graduation from the liberal arts college of his university. This was also some time after his father, in the best mid-Victorian tradition, had in righteous rage disowned him.

That denunciation, shortly after his mother's death, had finally terminated the father-son mutual antipathy and Capshaw had gone out on his own in the teeth of a national depression. In succession he drifted through a long descent of wasted days. This included having been, among other things, an ordinary seaman on a freighter, a dishwasher, an itinerant fruit picker, a section-gang hand, a sparring partner for an on-the-way-down third-rate pugilist, a carnival roustabout, a railroad yard worker, a street cleaner, a filling station attendant, a book salesman on commission, and, on and off, an ordinary panhandling bum. In this interval of instability he had done two things consistently—sharpened his observation of the world, and written about it. What he wrote could not sell. But it did ultimately land him his initial trial as a reporter on the *Record*, which, within a year, had passed into its current permanence.

The years of this relative security had not, however, changed Capshaw's character or his inclinations. It had only accentuated them. He had the dietary, sleeping, and sexual habits of a vagrant tom cat. And about as much respect for the world in which he moved. This was the sordid, shadowy, sleazy, and sometimes sinister environment of the *Record* office, the Charity, and the Criminal Court building mainly, and the places and people attendant on them. This was his element and he wrote about its parts and people with accuracy and perception because he was truly of it himself.

Capshaw lived alone, as he had for some years, in a two-room corner suite of the Hotel Andan on Velle Street. The Andan was one of the several older and shabbier semirespectable hotels in the vicinity. Its appointments were, like the clientele it served, rundown, worn, drab, and doubtful. Its chief patronage was from second- and third-rate theatrical and commercial transients. Capshaw, a permanent and solvent guest, had one of its better and specially rated accommodations. The two rooms and bath which comprised it were relatively luxurious. At one time or another, thirty years before, it had been the bridal suite and there were still pathetic touches of this elegance. Much of its furniture retained its overstuffed look of opulence, in spite of the spotted upholstery. The worn red plush of its draperies had not faded completely and the mange spots in the matching carpet were not too noticeable. The plumbing in the tiled bathroom was antiquated but still loudly functional. The most distinctive feature of it, at least during Capshaw's tenure of the place, was its enormous clutter of papers and books. The place was literally crammed with these. They were stacked with a kind of haphazard order on makeshift shelves, brackets, and sconces, and piled on the floor. The fire hazard was probably considerable. This and the rest of it, with the slovenly attention it got from the Andan's chambermaids, had been a long-time home to Hugh Capshaw. It suited his wants entirely and he spent much of his off time in it.

Capshaw had been on his way there to finish writing his day's copy when he had decided, as he often did, to stop by the Asterion for another priming drink. His fortuitous meeting there with Roy had turned out to be interesting. The doc was having the age-old difficulty of woman trouble. Capshaw himself had certainly had enough of that from time to time, and, as every man who has, he liked to commiserate with those in the same trouble. Capshaw was caught, as he often was, in the combined and pleasant spell of liquor and his own words. So was Roy.

"Men don't marry women, women marry men. A man chases a woman till she catches him so to speak. A smart woman goes after a man the way a smart hunter goes after an animal. First she studies his habits, points, and weaknesses, then she looks over her armament carefully to see which of her many weapons is best adapted to bring down that particular kind of male quarry. It turns out she has a very heavy arsenal to pick from. Her best weapon is the weakness of the animal himself. The human male is insecure and egotistical. Given any opportunity to do so by flattering his vanity he becomes an insensate, unthinking ass. A woman who will listen to him talk about himself will reduce him to this level shortly and thereby have him disarmed. Another item of the female armamentarium is a whole body of esoteric female knowledge passed on from mother to daughter which deals with these and similar weaknesses of the male and just how they can be best exploited. The goal of this exploitation consists in the permanent ensnarement by matrimony of the best possible male, or failing that, of a suitable male. The trick of this ancient game is to pick the male, induce his approach, employing the standard female bait, and then contrive to give him the illusion that he is the hunter rather than the hunted so that he runs unknowingly straight into the nuptial harness and corral. And he usually does. Usually, probably 99 per cent of the time, when he is up against a clever woman, but not always. There is still left a small percentage of recalcitrant rogue males who do not dupe easily, if at all. They will make the approach, give every indication of performing satisfactorily, then steal the bait and run out laughing. When this happens the particular female in the piece, and indeed all females, is outraged. He is a cad, a bounder, and a swine, because he has not played the game according to the ancient female matriarchal rules. Nothing exasperates and infuriates women more than to have this happen.

"So far as I have been able to determine, speaking generally, women suffer by comparison to men in only one respect. They are not profound. But this is of little matter because they can very easily exploit, one way or another, the men who are. Make no mistake about women. They are not inferior. They deserve a considerable respect.

"So don't do too much breast beating about this, Doc," Capshaw concluded. "About this one or any of them. The chances are they're smarter than you are where it counts and sure as hell they know better what's going on."

Capshaw grinned at him and drained his drink.

The evening clientele of the Asterion had begun to filter in. The traffic between the bar and the booths gradually increased and became constant. So did the clink of the cash register and the music from the juke box.

With the liquor and Capshaw's conversation, Roy was feeling better, a lot better. From time to time Capshaw eyed him judiciously.

"Come on, Doc," Capshaw said finally, "let's get out of here and find some excitement. I know just the kind we need."

On the way to the door Capshaw instructed Chris, "If that son-of-a-bitch, the city editor, calls over here for me, tell him you haven't seen me, will you?"

Almost all of the Asterion's booths and the bar were crowded now and the air filled with smoke and a continuous murmur. Above it came the throaty throb of the juke box:

> But forget all the heartache and blame
> Till another comes by and you make a new try
> Just remember they're still all the same
> It's part of the game with a dame.

For an instant Capshaw stood by the door with his head cocked to one side listening to it. He grinned at Roy.

"Hear that, Doc? Hear that song? That's the right idea. You remember that, Doc. Come on."

The door of the Asterion closed behind them.

3

Stasia Kondoleon ran an eminently respectable whorehouse, and, as whorehouse madames go, was eminently respectable herself. Both she and the house had been in business for a long time. As an old hand in the administrative echelon of the profession of whoring, she knew the value of public relations. She maintained hers with a consistent and scrupulous finesse. Her associations with her clients and the police were excellent. She kept a basic ethic with both. She never violated the confidence of her clients, and her payoffs to the law were promptly and regularly paid and in cash. Her credit rating was impeccable.

Over the years Stasia had become a woman of considerable substance. She knew the value of a dollar. She also had the inordinate Levantine intuition as to how to invest it. If the truth had been known, and it was frequently guessed at, Stasia Kondoleon had some startling holdings, including a substantial amount of real estate surrounding her establishment on Peake Street.

This was the corner of a row of solid-looking stone fronts flush with the street and continuous with each other. These had been built forty years before when the neighborhood was residential. Most of them had long since been converted to the purposes of the small-time commerce that had gradually encroached upon them. Printers, dry cleaners, radio repairers, confection hawkers, and bars had usurped their ground floors, and single furnished rooms for transients, their upper ones. Peake Street by day was a scurry of petty activity and a clutter of winking neon signs by night. Stasia Kondoleon's emporium was at the darker extremity of this. And there was, of course, no sign on it.

Roy stood beside Capshaw in the gloom of its side entrance. Capshaw pressed the bell again. This time the door opened. A Negro girl in maids' uniform stood in it briefly.

"Hello, Fanny," Capshaw said. "How are tricks?"

A flash of white teeth appeared in the indistinct face.

"Yes, sir, yes, sir. How are you, sir?"

She closed the door behind them. Roy felt his feet sink into thick carpet. There was music from somewhere, and a heavy permeating smell of smoke and perfume.

"Go tell the commander of Fort Kondoleon that a couple of scouts have just come in riding ahead of an Apache war party," Capshaw said.

Fanny giggled.

"Yes, sir. You want to see Miss Stasia?"

"Right away," Capshaw said. "We want to tell her all about the Apache uprising. Tell her we've got a couple of arrows sticking out of our stomachs."

"I'll get her right away, sir," Fanny said, giggling again.

She left them momentarily alone in a side room a little too small for its overstuffed, maroon plush furniture. Capshaw looked at Roy critically.

"How are you feeling now, Doc?"

"Drunk, but all right."

"Not sick or anything?"

"No. Just drunk."

"You just wait," Capshaw said.

There was a stir of the plush curtains. Stasia Kondoleon stood between them. Roy's first look at her in the subdued light gave him an impression of a sizable woman in a dark, severely cut dress. As he peered at her he saw that she was not so much fat as large and smooth-looking. There was much flesh to her. She seemed sleekly molded out of a single rich block of it. The contours of her flowed in curves, not bulges. Her face was Circassian, the complexion was an unblemished olive, and her eyes had the characteristic touch of obliquity.

They were full and black under her dark, plucked brows. The high prominences of the bones standing out from the softer folds and wrinkles of her face suggested that she had been much thinner in her youth. This arresting, flesh-contained face welled upward into a profusion of heavy black hair which she wore pulled into a large back knot. All of her features, particularly the full smiling mouth, gave a feeling of a compelling and forthright sensuality. She exuded above the general aroma of the place an odor of her own, something heavy and female, something of myrrh and musk. Her hands, for all of her considerable body, were slender and well cared for. The left one, resting on her hip, had a single ring on it. The set caught the light in the momentary cruciform flashes of a good star sapphire.

"Greetings, my queen," Capshaw said.

Stasia Kondoleon's wide mouth widened, showing some very even, very white teeth, possibly her own. Her voice was low and pleasant. Her eyes took in Roy in a sharp, lingering glance.

"Gentlemen." The dark, glossy haired head inclined slightly.

Capshaw turned to Roy with exaggerated politeness. "You indulgence, Doctor. Stase come here a minute."

They moved out into the dark hollow of the hall. Roy, the liquor fingering at his head, stood stupidly staring after them. He caught an occasional unintelligible phrase of Capshaw's voice, probably making the essential transaction. Capshaw came back, alone.

"Come on, Doc," Capshaw said, "let's circulate around a little." Roy followed Capshaw out of the alcove, across the expanse of corridor carpet into Stasia Kondoleon's general reception room. He was aware of signs of increasing activity in the place. There was an intermittent buzzing of electric bells, the low murmur of voices, sounds of muffled feet on stairs, and increasing music. It was Roy's first excursion to Stasia Kondoleon's or, in fact, any other whorehouse. But he was instantly and wholly aware of the age-old brothel atmosphere, a definable thing as ancient, changeless, and definite as commercial sin itself.

Stasia Kondoleon's salon (as she referred to it) was a huge room. It was much mirrored and filled with dark, dissolving light. In the carnal climate of it, there were characteristic movements and sound. The music was louder now with the continual mechanical tinkle of the high fidelity recorder hidden somewhere behind a reef of curtains. The movement was of a half-dozen bright-eyed, stark-fleshed women sitting or circulating around in the tempo of it. Roy was aware of Capshaw's voice.

"Sit down, Doc, and we'll look over the merchandise."

They went to one of the wide, upholstered, benchlike seats in a corner. Across the room Roy got an impression of indistinct male visages widely spaced from each other, not unlike those of patients he had seen in the Charity clinic waiting room.

Capshaw's glance toward them, casual at first, froze suddenly. He stared intently and said something under his breath.

"What did you say Cappy?"

"Nothing, Doc," Capshaw said.

The face Capshaw was looking at was momentarily lit by the flare of a lighter flame put to the cigarette in the man's mouth. Roy got a fleeting impression of the swarthy skin of it, small eyes, too close together, and the twisted lips pulling at the cigarette. The lighter flame flicked out and it was lost entirely in the general gloom. Capshaw's look relaxed and he sat back again.

"Want another drink, Doc?"

"I don't need any, Cappy. I'm still drunker than hell." He found himself speculating on the next face across from him.

That was a lean-looking one, probably belonging to a traveling salesman. But as much as anything he was aware of the women who periodically cut off the view between himself and the other sitters across the room. He listened to the low occasional laughter and smelled the odor of sweat, smoke, whiskey, and perfume and recognized them as all a part of the place. All were a part of the vicious, luxurious, bordello climate. This was a whorehouse. And what he was looking at were veiled preliminary transactions between the soft crafty offerings of flesh and those who had the need.

Capshaw said something he did not quite hear. He looked up. Standing beside the curtains where they had come in was Stasia Kondoleon, looking at it all.

"Hecate at a witches' Sabbath," Roy thought.

He turned to Capshaw. "What did you say, Cappy?"

"They'll all come around. Pick the one you like," Capshaw said.

He was aware that Capshaw was looking at him critically again.

"You know, Doc, I don't believe you've ever been in a whorehouse before. Have you?"

"Sure. Plenty of times. Why?"

"Well, well . . ." Capshaw said.

A slender girl in some kind of a diaphanous black-net dress stood smiling down at them. She was wearing red high-heeled shoes.

"Hello, Rita. Doc, this is Rita."

The slenderness and darkness of her reminded Roy a little of Katy. The whiskey was less with him now and he felt his stomach contract at the thought of Katy's body. He was also aware of something else beginning to stir through what was left of the whiskey in him. This was a feeling of revulsion for the place and the circumstance, something akin to guilt. He wished he were out of it right now. But now it was too late, he'd have to go through with it, but his lust, if he had ever felt any for this kind of gratification, was draining steadily out of him along with the whiskey. He was conscious that Capshaw and the girl were looking at him.

She stood, slender hand on slender hip, before them, smiling mechanically with her small overpainted mouth. Rita was one of Stasia Kondoleon's younger and more frequented girls. She was waiting to be taken or told to move on.

"Hello, Doc," she said.

"Rita's about as cute as they come," he heard Capshaw saying. "Aren't you Rita?"

Rita's mascared left eye closed in a slow full wink.

"You ought to know," Rita said.

"How about it Doc? Don't you think Rita's cute?"

"Certainly is," Roy heard himself saying.

"Knows her business and will treat you right too. You'll treat the old Doc right won't you, Rita?"

"He'll see," Rita said. Her jaws moved rhythmically. She was casually chewing gum. Roy hadn't noticed it before.

"How about it Rita? You like the Doc?"

"He's cute." Rita's winking left eye closed at Roy.

"Well, what's holding us up then?" Capshaw said. "Love at first sight—one of the things you read about and here it is. Just like that. What are we waiting for? Doc loves Rita and Rita loves Doc. Right?"

"Sure," Roy said sickly.

"Come on, Doc." Roy felt her slight palm in his. "Leave us cut out of here."

She pulled him to his feet. He followed her across the expanse of the smoke-filled room.

The music dimmed behind them as they crossed the corridor and went up the soft footway of stairs. He would have given anything to be out of it now. He felt an immediate and increasing panicky urge to bolt. His mind perversely turned now to the consequences of venery. The long, badly lit venereal ward of the Charity with the telltale searching stink of iodoform, balsam of Peru, formaldehyde, and Lysol hovering over it. He got a flash of the supine forms of those bedridden: long, short, fat, thin men lying in the various beds, all of them with sores, swellings, and discharges. And the others who had been that way and were a little further along on the doubtful cure, who moved about silent and shameful and to themselves. Syphilis, gonorrhea, hard chancre, soft chancre, lymphogranuloma inguinale, lymphopathica venereum. The signs and symptoms of all and sundry. There was a passage, too, now that he remembered, that had caught him in *Croke's Textbook of Venereal Disease, Diagnosis and Treatment*. Croke was apparently given in his medical writings to florid literary descriptions. What Roy recalled now was from the Preface: "Venereal Diseases are disorders which lick the organs by which they are acquired, and may bite the brain and heart long after there is apparent cure. Syphilis is perhaps the best example. . . ."

Nevertheless he went up the stairs.

For possibly five minutes after Roy had followed the girl out of the soft rustle and music of the room Capshaw sat on there. Then he got up and moved casually toward the alcove where Stasia Kondoleon stood.

"Come on out, Stasia," he said, passing her. "I want to talk to you."

He waited for her in the dim hall. She came through the curtains.

"Not here," Capshaw said, "this is on the way to the can. He might have to go."

She stood for a moment, and then moved down the hall ahead of him, where she opened a door. The room was small. In it were a desk, a sofa, and two chairs.

"Let's sit down, Stasia," Capshaw said, seating himself on the sofa.

"What's the matter, Cappy?" The long Levantine eyes looked at him.

"You've got a real bad boy in there, Stase. Do you know who I mean?"

"No."

"A guy by the name of Comalli. The one who's been talking to Agnes. I guess it's Agnes—the big blonde?"

"That's Agnes."

"You know who I mean?"

"Yes."

"Did he come alone?"

"Yes. I think so."

"You don't know him, do you Stase?"

Stasia Kondoleon looked at him.

"I said I didn't."

Capshaw returned the look.

"That's good. Then there won't be any trouble about it."

"What trouble? What trouble about what?"

"Look, Stase. This guy is going to get picked up."

"All right," she looked at him fixedly. "What's that to me?"

"Fine," Capshaw said. "Just as long as you know how it is. Where's the telephone?"

The dark, oblique eyes met his. "You're going to finger him?"

"Certainly," Capshaw said, "I'm a reporter. I don't give a Goddamn who I finger if there's a story in it. This could be a big one, an exclusive."

"I hope you know what you're doing, Cappy."

"I do. I want a telephone and not that pay one. I'm going to tell Rybecki."

"Now, just wait a minute." Stasia's eyes slowly came down to slits. "I haven't had any trouble here and I don't want any."

"Stase, you won't have any. They'll take him somewhere else. I'm just going to say Comalli is here. You read my piece about Di Genova? Well, Comalli didn't kill Di Genova. But he knows who did. So do I, I think, as a matter of fact. So does Rybecki. Now come on, baby, where's that phone?"

There was some silence between them.

"All right," Capshaw said, "who's side are you on Stase? I'll go out and phone from a drugstore somewhere."

She got up suddenly. The dark eyes looked at him opaquely. "Do what you want to. The phone's right there."

The star sapphire on her hand winked as she pulled down the panel of the desk.

"Now wait a minute, Stase . . ."

The curtains had closed behind her. He was alone with the telephone.

There was a wait after he got downtown Police Headquarters, another before he got Homicide Division, and still another before he got Rybecki. He had evidently interrupted Rybecki at some one of his more important chores. The inspector's voice came over with a timbre of distinct annoyance.

"Homicide. Inspector Rybecki."

"The whorehouse Kondoleon—Capshaw," Capshaw said.

"What the hell is all this, Capshaw? I'm busy."

"Yeah, fighting crime," Capshaw said. "Now listen, you're looking for the Kite, aren't you, for the Di Genova killing? That right?"

"Who says so? Who told you? I didn't say so. What—"

"Shut up and listen, Inspector. It figures, that's your number-one guy right now isn't it, the Kite?"

"Suppose it is. Now, Goddamn it, what—"

"Shut up and listen. I'm trying to do you a favor. Screw around with me and I'll hang up, see? I've never given you a bum steer have I?"

There was a momentary pause. The inspector's voice came back.

"All right, let's have it, Cappy."

"Am I right about the Kite, Inspector?"

"Now listen, Capshaw, that's confidential police business. You put anything like that out and you'll job the whole Goddamn case, for—"

"O.K. I'm right. You got any kind of a line on him yet?"

"That also is a matter of—"

"O.K. You haven't. Now I'm going to give you one provided you give me the whole works about it first, if and when you take him. Is that a deal?"

"Listen, if you've got any information about known and wanted criminals, you'd better—"

"Don't get official with me, you bastard," Capshaw said. "Is it a deal?"

"You really got something, Capshaw?"

"Yep."

"Like where we could pick up the Kite?"

"Not that good," Capshaw said. "But how would you like Iggy Comalli, who can probably tell you?"

There was a short silence.

"Yeah." The inspector's voice had a tone of suppressed interest. "Yeah. Comalli would be all right. Comalli will do. Let's have it."

"Good," Capshaw said. "Is it a deal?"

"All right, Goddamn it." The inspector's voice was charged now with annoyance and eagerness. "It's a deal. Where's Iggy Comalli? We've got a P.B.I. out on him. He's supposed to be in St. Louis."

"Well, he's not," Capshaw said sweetly. "He's right here in this decent and well-appointed whorehouse, owned and operated by our mutual friend, La Belle Kondoleon."

"You better be right, Cappy."

"I am right. Did you ever get a phony tip from me, Sherlock?"

"We'll be over." The inspector's voice was smooth now with a kind of subdued enthusiasm. "Is the son-of-a-bitch high on the hop? Is he heeled?"

"How the hell would I know whether he'd heeled or hopped up?" Capshaw said. "I'm not a public defender. You find out. That's your department. He's here though."

"We'll find out," Rybecki said. "We'll be right over."

"Now look, Stanislaus," Capshaw said, "we've got Anastasia to consider. No strong-arm stuff in her place. It's got to remain inviolable—like a church you know. I talked to her. She's real worried about this."

"You don't have to tell me about whores," Rybecki said, "or about Stasia Kondoleon or either one of her houses."

"You bet I don't," Capshaw said. "When it comes to whores, whorehouses, and whoring, I'll listen to Rybecki anytime. Just don't give Stase any trouble she doesn't need, will you? Take Comalli outside of the joint, will you?"

"We'll do that," the inspector said. "Anything I ought to know about over there?"

"Yeah. There's a lot of vice over here. People are getting laid right and left. Just don't forget our deal."

Capshaw hung up. He stood by the phone thoughtfully for a moment, half a mind to call the city editor and give him a good plausible lie about why he hadn't shown up yet at the *Record* office. Then he thought better of it. There was still plenty of time for him to get his copy in before the morning edition deadline. He went back to the climate of sin in Stasia Kondoleon's reception room.

Rita always handled her customers with a commendable professional dispatch. Almost before the door clicked behind them the girl was out of the flimsy sheath she was wearing and flat on her back, in bed. She held out her arms and wriggled her fingers at Roy.

"Come on, big boy, get out of them clothes and let's get with it. Rita's going to take care of you real good."

Roy stood irresolutely looking at the small overpainted oval of her face with its vacuous expression of expectancy and the bare lean stretch of her sinuous, small-breasted body. If she had had a sack over her head, the rest of her would look a lot like Katy. This idea did not stimulate him. There was in fact no lust in him at all. He felt no appetite for this. What he felt was a strange sort of guilt, and physically a little sick.

"Come on baby—whatsa matter with you? Get out of them clothes and come on. We ain't got all night." She wriggled her fingers at him again with impatience.

That gesture decided him.

"Listen, Rita," he said, "matter of fact, I'm not feeling very good and I'm really not up to this—"

The small painted eyes narrowed at him. She sat up suddenly.

"Whatsa matter? You think I'm not clean or something? Well, I am. I ain't going to give you any dose. I ain't done that to nobody yet."

"Look," Roy said, "I know that, I just don't feel like it that's all. I know you're all right. It's just that—"

She shot a hard suspicious glance at him.

"You queer or something? You want something special is that it? Like stomping on your or a whip? Well, I don't do none of that stuff. I'm a straight girl. Nothing fancy see? I'm a straight lay. You don't like it that way, I'm sorry. That's it. You want any of that other kind of stuff you better go downstairs and talk to Stasia."

"Jesus," Roy thought, "this is like a page straight out of Krafft-Ebing."

"Listen," he said, "it's not that way at all. I just don't feel like—"

"So you don't want it with me? That it? Well, that's all right with me too, big boy."

She was off the bed now, slipping into the skimpiness of the sheathlike dress. Whores have pride too.

"Listen," Roy said, "it's just that I don't want to get laid right now. But could you do something for me—for ten bucks?"

She stood there with her dress on, facing him and teetering into her high-heeled shoes. Her eyes narrowed at him again.

"What's that?"

"Just don't let on to my friend downstairs that I didn't do anything with you."

He pressed the crumpled ten dollar bill into her hand. She looked at it briefly and saw that it was a ten.

"You want I should tell him we did it real good, that it? That what you want?"

"That's it." Roy nodded.

She stood looking at him speculatively.

"Whatsa matter with you? You aren't a weirdo or a queer. You impotent?"

"No," Roy said, "but right now I am I guess. Tell my friend I'm a hell of a lay will you?"

The hard suspicion was out of her eyes now as she looked at him.

"O.K. I will. And I bet you are, too, when you get your mind on it."

She stuffed the bill in her stocking and Roy followed her out the door and downstairs again.

Before they left the place, Capshaw had a brief and private conversation with Anastasia Kondoleon which Roy, waiting in the anteroom, did not overhear. On the way out Capshaw was grinning.

"Come on Casanova," he said, "we'll have a couple of belts and then eat."

"I oughta to be getting back, Cappy," Roy said uneasily.

"Come on, Doctor, it's only nine o'clock. A satyr like you has to replenish his strength with food and drink frequently. Come on. We'll wind it up over at Chris's with a pizza and a drink or so."

Outside, as they walked down the almost deserted, neon-lit grotto of Velle Street, Capshaw looked back frequently. But there was no evidence of anyone looking like agents of the police.

"That stupid bastard Rybecki is screwing around getting here," Capshaw said thoughtfully to himself, "and he's going to lose him."

"What, Cappy?" Roy said.

"Nothing, Doc, nothing," Capshaw said.

There was something of the coming cold of winter in the October darkness. The clean sharpness of it began to clear Roy's head as they walked toward the Asterion. By the time they got there and pushed open the door into its intimate steaminess, Roy felt that he could eat.

"Katy," he thought. "Goddamn her anyway. Katy . . ."

The pizzas of the Asterion, along with the Greek salad (fresh lettuce, ripe olives, anchovies, chives, goat's milk cheese in thin slices, with olive oil and vinegar) were the house speciality. A little costly perhaps by comparison with the rest of the items on the Asterion's menu, but worthwhile—infinitely better than the less distinguished soup, spaghetti, and hamburgers, in any case. And compared to the Charity's notoriously lousy, cooked in quantity cuisine, it took on an additional opulence.

Capshaw finished his completely and hungrily just ahead of Roy. They sat back in overdistended satiation looking at each other. Chris pushed the coffee toward them and retired.

In spite of what had just gone down him, Roy was aware that he was no drunker but certainly no more sober, than he had been when he got there. He was also aware that Capshaw was looking at him with a kind of unexpected fixation.

"Doc," Capshaw said, "tell me something honest and true will you? Tell me now man to man, have you ever been in a whorehouse before? Before tonight at Stasia's I mean?"

"Why, Jesus Christ. Now Cappy I told you. Come on now." He had the wholehearted hope that Capshaw might believe his swaggering. "Why, for Christ's sake? Why?"

Capshaw looked at him steadily. And he saw at that instant that there was no lying to Capshaw.

"Sure, Doc," Capshaw said. He shook his head. "Don't try to shit me though. You're a good kid, Doc. You're a doctor all right. But you're still just a kid. Now you really haven't even been in a full-fledged honest-to-God whorehouse before tonight. Have you, Doc? Come on now, be honest. Have you?"

Roy looked back at the amusement flickering in Capshaw's eyes.

"No, I haven't," Roy said. "Tonight was the first time."

Capshaw sat back fingering his glass, still looking at him.

"Good. Now we're with each other. Now we can talk on the ground floor with each other. Tell me, Doc, did you ever read a thing by Ben Johnson called *The Honest Whore?*"

"No."

"Well, it's a lousy play. Lousy by comparison to any of Shakespeare's and Johnson was Shakespeare's contemporary. The point of it is interesting. The point is the title—there are honest whores. There were then. And there are now. There are honest whorehouses too. Stasia Kondoleon runs one in case you're ever interested again. Now . . ."

Capshaw took a battered wallet out of his inside coat pocket and removed a ten dollar bill. He pushed it across the table to Roy.

"There's your money back, Doctor. That's proof of it. At Stasia Kondoleon's you don't have to pay for what you don't get. See?"

Roy looked at the money and at Capshaw and felt himself redden with confusion. Capshaw's shoulders, he saw, in spite of his deadpan face, were shaking with suppressed laughter. . . . Then he found that he was laughing himself.

"Goddamn it, she told on me."

Capshaw shook his head, chuckling audibly. "That's right, Doctor. She may have told on you, but she didn't feel right about taking your money either."

"Well," Roy said, "well—"

"Well," Capshaw said, "you're a very fortunate man. You've learned two extremely valuable lessons today and real cheap too."

"Have I, Cappy? What's that?"

"Well, you've learned that there are honest whores. Very rare, but there still are some. And . . ."

Capshaw's pause was inordinately long.

"And what, Cappy?"

"And," Capshaw said, "the big one to remember is—whore or debutante, until you're married to her, and maybe not even then, never really trust a woman."

Before they left, Chris insisted that they have a drink on the house. They had it, and left the Asterion, parting at the corner across from the Charity.

"See you later Casanova," Capshaw said.

The minute that Capshaw closed the door of his suite at the

Andan he threw his battered hat in the general direction of the sofa, went to the telephone, and dialed.

There was a long wait before he got Inspector Rybecki. But he got him.

"Did you take him, Sherlock?" Capshaw said.

"Who's this?" Rybecki's voice sounded official, pressed, and important.

"It's Jesus Christ," Capshaw said. "Who'd you think it was? God?"

"Capshaw," Rybecki almost spit his name into the phone.

"Yeah. Capshaw. Did you get Comalli?"

"Listen," Rybecki's hoarse voice sounded defensive, "are you sure—"

"Look, I know by the way you're talking that you didn't get him. You got there too late, didn't you? He blew before—"

"We're going to get him, Cappy. We've got the line on him. Now—"

"Sure," Capshaw said, "you muffed the whole Goddamn thing because you didn't get over there when I called you to take him. You're a lousy sleuth, Stanislaus, and this is the last Goddamn time I stick my neck out trying to tip you. See? Comalli is chicken himself, but he plays with some bad boys I know about as well as you do. I could get my head blown off for tipping you, real easy. He saw me, I think, just like I saw him. I'll be Goddamned if I do this again and—Screw you, you incompetent son-of-a-bitch. My blood be on your head."

"Listen, Cappy. Now don't—"

"Up you," Capshaw said and rang off.

4

Back at the Charity, Roy slowly took off his clothes. He was drunk on a full stomach—the worst possible state of drunkenness. But he had the advantage of knowing it. He got himself into his bathrobe and went to the antiseptic and recently renovated bathroom the Charity maintained for its resident staff.

"I've got to be all right by tomorrow morning" kept pounding through his miasma of food and liquor. And with this urgency in mind he went to one of the metal-enclosed toilets and performed the ancient and effective self-treatment for impending hangovers. He leaned over, put his finger down his throat, and spewed up everything with which he had insulted his long-suffering stomach for the last six hours. He completed the ritual by brushing his teeth and taking a cold shower. It was probably the ill-advised cold shower that was to keep him awake awhile after he got to bed. . . .

He lay for some time in the darkness thinking and listening to the night-subdued traffic noises on the streets outside. He thought about Katy and wondered if he really loved her. At one time or another, in bed with her and out of it, he had certainly been sure he had. Even thinking of her now gave him a kind of twist in the belly. But then maybe Capshaw had the right idea about women. He had some ideas about them that Roy had never thought of. And Katy was right in there with his generalizations about them as he saw it now. And then the business of Capshaw knowing about him never having been in a whorehouse before and his Goddamn clumsy contrivance with that hard-eyed little whore Rita who reminded him of Katy. Capshaw had been trying to do him a favor, but Goddamn it, what with the liquor and the feeling about Katy's walking out on him, he just hadn't felt like it. And instead of being honest and saying so to Capshaw, he was so concerned with trying to look sophisticated and the rest of it, for his own and Capshaw's benefit, that he had given her almost his last ten bucks to go and lie about it to make him look what he thought he ought to look like. Capshaw was right about him. Had him figured precisely right when he had said, "You're a good kid, Doc. You're a doctor all right. But you're still just a kid." That was right. He was a doctor, but he was still just a kid.

He had all the trappings of the doctor. And he had earned them as they had to be earned. The years at Amityville Preparatory School, where he had gone from the eighth grade of the town of Tusculum's public school. And after that, the years, three of them, at the university, where he had kept up a surprisingly high scholastic average of his grades, till he had decided on what he thought he wanted to do. Be a doctor. And after that the competitive acceptance to medical school. And the tough hard grind of the four years of that, which he made *cum primis honoribos*, as his diploma obscurely stated in the usual conventional Latin phrases. Then, after that, his internship at the Charity following the gruelling examination to get it. The year's internship there that he had busted his ass for, and during it his decision that the specialty of surgery was for him, largely made because of the hero worship of those who had made it. Particularly, and beyond all others, the Old Man, whose rules were inflexible for those he took to learn under him. Especially about the pathology requirement in which you cut and described endlessly the Charity's lengthening list of dead to get the chance at it. When you had had enough of that (to satisfy the Old Man) you could then go on to learn the strange esoteric craft of surgery—what you really thought you wanted to do.

Meantime you hadn't learned much of anything else about living. You were too preoccupied with death. When you had a spell away from it you took what you could get in the way of living wherever you could find it. If you were lucky you met somebody like Katy who might sweat you through it. Like Katy who had a body (for you) like a bacchante. Who was smart and felt enough about you to listen to what you had to say after you, drunk or sober, had gotten through with having her—whenever and wherever you could. And she had a good idea about your mouthings and your clumsiness while you did it. But she was too much of a lady to charge you with it immediately after or at anytime after it.

"Katy," he thought, "maybe that's the reason I couldn't lay that little whore."

But it really was not. At least it was not the only reason. Much of it lay a little deeper than that, whether Roy recognized it or not. A lot of it stemmed from deeper roots. The fact was that Roy had a profound conviction about sin and sex. The two, from his cradle, had been almost synonymous. The chief component was a sense of guilt. These had been fostered in him by home (in Tusculum), the Amityville Preparatory School, and the Protestant Anglican Church. The sexual doctrines of these three were more or less identical.

At home particularly, and in the town of Tusculum generally, sex was never mentioned by that name, or any of its more pungent synonyms, such as copulation, fornication, or adultery. It was universally referred to as "doing wrong" or "being bad." So-and-so did not fornicate, copulate, or have sexual relations with so-and-so, they "did wrong." This home-Tusculum terminology was readily understood in light of the fact of the general admission that sex was nasty, forbidden, and obviously shameful. It was fraught with dire possibilities of infamy, illegitimacy, and disease. Those who indulged in it out of wedlock took terrifying chances with the occurrence of all three, and more than that on nameless divine retributions. Roy learned early through the gossip of the town and his home that fornication was the foremost sin of the world, and of Tusculum.

The St. Andrews Anglican Church of Tusculum heartily emphasized this concept. In the lofty sacerdotal language of Prayer Book and sermon, it sternly accentuated it by pointing out the mortal dangers of all fleshly connection except for the specific purpose of procreating more Anglican Church members. Sex was the original sin, the apple of Eve, the primary cause of human downfall. It was still first in the decalogue of human errors, chief source of the devil's harvest of souls, and principal propellant of man on his headlong flight to hell.

At Amityville Preparatory, where Roy had spent four years, these standard sexual dogma were variously repeated and reaffirmed. Every year that eminent molder of the plastic mind and arbiter of sound moral principle, the Reverend Luther Boardman Tringle, L.L.D., ST.D., Headmaster, gave regular and eloquent appeals to his adolescent charges. One of these was called "The Conquest of Self." It was almost wholly devoted to a certain terrible transgression of impurity of mind and body and its avoidance by prayer and physical exercise. It was delivered in a closed session. And it was very impressive because the Reverend Tringle outdid himself to make it so. Once heard, it intermittently haunted the mind of his listeners for months and even years to come. . . .

"Gentlemen of Amityville we are here in closed chapel session today to consider the most important subject in the world—yourselves. You, the boys of Amityville today, the men of tomorrow. Lucretius said 'Puer pater hominis . . . the boy is the father of the man.' What the boy is, the man will be, for it is the moral principles formed in youth that shape the character of maturity. What you do or do not do now, you will or will not become. Habits acquired now will determine the rest of your lives. There is nothing greater than habit. As Ovid says, 'Nihil ad seretudine majus.' Let us consider this closely. Here at Amityville every day we emphasize the habits of hard work, clean life, and fair play. This is the positive side of learning valuable habits. But it is also necessary, young gentlemen of Amityville, from time to time to point out and be aware of evil habits that we may put down and avoid them. This is what we shall do today.

"We shall begin pointing out evil habits by drawing attention to the great truth that all evil habits regardless of their nature arise from one evil habit—the greatest of all. This greatest of evil habits is yielding to the false call of the flesh. All evil habits regardless of their nature are born and grow into giants from yielding to this false call of the flesh. Remember this, young gentlemen of Amityville, all evil habits arise from this one greatest and evil habit, yielding to the false call of the flesh. But to yield to such a call one must first hear it. But it is always heard and will be heard by each and every one of you. And how will you recognize it for the evil, monstrous, devil-spawned thing it is? You will recognize it because it will beckon your mind to dwell upon impure thoughts and your body to act upon them. This call of the flesh beckons you to defile your mind, your spirit, and your body, and hence to the first step in their destruction, in the sight of God and in the sight of yourself. Listened and yielded to, this destruction is inevitable because it is the first step in acquiring the most powerful and malign of all evil habits and the source of them all—yielding to the false call of the flesh. Let us recognize this false call of the flesh by another name by which it is familiar. It is called lust. This greatest and father of all sins is lust—the false call of the flesh. Lust means to be fleshly or carnally minded. And what does the Bible say of this? In the New Testament, Romans VIII, 6, it says, 'To be carnally minded is death.' And so it is. And so it is for it is the source and wellspring of all evil habits because it is the first false call of the flesh which, when listened and succumbed to, makes possible itself and all others, such as smoking, gambling, and the taking of alcohol. Burton, in his magnificent Anatomy of Melancholy, which some of you in the fifth form will well remember reading, says:

" 'Burning lust, a disease, frenzy, madness, hell. . . . It subverts kingdoms, overthrows cities, towns, families: mars, corrupts, and makes a massacre of men: thunder and lightning, wars, fires, plagues, have not done that mischief to mankind as this burning lust, this brutish passion . . .'

"Recognizing this, what is to be done? What is to be done to destroy this origin of sin, this fountainhead of all iniquity? This is to be done. The call of lust when heard is to be denied with all the strength of mind, soul, and body. And just as it will destroy mind, soul, and body by the habit of yielding to it, so will the habit of its complete denial by the mind, soul, and body subdue and destroy it. How can the mind deny its temptation? By recognizing it for what it is—the source of incalculable evil, an age-old device of the devil to ensnare and delude. Recognizing that, yielding to it is the first step in debasement, dishonor, and final destruction. How can the soul resist it? By calling upon the Lord in prayer fervently and again and again until the wicked whisper of its beckoning is past. And last, how can the body, as a proper temple of grace, defend itself, and aid the mind and the soul, in their resistance? This can be done by strengthening the body in the pursuit of manly sports and hardy exercise. When such temptation comes, go to the athletic field and the sweat and fatigue of the body will subdue the beast.

"What is the secret then of greatness and character? The conquest of the lusts of the flesh. The habitual victory of the mind, the soul, and the body over its temptations—the conquest of the baseness of self. Remember the words of Titus, "He who ruleth himself is greater than he who taketh the city. . . .'"

There was more of this in the hour that the Reverend Tringle devoted to it before his final prayer for the chastity of the young gentlemen of Amityville. Invariably Roy and the rest of the young gentlemen left this closed session chastened, fearful, and ashamed. They also left with a sense of secret guilt and a desperate resolve to substitute the Bible, the chapel, and the quarter-mile track for some other adolescent inclinations.

It was not particularly strange then that Roy, with the Tusculum, St. Andrews Anglican Church, and Amityville sexual dogma instilled in him, had for a long time distressing reaction from his early lapses into carnality. On this account they remained relatively few and far between. With his attitude any lasting or generous physical relation with a woman was unlikely if not impossible. It was some years before any woman with whom he had bodily to do was otherwise than an embodiment of guilt. Once he had to do with one, he wished not to see her again, and usually did not.

Gradually, through a succession of hit-and-run amours in college and medical school, he became more acclimated and his sexual perspective changed to one of a little more maturity. By the time his relationship with Katy Winter was established he could regularly consort with a woman, and had even learned he could like her a little afterward. But now, if he was going to do what he said, he could not afford any encumbrance on the way to his objective, particularly the possessive female type of encumbrance that such relationships are likely to impose. Katy Winter had recognized this, almost from the instant he had begun to tell her about his commitment with the Old Man.

Katy was mad, hurt, and disappointed. And she was no fool. It could be said for her, among other things, that she loved Roy as much or more than she would probably ever love any other man. But she had given herself to him not without a good deal of the usual female calculation. A calculated risk so to speak. Her gamble had been that Roy would marry her without further ado or other male nonsense that year as she suggested. She had staked her plans and one of her best assets—her pliant and attractive body—on it. Instead she had lost. He had, like a cad, taken the bit in his teeth ("stolen the bait" in Capshaw's parlance) and run out on her. Given her up, betrayed her, and preferred to go on starving in that damned pesthouse for God knew how much longer under the Old Man. Doing that, when he could be out in practice making money, like all doctors invariably did, and with her in holy wedlock helping him and having such a wonderful life climbing together. But he was going to do what he had told her he was going to do, and he was asking her to wait around when he could have her now—the ideal wife for a rising young physician (all women are convinced that they can be superb at this because they are so diplomatic and understanding). Doing what he was going to do, instead of what he had given her every reason to believe he would and could do. Marry her now and get started. Well, he wasn't going to do that. That was that. She knew it now. She had made a bad bargain and she might as well face it along with the humiliation. And that humiliation would be considerable, too, because she had hinted to "the girls," the nebulous group of similar females of her circle who thought that it was ring- and blossomtime for her, too, as it had been for quite a few of them recently. She had been so sure he would be submissive that she had, prematurely, in the coy way that women have, let it be known among "the girls" that there was that final sweet understanding between herself and the doctor (date to be announced anytime now—or maybe, as she had archly suggested, the announcement that they had gone and done it on the sly and that she was already Mrs. Dr. Roy Maines). She knew for a fact that Lucille and some of the other girls were planning a shower for her. But now, on top of everything else, there was the necessity of the absolutely humiliating hell of some proper explanation, particularly to the girls wed, about to be wed, and otherwise. In this, as in other things, Katy Winter was a realist. The hard chore of satisfactory explanation to them had to be done. The sooner the better. And after the immediate reaction period of tears that followed her meeting with Roy, she began it at once. She had dried her eyes, had two large, comforting drinks of bourbon, and picked up the telephone. At the moment Roy, in his bleak bed at the Charity, was going to sleep thinking of her, she was still on it:

"I just told him simply and frankly, Lucille. You know how I am. I am a direct person and I have to be direct. I simply told him no, that I would not marry him right away under circumstances like that. . . . What? Oh yes, Lucille—it's all over. I'm through—definitely through. . . . Yes, he's tried to reach me several times. . . . No, I certainly won't. I just hang up. . . . Yes, I intend to . . . What? . . . Yes. And you know out of it there is one thing that I'm terribly glad about. Through it I managed to keep my head. Fortunately there wasn't any of that to complicate things. It's so hard to make them understand that it means so much more to a woman. I will say this for him though, once he understood that I wouldn't until we were married, he was really all right about it. . . . What? . . . Oh, I'm sure. It isn't that there's anyone else . . ."

Capshaw's comment on that conversation would have been interesting if he could have heard it. But he was then asleep, with his clothes on, at the Andan. And so by that time was Roy, at the Charity, in one of its narrow iron bedsteads.

Roy woke up later than usual that morning. But due to his previous emetic performance before going to bed, he woke with no headache and a commendably clear head. The first

thing he did was call the switchboard to locate Blinn. Blinn
had gone to breakfast earlier but was still in the dining
room. Roy dressed hurriedly and went down. He pushed
open the swinging doors and went in. The familiar, faintly
sour smell of the place rose in his nostrils and then receded.
There was the low buzz of conversation and the scrape
and chink of metal and crockery. Over in the corner he saw
Blinn sitting alone. He went to his table and sat down.

"Hi, Maines." Blinn gave him a friendly nod. "I was just
getting ready to try to find you. I guess you're going to be it
now."

"I'm sorry as hell to hear about your father, Ted. I hadn't
heard until the Old Man talked to me yesterday."

"Thanks," Blinn said. "Well, you know, one of those
things. I talked to the doc back home again this morning,
who's taking care of him. So far he's coming along all right.
I'm taking the four o'clock train out of here."

The waitress was beside them.

"Just coffee please, Nola," Roy said.

"Make it two please, Nola," Blinn said, and turned back to
Roy. "The Old Man said you'd be taking my place and to line
you up with the service from my end of it."

He pulled a paper from his pocket and pushed it toward
Roy.

"This will help. It's a list of the patients on my ward with
the diagnosis and a few notes about them that will save you
going through a lot of charts. I can meet you later up on
the ward and go around a little and look at them if you want
to." Roy pocketed the paper.

"That'll be fine, Ted. Any time you say."

"I've still got some stuff to do before I clear out of here.
How's about one o'clock for you?"

"Fine," Roy said. "I certainly appreciate all the trouble
you're taking for me."

"Not at all, Roy. I want to have the service with everything
straight before I leave it and you're the guy who is coming
on."

The coffee came and they cautiously sipped at the bitter
black scald of it.

"Anything you want to ask me about, I'll try to give you
the right answers." Blinn looked at him expectantly.

"Well, you've given me the list and we're going to look
around together at one o'clock. I guess the only thing right

now is Santry. What's the best way to work under the Smiler?"

Blinn gave a mirthless chuckle. "That's a good question, Maines. I wish I could give you a good answer. I really wish I could. I don't know the best way to work with him or under him. I've been with his end of the Old Man's service for almost a year now and I still don't know. I can tell you how I've done it—that's probably not the best way though."

"Well, tell me about him," Roy said. "I've heard. And I'm in the barrel with him now."

"That's right, you are. Well, let's see. I'll try to be fair about it. Now this is just my side of it—"

"Sure," Roy said, "go ahead."

With his thin, pleasant face, Blinn's eyes had become suddenly hard, with a thoughtful kind of hardness. It was the kind of an expression a man gets on his face when he is trying to be honest about a difficult and personally distasteful subject.

"You've got to understand to begin with that I hate the son-of-a-bitch. So that anything that I say has to be interpreted in terms of that. I've been with him all this time and that hasn't changed a bit. I hated him after the first week on his end of the service and I hate him more now. He's a hard guy for me to talk about. But I'll try.

"I've spent a whole year looking at him from a worm's-eye view, me being the worm. In the first place, make no mistake about it, he's a master surgeon. Not in the Old Man's class of course, but good. Very good as a technician. As good I think as either Tom Wilder or Wild Will Wortle. Honestly, I think that, and I've been with all three on emergencies. And he knows his surgery. He's not very often wrong—on diagnosis either. In fact, at times the son-of-a-bitch is like the Old Man in that. He's a little uncanny. But when I've said that, that's all that's good I can say about him. The rest in my book is all bad—"

He looked at Roy suddenly.

"You know, Maines, I really hate to feel this way about him. I hate to feel this way about anybody. I hate to leave the Service and this place for good feeling this way. But I can't help it."

Roy shook his head. "I know," he said, "but anything you can tell me will be a help."

"He really is a fantastic guy," Blinn went on. "He's the one person I've ever seen without one iota of human warmth in him. I don't believe he ever had any. Or if he ever did he's schooled it completely out of himself. Personally I think he was born without it. Anyhow he hasn't got any at all. He's as cold, unfeeling, and impersonal as a snake. He has absolutely no regard or concern for anyone or anything but himself. He's consistent in this, though, as in everything else. Whatever he is, he's a very consistent guy. If he has any more emotion than a wooden Indian he never shows it. He does have two emotions, though, at that, vindictiveness and contempt. He has contempt for anybody under him and vindictiveness for anybody who crosses him on anything—even the slightest thing. His ego is simply unbelievable—with him it's a regular Moloch. He'll throw anything into it to keep it appeased. You'd never know any of these things though, maybe on casual acquaintance with him, except for one thing. The son-of-a-bitch is a smiler. He's always smiling. It looks like a smile, but after you've seen it often enough you recognize it as more of a device to conceal something. It's a pretty eerie thing that smile of his. It's always there, just more or less so at times. Tell him anything, he smiles. It's never off that face of his. I've lived around it and hated it, yes, and I guess even feared it for almost a year. He smiles when he operates, smiles when he eats, smiles when he's chewing somebody's ass out for something, smiles when somebody's died. It's pretty weird.

"The bastard really isn't quite human I do believe—I think he's some kind of real smart lizard that turned anthropomorphic somehow. He's a very creepy guy. He'd throw his own mother to the wolves, too, and never think twice about it if it happened to gain him a point."

Blinn looked at his watch. "Hey! It's damned near nine, Maines. Look, I've got to go. There's still a lot for me to do before traintime. See you on the ward at one and we'll finish things there, O.K.?"

"Sure, Blinn. Thanks. And I'll see you."

He was on the point of leaving when Ransahoff fanned through the swinging doors, saw him, and came over.

"Jesus!" Ransahoff said, hitting Blinn's vacant chair heavily. "Hey, Nola, just coffee, please will you?"

"Hello, Doctor." He turned to Roy. "Christ, I'm in terrible

shape. I don't know why the hell I don't just die and get it over with."

Roy looked at his pale face, the dark shade of his eyes, and his stubbled chin. "You certainly look like hell. What happened to you?"

"Last night is what happened to me. I worked on this hangover from the time I left you at the Greek's until two-thirty this morning. And, let me tell you, this is without a doubt the Goddamndest post-alcoholic depression on record. With this one I am now grand champion. Christ, it's ridiculous that you can still stay alive and feel like this. It's like having cerebral palsy, the clap, cancer, and the menopause all together and rolled into one. Look at that . . ."

He held up a quaking hand.

"I may live at that, though. It's been a whole hour since my last puke."

"What happened in the l'amour department? How did the big seduction go?"

"Oh, that, for Christ's sake." Ransahoff made a gesture of disgust.

"Well, what happened?"

Ransahoff reflected on this moodily for a moment.

"I failed, chief. I didn't get it. I'll turn in my badge, but I'm all through with that one. It just simply can't be done. I don't care about the money I spent trying. I'm just happy to be alive even this way."

"Go on."

The waitress was beside them.

"Listen," Ransahoff said, "if you're going to eat I'll leave. I can't bear to watch you. Today it's curds and whey—those lousy eggs with that creamed crap on them—"

"I'm not eating either," Roy said. "Come on, let's have it."

"Well, after I left you at the Greek's I came back over here and got dressed. How many beers did we have there? Six or eight, maybe? Anyhow I was far from blistered. I got all tuned up in my sharpest. Shower, shave, deodorant under the arms, and the pick of my extensive wardrobe— that imported English tweed suit I got at Marsten's close-out sale. I had about thirty bucks left. Hell, I figured I was irresistible. I go over to Kinerem's—that's her name, Kin-erem—apartment in Kilroe's car to pick her up and I'm right on time—right on the button. And in I go. She's not like most broads. She's all dressed and waiting. And let me tell you something, this dame, Ruth Kinerem, in street clothes is really something. They just don't come any better built—not possible. She knows how to dress too. I take one look at her and begin to gloat. But you know me—no off-hand preliminary plays. I'm the suave diplomatic type. I asked her where she would like to go. She says, 'Anywhere, is there some place we can dance?' I asked her did she like Hungarian food. Certainly. Fine, then we'll go to the Tokay. You know, that fairly fancy hunky restaurant with gypsy orchestra over on Linden Street? They've got a bar and the goulash is pretty good. Well, that's where we go. For openers she put down three double bourbons, and not to be outdone I ride right along with her. I might as well admit it, by the time we're ready to eat I'm fairly well boiled. Not her though—no indeed. She's just dandy—just more bright-eyed and bushy-tailed that's all. To give the business at hand the continental touch, I ask her would she like some wine? 'Oh, certainly.' Hell, yes. Of course. It will be fun. We have a couple of the large economy size with the goulash. Meantime we get up and throw it around on the dance floor a little. And let me tell you another thing, just as an aside, this girl is quite a kid on her feet. A regular Madame La Zonga. She does the rhumba, she does the Conga. I'm not Hungarian and neither is she, but the gypsy braves play a couple of czardas and we do that. We go back to the table and finish the goulash. It's an off night and there aren't many customers, so we get a lot of attention from the help. The gypsy orchestra leader, the violin player, Ferenc something-or-other, comes around with the cymbalum player, who doubles on the accordion. We get a private serenade. 'Faded Lilacs' and 'When a Gypsy Makes His Violin Cry,' as I recall. We're sopping up the booze all this time of course, and I'm getting more sentimental by the minute. I'll say this for me though, I only do it when I'm good and swacked. Anyhow I figure it's a good pitch and I tell her the story of my life and hard times. I let her in on the fact that I'm a pretty tragic figure—alone, valiant, and misunderstood, like a hero out of A. E. Housman's poetry. We're drinking all this time mind you. This girl is listening to me maunder with both ears. That's another thing—she's a great listener. You have to watch that. When they're that way you'll blat your brains out before you know what you're doing. Well, to make a long story short, we close the Tokay. I'm blind. The bill is more dough than

I've got. She lends me ten to get out of the place. From here on it gets pretty hazy, but she drives Kilroe's car back to her place. I have a vague recollection of coffee and a phone call. Apparently she got me back to the Charity and turned me over to Kilroe at the back door. That's about the last thing I remember. I got up at six-thirty officially, but I threw up three times before that, and a couple of times since. I don't know where that dame puts it. She polished off the booze with me drink for drink. I wind up stoned to the eyes and she's apparently cold sober. I wonder how she feels today though."

"My, my," Roy said, "and she looks fine."

"That dame is in league with the devil or something," Ransahoff said. "Wait a minute—how do you know how she looks?"

"Saw her on the way down here."

"Well, Goddamn it. At least I know when I'm outclassed. I'm only mortal. I was a fool to think I could go up against the Witch of Endor. She's not that though—she's really Circe—turns unsuspecting guys like me into swine. One last word of advice, don't ever try to ply that kid with liquor to get at her—you'll end up broke, walking on all fours, and talking to yourself."

"Why don't you go lie down awhile, Ransahoff? You look like hell. You're not worth much feeling this way."

"You're the doctor," Ransahoff said. "Thank God there's nothing cooking right now. I'll tell Kilroe to take my calls for a while."

They left the dining room.

Roy met Blinn on the ward at one o'clock. They spent more than an hour shifting from bed to bed looking at the patients that lay in them with Roy trying to beat their faces and diseases into his memory. It was obvious that Blinn knew them intimately and had taken a lot of time with them and with their charts. Roy found himself hoping enviously that he would be able to do as well or even almost as well. There was an end to it finally.

"Well," Blinn said, as they stood by the desk again, "I guess that's it, Maines. It's all yours now. Good luck. It's about time for me to shove off."

"Who's taking you to the train, Blinn? I could."

"All arranged, thanks, Maines," Blinn said. "I've got to

do this alone—" Blinn looked at him with his face suddenly empty.

"The Smiler is going to be in his office just about now. I'm going down to tell him off. I've been waiting for this a long time."

They shook hands. He watched Blinn's wiry erect figure, now in street clothes, out of the ward, then he turned back to the charts.

He had gone over them for another hour and was back in his room, when the phone rang.

"Dr. Maines? . . . Dr. Santry. One moment please." Santry was in his office and wanted to see him.

He hurriedly put on a clean uniform, smudged off his white shoes, and got down to Santry's office, wondering as he went what Blinn had said to him.

The Smiler's office in the Charity was like the desk in it, the neatest in the place. And the Smiler was behind it, and he was also a very neat man. At the moment he was wearing, as always, a dark, meticulously fitted suit, impeccably white shirt, and precisely knotted tie. The general impression of his quietly expensive clothes was accentuated by the gold wrist watch and the massive gold links in the spotless cuffs. But it was not this sartorial elegance that Roy looked at. It was the face. He had seen it enough times in and about the Charity in passing. But this time it was turned full visage on him and close enough for a good examination of it. And it made a lasting impression. It did this because as he looked at it, Roy instantly and instinctively felt some primordial alarm system in his subconscious burst out in warning.

Santry's face was abnormally and finely cut, like his clothes and like his body. He had a rather small head with a high brow line. The face under it was long and narrow with narrow and distinct features, ending, as sharply as they started, in the pointed chin. The eyes, set too close together over the thin nose, were light, with a certain flat look about them. Fixed on Roy now there was something behind them that was calculating and watchful. It was not the eyes, though, so much as the mouth that caught Roy's attention and held it. It was the mouth. It was smiling. This smile was simply a mirthless, upwardly concave crease in the thin lips which left just a glint of incisors showing. Really it was no smile at all but a smirk, a cold impersonal, colubrine kind of smirk. It was a fixed and habitual thing that probably was seldom off that face, Roy was to find. And he instantly felt something ominous in it.

"If snakes could smile," Roy thought, as he looked at it, "a cobra would have one like that when it was poised with its hood spread. I wonder what's really behind it? Whatever it is it's eerie and wrong. It's part of something diseased. Something sick as hell that made Kilroe, and Blinn, hate you, and a lot of others too probably. You're the one Chaucer wrote about, 'The smiler with the knife under the cloak.' Blinn had it right. That smile is really something. It's reptilian. That kind of a smile really has no right on any man's face. It's the smile of a reptile hiding in the body of a man."

Santry made a casual gesture toward a vacant chair with a white, well-manicured hand.

"Sit down, Maines," he said, in a toneless and cultured voice.

" 'He surest strikes that smiling gives the blow.' " (This quotation rising from somewhere into Roy's head as he sat down.)

"You're taking Blinn's place beginning tomorrow morning, Dr. Hand tells me."

"Yes, sir."

"You've spoken with Blinn, suppose?"

"Yes, sir. I've been around with him on the ward and gone over most of the charts. I've got a pretty good idea about the patients. I'll try to catch them all up as soon as I can."

The small elegant head nodded at him.

"I see. Very commendable. And on a day off for you wasn't it? Dr. Hand suggested that, didn't he?"

"Yes, sir."

"I see. Very good. Very conscientious. And what else did Blinn have to tell you about my end of the Service, Maines?"

Roy looked at the face and the smile and went on guardedly, wondering what Blinn must have said in his final confrontation.

"Well, about time off and time on, the operating schedule, and the clinic."

"I see. Did he tell you anything more about the Service? Or about me?"

Roy hoped his air at the moment looked ingenuous. "No, sir."

"I see. Well then suppose that I round it out for you then. So that we understand each other."

"Yes, sir."

Santry passed his well-manicured hand lightly over the pointed chin, reflectively. The smile, though, remained the same.

"I run my end of the Surgical Service quite tightly, Maines, as you will see. By that, I mean I tolerate no sloppiness. Operations are on time, rounds on time, and the resident's work is done no matter how long it takes and regardless of his schedule of hours on or off. I don't accept excuses. All I am interested in is whether or not the work is kept to my standard. If a resident cannot keep it that way, I make other arrangements."

His cold eyes flickered over Roy, at his reasonably clean white uniform and fairly clean white shoes.

"I am rather particular about the resident on my division presenting a good appearance at all times. By that I mean a clean neat appearance since he represents me before the patients and the public. Dr. Wilder and Dr. Wortle are more liberal about this, I have observed. If they wish to let their residents go around looking like street cleaners, as they do, that is up to them. My resident does not. He looks like what he is—my representative. His uniform and shoes are clean. Always clean and neat—"

Roy thought of the Old Man, Wilder, and Wortle as he had seen them often, disheveled, pants bagging, in long white coats that were never free from stains and spots, and never immaculately clean.

"So much for that," the flat precise voice went on. "Now. You spend time here in the hospital that I cannot. You see and hear things that I cannot from patients and other sources. These things, you know, Maines, can be quite important. I am going to depend on you to keep me informed about details, about these things. They can occasionally be critical—even small things, like what is going on in the other parts of the Surgical Service. Dr. Wilder's or Dr. Wortle's division, for example, or what Dr. Hand himself might do or say. I'll depend on you to report little things like that to me—not because they are of much consequence in themselves, but because knowing about them makes for a smoother more integrated Service from my end of it."

"Sure," Roy thought, "that's in character—that suggestion that I come sneaking to you like an informer. That I act as your personal stool pigeon. The day I do, that will be the day."

Roy listened to the flat impersonal voice go on for another five minutes about what would be required of him. There was an end to it finally.

"Now, any questions, Maines?"

"No, sir. I guess not at the moment."

"Very well. We'll see how things work out. That's all."

Santry nodded slightly. The interview was over.

"I'm in for trouble," Roy thought as he left the room. "I hate the son-of-a-bitch just looking at him and that smile of his. I'm in for trouble before I even start with him. I could take anything from the Old Man, or Wilder or Wortle. But not from this one—not from him."

He still had until tomorrow morning off and he realized with a sudden pang that he would not be seeing Katy tonight. He wondered if she had cooled down enough to try calling her. Probably not yet. He'd take Capshaw's advice and give her a good letting alone for a while, say a week or so. But right now, he had time on his hands and he acutely missed her. Maybe if he just gave her one nonchalant phone call right now to feel her out. . . . He fought down the temptation. Instead, he ate early at the Asterion, and then, bored and alone, walked down Velle Street toward its line of theaters. His choice was unfortunate and he arrived in the middle of the feature. It was an outstandingly bad English film called *The Cholmondoley* (pronounced Shumley) *Affair*, in which lovely Lady Penelope Cholmondoley and other members of the ancient Cholmondoley lineage honked nasally at each other across the drawing room about the missing Cholmondoley heir who turned out to be the butler. Out of sheer boredom he sat it through to the dreary donouement. The following newsreel was considerably less static. This was largely a series of staccato scenes of the rising Nazi war ferment in Europe—marching Storm Troopers, Jews herded behind barbed wire, and then the hypnotic hysterical face of Hitler spewing threats from a platform in Munich. To Roy at this point, it had little significance. War, if it did come, would be in all probability a remote European contest which the United States could regard as a spectator and without involvement—hardly a matter of concern for a Charity surgical resident, or for anyone so far away from it. If people let those Nazi bastards push them around that was their affair. Americans wouldn't stand for it in this country. . . . He left at the end of the newsreel, wandered back along Velle Street to the Charity, and went to bed.

Out of habit he turned on the battered radio to help lull him into sleepiness.

"Ladies and Gentlemen, the President of the United States . . ."

The announcer's introduction was shortly followed by the smoothly measured patrician voice. The words came with a convincing earnestness.

"My friends and fellow countrymen . . ."

There followed a concise summation of the official position of America toward whatever new signs of conflagration were imminent in Europe. To Roy, dozing by this time, it sounded as it ought to sound . . . semidetached and reassuring.

He turned off the radio and went to sleep. But before he had completely slipped into the comforting blackness, he thought of Katy. . . . He hoped she was feeling as bored and alone right now as he was.

5

That first morning of ward rounds on Santry's division of the Service was on Friday. This was the day that the Old Man saw every patient on every division, Wilder's, Wortle's and Santry's. Because of this, Friday was the official day of "grand rounds." But any day the Old Man came on the ward, so far as the surgical resident was concerned, was almost that.

Roy was there forty-five minutes ahead of time, making sure of what he had been over with Blinn. They came finally, the Old Man and Smiler Santry a little ahead of the hour with the full retinue of the Old Man's staff, including Wilder, Wortle, residents, interns, and medical students. This time there were no visitors. But you never could tell when there might be. And you never could tell who those visitors might be. Some insignificant-looking stranger who the Old Man addressed off-handedly by his first name could be someone of considerable consequence, for example a familiar author in medical literature, a professor of surgery somewhere. If he were, this fact would be gradually exposed in the slow progressive shift from bed to bed. He would then let out that he had done something definitive, like writing a well-known textbook, devising a new operation, or doing a piece of current and possibly controversial research. On the other hand, the stranger might be an undistinguished rural practitioner, in the Charity to learn what he could, and who, in one way or another, had managed the distinction of an acquaintance with the Old Man, for the Old Man treated all of them the same.

There were no strangers this time though. Roy nervously noted this as the string and line of them came on the ward. Roy and the ward nurse apprehensively went forward to meet them with the charts and dressing cart.

The entourage halted before the first of a long phalanx of beds. Roy took the chart from the nurse and handed it to the Old Man. Then he recited generally to the expectant group, but specifically to the Old Man. He made a comprehensive but inclusive presentation.

"This patient is a fifty-five-year-old white male, admitted five days ago at four in the afternoon from the outpatient department. His chief complaint was vague upper-abdominal pain and occasional vomiting of approximately two months duration, progress gradually worse . . ."

He followed with a memorized recital of the X-ray and laboratory reports and then stood expectantly. The Old Man and Santry asked a series of routine but essential questions and got immediate and exact answers.

"All right, Maines," the Old Man said. "What's the diagnosis and what do you want to do about it?"

"Malignancy of the stomach, I think. He's tentatively scheduled for operation as the first case tomorrow. There are four units of blood available for him. He's been talked to about it, has given his consent, and the operation permit signed. Family's been notified."

The Old Man nodded. He turned to the attentive column behind him and gave a terse dissertation. He nodded to Roy again and they moved to the next bed. This bed by bed progression went on slowly but steadily for an hour. When it finally came to an end, the Old Man, Santry, and the rest of the straggling cavalcade left the ward. His first set of rounds as resident with the Old Man and Santry had gone well.

Sweating with relief, Roy sat down at the ward station desk with the stack of charts to write the comments and orders.

One thing was certain. The Smiler hadn't tried to make him look bad by asking a lot of questions about the patients that he might not have been able to answer. Blinn had warned him that Santry frequently did this. But he hadn't this time. But maybe that was simply because the Old Man was around. Anyhow it had gone well and gradually he felt the tension of his first ordeal on the Service loosen and leave him.

The existence of the Charity resident was by necessity narrow and confined. It was a microcosm bounded by the wards, the operating suite, and the emergency rooms. Its activity was continuous, intense, and sometimes disordered, but it was governed by an inexorable and grinding routine. There was a monotonous pattern of sameness in its days.

They started at six in the morning. The reveille was, for Roy, a battered alarm clock or a call from the telephone switchboard. A nasal, gum-chewing voice came over the wire, "It's six o'clock now, Doctor." If this did not stir him the alarm clock did. He lay, listless and gaping, for several minutes looking at the cracked, yellow-calcimined ceiling. With considerable effort he heaved himself out of bed. If the window was open he shut it. He went to the washbowl with the medicine cabinet over it and stood there momentarily collecting his strength and his wits. He yawned, he scratched, and farted. If he had been at the Asterion the night before on off time he was likely to be somewhat aware of his head. He reached into the medicine cabinet and got the usual two aspirin. He looked in the mirror to decide whether or not the stubble on his chin warranted a shave. He shaved, usually, and brushed his teeth. Then he wrapped a towel around his bare belly, put on his wooden clogs, and went to the shower room. The water revived him all the way. He came back fully awake. If his laundry had come back and his old uniform was too dirty, which it usually was, he put on a clean one. He made sure he had his watch, money, fountain pen, keys, and stethoscope. He went down to breakfast. In the dining room he had two cups of scalding coffee strong enough to tan rawhide, and if he thought his stomach would stand it, a rubbery fried egg. At about this point he usually reached a state of full correlation with his environment. He pulled out his notebook, his day's list of chores. Then he went to his ward. By this time it was seven o'clock or almost. For half an hour or a little longer he shuttled around its stretch of beds with the nurse, the charts, and the dressing cart. By the time he had finished this, he had a fair idea of what had gone on during the night with his patients. If there was any time left he wrote orders and notes, but at ten minutes of eight he was in the operating room. There he changed into operating clothes. These came in two sizes, too big and too small. He checked the first case chart and its patient and snarled at the anesthetist for being late. He usually exchanged a few traditional sarcasms with the supervisor. She was a large, graying, inflexible woman with years of service and an enormous experience. She had seen generations of young, smart aleck surgical residents like him come and go. She had no respect for him and he knew it. In fact she considered him and all surgical residents as a passel of impudent young whelps with misplaced medical degrees. The only ones she had any real respect for were the Old Man, or Santry, Wilder, or Wortle. Around them she was coy, almost girlish. She bridled, smiled, and blushed like a girl. She was one, too, once, they said, a long time ago, and just about the time the Old Man was doing what his residents were doing now.

By that time the patient was insensible and the anesthetist sending out to the resident to ask what the hell he was waiting for. He would send back word to the anesthetist that he (the anesthetist) knew what he could do. At this juncture the resident was reinforced by the intern and they began the business of scrubbing. Ten minutes later they were gowned, gloved, waiting for the Old Man or one of his duly appointed attending surgeons to appear. The patient was painted and draped in the trappings of sterility. The red ritual began and ended. It was repeated at irregular intervals while the day crawled on into the afternoon. Sometime around one o'clock or one-thirty the last specimen was out into formaldehyde and the last case was wheeled out. The resident peeled out of his sopping operating clothes and put on his uniform again. He usually got down to the dining room just under the line before they locked the doors. He ate whatever was left on the steam table that looked edible, drank a lot of water followed by coffee, followed by more water. He did not linger usually because it was late and there was nothing to linger over. Half an hour later he was back on the ward and there he spent the rest of the afternoon. He changed the dressings he had not done in the morning, did the histories and physical examinations on new cases admitted while he was in the operating room, listened to new complaints and investigated the old familiar ones, wrote further orders and notes, drew blood, gave blood, and reviewed X-ray films. During this he was likely to be interrupted by ward rounds by Santry or the Old Man, visiting hours, an autopsy, calls on the telephone from other residents, consultations with other services, and unscheduled trips to the emergency room. This went on usually until five or six o'clock. From there on it depended. If he were on call on that particular night he covered his own ward and the ward of his alternate resident. The emergency room became his big concern, for he was likely to put a lot of the night into it. If he were off call what he did was his own business until next morning at six, when the cycle began again and progressed and ended in the same way.

Once in this pattern, the order of his existence became almost automatic. In the long descent of toiling days, time had a tendency to stop. He counted it not by the calendar but fixed it by events. The day that he did this, the night that that happened, the afternoon that something else occurred. His vision was that of a man looking through a tunnel. He saw not to either side but only straight ahead. His only concerns became a series of immediate objectives. He was like a man putting out many small recurrent fires. He extinguished one and passed on to the next, that done to the next, and the next, and finally back to the original place where the fire had sprung up again. It was a hard pattern of existence and the unremitting grind of it required stubborn conviction and the bowels of a badger. But there was no substitute for it and anyone who accepted and lived it long enough, consciously or otherwise, learned much.

In the weeks that followed Roy became fully acclimated to it. He became an intimate and dependable part of the pattern. He learned much of which he was aware of learning and more of which he was not. His only regret and one over which he fretted was that he had not yet had a chance to operate with the Old Man. Junior residents like himself seldom get the opportunity. There was good reason for this. The Old Man was a brilliant but impatient technician, and as such he set a very hard pace for even his most experienced assistants. For the neophyte he was almost impossible. To get used to it usually required a prolonged and gradual period of breaking in. Besides this, operations with him were considered distinctions by his senior residents, who did the scheduling of his cases and invariably booked themselves to work with him. Most of Roy's time in the operating room was passed as a first assistant to Santry.

There was no doubt about it. Blinn was right. Santry was an excellent technician. He operated with a cold, methodical deliberation. He was to Roy's mind a little slow and overmeticulous, but the work was accurately and completely done. It was also done silently for the most part. No one spoke in the operating room when Santry operated except Santry himself. This was in contrast to the Old Man, and for that matter to Wilder and Wild Will Wortle. The Old Man constantly questioned everyone on everything, particularly the anatomy. Wilder kept up a running instructive commentary of explanation and Wild Will Wortle did both loudly and profanely. But not Santry. Santry did not query or explain to his assistants. When Roy asked him about the anatomy or the technique, the cold too-close-together eyes flicked up at him over the mask, and the flat measured voice came from behind it:

"If you don't know that, Maines, you had better look it up. That way, you'll remember it longer. Just watch what we're doing right now."

After a little of this, Roy kept his mouth shut. This was difficult at times because his honest urge to ask was often hard to suppress.

Occasionally though, the Smiler got very articulate. This happened almost invariably when things were not going well, or well enough to suit him. At these times Santry's voice took on a particular low, hissing quality and the words and phrases came in questions.

"Don't you see what I'm trying to do here, Maines? Then use that retractor where I need it."

"Do you ever look at an anatomy book Maines? Then don't put your retractor there, you're going to tear into that vein."

"What's the matter with you, Maines? Tired today? Maybe a little too much beer at the Asterion last night? Come on, give me some exposure. See? Right there is where I want it. . . ."

Roy felt a high hot resentment building up in him during these episodes. But Blinn had taken it and so could he. There was one thing though that Santry did to his assistants when he was particularly annoyed or uncertain. It did not happen often, but when it did it made Roy furious. This was when Santry rapped him over his gloved knuckles with whatever instrument he happened to be holding in his hand. Usually it was a hemostat, but then it could be anything short of the knife. It could be a scissors, a forceps, or a needle holder. But the very fact that he was hit on his obedient well-meaning hands with it and by that quiet smiling son-of-a-bitch roused Roy to a height of uncaring rage. He suppressed this, as he knew that Blinn must have done before him, the best that he could and for quite awhile. And so for a time, as Blinn had done, he endured it. But his preconceived and inherent hatred of Santry continued quietly to grow.

"Jesus Christ," he thought at times, "I wonder if I'll ever get to the place where I'll be with the Old Man? Or Wilder or Wild Will Wortle."

Meantime Roy's first hectic days of getting acclimated to the service were beginning to fade into weeks and months. He realized suddenly one Sunday afternoon that he had not tried to call Katy. The fact was that he had been too preoccupied with the work and too tired following it to give much to anything but the matters at hand. It had been long enough now that he ought to give Katy a try.

Katy's voice came coolly over the phone:

"Oh, hello, Roy. How are you?"

"All right, I guess, if you use the term loosely. How are you Katy?"

"Perfectly fine."

"Uh, Katy. This is really the first time I've had off since I started the Service. How about tonight? I'll get Kilroe's car and pick you up and we'll go out on the town a little. Will—"

"I'm sorry, Roy. But no."

"I see. Another date or still sore, is that it?"

"Let's just leave it at no, shall we Roy? I've really been very busy these days myself."

"Oh, come off it, Katy, will you? I really miss you like hell. Got a lot to talk to you about. I'll be over around six-thirty."

Katy's voice now had something of edge in it, and something a little triumphant.

"No, Roy. I'm sorry. I'm going out."

"Well, I'll come over for a little while right now then. Just for a few minutes. I want to talk to you."

"I know what you want, Roy. And the answer is still no. Just let it go at that."

"Still sore, huh, Katy? All right. You name the time then and I'll get covered and be there right on the nose."

"There aren't going to be any next times, Roy. Now please, I'm late now."

"All right, if that's the way it is." Roy tried to keep the frustration and pique out of his voice.

"That's the way it is, Roy. Good-by."

Roy began to say something sharp that would salvage his pride a little. But he was talking into a dead phone. Katy had hung up.

"Going out," he snorted to himself. "In a pig's eye. Probably going to sit around over there at home with a book. Going to teach me a lesson. O.K., to hell with her for another couple of weeks."

But Katy was going out and almost immediately. The cut-off with Roy might not have been that abrupt if she had not heard the doorbell ringing. She hurriedly revised her lipstick before answering it.

"Well, hello, Preston." She smiled as she held the door open. "Come in. You're right on time, aren't you? Sit down. Be with you in a minute."

Still fuming, Roy was on his way over to the Asterion. He found Inspector Rybecki and Capshaw seated near the bar engaged in beer and learned dispute.

"Hello, Doc." Rybecki's gold teeth glinted at him. "Sit down and listen to the ambassador here trying to horseshit me about international politics."

He turned back to Capshaw. "Like I said, Cappy, how the hell can there be a war for us? Them Nazi bastards ain't got nothing to fight us with. The German financial state won't stand for it. Besides the German people ain't forgot the last time yet when they got the Jesus licked out of them. That guy Hitler may do a lot of yapping around, but when it comes down to hot scratch, why hell, he ain't really going to get into it against the whole world—particularly us—"

"Stanislaus," Capshaw said, "I like to hear you talk about

war because you're a pretty good barometer of uninformed public opinion about the Goddamned cataclysm we're headed for. The average American right now thinks just about the way you do. He sits on his ignorant happy ass right over the powder keg with that queer mad dog son-of-a-bitch Hitler lighting the fuse. What the hell do you think the Spanish Revolution was about?"

"What's that got to do with it?" Rybecki said. "This here's Germany fighting England and France now we're talking about."

Roy was surprised at Capshaw's seriousness.

"I'll tell you what it's got to do with it, Inspector. The Spanish Revolution was a rehearsal for what's coming—a sort of a road company preview of the big one that's now on the way. There's no doubt about that. Ever been in Europe?"

"No, and I ain't about to go there," Rybecki said. "I like it here."

"Well," Capshaw nodded, "I have. I've been all over the whole European eel bucket. At one time or another I've been in every country that had a port you could get a ship into. I was an ordinary seaman on cargo tramps mostly. Two years at it and I got a pretty good look-around, including Spain. The seeds of explosion were all there in Spain before if you knew how to recognize them, just like they are in Germany now. They were in Germany then too, only it's taking a little longer. But it's going to blow for us, Stanislaus —and in not so long now. With Germany at the center of it. And when it does it will make any other war the world has ever seen look like a small fire in a country backhouse. Nobody will be able to stay out of this one including our own fat complacent country, the United States of America—in spite of a couple of thousand miles of protective ocean."

"The President don't think so, I heard him talk the other night. He don't think there's much to get steamed up about," Rybecki said.

"I heard it too," Capshaw said, "and you're wrong there. I thought it was pretty good. The thing about that that is significant is not so much what he said but what he didn't say. This isn't the time to raise any alarms, although there's plenty of cause for it even right now. I see what comes in over the I.N.S. tape, and believe me there is—"

"What's the I.N.S.?"

"International News Service, the ticker. Not all of it gets in

the paper—can't—because of space. But the signs are there
and it's on the way."

The inspector was showing signs of wearying under the
argument. "Well, we'll see, Cappy. We'll see. Every man
to his opinion."

"Yeah. We'll see all right and not too long hence. We'll
see the tough way too, because we're up to our ass in it and
it'll chew up a lot of nice brainy young guys like the doc
here before we're through with it."

Rybecki looked at Roy and winked. "Hear that, Doc?
Hear what the Secretary of War here says? You better get
drinking while you still got the chance. Come on, drink
up. . . . Hey Chris—three more. . . ."

6

Long before the end of that first year on Santry's division of
the Surgical Service, the cat and mouse relationship that Santry invariably imposed on any subordinate was thoroughly established between himself and Roy. Santry was well aware of
Roy's smoldering dislike of him, as he had been of Blinn's.
And in turn Roy recognized also, as Blinn had done before
him, that Santry was contemptuously amused by this and was
waiting to clip him whenever and wherever he could.

There were opportunities for Santry to do this and he
seldom missed one. He could, for example, expose Roy's
neophyte ignorance publicly in the operating room or on
the ward by a word, a phrase, or a gesture. And this he frequently did, always with the habitual smile. Long practice
had given Smiler a considerable finesse in this kind of slow
assassination, and, like a sadist, he enjoyed exercising it.
Particularly with smart, churlish young upstarts like Blinn
or Maines, who had the audacity to stand up against him.
He enjoyed such unequal contests immensely. He was like
an accomplished unassailable duelist with a rapier who delighted in pinking novices whenever and wherever he chose,
so that they bled slowly to death. Santry liked blood, in spite
of his meticulous control of it in those he operated. He particularly liked the hemorrhages of wounded pride, not his

own of course. Santry had never really had his own pride violated for many years now. He had been very fortunate in that. Sometimes he used to wonder what would happen if it were demolished as it once had been. But he did not like to think on that and seldom did.

Roy frequently left the operating room or the ward with his teeth clenched and almost exploding from keeping his mouth shut. He understood that the Smiler was trying to goad him into opening it. He did not do it though for quite a while. On these occasions the thinking through his rage had a sameness of pattern:

"I won't let the son-of-a-bitch get to me. That's what he's trying to do. I won't let him trap me into anything. I'll work my head off, till I get the chance to be with the Old Man. But, by God, once I get out from under Santry and that smile of his. . . . The son-of-a-bitch is a disease not a man, I've got to remember that. I don't know what he is but I've got to remember that. . . . He can dish it out all right. But can he take it? I wonder?"

On this Roy's principal and mounting tension fed and grew.

On that particular morning things had begun badly in the operating room. Roy, fatigued and frowsy from intermittent calls to the emergency room the night before, arrived with a headache that pounded on in spite of all the aspirin. The first patient had developed upper-respiratory symptoms including a temperature, and had had to be canceled. The second had vomited after his preoperative medication and the anesthetist had trouble getting her to sleep. When Santry arrived, as usual precisely on time, the anesthetization could not be begun at once. There was a twenty-minute wait in which they had stood around gloved, and gowned, waiting to get started. Delays of this kind, reasonably explained or not, were of special annoyance to Santry. He never excused them and he invariably vented his irritation on his assistants.

Beside this, when it got under way the case turned into an unexpectedly long and difficult procedure. Almost at once Santry began his quiet and brutal abuse.

"How did you ever get through medical school, Maines? Come on, watch what you're doing there . . .

"Come on, Maines, get a clamp on that vessel. This is an operation, not an autopsy, or didn't you know?"

This went on for an inordinately long time, and as it did Roy's seething resentment was gradually transformed into a cold, uncaring rage.

When they were out of trouble at last and beginning the closure, Santry rapped him briskly over the knuckles with a hemostat. Then it happened another time.

"Goddamn you," Roy heard his own voice come out in a strange snarl, "never do that again."

The sheer surprise of it caught everyone in the operating room, particularly Santry. There was an instant's dead silence in which Santry's hands stopped their work and hovered poised and immobile over the gaping wound. The narrow eyes over his mask returned Roy's glare for a moment, then dropped back to the field and his hand moved on.

"Pay attention to the operation, Maines, and incidentally to what you say to me."

Two minutes later Roy felt the hemostat on his knuckles again. For one blazing fraction of a second, the impulse to smash his fist into Santry's masked face was almost uncontrollable. Instead he turned to Kilroe, who was second assisting.

"Here, Kilroe, take my place."

He turned from the table, stripped off his gown and gloves, and almost ran out of the room. There was no one in the dressing room. He sat down on one of the benches before the line of lockers, trying futilely to still his shaking hands and what was stirring in him. Some minutes later Santry came in alone, still gowned and gloved but with his mask down. The smile on his face was not the usual. But now the whole line of his upper teeth was showing.

"Maines, you're coming with me to see Dr. Hand. You're going to—"

That was as far as Santry got with whatever else he was about to say. Roy got up, measured him for a split second, drove his left fist into the gowned belly and his right straight into Santry's smile. He was vaguely aware of a gratifying difference in the sensation between his two hands as he did it. This was the feel of a solidly connected body punch and head punch of a well-landed right cross. He was also aware that Santry was down on the floor making inarticulate noises. He stepped by him and out the door. In the corridor Kilroe was just coming in.

"Did you belt him, Roy? Did you?" Kilroe's voice was almost

a beseeching whisper. "Jesus. I was sure you were going to right there in the op—"

Roy jerked his head toward the dressing room.

"He's in there."

He walked out of the operating-room suite and down the main corridor. The shake was out of his hands now and the hard murderous fury in him was gone. Suppose Santry had hit his head when he had fallen? Suppose he had a fractured skull? Suppose he had killed him? Suppose Santry was dead? Maybe he was, things like that happened when they weren't intended. Well, if it happened, it happened. One thing was certain, he was through at the Charity now as a surgical resident or anything else. No resident, no matter what, could get away with hitting an attending surgeon. They were sacrosanct no matter what they did, almost like the Old Man. He was through all right, but he was going to make a gesture, just for himself. He went to his room. It took him only five minutes to do it. Probably it should have been properly typed and signed. Instead he wrote it longhand. It was written on the cheap official Charity Hospital stationery and addressed to the Old Man of course.

Dear Dr. Hand:

This will constitute my resignation as junior resident from Dr. Santry's Division of the Surgical Service of the Charity Hospital.

I am sure that the reasons for this will be made very clear to you by Dr. Santry.

I should like to thank you personally, Dr. Hand, for the opportunity you gave me. I will always be grateful for it and I am very sorry that it could not work out.

Thanking you again, I am,

Sincerely,
Roy R. Maines

He sealed it, took it to the Old Man's office, and gave it to the secretary. He had nothing to lose now. He would be sick about it later, probably whenever he thought about it for the rest of his life. But now he felt a queer sense of freedom and something akin to elation. All of it had happened very fast. All in one morning. The hands on the big bald electric clock in the Charity voyer were clicking on twelve noon as he went through it on the way to the Asterion.

Capshaw was there in the booth by the phone having his lunch—coffee and bourbon. Chris, just then, was hovering over him.

"Sit down, Aesculapius. How are things in your chamber of horrors?"

"Give me a boilermaker, Chris," Roy said.

Chris arched his eyebrows.

"A little early for the hard stuff isn't it, Doc?" Capshaw said.

"How are you, Cappy? You're having some, aren't you? Chris, a boilermaker."

"Yeah," Capshaw said, "but I'm an old alcoholic and you're not. Day off, Doc?"

Capshaw leafed casually through the newspaper beside him, folded it expertly to one of its secondary pages, and turned back to Roy.

"Day off," Roy said. "They're all going to be days off from now on, Cappy."

"That so?" Capshaw said, watching Roy down the whiskey and then the beer. "How's that, Doctor?"

"I'm through," Roy said. "I've quit."

"Quit? What do you mean, quit? Quit the hospital?"

"That's right. Quit the hospital as of now."

"Hmmmm. Well, well, is that a fact? Chris, two more boilermakers. How's that, Doc? How'd you happen to do that?"

Two boilermakers later Capshaw knew and in complete detail.

"I see," Capshaw said. "Don't blame you, Doc. What are you going to do now?"

"I don't know," Roy said. "Go back home I guess. Go into general practice there. I could do that. I really don't know. I'll see what turns up."

"Uh huh." Capshaw took his folded copy of the *Record* off the table and put it away on the bench beside him, "That might be a good idea for a while. Till our part of the war starts anyway. You're going to have to fight it."

"Jesus," Roy said, "let's not get on that again. I've heard it all with you and the inspector the other day."

"All right, Doc. Let's skip that. Tell me about this guy you just clipped who's going to get you fired. This guy Santry who smiles all of the time."

Roy, with his liquor-loosened tongue told him about all of it with his own interpretations.

The phone in the booth behind them rang. Chris answered it:

"You, Cappy."

"Back in a minute, Doc."

Roy was on the point of another drink. Instead he idly picked up Cappy's copy of the *Record* and began to read where it was folded, on the society page.

There was a fairly large caption and under it a small but fairly good picture of Katy. Miss Katherine Wells Winter was about to marry Mr. Preston Johns Knox it seemed. Date to be announced. The bride-to-be was a graduate of Hilton College where she blah-blah-blah, and was currently employed blah-blah-blah. Preston Johns Knox, graduated from, listing of preparatory school, undergraduate and law school, was currently associated with the firm of . . ."

Capshaw came back as Roy was looking at it with a feeling of considerable sickness. He had the sudden wild impulse to call her, to see her right then and tell her that everything was different now, that he would do anything she wanted now, marry her right today for instance. Too late, though, too late . . .

Capshaw sat watching Roy for a moment with amused compassion. "Just happened to catch that this morning, Doc. Thought I remembered her face. That's the dame all right isn't it, Doc?"

Roy nodded.

"I wasn't going to show it to you, but after what you told me happened with you this morning—"

Roy grinned sickly.

"This is as good a time as any I guess, Cappy. Have to find out sometime. No wonder she was never home or hung up on me when she was."

"Well, that's the way broads are, Doc. Remember that. Also remember that after if you've been really gone on one the first time and gotten the heave-ho from her, it will never be that tough again. You're vaccinated so to speak."

The phone rang.

"You, Doc," Chris said.

The Old Man's secretary was on the other end.

"I've had a terrible time locating you, Dr. Maines. Why on earth didn't you tell the switchboard where you were going? Dr. Hand wants to see you over here right away." Roy hung up.

"The Old Man wants to see me, Cappy."

"Not with that breath on you he doesn't, Doc. Hey Chris, a double black coffee and a package of those booze-killer mints. I'll be around here. Let me know how this comes out . . ."

The Old Man was slouched over the litter of his desk, his elbow on it and his chin leaning on one hand. Roy immediately recognized the paper before him. It was his letter of resignation.

"Sit down, Maines. I've just talked to Dr. Santry. Let's hear your end of it."

Roy gave it all to the Old Man and factually as straight as he could make it. The Old Man's steady sleepy gaze was fixed on him as he spoke, and for a long moment of silence after he had stopped. Then the Old Man rubbed his chin reflectively.

"Tell me, Maines, along with everything else you don't like about Dr. Santry, what is it you dislike most? What was the underlying thing that made you hit him? It's not unusual for pup surgeons to be rapped on the hands with hemostats. So that wasn't it."

"Well, sir, I guess it was everything in general about him, but more than anything else, he hates me. He hates people. He hates everything, and . . ."

Roy was aware that it was going to sound preposterous, and he hesitated. Still it was damned true.

"Yes?"

"It's that smile of his."

Strangely enough the Old Man didn't bat an eye. But then the Old Man never seemed surprised at anything. Anyhow the Old Man did not pursue it.

"All right, Maines. Now you listen to me. I am putting you on probation, understand? And you will be on it till I tell you that you are not. There will be no more episodes of this kind no matter what the reason. From now on you will work with Dr. Wilder, Dr. Wortle, or with me, and not with Dr. Santry. This will create some problem in scheduling but it will be arranged. You will begin with Dr. Wilder tomorrow morning. Do your work as you have been doing, and stay away from Dr. Santry. Is that clear?"

"Yes, sir."

"Now, you have from now till tomorrow off. Do some thinking and let's have no more lapses of self-control."

The Old Man picked up a single sheet of paper from the

top of his desk. "Here, take this with you." He handed it to Roy. "That's all, Maines."

Roy left the Old Man's office a little dazed, with his letter of resignation in his hand.

For some time the Old Man sat with his chair swiveled toward the window, staring out of it. Then he turned back to the desk and pressed the outer-office button. His secretary came in.

"Bertha, we are not going to start any more junior residents on Santry's division of the Service. There's been trouble of one kind or another every time. Trespach, Blinn, and now Maines. So we won't try again. From here on out we'll only assign senior residents to Santry's side. Now about Maines' schedule—it's a little early for him to begin this, but he'll be working between Wilder, Wortle, and me . . ."

Capshaw was still at the Asterion when Roy got back. He listened to Roy's confused, exultant account of the interview with the Old Man.

"And I'm not fired for smearing that smiling son-of-a-bitch. Only on probation. And I'm going to work with the Old Man too now, and Wilder and Wortle. And on top of it all, he told me to take time off till tomorrow."

"I wish to Christ that I had a city editor like that," Capshaw said feelingly. "Tell me, Doc, what church do you go to?"

"Church?" Roy said. "What the hell do you mean 'church'? I don't go to any church. Don't belong to any—"

"Well, if you did, I'd like to join it. Only reason I can think of for your kind of luck."

Capshaw looked at him and tapped the folded newspaper. "You don't fell so bad about this now, do you?"

"Why, hell no," Roy said, "I don't feel bad about it at all. I'll tell you something though, that little Rita over at Stasia Kondoleon's reminds me a lot of Katy—you know not really, but the way she looks bare-assed and everything. I'd really like to see her sometime now when she wouldn't give my ten bucks back . . ."

Capshaw looked at him for a long instant and chuckled.

"Well, well, Doctor, is that a fact? Now you're getting smart. Smart like an art dealer. You can't get the original—get a reasonable copy. One's as good as another if you're drunk enough, and you like art. What are we waiting for? Come on."

On the way to the door Capshaw paused suddenly and listened to the blare of the Asterion's radio. "Wait a minute, Doc," he said, "let's listen a minute. That's a news broadcast from Berlin."

Roy stood with him a little impatiently while the high-pitched hysterical voice that was coming from the box above the bar went on rising and falling in an unintelligible spate of German.

"*Ein Reich* . . ." it said and paused. "*Ein Volk* . . ." another pause. "*Ein Fueher* . . ." If there were anything else it was lost in the pandemonium of applause.

Then it faded out and the announcer came on. Capshaw looked surprisingly thoughtful.

"What's the matter, Cappy?" Roy said, looking at him.

"Hear that, Doc?" Capshaw looked at him abstractedly.

"Sure," Roy said, "what about it? German isn't it?"

"Certainly," Capshaw said. "Understand any of it?"

"Hell no," Roy said. "I don't know any German. What's the matter, Cappy? What is it?"

"Hitler addressing his sons-of-bitches at a Berlin sports *Palast* Nazi conclave. Hear that applause? 'One state, One people, One leader.' Listen to that applause."

Capshaw's abstracted gaze broke and he looked suddenly and almost sadly at Roy.

"That's the voice of doom, you poor withdrawn, uninformed, young son-of-a-bitch. That may get you killed pretty soon—"

"What the hell are you talking about, Cappy?" Roy said.

"Never mind," Capshaw said. "Let it pass, Doc. Come on. Let's go see Stasia."

It was an off hour at Anastasia Kondoleon's. But with Capshaw's inevitable entree they got in. Capshaw sat with Anastasia in the small alcove while Roy was upstairs with Rita.

"What's the matter with you, coming in now?" Stasia looked at him.

"Favor to a friend, Anastasia. Besides that I always like to ride my drag with you."

"Isn't that the same kid, a doctor or something you brought in here a while ago. And Rita—"

"That's the one," Capshaw said.

"The one who wanted to pay her for nothing—"

"That's the one," Capshaw said.

"I think all of them must be crazy or queer," Anastasia said. "Rita seems to draw them."

"Oh? How's that Anastasia?"

"Once in a while I let the girls go out on a trick if there's money enough in it. If there isn't they don't go—"

Roy appeared with Rita. Capshaw noted with amusement that he looked sheepish, satisfied, and a good deal more composed. Somewhere there was the sound of a muffled buzzing.

"That's the phone, Cappy. I'm expecting a call," Anastasia said and left them.

Now that it was over Roy was feeling the inevitable novice's urge to bolt out of the place, to be somewhere else—anywhere, but the scene of his turpitude.

"I ought to be getting back, Cappy. There's a few things I ought to check about tomorrow," Roy said lamely.

Capshaw's grin was sympathetic. "Sure, Doc, sure. You better do that. Go ahead. I'm going to stick here for a while. See you around."

"Sit down and talk to your old uncle, Rita," Capshaw said as Roy followed the maid out. "Tell me, how'd it go this trip?"

"Say!" Rita rolled her eyes. "He's really something. Nothing wrong with him, this time."

"You remember him, huh Rita?"

"Sure—didn't want to go last time and gave me ten bucks to say he did. Is he really a doctor? He's awful young."

"He's a doctor all right," Capshaw said, "a good one too. And a good guy."

"Some of them doctors are real creeps though," Rita said. "I thought maybe he was, that first time. But he sure ain't. He's real normal."

"They are, Rita? How's that? Tell me about that."

"Well, I seen one that was. A real weirdo. He scared the hell out of me. That's why I say some of them must be creeps."

"Why, what happened, Rita?"

"Well, you know Stasia gets calls for us to go out sometimes. And if the setup looks all right she sends us. If it ain't, she don't. I don't mind doing it, don't take long usually, and the money's real good, twenty-five bucks anyway, maybe more if there's a convention or something, you know?"

"Yeah, I know," Capshaw said.

"Well, anyway Stasia got a call to send someone over to the

Cassalis Hotel. You know just off Martin on Third? That's a right joint—never any trouble. Stasia knows the night man on the desk and it's square with the cops and everything, so she sent me. Turns out that the mark is alone with a nice room there.

"But he turned out to be a real bad one—a special kind of a nut or something. Know what he wanted? First he offered me double the money if I'd let him hit me a few times with a heavy gold watch chain he had, before we did anything. Well, I wouldn't do that. I told him I was a straight girl and nothing else. Then he offered me three times the price if I'd let him burn me on the breasts a couple of times with a lit cigarette. Said he had to do something like that or else he couldn't go. He began to get real excited like he was hopped up or something and he started pushing money at me—a whole handful of it, tens and twenties even. Asked me, didn't I want to know what it was like to have it with a superman. Jesus, I got scared, he acted so crazy. All I wanted to do was get out of there. I did, too, finally, without him touching me, by threatening to yell my head off. I came back right away and told Stasia about it."

"What about the doctor part, how did you know he was a doctor?"

"Oh, I didn't then. I found that out later. I saw him a while afterward—a couple of weeks I guess, at the hospital."

Capshaw sat forward. "At the Charity?"

"Sure. I seen him there in one of them long white doctor coats they wear when I went over to the clinic for a flu shot—they're for free over there, you know. He was a doctor all right. I asked."

"Maybe it wasn't the same guy, Rita. People can make a lot of mistakes on that."

"Oh, it was the same guy all right," Rita said. "I remembered everything about him. He scared me so damned bad. I'll never forget that face of his if I live to be a hundred, mainly that God-awful smile."

"Well, well . . ." Capshaw said, "very interesting, Rita. Very interesting."

Anastasia Kondoleon came through the curtains.

"Skip out now, honey, and leave us alone," she said to Rita. "We've got some private talking to do."

She sat down by Capshaw. "Well, what is it, Cappy?" Capshaw's face lost its bemused look. "I want to know about that cheap hood Comalli, Stase. The one I fingered for the inspector that night and he muffed taking in because the boys didn't get to him in time. Remember?"

"I remember."

"Well, has he been in here since?"

"No."

"Are you sure, Stase?"

"Of course I'm sure. Don't you think I know what goes on here? I'm sure or I wouldn't say so."

"All right. Now look, if he ever shows again, I want you to call me, Stase, and you can't get me, get Rybecki."

Anastasia Kondoleon looked at him steadily. "You know I'm no stool pigeon, Cappy. Don't put me in a spot like this."

"Look, Anastasia, I know you're no stool and I'm not trying to put you on any spot. I may be in one myself I kind of think. I'll give it to you straight. I want Comalli picked for whatever story there is in it, sure. I'm certain he's a lead to a big one like whoever killed Guida Di Genova. But also because that guy around loose makes me a little nervous. It makes me that way because I'm sure he recognized me that night. And he could very well have the notion that I fingered him. He'd be right. The point is it's a lot more healthy for me, aside from everything else, if that guy cools in the bastille for the time being if he's got any ideas on evening up with me. See what I mean? The quicker he's in there the better for everybody, including me. See baby?"

It took Capshaw a little while longer before Anastasia Kondoleon reluctantly agreed.

7

Capshaw's contacts as a crime reporter were intimate and varied. He tweaked Inspector Rybecki about this occasionally when they were both in their cups at the Asterion.

"Stanislaus, the *Record* beats the Police Department almost every time about any real good lead for one reason. Know what that is, Stanislaus?"

"No," Rybecki said, sourly mouthing his bourbon, "you're so Goddamned smart, you tell me."

"All right, I will," Capshaw said. "It's because the *Record* treats its informers and stool pigeons a whole hell of a lot better than the Police Department does. That's why. Right?"

Rybecki considered this before emptying his glass. "Yes, that's right. That and the fact that the *Record* has a dissolute bastard like you drinking and whoring around as its big-time city reporter."

"Flattery will get you nowhere with me or the *Record*, Stanislaus," Capshaw had said.

But what Capshaw had said was true. And they both knew it. The *Record* had sources of information that the police did not simply because the *Record* had more money to pay for them. And Capshaw dispensed it with a free hand—a great deal of what there was of it with a knowing hand.

After Capshaw left Anastasia Kondoleon's he decided that it was time to spend some more of the *Record's* underground intelligence money. He went to a pay telephone in a sleazy drugstore off Velle Street and dialed a number.

Finally a cautious nasal voice came on.

"Rip," Capshaw said, "that you? . . . Good. Meet me at Chris's. Can you do that? . . . Good. All right, at Chris's, in about an hour. . . . Who? . . . He's with you now? . . . Klaus who? . . . Never heard of him. Ditch him. . . . What? . . . You personally vouch for him? . . . All right, bring him along."

At the Asterion, Capshaw stood at the bar with a drink until they came in.

Capshaw's introduction to Klaus was minimal. "Cap," Ripstein said, "this here's Klaus. He's a right guy."

Capshaw nodded without shaking hands and they retired to a back booth. There was an interval in which they sat with a round of Chris's cheap whiskey without saying anything. Capshaw drained his glass and began to talk.

"Rip," Capshaw said, "you know Iggy Comalli?"

"Yeah—one of the Kite's boys."

"That's right. Supposed to have powdered out for St. Louis awhile back when things began to heat up for the Kite after Di Genova got it. Well, he's back in town."

"So I hear," Ripstein said.

"Yeah. He's back. Have you seen him around?"

"Not yet. I probably will though."

"All right. Maybe. Maybe not. But he's here. Do you think you could find out where he is?"

Ripstein's eyes shifted away from Capshaw's expressionlessly and back again.

"I could try."

"I want you to try. And try hard."

Capshaw took his battered wallet out and extracted three twenties and four tens and put them on the table between them.

"This hard."

Ripstein made no move toward the money. His eyes flicked at it, then back at Capshaw.

"That's just the retainer," Capshaw said. "Find out in the next twenty-four hours and I'll double it."

"O.K.," Ripstein said, "maybe I could make a phone call right now since you're in a hurry."

"Yeah," Capshaw said, "I'm in a hurry. Suppose you do that, or anything else you need to do. If you can't get me, get Stase Kondoleon. She'll get through to me."

"O.K.," Ripstein said. He got up, casually swept the bills into a side pocket of his baggy pants, and went to one of the phone booths. Capshaw watched him close the door, insert a coin, and begin to dial. He turned to Klaus.

"Same goes for you too, friend," Capshaw said. "You find out where Comalli can be picked up, you get the same treatment and the same bonus."

Klaus gave a mirthless chuckle that made Capshaw glance at him sharply. He was a short, faded little man in a spotted brown suit. Somewhere, Capshaw guessed, in his late forties. He had the characteristic down-at-the-heel nondescript look of the bum about him, and the bum's aura of furtiveness and failure. Capshaw was shortly thereafter amazed at what he said.

"Not in my line," Klaus said. He reached somewhere in the folds of his sleazy jacket, took out a ratty-looking billfold, and produced a plastic-encased card, and a badge. These he passed to Capshaw.

In spite of his surprise Capshaw examined them both carefully and impassively. They were authentic all right—as Capshaw instantly recognized the usually presented credentials of the Federal Bureau of Security.

"Well, Jesus Christ," Capshaw said feelingly, and put out his hand, "glad to know you Mr. Schneider. If it's not too much to ask in confidence on short acquaintance, what the hell are you doing around here with a Goddamned slob like Ripstein?"

"Rip's all right," Klaus Schneider said. "He's on the right side of the fence, with us anyway. His nose is clean. Matter of fact he's a very reliable contact—very useful, particularly now."

"That so?" Capshaw said, looking at the little nondescript man with a good deal of respect and a consuming curiosity. "Mind if I ask why?"

"No." Klaus Schneider rubbed his thin nondescript hand over his thin nondescript nose. "Ripstein is a nasty, on the make ex-con and stoolie. But there are a couple of things go-ing for him. Maybe three.

"The only ones I'm interested in are that he takes his American citizenship seriously and that he can speak German as well as I can. And I was born there. I don't care what else he's mixed up in."

Capshaw looked at him. "Mr. Schneider, I don't speak German too well but I take being an American pretty seriously."

Klaus Schneider smiled thinly. "You're anticipating me a little, Mr. Capshaw."

"Name's Cappy," Capshaw said. "I hate formality and I'm calling you Klaus."

"All right, Cappy," Klaus Schneider said, "that's fine with me. And about your loyalties and sympathies as an American, you can spare me that. Yours, or your editor's, or newspaper's. They've been pretty thoroughly established."

"That so?" Capshaw said, arching his eyebrows.

"Yes. Matter of fact, very thoroughly—or I wouldn't be here talking to you like this. You see if on pure chance you had not made this meet with Ripstein, I would have contacted you. I've talked to some people, including your publisher, and there was a general agreement that you know the ass end of this city like no one else."

"Thanks," Capshaw said, "I flatter myself that I do. I've been around and writing about it for quite a while."

"Well, apparently you do. That's why the Federal Bureau is interested in you."

"Uh-huh." Capshaw sat back and looked at Schneider almost dreamily. "Look, Klaus, a while back you said I was anticipating you a little. Want to hear me anticipate a little more? Like why you're here and we're talking like this?"

Capshaw signaled Chris for more whiskey. In the phone booth Ripstein was putting more coins into one of the slots.

"Go ahead," Klaus Schneider said.

"The German-American *Bund* in this town," Capshaw said. "That's what you're around here sniffing at. The bastards are getting a little out of hand, aren't they? What with their God-damned hysterical meetings, bought radio time, appeals to the malcontents, and the rest of it, and whipping up the sympathy and cooperation of stupid bastards who can't or won't think for themselves. That's right, isn't it? And us not in the war yet—" Capshaw was aware that Klaus Schneider's eyes were fully on him.

"That's close enough, Capshaw. We know all about their open propaganda. That's still legal. My end of it here is their subversive recruiting and who they've already got lined up—"

"For a potential undercover apparatus just in case the fat, dumb United States really gets into it by declaring war," Capshaw said.

"That's also good enough," Klaus Schneider said. "They've done quite a job in some other places and made a pretty good start here in this town too. The ones they get to first and easiest are the crackpots and the small-time criminals. The Nazi brand of fascist ideas apparently has a lot of appeal for intellectual nuts and the hoods love their easy money."

"I know," Capshaw said, "I wrote a whole Goddamned beautiful piece about that. In the *Record* a couple of months ago. One of the few things editor Coles didn't castrate."

"It was pretty good," Klaus Schneider said. "You've got a tendency though to get too virulent. Too virulent for now anyway."

"You read it?"

"Certainly. It's part of the file."

"Oh ho," Capshaw said, "you mean I've got a file on me with the Federal Bureau?"

"Certainly. Don't be naïve with me, Capshaw. You look pretty good from what's in it too, or I wouldn't be here talking to you."

"Well, well," Capshaw said, "think of that. Me on record with a personal file in the Federal Bureau. Fame at last. Thank Christ I have not lived and written in vain. By the way, does it say anything about my having been hit at Guadalajara with the American Lincoln Brigade?"

"Yes, it does," Klaus Schneider said thinly. "It also says that you got out of Republican Spain when the Communists began to take over."

"I sure as hell did. Just as soon as I realized that there was no Goddamned difference between Fascism and Communism. I learned it pretty cheap—just a flesh wound in the ass retreating from action with a pad and pencil in my hand writing about it. No gun you understand."

"We're not here to discuss your past convictions, Capshaw, or your current philosophy," Klaus Schneider said. "Here—" He pushed a paper under Capshaw's nose.

"There's a list of names and aliases. Assorted nuts, wanted, and bums. Can you give me any help with it?"

"Let's see. It takes one to tell one, doesn't it? I'm quite an authority."

"Keep it. Look it over and tell me what you can about it later."

Capshaw was comfortably drunk now. He was sentiently drunk—drunk the way he usually was when he wrote his copy for the *Record*. His alcohol-sharpened eye went down a tabulation of names. One of them he caught almost automatically because of the letters M.D. to the right of it. The name was Lothar Gamaliel Santry, M.D., Surgeon, Charity Hospital.

"This might take a while," Capshaw said, examining it closely.

"No hurry. We'll be doing some talking from time to time. I'll be around."

"There's a doctor's anme here, Lothar Gamaliel Santry."

For a moment Klaus Schneider looked thoughtful. "Yeah, Santry," he said reflectively. "That one. Never saw him. Don't know him. You do?"

"Indirectly," Capshaw said. "A whorehouse connection."

"Well, what about him?"

"I don't really know about him," Capshaw replied, "but I can find out."

"Maybe you'd better do that. The Bureau could be very interested in Dr. Santry. So far we have been able to determine an enthusiastic supporter of the local *Bund* and he's got some friend or friends in Washington."

Ripstein was through with his phone dialing, and came back to the booth. "I don't know about Comalli," Ripstein said, looking at Capshaw and at Klaus. "I did the best I could—I'll keep pitching."

Capshaw looked at him briefly and at the expression on his inert face. "Fine," he said. "You do that."

"I may have a kind of line on him. I'll call you, Cappy, or Stasia Kondoleon."

"Good," Capshaw said.

Ripstein sat down in the booth beside Schneider. There was another drink. And then Capshaw rose suddenly, paid the bill, and went out. He went back to his lair in the Hotel Andan. He went to his bed, threw his hat on the floor, and lay down on it with his clothes on. For a while he slept. Then his bedside phone rang.

"Hello," the voice said. "Rip."

"All right, Rip. What's with it?"

"Comalli's at Stasia's."

"You're sure?"

"Sure."

"Good," Capshaw said and hung up. He thought briefly and then dialed. There was a wait before the low, quiet voice of Anastasia Kondoleon came on.

"Stase? Cappy."

"He's here," she said.

"Comalli?"

"Comalli."

The line clicked off.

Capshaw instantly put in a call for Rybecki. He waited while the line went through the routine of the central desk and then to Homicide. Finally the inspector's voice came in.

"Hello, Javert," Capshaw said. "This is Jean Valjean."

"What? What?" Rybecki sounded very preoccupied.

"It's Capshaw, Sherlock. Can you hear me?"

"Yes, I can. I can hear you very well."

"Good," Capshaw said, "I'm glad you can. It's important. Comalli is at Stase's. You jobbed it up the last time. You think you can take him now? Or are you too busy with traffic violations?"

"Listen, Capshaw—"

"I mean it, Goddamn it," Capshaw said. "He's over there again. Now get him. I want him in the can as bad as you do. I think he knows I fingered him the first time. I want to stay healthy, and I won't if he's around loose. Now—"

"O.K. O.K. He's there, we'll take him."

"Right away?"

"Yes. Right away."

"Fine," Capshaw said, "I thought maybe you might ask Anastasia to do it for you——"

But Capshaw was talking to himself. The other end of the line was dead.

8

Inspector Rybecki stood looking at his quarry reflectively for a moment and then gave him an open-handed slap that almost bowled him out of the chair. The man made an involuntary movement with his handcuffed hands and slumped back again. With the hard glare of the light upon him, the red welts on his face stood sharply out. Trickles of sweat ran down his neck to his soaked shirt. His left eye was almost swollen shut. The interrogation had been going on for some time now. It was about the fourth in a hitherto unproductive series.

"All right, you son-of-a-bitch," Rybecki said casually, "just keep talking. Don't stop like that if you want any face left. Now then, let's try it again. We know the Kite knocked off Di Genova. Where's the Kite now? Where's he holed up?"

"I tole you I ain't seen . . ."

This time it was a slow backhand full in the mouth. It was a good thing for Iggy Comalli's face that the inspector had taken his ring off.

"Where is he?"

"I tole you . . ."

Wham. The hand came in again.

"Where is he?"

"But I don't . . ."

Wham.

"Where?"

"I don't . . ."

Wham.

The inspector rubbed his reddened fingers. He nodded to one of the figures in the shadow behind the light. "O.K., Manny. Let's make a night of it. My hand's getting sore. You take him awhile. Just keep it nice and easy like I been doing it."

Manny moved heavy-footedly forward into the glare. He

took off his coat and shoulder holster methodically, laid them on a chair, and went toward the slumped figure in the center of it, limbering up the thick palm of his right hand.

The man's swollen lips moved and spat. "Jesus, wait. Can't you wait a minute, for Christ's sake?"

The inspector nodded to Manny. Manny lowered his hand. "O.K., bastard. Get talking. What you got to say? Where's the Kite?"

"I got to have protection. I tell you I got to have protection."

"You'll get protection, pimp. Where is he?"

The man's tongue moved slowly over the puffy lips. "He's holed up over on Velle Street." The words were thick but intelligible.

"Where on Velle?"

"842. Second floor. Back apartment."

The inspector's gold teeth glinted pensively.

"You know what we do and you're lying, Comalli? We'll turn you loose and pass the word around. The Kite's friends like canaries like you. You get what Di Genova got—the Charity morgue slab and a tag on your toe."

"I ain't lying. You said I get protection."

"You play ball and you get it. Is the Kite there now?"

"I don't know. Must be. Gotta be. Can I have a drink, water, anything?"

"All right, boys, you heard. Stuff this son-of-a-bitch back in the gow. Manny, you and Ed come with me in the squad car. We'll go over and take him right now."

There was a short period of milling around and more orders and Rybecki's herd of sleuths clumped downstairs behind him. Going out the entrance of the Central Precinct Station they almost ran down Capshaw on his way over from the Press Building for his nightly look at the blotter and anything else.

"What's up, Inspector? You got him?"

"Comalli's a live one all right, Cappy. Stick around. I'll give you that fast headline on the Di Genova homicide."

"Come on, Inspector, if it's hot let's have it. Goddamn it. Remember, I tipped you. I'll give you a hell of a play when I write it."

"O.K., deal," the inspector said, climbing into the front seat of the squad car. "We're going for the Kite. Stick around, be right back. Comalli finally sang."

The Kite, actual name unknown but so called because he was usually high on heroin, was seated in a sagging over-stuffed chair in his undershirt. He now, as he frequently did, sat staring at nothing, before a tinny radio with a .38 automatic close by. He had been holed in with his heroin and the gun ever since he had emptied it into a man named Di Genova.

The inspector's black sedan and another squad car boiled away from Central Precinct. "Now, listen, boys." the inspector said, "this caper may not be so easy. That Kite son-of-a-bitch is heeled ten to one and he's likely to be ornery. He tries any kind of cute move before we make him, we let him have it right there. See?"

Some minutes later they pulled out of the traffic on Velle Street. The inspector squinted at the passing teethlike rows of darkened store fronts. Suddenly he pointed to a litter-strewn doorway.

"That's it. Turn right on the next block, Manny, and park." He glanced back through the car's rear window.

"Good, the rest of the boys are right on our tail."

Manny signaled a right turn, went halfway up the block, and stopped. They got out. The street was deserted.

"O.K.," the inspector said, "we play it routine. They cover the front and back of the alley, and we take him. Come on."

They walked rapidly down the darkened block and turned the corner, the inspector and Manny leading and Ed five paces behind. Without hesitating they swerved into the semi-darkness of the doorless entry numbered 842. The inspector held a flashlight on a row of battered, brass wall boxes.

"That's good. Only one apartment on each floor of this trap. Second is A. Kosin. That's got to be it. Let's go."

The ragged carpet on the creaking stairs helped muffle their beefy ascent. A single shadeless bulb lit the hallway and shadowed a door at the end. . . . They advanced on it and stopped. The inspector motioned Manny to one side of it and Ed to the other. Guns in hands now, they stood listening. From the other side of its paint-scaled panels a radio mooed out soft music. The inspector took the knob deftly in his free hand and leaned his full weight steadily on the door. Then he turned the knob. There was a faint but very audible click. The door was locked. On the other side of it there were vague sounds of movement. The inspector made a motion with his gun hand, took two steps back from the door, and let go

a Homeric kick against it. The door flew back and open. At
that instant the inspector felt a hot slamming pain somewhere
near his navel and heard the report of the shot that made it.
As he went down he got a glimpse of a thin man in an undershirt holding an automatic. He saw a black hole suddenly
appear over the Kite's left eye before the face dropped away
from his sight. He also got a look at Manny's tan number-
twelve shoes now on a level with his own face. Manny emptied his gun toward the target on the floor. The hot slamming
pain eased away from around the inspector's middle. Instead
his belly began to get numb. He had a sensation of spreading warmth in his crotch and down his legs. He felt suddenly
tired and curiously thirsty. He saw Ed's flat, broken-nosed
face bending down toward him.

"Son-of-a-bitch got me square in the belly, Ed."

"Yeah. Yeah, just you lay right still, chief, just lay right
still."

Ed's face gradually dissolved in a void of blackness. It was
fifteen minutes past midnight. . . .

About the time the inspector's action was beginning at 842
Velle Street, Roy went to the emergency room for a routine
look around. The emergency room of the Charity was actually
not a room at all but one area of the ground floor of
the hospital that took up a sizable part of its Mercer Street
side. Behind it sliding doors opened onto a loading dock
with a ramp for the string of Charity ambulances that moved
in and out of its quadrangle. Inside, the area was divided
into a railed-off space filled with a clump of battered steel-
topped desks and a periphery of fourteen doorless, white-
tiled rooms. The place operated day and night in a blare of
eye-scorching light. Its usual routine of management of sick
and wounded citizenry was simple, direct, and efficient. The
ambulance backed up to the loading dock. The driver and attendant rider got out, opened the back end, and slid the
stretcher onto a high, rolling cart. The driver opened the
sliding door and the stricken citizen passed into one of the
doorless white-tiled rooms. A clerk from one of the desks
followed him in with forms and a pencil and filled the forms
out with information taken from the citizen, driver, attendant,
or not infrequently from an accompanying policeman. He returned to his desk and was succeeded by an intern who examined, diagnosed, and filled out more forms, and called

the resident. The resident read the forms and looked at the stricken citizen. The resident filled out more forms. Following this there was a definitive disposal. The citizen was given indicated treatment and sent home, to the operating room, or to the ward. Not infrequently he was sent to jail, and occasionally to the morgue.

At times the emergency-room activity reached a pitch of intensity akin to the complete chaos of a whorehouse fire or a sinking ocean liner. At these times the white-tiled rooms were jammed with stretcherloads of bawling lacerated drunks, beaten-up prostitutes, maundering psychotics, confused derelicts, old ladies with broken hips, extensive burn cases, stabbings, shootings, attempted suicides, perforated peptic ulcers, unruly prisoners disciplined by the police, abortions and premature labors, food poisonings, gas asphyxiations, hemorrhaging consumptives, acute venereal cases, street accidents, and hysterics. Stretcher carts full of them reached in irregular tentacles down the hall between the desks and the rooms, past the sliding door onto the ramp, with more loaded ambulances arriving every other minute. Interns, residents, nurses, clerks, and police milled about the general disorder like feverish albino ants, until the tidal wave of screaming, bleeding, hurting, puking, pissing protoplasm could be contained, which strangely it always was. In one way or another such periodical holocausts subsided gradually and the steady, ceaseless train of diseased and their ordered routine of management restored. While there was no precise accounting for these cataclysmic pathological outbursts at the Charity, some predisposing factors were known.

One of them was payday. Paydays were every two weeks in the moiling mills of Hastings Hill. There was a surfeit of money, and the bars, bawds, and dice games were overwhelmed with loaded customers. Saturday was payday and Saturday nights in the Charity Emergency were always active. Another casual agent was hot weather. It is a well-known fact about humans that heat makes them not only sweaty, but thirsty, copulatory, and generally restless. They react by drinking in cooled saloons, copulating indiscriminately or indiscreetly, and generally moving around in strange neighborhoods. Another cause may be astrological. Possibly Mars moves in on Venus and Saturn.

When Roy went down to the emergency room the place was ominously quiet. Two clerks leaned over papers at the bank of desks. A nurse followed by an anxious-looking woman carried a baby down the hall. An intern, lolling, feet up on a row of the straight-backed chairs before the desk railing, thumbed a magazine. The only sign of impending action was on the loading ramp. There was noise out there. An ambulance had just pulled up. Roy pushed open the door and went out. The noise became louder and more interesting as the back end opened and two policemen hauled a struggling man in a regulation strait jacket out of it. Expertly they pinioned him on a stretcher cart and pulled the straps down tight.

"God! God! Strike them God! Help Thy Son, God. Kill them. Oh, God! Smite the defilers and unbelievers!"

"What's going on, Sergeant?" Roy said to the one with the chevrons on his sleeves.

"We got Jesus Christ here," the sergeant said, pushing the stretcher cart toward the door.

"That's a hell of a way to treat him," Roy said. "What's his trouble?"

"He's a Goddamn special kind of religious nut or something," the Sergeant said. "He started waving a Bible around and yelling over on Peake Street and beat the shit out of a couple of people who tried to make him pipe down."

The sergeant grinned and jerked his thumb toward the other policeman whose hand was wrapped in a handkerchief. "He bit Lew there on the hand."

"The son-of-a-bitch," Lew said solemnly. "I had to kick him in the balls to make him let go. He's strong as a Goddamn ox. Say, Doc, can a thing like this here give you the blood poison?" He waved the handkercyhiefed hand at Roy.

"Probably not," Roy said. "Come on and I'll take a look at it."

They went through the sliding door. Roy took Lew into one of the rooms. He was cleaning and dressing the wound when he caught the first sound of a far-off siren. The intensity, low at first, swelled steadily into a high moan, and then to a full-pitched scream.

"Man, he's coming in fast," Lew said.

Roy hurriedly finished the bandage. There was a squeal of brakes. The siren died off. The brakes squealed again. A squad car swung into the ramp. Roy went out on the loading dock. The car with its red signal light still flashing backed into the brilliant light of a loading dock. The doors flew open simultaneously and three plainclothesmen churned out of it.

The broad flat face of one of them turned whitely up at Roy. "Give us a hand. Get a stretcher. We got the inspector here, hit in the belly."

A minute later the inspector was on the cart and rolling through the sliding door. They wheeled him into Room 1 and Roy began the action.

Rybecki's squat, thick body lay inert and flaccid on the stretcher. His moonlike face and the hamlike hands had the white, pinched waxiness of exsanguination. A large irregular stain mottled his clothes from his belt to his knees. Roy yelled for an intravenous setup, took out his bandage scissors, and began cutting away the saturated cloth. He exposed a single oozing hole just above and to the left of the navel. He put a stack of sterile gauze squares over it and strapped them tightly against the skin with adhesive tape.

"Take his blood pressure on the other arm," he said to the intern. "Tell somebody to get the lab down here right away for a stat type and cross match for transfusion. Tell them we'll need all the blood they've got of whatever type he is."

He slit the inspector's coat sleeve to the shoulder, threw a tight rubber tourniquet around the massive biceps. The veins were collapsed but he found an easy one near the elbow. The needle slid into it and a fast yellow drip of plasma began from the bottle.

"Seventy over forty," the intern released the blood pressure cuff and pulled the stethoscope out of his ears.

"Call the operating room and tell them to get set up and stand by. All the stuff for an abdominal. Is this the only place he's hit—just in the belly?" Roy turned toward his silent spectators.

"I think the bastard only got him once," the one with the broken nose said. "He only got that one shot in anyway, I think."

Roy rapidly cut away the rest of the inspector's clothes to make sure.

"Is it pretty bad, Doc?"

"Yeah, it's bad," Roy said. He put three blankets over the inspector and connected another bottle of plasma into the intravenous setup.

"Think he'll make it, Doc?"

"He's got a chance."

"Going to operate him right away?"

"Soon as we can. Like to get his pressure up a little."

"Anything we can do?"

"No. Can't think of anything right now."

"All right if we stick around with him?"

"Sure, stick around."

A laboratory technician, a nurse, and another intern came in.

"Keep that plasma pouring into him," Roy said, "till we get the blood. And watch his blood pressure. We won't take him upstairs till I've talked to the Old Man."

He went to the central desk and got the Old Man on the phone. The Old Man listened without comment until he had finished.

"All right, Maines, it sounds like that's all you can do for the moment. Get the blood into him as fast as you can and take him right up to the operating room. I'll be there in about twenty minutes."

Roy hung up and went back to the inspector. His pressure had come up to ninety over sixty. He waited until the blood came down from the laboratory and started it before they moved the inspector to the operating room. The Old Man arrived on cue, went over the inspector, and nodded. Roy and the rest of the operating crew got rapidly into motion. The inspector was anesthetized, his belly shaved and painted, and operating field draped, when the Old Man walked in, hands dripping from scrubbing. He dried his hands and slipped into his gown. The circulating nurse tied it behind as another sterile nurse held his gloves. The Old Man worked his hands into them quickly and moved to the right of the table.

"Maines, you first assist. You," he pointed to one of the interns, "stay on that side of the table, and you," he pointed to the other, "over here by me."

The instrument nurse passed the knife. The Old Man took it and made a clean, sweeping incision over the exposed antiseptic-painted skin. The flesh fell apart in a clean red gape. Roy sponged and clamped the bleeding points. "Ties, now," the Old Man said. Smoothly and evenly he threw ligatures around the bleeding points and ran the knots down square and firm. "Cut the ends right on the knot," he said to the intern holding the scissors ready. He took a clean knife. In no time he was in the abdomen. There was an instant weltering deluge of blood and clot into the gape of the incision. The Old Man pushed a hot wet sponge against it and placed two retractors. "Hold these just where they are," he said. A moment later he had his hand under the pressing coils of bowel. Quickly and deftly his hands shifted and probed in the depths. Methodically he exposed and examined. "All right, here we are. Bring the light in more to the left." The circulating nurse swung the heavy overhead lamp in a short arc. "That's it. Now hold it. Look here." Roy craned closer over the incision. There were several perforations and a long linear laceration in the small intestine close to its vascular attachment. Behind this was a hole in the iliac vein. This had opened and the blood was pouring out of it. The Old Man put on two clamps and the terrifying hemorrhage stopped. "I can feel the bullet in the psoas muscle," he said. "We'll take the vein first, take out as much bowel as we have to, and then get the bullet." In twenty minutes the vein was securely tied off and two and a half feet of bowel and the bullet were out and on a towel-covered tray. He sewed the severed ends of the bowel together and explored the rest of the abdomen. There was nothing else. "How is he now?" the Old Man said to the anesthetist. The anesthetist nodded. "Pressure's coming up, it's one hundred and five over sixty-five." "Fine," the Old Man said, "let's close him up." Fifteen minutes later the inspector was off the table with a tight supporting dressing on his belly. . . . The Old Man went downstairs to talk to the waiting delegation from the police department.

Roy felt a little smug about this initial operative experience with the Old Man. He had, he felt, done just about right with it. He had handled the inspector's emergency treatment well from the start and in the operating room he had done pretty well too. He had kept up with the Old Man's notorious pace and he hadn't had to be corrected for any slips. It had gone so well that he was disappointed that the Old Man never gave compliments or commendations of any kind directly to his staff even when their performance had been outstanding. He dismissed it with no comment. The absence of criticism from him was in itself laudatory. Criticisms from him were generally feared and rightly so. They were open, honest, and lacerating. They hurt more because they were justified and therefore hard to rationalize for those on whom they fell. They were very embarrassing because they were nearly always delivered publicly or wherever the Old Man happened first to confront the culprit after his transgression. In some instances they were devastating and they who had been verbally disemboweled by the Old Man never forgot it and did not make that particular mistake again. Openly, the Old Man showed no sentiment whatever for the residents and interns on his Service. Secretly he had a good deal of sneaking affection for them. Although he frequently snarled at them for their ignorance and excoriated their errors, this was his privilege. He allowed no one else to do so. Covertly he approved of their unshaven faces, dirty uniforms, cynicism, profanity, and horseplay, because he regarded such as natural in the hard serfdom of his Service. He had served this high, hard apprenticeship himself and, as he remembered everything else, he remembered those many lean years very well. Behind his impersonal façade the Old Man had his favorites among his boys, but he took precautions to conceal this. These favorites of his were usually, but not necessarily, his most apt or talented neophytes. Usually there was some specific trait or quality discovered in them that first intrigued him. The Old Man had a rigid discipline of honesty and he liked to see it in others. An absolutely honest man could really do no wrong with him. He understood the anatomy of courage. He possessed courage in the extreme himself and he recognized it in others. Anyone with it went far in the Old Man's estimation though he might have little else. He had a surprising regard for generosity of a certain kind. This was generosity in the form of the *beau geste*—the high magnificent gesture made in an offhand and wholly casual manner. He was very vulnerable to a sense of humor. The Old Man had it in quantity although he was seldom articulate with it. But anyone who was had a good deal of advantage with him. Anyone who could get under his impersonal deadpan exterior with wit of the laughable kind partially disarmed him. If he could make the Old Man laugh outright, which no one remembered ever happening, the Old Man was temporarily at his mercy. There was one other thing, and this was loyalty. On this he was fanatic. His insistence upon this was adamant and without qualification. This meant unswerving, sacrificial, and absolute devotion, first to established principle, then to the surgical service, and then to himself. Breaches of loyalty infuriated him with a cold unpardoning anger. And they were accordingly punished. Aside from his natural aptitude, Roy's ultimate place in the Old Man's regard probably came about

through the Old Man's observation of his honesty and sense
of humor. Of his complete loyalty there was never to be any
question.

It is doubtful that Roy abstracted much specific knowledge,
technical or otherwise, from this first operation with the
Old Man. The whole procedure had gone too rapidly. His
attention had not been concentrated on what might be
learned from the Old Man's technique and kept, digested,
and applied elsewhere. It had been focused upon his own
personal end of it—of assisting the Old Man and doing it well.
Nevertheless it made a profound and lasting impression upon
him. It instantly and permanently established the Old Man in
the Old Man's own tradition. It proved for Roy what he ached
to believe, that the stories of the Old Man's phenomenal vir-
tuosity were true, that there were men like him who looked
resolutely into the dirty, bleeding face of death and, with
high and ghostly courage against odds, struck at it and drove
it away; that there were men whose sincere integrity and
enormous skill gave them the right to take unfalteringly the
last clear chance with another's life and breath; that there
were men who saw, recognized, and accepted perilous battle,
were unshaken by it, and on the instant made irrevocable decisions about it. It proved that there were men who
held knives who were saviors instead of assassins. It proved
that such men at certain terrible moments became as much
the selfless instruments of an idea as the knives they held.
It proved that such men were very, very few. It proved that
while they existed the age of the demigods of healing had
not really died out entirely, that something of Hippocrates,
Albucasis, Avicenna, Roger of Salerno, Pasteur, Lister,
Ehrlich, Cooper, and others in the long-dead apostolic succession of greatness still survived. It proved for Roy that
the Old Man was an embodiment and a symbol, for he now
recognized that the Old Man was one and the same with
them.

Privacy for patients was not an outstanding feature of the
Charity. On the wards there was none whatever, but there
were a few small rooms on every floor for sequestration purposes. Disturbed, moribund, and contagious cases were generally put into them. Occasionally they were occupied by
sick members of the house staff and more frequently by alco-

holic city politicians. Inspector Rybecki went from the operating room into one of these.

The inspector's survival did not remain long at issue. In twenty-four hours he was bellowing for water and in forty-eight for food. From there on he charged into full convalescence with an incredible and bull-like vitality. His room, off Roy's ward, became the unofficial social annex of the hospital. The inspector had an immediate and enormous popularity. His room was too small for it. There were impressive daily deliveries of liquor, candy, and fruit, swarmed upon by the house staff. Beside solicitous delegations from the Police Department his room bulged with other deputations of well-wishers. These included City Hall workers and politicos, assorted stool pigeons, sundry anonymous ladies obviously not social workers, and the press, invariably headed by Capshaw. The inspector's news notices to his delight were panegyric and sustained: DI GENOVA DOPF SLAYING SOLVED IN BLAZE OF GUNFIRE—SUPERIOR SLEUTHING; HERO COP IN JEOPARDY; RYBECKI FIGHTING THROUGH. There was a series of feature articles by Capshaw. In one of these, Capshaw, inspired by five straight hookers of whiskey at the Asterion, surpassed himself. This gem, printed in the family edition, was headlined as follows: ONLY HIS DUTY.

"Today a police paladin lies grimly fighting for his life in the Charity Hospital. He is there because he made his body a shield to save his men from injury or death. That man is Inspector Stanislaus Rybecki, who, without thought for himself, took the desperate bullet fired from a criminal gun. The price for his kind of courage is likely to be high, but Rybecki is gladly paying it. When asked of this in a brief interview with him today, Rybecki said 'Only doing my duty.'

"Rybecki lay as usual in his narrow hospital bed. As usual, too, his face was pale and smiling, drawn by pain but smiling. Today flowers brightened the barren room. A little bunch of wilted violets from his friend, the crippled newsboy on the Charity corner, were in a drinking glass beside his bed. . . ." Capshaw had several more drinks to keep from throwing up as he read what he had written. But the public loved it as he knew they would.

Shortly before Capshaw had retired to the Asterion to give birth to this masterpiece, he had visited the inspector. The inspector was putting down his second pint of ice cream.

"You know, Cappy, I just been thinking—ain't it a shame I didn't even get one damn shot into that Kite son-of-a-bitch? Manny nailed him right through the eye with his first one, and that Manny is the lousiest marksman on the force. He can't hit a bull in the ass at ten feet with a shotgun . . ."

That particular piece of Capshaw's remained unsurpassed in the press reader reaction. The inspector's fan mail became overwhelming. The mayor personally pinned another police decoration on his pajamas. Capshaw turned down a promotion to a feature writer's desk.

When he had the time, Roy frequently dropped in on the inspector, usually late after visiting hours. At these intervals the ward had settled into darkened inactivity and calls even from the emergency room were likely to be few. In those impromptu sessions with the inspector, Roy got to know him very well. He also got a good deal of information on the inspector's views of the city, crime, the Police Department, sex, religion, politics, medicine, the Charity, and life in general. Roy sat for long stretches facing his bed, listening to him.

"Now you take a guy like me, Doc. For what I started out as I ain't done so bad. One of five kids, the middle one, poor as all hell and only an eighth-grade education. Christ, when I think back on it I wonder how we ever got along. My old man was a steel puddler. They make pretty fair dough but they earn it. That kind of work tears the guts out of anybody. The trouble with the old man was he was a booze fighter. Jesus, how he used to belt that stuff. He'd get paid, hit the nearest saloon, and stay there as long as the dough lasted or until they threw him out. He'd come home blind and depending on what he felt like, slap Ma or us kids around or maybe just go to bed and sleep it off. The only dough we got from him was what he had left after he'd been out on one of his payday bats. I can still see my mother bringing his pants out of the bedroom into the light and going through his pockets and counting it up. Ma had to hire out with a mop as a night scrubwoman in an office building to make ends meet. She was a great old girl, my mother. A lot of times she didn't eat much or at all just so us kids could have more. She did a damn good job too, considering what she had to do it with. She always kept us pretty clean and saw that we went to school and St. Konrad's Church. We didn't turn out so bad either. My oldest brother is an ordained priest right now on the Coast. My sister's dead, died in the flu epidemic, but when that happened she was training for a nurse. I got another brother that's a contractor in Dallas. Made a lot of dough too. My baby brother died of black whooping cough when we were just kids. Me, well hell, here I am, inspector on the police force. That ain't bad for anybody with nothing and two strikes against them to start with. You know, Doc, my mother couldn't speak English at all and the old man just enough? Around home we always talked Polish.

"We had a hell of a time. All of us had to get out and work after school the minute we were old enough. I got a job running packages when I was ten and that was quite a deal. We had a tough gang of kids in that neighborhood and these little bastards used to jump anybody. They used to jump me just to see what I had in the packages I was delivering and I had to fight like a son-of-a-bitch to keep them from doing it. I got pretty good doing it too. I was a big kid for my age and I got real handy just from dodging around trying to keep from getting hit when the old man had a mean can on and fighting off the neighborhood kids. Hell, when I was twelve and thirteen I was taking them on three and four years older than I was and licking some of them too. Anyhow they finally got to let me alone. About that time I got a job as runner and general errand boy at Vulcan Steel. I made more dough than I had ever seen before . . . fifteen bucks a week. But I worked like a son-of-a-bitch for it. I was all over the joint. I kept the salt-water buckets filled for the guys working the slag and on the furnaces. I got coffee for the crane men, ran messages all over, a lot of other things. They kept me busier than a blind dog in a meat shop.

"One day I was sitting down at lunch hour eating and this mick son-of-a-bitch by the name of Bucky Sheehan, a puddler's assistant, comes up. I had some Polish sausage in my lunch bucket—

" 'What you got in there, Pollack?' he says, and before I can stop him, he reaches in my bucket and pulls out one of the sausages and looks at it and smells it.

" 'I always thought Polacks ate shit,' he says, 'now I know it,' and he throws the sausage on the ground and laughs at the other guys sitting around eating. I was madder than hell and I went for him and we had it right there. He was bigger and older than me and he was pretty good too. What I didn't know was that he'd already had a couple of fights in the amateurs and had an older brother who was a welterweight pro. Sharpy Sheehan, name he fought under. Anyhow I was so Goddamn mad, all I wanted to do was get at him. He could outbox me easy and he cut me up some, but he couldn't hit hard. You know something, Doc? That's something that a man can do or he can't. He learns it early or by instinct does it right or he never really can do it. Well, anyway, I got in maybe a half a dozen solid ones right from my heels, mostly lucky, that slowed him down. The best one Goddamn near took him. Right in the belly just under the ribs—solar plexus. About this time the foreman sees everybody standing around yelling and comes over and stops the fight. Bucky was ready to quit. Not me, I'm still so mad they got to hold me to make me stop. I'm crying, I'm so mad. Finally I get calmed down on account of the foreman being there and I tell Bucky:

" 'O.K., you dirty mick son-of-a-bitch. Wait and see.'

" 'Any time, Polack,' he says. But after that he stayed away from me. One day a while later he comes around.

" 'Listen Stan,' he says, 'can I talk to you a minute?'

"I'm not all the way cooled down yet and it's been a couple of weeks. I think maybe he's been thinking it over and wants to make a meet somewhere and finish the fight.

"I ask him what he wants.

" 'Look, Stan,' he says, 'about the fight. I was way out of line. I'm sorry.' And he sticks out his hand.

"Well, Doc, when a guy does that and means it there ain't much you can say or do. We shake hands.

" 'Tell me something, Stan,' he says, 'you only sixteen?'

"I tell him I am.

"'Well, hell,' he says, 'one of the guys said you was. I'm eighteen and I want to tell you something. Right now at sixteen you got it. Ain't many guys can hit like that no matter how old and you're just a kid. A couple of times when we was mixing it up you really hurt me. Guy that can hit like you ought to do something about it. Ever hear of Sharpy Sheehan? Well, he's my brother. He trains over at the gym on Price Street. I go over with him a lot. How's for us going over together sometime? Sharpy can show us a lot of things.'

"I tell him I will, and we do. I get going over there with Sharpy and Bucky and working out all the time. Bucky got to be my best friend. Jesus, that's a long time ago, Doc, when

I think of it. Bucky's been dead for years now—killed in a chain break off one of the plant cranes along with another guy—and Sharpy, the poor punch-drunk son-of-a-bitch, is up at Greengate Asylum. Don't know anything now or anybody, last time I saw him, just sits there in a dirty bathrobe looking at nothing, with his fists balled up waiting for the bell.

"Anyhow that's how I got started fighting pro, Doc, working out with those boys. I started fighting around in prelims at clubs and places. Fought under the name of Young Stanley. Fifty bucks a fight if you won and twenty-five if you didn't —manager gets half either way. Mine was the same one Sharpy had, name of Solly Parsons, a skinny ex-lightweight with little mean eyes and a mouth that had been clipped so much it looked like a scarred up ass hole. Always wore a red necktie. The buck-hungry little son-of-a-bitch would sell his own mother, if there was a dollar in it. The little bastard didn't have an ounce of decency in him. He ruined more good young fighters than booze and broads put together by deliberately overmatching them to get bigger purses. He put Sharpy where he is today and a lot of others just that way—getting their brains kicked out for an extra buck or two. He did it to me too, finally. I was young enough and dumb enough I'd be dead or a bum myself now if something hadn't happened that got me out of the whole Goddamn dirty fight racket entirely.

"I was just nineteen then and going pretty good in it. Forty-three professional fights. Sometime—just for laughs, I'll show you my press notices. I was on the long end of thirty-two knockouts including eight T.K.O.s, six decisions, and five losers, four by decision and one knockout on me, the last one.

"That's the one that did it, the last one. Remember now, Doc, I'm working in the mill right along and doing my training at the gym catch as catch can—nights, time off, and like that. Anyway, this one day Solly comes around to the mill and talks to the foreman and then comes over and gets me.

" 'Kid,' he says, 'you're on the way up and I'm going to put you there. This is it. This is where we make the big pitch that starts it all. One month from today you're going to fight Abby Balzano and you're going to lick him by knockout or T.K.O., anyway. What do you think of that?'

"Well, you're too young to remember, Doc, unless you

been following the fights from a high chair, but Abby Balzano was a ranking welterweight. He was always around four or five down from the top. He never got any higher, but he stayed around there for a long time. He was way past his peak then, hell, he was damned near thirty-five and on his way down but still up there and he was good, very good, but his legs was giving out. You got to keep the old legs, Doc. The old legs are a lot of it, they hold you up. They go—you go. Anyway, Abby still had everything else. He had all the ring experience in the world, he could hit, and he could box. Hell, he was a veteran and he had it. Putting me in against him was like a night stick against a .38. And I knew it and I said so—it sounded like a lousy joke.

" 'Listen, kid,' Solly said, 'wait'll I give you all of it. Sure, Abby can take you but he ain't going to, see? He ain't going to. He's ready to pack it in. He's going to quit and he wants to make his last bundle. It ain't this fight or any other fight with him now. It's the old ro-de-o-dough. And you're going to lick him for it. The odds will be way up on his side and he's going to have a big piece down on the fight, only it ain't going to be on him, it's going to be on you, see, at eight or ten to one maybe? So you win the fight and the winner's end of the purse and he gets enough bucks he don't have to care. You jump way up there, he gets the moola, see?'

" 'You mean he's going to take a dive for it?' I say.

" 'You ain't taking the dive,' Solly says. 'Sure he's going into the tank. Who wouldn't for what he's going to get for it? Do I have to spell it out for you kid? You get the glory, he gets the dough. We do pretty good that way too. The winner's end is ten thousand bucks. Ten thousand bucks and your nose is clean. He takes the dive, you don't.'

" 'What do I do?' I ask him.

" 'You just fight,' Solly says. 'You just get in there and try to kill him see? For you it's all on the up and up. Just get in there and try to murder him, kid. That's all you got to do. He'll make it look right. He'll cut you up a little early on, sure, but you got to expect that. You got to take that. But he's old, you're young, and as it goes you stand the gaff better. Along 'bout the eighth or maybe earlier you start to land them. Then there's the lucky punch. You won't even know when you throw it. He'll take care of that. All you got to do, kid, is fight. Abby'll take care of all the rest.'

"You know, Doc, I bought it. I bought what Solly said. That

conniving little son-of-a-bitch sold me real easy. The real pitch was, of course, that they were building Abby up for a swan-song crack at the title, and he needed a string of easy straight wins by knockout to qualify for it. He never got the crack at the title though, but he got a lot of straight wins by knockout. He assassinated a string of bums and beginners like me. I fought him though and he took me apart.

"I'll tell you something, Doc, a man can take maybe one beating like that in his life and live to get around all right.

"The son-of-a-bitch broke my nose and closed my eye in the second round and floored me twice. See this ear? It don't look too bad now—I got that in the second too. My nose was busted again by the third so I went in without my mouthpiece in the fourth because I couldn't breathe with it in. See these gold teeth here in front? My real ones went in that third too, and he closed my left eye. Along toward one minute of the bell at the end Abby made a deliberate clinch away from the referee and says out of the corner of his mouth, 'Lie down with the next one, kid, or I got to hurt you.' Well, Doc, I still don't get the score. I keep thinking of what Solly told me. Anyway I don't lie down. I just get knocked down twice and on the last one saved by the bell. The fourth round was it though. There was one clinch early. In it Abby says into my ear, 'I told you, kid, lie down.' The referee broke us and Abby came in. I about halfway saw the first part of the right cross he threw into me. The next thing I saw was Mike Tendler, my handler, in the dressing room. Mike had been working on me for almost a half an hour. The doctor had been in and out already and said I'd come around all right. He'd stitched me up and gone back to the ring for the mercy bout. That's the one they put on when the main event don't last too long to satisfy the customers. Mike got me into a shower and into my clothes. Solly was nowhere around, but Mike gave me an envelope. There was seven hundred and fifty dollars in it—all I ever got out of the fight. Mike asks me am I all right and I say I am. I ain't though, I just think I am. My head feels funny and I'm really fuzzy as hell. But I can walk good it seems, and I fell dry and hungry. I make it out of the arena all right to get a cab and figure to maybe go somewhere and get something to eat. I step off the curb to flag a taxi and a car I don't even see hits me. I don't even remember anything about that. What I do remember is waking up right here in this hospital with a real pretty nurse over me. They got my right leg strung up in ropes and pulleys—it's broke in a couple of places. I'll tell you something else, Doc. You know who took care of me just like you're doing now? Your boss, the big boy, the Old Man, you call him. He was in the white suit then just like you are now—just about as old, too, maybe. I remember a couple of things about him from then. He was skinny like he is now and he never slept any. He was always sniffing around day or night. They tell me he still does. His ears stuck out and he had a hell of a sense of humor, the real deadpan kind. He had a great pair of hands too. I used to dread dressings on that leg of mine—they hurt so Goddamn much—except when he did them. Then I didn't mind a damn bit. He had the easiest, gentlest hands I ever saw. He'd come around with the cart and the nurse and kid around with me while he was doing it. 'Pugilist,' he'd say, 'I've come to admire your leg again.' 'Is it going to hurt, Doc?' I'd say. 'Why, how you carry on about nothing,' he says. 'How can a compound fracture of both bones of the lower leg hurt anybody? All I'm going to do to-day is tear all the skin off of it and pour on a quart of iodine.' Hell, he could have done it too and I wouldn't have let out a peep. He could have done anything to me he was so easy and gentle. He was a great guy then, and I guess he's the greatest there is now ain't he, Doc?"

Roy said the Old Man was.

"Well, Doc, anyway, that busted leg ended me in the ring. Actually it was a blessing in disguise as they say. That hadn't happened and I might be where Sharpy Sheehan is now at Greengate Asylum. That's really how I got into police work. The leg healed up just fine. After a while I managed just as good as always—didn't even have a limp, but I knew better than ever to try fighting again on it. I did a lot of thinking while I was laying there waiting for it to heal and I figured about the only thing for me was going back to the steel plant. One day while I was laying there a cop with a lot of gold braid on him came in to see me just to say hello. He'd come in to see another cop who was hurt and he stopped off to see me when he heard I was in there. That was Captain Forham of the Twenty-third. He was an old fight fan. I'd been on the card a couple of fights he'd been to and he remembered me. We got to talking and this and that and I tell him about myself. He dropped around every once in a while after that. He came in one time just before I was ready to leave the hospital and says:

"'Kid, the doc says you're going to be as good as new. I got a good idea for you. Come around and see me when they spring you.'

"I did. I went to see him over at the Twenty-third Precinct and six months later I was a rookie cop, and I been a cop ever since. I had to work my ass off to get in—about all I could pass at first was the physical examination. I went to night school and took Saturday courses and finally passed the examinations on the first crack. Captain Forhan pinned the badge on me himself. From there on out I got a lot of good breaks, a good many of them on account of Captain Forhan. God rest his soul. He was like a father to me. And some of it was just plain Goddamn Polish luck. I was only in uniform two years before I got made detective and from there on out it's been right straight up. I been inspector now for almost five years and hell, I ain't too old yet—fifty-three. That ain't bad is it, Doc, for a thick-headed Polack son-of-a-bitch with no education or much of anything else to start with?"

Roy said that it not only wasn't bad, but that it was very good. The inspector lay back on the pillows and sucked his gold teeth meditatively for a moment. A lot of things were probably running through his head. The teeth glinted in a chuckle.

"You know, Doc, I'm fifty-three and I ain't married. How many guys you know that old who ain't married or haven't been?"

"Not many, Inspector. Can't think of any right now. Why aren't you?"

"That's a funny thing too, Doc. When I might have, when I was a hell of a lot younger, I figured I couldn't afford it. When I was older and could, I got out of the idea. I don't know, from some of the guys I've seen and their wives maybe I been lucky there too. You married, Doc?"

"No, Inspector, I'm not."

"I thought not, Doc. You guys have to work too hard to have any time for a wife till you get through with it. But you got to watch out, Doc. Let me give you a straight tip, the finger's on you, boy. Look out." The inspector's teeth flashed broadly.

"What finger on me for what, Inspector?"

"On you, my boy, and for the old ring, that's for what. You don't know that, huh? You ain't noticed that? I thought not. You ain't caught the pitch yet—it ain't open enough yet, but it's there. It's real plain where I sit, real plain."

"Well, maybe you better tell me, Inspector. I think you've got a wrong reading."

"No, I ain't, Doc, and I'll tell you. It's your ward nurse in there, on in the daytime and the rest of them too. The one that comes in here with you and the big boy on rounds."

"You've got that one wrong, Inspector. They're too smart to get any ideas about surgical residents. She's probably someone else's girl."

"That's right she may be someone else's girl. But she's got ideas about you, Doc. Look, maybe you know this or maybe you don't, but there's a certain way a broad looks at a guy she's that way about. When you see it, it means just one of two things—it means she has or she will with the guy. She's on the make for him. Anybody knows that, they can pick it up every time. That's the way they look at you, Doc boy. That's just the way. I caught all of them at it the first day after I could sit up a little and I seen them at it since. It's all yours for a crook of the fingers. That's all you got to do. Just be careful unless you want it for life. Any one of those babies look to me like they're right in there trying to hang a ring job on a real serious guy like you. But that's up to you, but I'll tell you one thing"—the inspector gave a golden chortle— "if they looked that way at me, old as I am, I wouldn't waste no time. All of them around here are cute."

An orderly came in. "Dr. Maines, telephone. Admission in emergency."

"Grab some more of that fruit, Doc." The inspector waved at one of the baskets. "I get a bellyache looking at it. Come back whenever you get a minute."

Roy took an apple, winked at the inspector, and went out.

The day the inspector was discharged from the Charity he got a final blast of applause from the press. There was a full-length picture of him standing at the front entrance waving his hat. This made page two in both editions.

Roy finished in the operating room and hurried down to the floor to see him off. The inspector, aware of the presence of waiting photographers, had accentuated his natural bent toward sartorial magnificence for his public's benefit. His suit, tailored by Klopstein Klothes, had been delivered with imperative haste for an emergency fitting. With commendable dispatch a trusted emissary of the brothers Klopstein took in the belly slack of the pants and padded the shoulder sag caused by the inspector's loss of weight, and returned it in time for the exit ceremonies. This suit was a paragon of Klopstein craftsmanship. It was a delicate off shade of magenta with a black pin stripe. The peaked lapels and other features of its acute pattern were artfully emphasized by obvious hand stitching. The effect of this startling garment was enhanced by a mauve shirt, socks, and handkerchief and a Paisley-type tie. There were the additional items of new tan shoes and a pearl-gray Homburg hat. In this ensemble the inspector shone and rotated among his waiting henchmen like a lyre bird in a flock of Plymouth Rocks.

"Come in, Doc, come in," the inspector said when he saw Roy standing at the door of the smoke-filled room.

"You guys," he turned to the waiting aggregation, "mind leaving me and the doc a couple of minutes? We got a little private talking to do."

They filed out into the hall and the inspector closed the door. His words were halting at first, almost shy.

"Look, Doc, I ain't said this before to you because things like this are real hard to say. Hard for anybody I guess, but more than that for me because I don't know the kind of words it ought to be said in. Anyhow, Doc, what I'm trying to say is this. I know what you and Dr. Hand, the Old Man you call him, done for me. I know if it hadn't been for the both of you I'd of been a front carry in a box out of Lopardi's point long ago. Look at me now—good as ever.

"I ain't ever going to forget it. With me and the rest of the boys over at the department you and your boss can't do no wrong."

He took a large folio envelope from inside his coat.

"This stuff I got here ain't just from me, Doc. It's from all of the boys, Manny, Ed, Tip, Mig, and the rest you've seen around. We talked it over and we all felt the same way. We know we're backed up real good, best we can be as long as there's doctors like you and Dr. Hand around to work on us when the chips are down. You'd be surprised how much that means, Doc. On account of that this here's for you. Your boss has had one for a long while."

He handed the envelope to Roy.

"Don't bother to open it now, Doc. Save it till later. I think you'll get a belt out of it. It ain't money or anything like that. And these here," he pulled two oblong packages out of his pocket, "one for him and one for you. Here, this one's yours. His is just the same. Give it to him, will you, Doc?"

Rybecki gave him the two packages and stood a minute sucking his gold incisors meditatively.

"I guess that's all I got to say, Doc. Except maybe for one more thing you might like to hear. You know, Doc, except he's a lot older and the best there is, you and him are a hell of a lot alike. See you later, Doc."

The inspector opened the door. "All right boys, let's go. I don't want to keep them photographers waiting."

Roy stood listening to the inspector's stampede of attendant sleuths clump away down the hall.

He opened the envelope. In it was an embossed certificate with an identification card, both with the seal of the City Police Department. Both said that Roy R. Maines, M.D., was an Honorary Police Surgeon and "Entitled to All Rights and Privileges Pertaining Thereto." In the package with his name on it was a gold chronometer wrist watch in a velvet box. On the back of its casing were three lines of engraving: Roy's name, the date of the inspector's operation, and "Remember Rybecki."

For a while after the inspector's celebrated interlude at the hospital, there was nothing to relieve the sameness and the unrelenting grind of work. The days and nights, long in themselves, drifted imperceptibly into each other, and into weeks and months with a rapid fluid facility. Almost before he knew it Roy had finished that hard and trying first year of surgery at the Charity. During it Roy's living had become set almost automatically into an unvarying schedule. Out of the hospital he spent much of his time off at the Asterion—where he got mildly drunk before going to bed. Frequently he saw and consorted with Capshaw there.

One night Capshaw waited until they were both suitably reflective on Szabo's Bohemian Beer and then handed him a fresh, ink-smelling copy of the press, neatly folded to the society page.

"For your files, Doctor," Capshaw said gravely, and watched him as he read it.

There was a picture of Katy Winter, looking very virginal

in a veil. She had done it. She was married, Goddamn it, married—and to someone he didn't even know. He passed the paper back to Capshaw with something like an egg beater churning in his belly.

"Well, good luck to her, and good luck to the guy, too, whoever he is," he said with a casualness he did not feel.

Capshaw looked at him with a slow, appraising smile. "That the way you feel about it, Doc? All over it now, eh?"

"Right," Roy said, "has been for a long time. I'm fine."

"Sure you are," Capshaw said, "in a pig's ass. Your first real love takes a long time to get over, Doc. A long time. You're not over it yet, but I think you're getting there. Come on let's have another drink. That's indicated for all lovelorn bastards. Remember what I said about emotional vaccination . . ."

9

At the end of the Charity's fiscal year (July to July) there was a good deal of confused activity. New interns and residents came on and others left in the midst of intemperate celebrations. The Charity surgical staff banquet was part of this and every year during it the Old Man gave a speech. In it he usuall began with comments on the Service statistics for the year. After this he announced changes in staff appointments and generally reviewed the state of the Service and the hospital. Then he held forth on some subject of his own choosing. The first time Roy heard one of these the Old Man, loosened by a bourbon bottle, had given quite a dissertation, parts of which Roy never forgot.

"What I say now," the Old Man had begun, "does not concern what we do, but what we think about what we do. From time to time it is necessary for any man who performs an essential kind of service such as ours, to consider why he does it. To do this he must look at his work in general, and himself in particular, if he is to come to any significant conclusions about either one. And these conclusions are necessary if he is to continue to function in his best capacity.

"Let us never forget that we deal in fundamentals. We are dealing basically in human protoplasm—the same protoplasm of which we ourselves are made. Let us not forget this. Let us not forget that the same human stuff that we cut, ligate, and sew, is the same stuff of which we, the cutters, are composed. And that when we cut and sew upon it we are in a sense cutting and sewing upon ourselves. In what we do, then, let us be true to ourselves—true to our own protoplasm. If we will remember this, although we may not be able to help it, we shall do less to injure it. First then let us be aware of and respect all protoplasm, the fundamental stuff of which we are all made.

"Next let us remember that in an ultimate sense we deal in time. We are merchants of time. We deal in time in terms of its length and its quality. The time of human protoplasm is not long and much of that time is not good. It is a transient and delicate stuff. The arch enemy of its length is death and of its quality, disease. What we do fundamentally is to prolong the time of protoplasm by postponing its death, or, failing this, to change the quality of the time of protoplasm by making its existence less painful. We deal then in time, its length and its quality. This concept has many implications. *Shall we prolong time if we can, when its quality is such that it is not desirable? Shall we give time at the price of suffering? Shall we do this? And who is there to say?*

"There is no one to say. No one except ourselves. Because we do what we do, we are the sole arbiters of this. We do not know why God so often abandons the protoplasm he has created to its natural enemies. That is neither here nor there. What is significant is that, because of what we are or what we hold ourselves to be, we must support and defend what is apparently abandoned. We must assume, whether we will or not, at certain times the terrible decisions of some lost deity. We must do this in spite of our ignorance and ineptitude because there is apparently nothing else to look to and no one else to do it. But, since we must do it, let us do it as any human act of significance must be done—honestly, bravely, and generously. And, in so far as we are capable, in the awareness that for the instant we are mortals assuming the trappings of divinity.

"When we do this honestly we have fulfilled our highest function as beings, as creatures of protoplasm, and as healers, for, at these times, we are the selfless instruments of an ideal. When that happens we possess for a while perhaps the truth of whatever absolute there may be. For that short and awesome space we cease to be stumbling, faltering, and blind for we have closed as intimately as possible with a principle. We are then perhaps the principle itself.

"Let us reflect a little further on this. Let us examine the abstraction of our relationship to the general principle.

"The serious work which we do of cutting disordered living protoplasm to its benefits involves these elements: the main one is the idea of trying to cure. This idea is the prolongation of life with a minimum of pain or discomfort. The second is the disorder which must be removed or modified to realize the idea. The other two elements are the means by which the idea is to be fulfilled or accomplished. These are a being who holds a knife and another who is under it. In the ultimate then, our work is striving for the realization of a principle or idea through human agency. It is at point here to note that in our work the disease, the holder of the knife, and the being under it differ and change from time to time. But the principle or the idea does not.

"As the holders of the knife, then, we are the active instruments of the idea. Those under it, and their diseases, are the passive parts of it. The importance of this is that, to be a part, either active or passive, of this particular principle or idea, is a perilous business. He who is under the knife with his ailment may lose his life, but the holder of the knife can lose his head, his heart, and his soul. Let us not forget this.

"We as holders of the knife are the active personal elements of the idea and at certain times we become, or are like to become, its greatest one. There are times when we are at one with it. We may come to be its sole element because all our decisions are final. Remember that what we do and the way we do it is related to everything we have ever done before, everything we will do after, and everything we are. What we do then is the essence of the sum total of all our past and previous existence. It is not then a question of a man with an idea but of an idea with a man. Ideas possess men, men do not possess ideas.

"An idea possesses a man when he instantly and irrevocably exercises decisive action in terms of the idea he holds and his capacity to realize it. When he does this he can probably, for certain brief and terrible moments, assume a certain immortality. This, because in these moments he is absolutely alone with the idea itself. He becomes the complete and selfless implement of the idea and an agent of its truth as well.

"Let us remember then that we are not simply holders of knives. We are best agents of truth, or we should be striving to be so. And as such, we will hold fast to it no matter how charged or set upon we are by circumstances. When we are overwhelmed or annihilated in the support and search for truth, we will stand or fall with it—even though an act of truth as we see it, may be our last—the last act of our lives. In a sense, gentlemen, if I may mix my metaphors, we are pilots of protoplasm, but instead of a tiller we use a knife. Let us be the best pilots we can.

"Remember the words of Seneca:

" 'He who has been able to say "Neptune, you shall never sink this ship except on an even keel," has fulfilled the requirements of his art.'

"This was true when Seneca said it. . . . It is true now."

The Old Man sat down.

10

Roy now had little or nothing to do with Santry or Santry's end of the Service. He worked alternately under Tom Wilder, Wild Will Wortle, and the Old Man. His encounters with Santry in the wards, corridors, and operating rooms were only passing and relatively infrequent. When they occurred they ignored each other. The silence between them was stony. Roy gave Santry a transient glowering glance and Santry returned it with his habitual smile. The flash of hatred that Roy felt at these times he knew was returned, but this had no importance now. He was too pressed with keeping up the pace of the work to think much on it. At this point he was particularly preoccupied with the taxing tutelage of William MacTavish Wortle.

Wild Will Wortle in his twenty years at the Charity had become almost as much a part of its surgical tradition as the Old Man. Wortle was a chest surgeon and confined himself wholly to that specialty. He was a surgical swashbuckler. Wortle was irascible, impatient, unrelenting, and loud. He was also astute, courageous, and a dazzling operator. His ego, like his talent, was enormous, but so was his humor. Wortle's arrival on the ward, in the operating room or anywhere else for that matter, was catalytic. Explosions of activity followed in the wake of his prodigious energy. Patients and medical personnel were likely to be blown out of their beds and their complacency. He hit places and people like a cyclone and left them jarred, stimulated, and breathless. He had an amazing command of profanity.

"All right, Goddamn it, what are we waiting for? Is this an operation or a wake? We're five minutes late starting this case now. Want the patient to die of old age before we get the steel on him? Come on, off your asses and get the show on the road, Goddamn it."

The show, whatever it was, instantly got on the road, and forthwith Wortle, its star performer, blazed through it with a magnificent demonstration of technique and a torrent of exhortation, invective, and profanity. Wortle was roundly effective as a surgeon and as a man. He was a bitter enemy of hypocrisy wherever he encountered it. His judgments of others and himself in any situation were instantaneous, loudly announced, and usually correct. He lived hugely and most of the time in a lathered gallop of activity. In spite of a contempt for money he made it and spent it in quantity. His style of living outside of the fever of his professional activity was baroque. He was a fancier of exotic and outlandish food which he went to much trouble and expense to get and eat. His prowess with liquors was extraordinary, but his habit of drinking was meticulous. He never drank when he had work to do or worked when he had been drinking. These dietary and bibulous excesses had had astonishingly little effect on his physique. Wortle had the muscular durable frame of a gladiator in spite of the abuses he put upon it. His body to all appearances was much younger than his face. His face showed something of the stigmata of his fifty furious years of living. Wortle had kept all of a thick head of hair but this was almost completely white. Beneath it his eyes flashed above tremendous bags of dark-hued flesh. His brow and cheeks were seamed with wrinkles. It was a strong face and a wise one. Dutch Ransahoff's simile about it was to the point:

"You know what Wortle reminds me of when I look at him, Roy? A Goddamn bloodhound that's had a shot of adrenalin."

Roy's association with Wild Will Wortle began one day when the Old Man called him into the office after morning rounds:

"Maines, how do you get along with Will Wortle?"

"Why, fine, sir, I guess."

"That's good. He thinks you do. He's picked you to come on the chest service if you want to go. I'm asking you because not everyone can work with him."

"Well, sir, I'd rather stay on surgery with you, if it's up to me."

The Old Man swiveled in his chair.

"I think it might be a good idea for you to go on with Will for a while and pick up chest technique. You're far enough along now to get something out of it. It may be a help to you too with the surgical board coming up. Suppose you try it for a while. With the amount of work Will's doing he needs somebody . . ."

Roy went on chest surgery with Wild Will Wortle. Whatever misgivings he might have had cleared as he came to know Wortle and the work. Underneath Wortle's bombast was a tremendous specialized knowledge and skill and this when he was so minded he could impart with emphatic clarity. Roy began to absorb it. Wortle pushed him and in three months Wortle was letting him do an occasional case on his own. Wortle did not have the Old Man's reticence about commendation. When a man did well with him he was to say so loudly, with conviction, and usually with blaspheming emphasis.

Roy almost immediately developed a solid and satisfactory rapport with Wild Will Wortle. He worked very well with him and as the work went on he got a good deal of enjoyment out of Wortle's pyrotechinics as a surgeon and a man. There was also the fact that there was a militant and long-standing enmity between Wortle and Santry. This enmity Roy understood and considered as a common bond with Wild Will.

"I hear you clouted that smirking son-of-a-bitch," Wortle had said to him.

"I'm still on probation for it," Roy said.

Wortle snorted. "The Old Man should have hung a medal on you instead. One of these days I may knock him on his ass myself—I've had an itch to do it for years."

Roy could well imagine Wortle doing it, too. Aside from his vast talent and honesty, Wortle was a vastly physical man.

A great deal of Roy's working time was still spent under Wilder. Wilder was the antithesis of Wild Will. For Thomas

Wilder had an almost unbelievable gentleness of heart. He was truly a gentle man. In all probability Wilder should have been a professor of philosophy instead of a surgeon. He had many of the traditional professorial attributes. He was mild mannered, forgetful of practical considerations, and he loved to talk. He was devoted to learning of any kind and he had tremendous knowledge pertinent to medicine and of matters far removed from it. He had a phenomenal familiarity with medical and general literature. He was fond of abstractions, principles, and aphorisms, and he was an inveterate quoter. Wilder was a man of perpetual fretting concerns, necessary and otherwise. He had immense solicitude for everything and everybody within his immediate environment. With patients this solicitude was endless. He spent hours listening to, investigating, and soothing even the most trivial complaints. He treated his subordinates, particularly the residents, with consummate consideration and he took infinite pains with their instruction. He had boundless patience with their mistakes.

As an operator he was an exquisitely meticulous but a painfully slow technician. The selection and use of each instrument was always weighed and deliberated. Compared to the high authoritative flash of the Old Man's technique, he was a surgical tortoise. It took him three times longer to do a comparable case, but his work, when he was finally done with it, was similar. It was beautifully and correctly done.

With Roy and others he shared a common idolatry of the Old Man. This was embarrassing at times, for he never defended himself from the Old Man's occasional petulance or his irate criticisms, however misplaced. That Thomas Wilder was a good doctor and a good man and a humble one was generally recognized. He was frequently and covertly referred to as "Saint Thomas." Actually he was something of a martyr. His martyrdom was mainly matrimonial. For twenty-nine of his fifty-seven years he had gently and forbearingly endured a domestic hair shirt. This was his home life with one hundred and twenty-odd pounds of spoiled, sarcastic, vain, nagging, sophisticated, unhappy woman. That was Mrs. Estelle Solton Wilder, his wife. Mrs. Wilder and his long-established pattern of escape in overwork were the principal elements of Wilder's sustained personal tragedy. But there had been other long-standing ordeals for him before that.

Sadness, bad luck, and bad health, of one kind or another, had haunted Wilder for much of his life, beginning early.

Wilder's mother died bearing him. At the age of five polio-myelitis had left him with a slight permanent limp in his right leg. At fourteen his father was bankrupt. His suicide a year later left Wilder for the next seventeen years under the tyranny of his tight-mouthed, overly strict, and overly religious grandparents. They died within a month of each other during his first year in medical school, leaving him enough money, and barely enough, for him to finish on. It would have been enough, too, and even a little more, if young Tom had not come down with tuberculosis during the grind of his sophomore year. After his year in the sanitorium, there was just enough. Alone then, he had gone on through internship and the surgical residency at the Charity. Then he had met and married Estelle the first year he was out in practice. That in many ways had been almost the greatest misfortune of all in his continuous chain of ill luck. But it was not the last.

After that came the early morning when he was operating as usual at the Charity with Roy as his first assistant. And as his other misfortunes this castastrophe had come to Tom Wilder when he was least expecting it.

This time the pain came on with sickening suddenness. There was none of those previous warning twinges he had tried to ignore before. This time he had felt perfectly all right one instant and the next was like having his chest fast in the jaws of a closing vise. There was a queer, dead numbness with it down his left arm and into the fingers. He found himself breathing heavily against the slamming hurt of it. He began to sweat.

Across the table from him, Roy saw the unexpected slowing of his hands and looked at him. No one else seemed to have noticed. The instrument nurse apparently hadn't, and neither had the anesthetist.

"Anything wrong, Dr. Wilder?" Roy's eyes looked at him over his mask.

"No, just a stitch in my back," Wilder said. He was surprised how casual his voice sounded.

"The table's set too low." Roy turned to the anesthetist. "Bring the table up, will you, John?"

The anesthetist stopped tinkering with the patient's pressure cuff and started pumping the hydraulic treadle under his foot. The table and the body on it rose about four inches.

"How's that, any better?"

"Better," Wilder said. The pain was easing a little now. He

ought to be able to finish if it got no worse. All he had to do was close the incision anyway. The tumor was out, so the difficult part was over. His hands started to pick up the tempo of their work again. Gradually he began to breathe easier. The vise around his left breast was loosening perceptibly and the numbness in his arm was going with it. Immediately all of it was gone, just as it had hit him. The whole episode was over in less than two minutes. What was left was the clamminess of sweat. He was still sweating. Fifteen minutes later the patient was off the table.

Roy untied his gown for him and he peeled out of his gloves. They left the hot, heavy smell of the operating room and crossed the hall to dress. There wasn't a sign of anything now. It was just as if it hadn't happened. Wilder took off the sloppy wet tunic and trousers, mopped his face with them, and threw them into the hamper along with Roy's. Then he opened his locker and commenced putting on his street clothes.

"That was nice," Roy said. "I wonder if I'll ever be able to do one like that?"

"Sure you will," Wilder said. "All you have to do is a lot of them."

"How many have I done now?" Wilder thought. "I wonder how many. I lost count so long ago."

He pushed the locker door shut, locked it, and joined Roy at the long mirror. His face looked a little drawn and whiter than usual. He saw that there was a barely perceptible tremor in his hands as he fixed the knot in his tie.

Roy had finished and stood eyeing him solicitously. "You feel all right, Dr. Wilder?"

"Certainly, why?"

"I don't know, just thought you looked kind of pale."

"The older I get the more I feel the heat. It's a little too hot in there is all."

"It sure is," Roy said. "Every damned one of those operating rooms ought to be air-conditioned."

They went out into the corridor and forward through the swinging door to the elevator. A moment later they were in the lobby.

"Same time tomorrow for starting?"

"Why yes, Maines, I guess so."

"All right then. So long, Dr. Wilder. See you tomorrow morning."

He watched absently for a moment as Roy turned back toward the elevator. Then he went to the information desk. The pleasant, horse-faced girl sitting there greeted him brightly.

"Is Dr. Bauer in the house?"

"I'll see, Dr. Wilder."

She picked up one of the battery of phones.

"I've put it off long enough," he thought. "Now we'll see for sure."

The girl looked up at him.

"He's not here. He's in his office. Shall I get him for you?"

"No, don't bother. I'll get him."

He crossed the lobby to one of the chain of pay phone booths and carefully shut the door. There was a little wait before Bauer came on the wire.

Bauer's heavy voice boomed at him. "Yeah? This you Tom?"

"Yes. Are you busy right now?"

"Not very. What's on your mind, Tom?"

"I'd like to see you if you can make it."

"Now, you mean? Where? Here or—"

"I'm at the hospital. I can come over."

"Sure. Come ahead. Anything wrong?"

"I'll come over."

"O.K. Come ahead."

He checked with the information desk and went out into Velle Street and started for the car. Then he decided he'd walk it instead. Bauer's office was only six blocks away. On the way to the corner, an intern and a student nurse, much preoccupied with each other, respectfully said hello to him. The sun was beginning to heat up the street. It was almost noon. He crossed through the straggling line of traffic and began to walk briskly. He was almost there when he felt the peculiar twinging numbness begin in his chest and arm. Then the sweating started. He slowed down, stopped, and pretended to be looking at one of the line of shop windows. The feeling disappeared almost instantly. He stayed there several minutes, waiting to see if it would come back, and when it did not, he went very slowly the rest of the way.

He found Bauer sitting behind a litter of charts and tracings that covered the huge desk and overflowed onto the floor. Bauer looked spent as usual. His big frame slouched in the swivel chair. His white office coat was frayed at the sleeves, and not too clean. His neck bulged thickly over his collar and the sleazy half-knotted tie. As always he needed a shave.

"He's the sloppiest human living," he thought, "and he's also the best damned doctor I know."

Bauer peered at him through his thick, gold-rimmed lenses and waved him to a chair. "Well, well, Tommy boy," he boomed jovially, "sit down."

"Hello, Otto," he said, sitting down, "you look busy." He pointed to the litter of papers.

"Oh, this. They didn't agree with me on the statistics last time. This one I'm going to shove down their throats. What's on your mind, Tom?"

It took less than five minutes to tell Bauer, but almost a half hour to answer his questions. At the end of it Bauer looked at him thoughtfully. "Come on," he said, "we'll look you over."

Bauer always moved slowly and methodically, so that it was almost another hour before the examination was done, the heart tracings taken, and read, and they were back in the consultation room. Up to then neither of them said much. Bauer drummed on the desk for a moment with his thick fingers.

"Tom, you know what this is as well as I do," he said tentatively.

"I guess I do. The question is how bad is it?"

"Well, we'll say it's bad enough. The real question is what are we going to do about it?"

"What do you want me to do about it, Otto?"

Bauer rubbed his nose. "Tom there's a lot of people I would rather say this to. But I probably better give this to you straight. You've got to do two things. You have to stop working for a while and take things a little easy. And I want you to take some medication. You won't have to take it regularly, but just as you need it."

"What's that?" he said, "nitroglycerine?"

Bauer made a deprecatory gesture. "I wasn't thinking of nitroglycerine. My idea was amyl nitrite."

"What's the difference? They both do the same thing, don't they?"

"Well, yes . . . but for you just now I think maybe amyl nitrite is better."

"All right, I'll take your word for it. What else?"

Bauer rubbed his nose again. "That's it. The main thing is to knock it off for a while. I want you to stop working and take it easy, and we'll see how things go."

"What do you mean, stop working?"

"I mean stop working . . . entirely and now."

"But, look Otto, I . . ."

Bauer eyed him levelly. "'You heard me. This is angina, Tom. You know that as well as I do. From now on, Tom, you've got to take care of yourself."

"I can still do a little work though if I take it easy with it?"

Bauer shook his head. "Don't be a damned fool, Tom. I don't have to tell you these things. You're no child in this business."

"I didn't think it was that bad," Wilder said.

"Look, Tom, who can say how bad a thing like this is? You might go on like this quite awhile. On the other hand you might not. You've given yourself a hell of a kicking around for a long while. Now it's time to stop. Just take my word for it, will you?"

He wagged his finger.

"You know I'm right. Now look, I'm going to give you some advice you've given a lot of other people. From now on no more work till I say you can. From here on out, the times you ran, you're going to walk. The times you walked, you're going to stand still. The times you stood still, you're going to sit down. And the times you sat down, you're going to lie down. Meantime"—he wrote a few scrawls on a prescription pad—"you know how and when to take this—just whenever you get the pain. I want to see you twice a week for a while."

There was more of this before he left Bauer's office. On the street, cars and pedestrians streamed busily through the copper hotness of the afternoon. He threaded his way among them slowly, back toward the hospital.

The session with Bauer had left him with a sensation he had not felt before—a sinking sensation with just a tinge of panic in it.

"Reaction to hearing it straight, that's all," he thought.

"One of the things you get used to. I've made a lot of people feel like this at one time or another. It'll wear off though. I really knew it all along so it's no surprise. What could I expect? I'm almost fifty-seven . . . will be next month. Not so old maybe, not so young either. This business has been going on with me a lot longer than I thought probably. So, it's here now and I don't like it. The thing is that I'm not being any more philosophical about it than anyone else . . ."

He was abreast of the hospital now and he stopped and looked around absently for the car. It was where he had left it, across from the entrance. He got in and a minute later was moving downtown with the tide of traffic.

At the office he put on his white coat and looked at the appointment list Reba Cole, his nurse, gave him. As usual he went through them in turn. The only difference was that, as he listened and examined his way through the line of them, his mind wasn't quite on it.

"I've got to stop this," he thought. "The trouble is I'm not used to the idea yet and I don't know just what I'm going to do."

There was an end to it finally, when the door closed on the last of them. He sat at the desk for a while and then buzzed for Reba.

"Reba, what's on at the Charity tomorrow?"

"Just the two operations beginning at eight."

"I may have to cancel them, Reba, I've got some business to attend to tomorrow morning," he said.

"Do you want me to do it now?"

"No. I'm not sure yet. If I have to I'll call the hospital myself. Right now I'll go on home."

He hoped no one would be there. The way he was feeling it would be a good thing to sit and think by himself for a while. It wasn't to be that way though. Estelle's voice came down to him stridently, almost before he was in the door.

"Is that you, Tom? Here, I'm in here."

He went resignedly into the living room. She was sitting, as he knew he would find her, with her feet up on the sofa.

"You're home early." Her pale eyes swept up at him.

"I thought I would take the afternoon off—it's pretty hot and there's not much doing."

He sat down in the big chair opposite her. She smiled at him noncommittally. "It was even hotter yesterday."

He understood what she meant by this. It meant that he hadn't come home early yesterday when she had asked him to. She was having some people in and wanted him around. He had said he couldn't because he had work to do. The idea was that she knew he could have if he had wanted to. He decided to let it go and he hoped she would.

"It's hot enough now and from the reports it's going to be for a while."

"Anyhow this is a nice surprise," she said. "Besides I want to talk to you."

"All right, Estelle, what's on your mind?"

"Well, there are several things that I simply have to discuss with you. You are not doing anything now, are you, so that you can give me a few minutes?"

"I'm right here," he said.

"That's just fine. Do you suppose you can stay long enough to listen without thinking of something you forgot, or running to the telephone, or getting too bored or something?"

"I'm listening," he said.

"Well, the most important thing is about Allen—he's coming home tomorrow."

"What? What's he coming home for? He just started up there in summer school."

"Well, he's coming home. I just talked to him on the phone after lunch, and he'll be here tomorrow. He's not going to continue and I can't say that I blame him."

He fought down the instantaneous surge of frustration and disappointment. The old story. "What's the trouble this time? What in God's name has he done now?"

"Now just a minute, Tom. Just a minute. You're always so ready to blame Allen. Let's try to have you be a little fair this time. You see—"

"Just tell me what's happened," he said.

"Allen hasn't done anything it just so happens. But you know very well you can't treat a high-spirited boy like Allen as if he were a clod. I told you Milhaven wasn't the place to send him in the first place. But no, you wouldn't lis—"

He tried very hard to keep his voice level:

"Milhaven is the only tutorial school where he'll have a chance of getting back into prep school. Now just tell me what happened."

"All right. Allen and two other boys had some kind of a minor accident with a faculty member's car. Nobody was hurt and the cars only very slightly damaged. Everything would have been all right—but the boys made the mistake of trying to argue with the police. The car they were in belonged to one of the boys Allen was with. There wasn't much damage to it either and it is fully insured. There would have been no trouble if they hadn't tried to argue with the police. Where are you going?"

It took only fifteen minutes. The headmaster of Milhaven was sympathetic, but very firm about it. All three boys were expelled—drinking was not tolerated at Milhaven. When he came back to the living room Estelle was sitting just as she had been when he left her.

"You just can't take my word for anything, can you?" she said as he sat down.

This was true. It certainly was true as far as the subject of Allen was concerned, but he did not say so.

"I wanted to find out if there were any possibility of his finishing his summer work in spite of this—there isn't. They won't take him back."

"There are other schools," Estelle said.

He looked at her. It was very hard to keep his voice even. "Are there? Where would you suggest with Allen's record? He's been thrown out of Lawrenceville, Mercersburg, Andover, and now Milhaven. He's classified with all of them as a problem case and none of them want him."

"Who's fault is that, Dr. Wilder? You're such an eminent physician. You understand things like this. You tell me. Or suppose I tell you? Allen's the way he is because he's a high-spirited boy who's had the great Dr. Wilder for a father. That is to say no father at all. The great Dr. Wilder has always been too busy being a white-winged angel of mercy for everybody else to pay any attention to his only son—or his wife. No time for the petty problems of his own house—he's much too busy doing his great work. Then the good doctor is so surprised and so upset when a seventeen-year-old behaves like a seventeen-year-old. Really, Doctor!"

There was considerably more of this. The acrid edge of her voice fell into the full vein of bitterness he knew so well. He listened to it, wincing inwardly. He stood it as long as he could, probably longer than usual. He found himself thinking of her and how she spoke rather than what she said to him.

"Can it be possible," he thought, "that this sleek, aging virago was the melting creature he had married twenty-odd years ago? Could this handsome, self-willed, high-styled matron be the one?" He looked at the thin, small-set mouth almost as if it were that of a stranger. Had he made her this way? If he had, how had he done it? Security was what most women wanted. She had it now because he had gotten it for her. The house and the clothes she liked, and enough money. They had gotten security all right and lost about everything else. There wasn't much left between them now except tolerance of a kind. Then there was Allen.

The phone rang. . . . Mary's fat, brisk figure, sacklike in her maid's uniform, appeared in the doorway.

"Phone for the doctor."

Glad of the interruption, he followed her out. Edelstein's impatient nasal voice came over the wire:

"Hello, Doctor? Edelstein. Sorry to bother you at home. Tried at the office. I've just finished a session with the Bureau of Internal Revenue on your last year's tax. Thought you ought to know about it right away in case you want to go to litigation on it."

"What's the trouble?"

"They want to stick us for some more money."

"How much? Didn't we just pay them?"

"That's right. They want quite a lot more."

"How much?"

"No exact figure set yet, but they're thinking in terms of around ten thousand additional."

"How can that be?"

"They won't concede our deductions. I'll have to show you the figures."

"What do you suggest then?"

"We've got a damned good case. We may have to pay them some more, but nothing like the ten thousand they want. We ought to contest it." Edelstein was the best accountant in the city. There wasn't much for him to do but take his advice.

"All right, if that's what you think."

"That's what we ought to do. We'll have to go over the business together a little. Any free time tomorrow when I can see you?"

"Late in the afternoon maybe. I'm not just sure of my schedule."

"I'll call you tomorrow noon and we'll set it up."

"All right. Tomorrow noon."

He hung up and went back to the living room. Estelle was off the sofa, standing by the window by the bird cage, watching the birds.

"I think I'll go up and lie down awhile."

She looked at him questioningly. "What's the matter?"

"Nothing," he said, "I just feel like stretching out is all."

"You'll be here for dinner?"

"Yes, I'll be here."

"Anything you particularly want?"

"No—anything. Anything at all."

"We'll have cold cuts and salad then." She turned back to the birds again.

"Sounds fine."

At the top of the stairs he was no more winded than usual. He went down the hall to his room at the end of it, went in, and closed the door. It was the only room in the house that did not somehow remind him vaguely of an elegant hotel. The rest of the house always had. The expensive decorator Estelle had hired had made it look that way. His room was different because he had absolutely refused to let them have anything to do with it. The books took up all the wall space from ceiling to floor. There was his desk and chair at the window and his hard narrow bed at the other end with the phone on the night table beside it. That was all except for two comfortable nondescript chairs. He got out of his coat and hung it over the back of one of them. Then he took off his shoes and stretched out on the bed.

He would like to have slept a little before he did any thinking, but as on other countless times he had lain there he did not. He found he was not thinking very well either. Decisions of this kind could be made in time if you had the time. He hadn't come to any conclusion yet, but then he had only seen Bauer less than three hours ago. He had the facts though. Bauer had given him the facts. The thing to do was evaluate them as they related to everything else. That was the problem and right now he apparently wasn't doing much with it. Maybe if he cleared his head a little. . . . He snapped on the reading light and turned to the night table. Without changing his position he fished blindly in one of its shelves, pulled out a book, and opened it, somewhere past the middle, at no particular place.

He saw that it was one of his battered Shakespeares and he was somewhere in Henry the V, Act II, Scene III. He began to read.

"By my troth. I care not. A man can die but once. We all owe God a death. And let it go which way it will, he that dies this year is quit for the next."

He read it casually enough the first time and went on a few lines. Then he came back to it. He read it again.

"By my troth . . ."

The words caught him. He read it aloud. After the fifth time he found he had it memorized. He put the book down, closed his eyes, and lay back, thinking about it. He found he was thinking very clearly.

Vaguely he heard the phone ring downstairs and Mary answer. Almost immediately the one beside him buzzed.

"It's Miss Cole from the office."

"Put her on, Mary," he said.

The switch clicked over.

"It's Reba, Doctor."

"Yes, Reba?"

"I thought I ought to remind you about tomorrow."

"What about tomorrow?"

"You said you might not be operating. Did you call the hospital to cancel the cases?"

"No, I haven't, Reba."

"Then you will be operating?"

"That's right. Starting eight o'clock as usual."

"I just wanted to make sure. I'm sorry if I bothered you."

"No bother, Reba. Thank you. I'm glad you called."

"All right then, good-by."

"Good-by Reba, see you tomorrow."

He put the phone back on its table. And almost instantly he was sound asleep.

The confidential session between the Old Man and Otto Bauer took place in the Old Man's office a month after Bauer had given Wilder the verdict about his heart. Bauer sat slumped before the Old Man speaking slowly and deliberately. Across from him the Old Man leaned his elbows on the littered desk, his chin in his hands.

"Now, for Christ's sake, Amos," Bauer went on, "don't ever tell Tom Wilder that I came around to you about this. You know Tom. He'd never forgive me or trust me again."

"Go on, Otto," the Old Man said. "You don't have to tell me about keeping confidences."

"Well, as I said, he's got all the signs and symptoms of a damned bad coronary insufficiency. Had them when I first saw him and has them now. Couldn't help but have them. But he hasn't done what I told him. Hasn't even been back to see me. He's working even harder if anything and it looks like he's going to keep right on that way. He hasn't talked to you, of course?"

"No," the Old Man said.

"And he's not going to either, I guess."

"No," the Old Man said, "that wouldn't be Tom Wilder."

"Well," Bauer said, "he'll probably go on this way till the first big one hits him. And that will be the last one, too, probably from all indications. I just thought maybe if you knew about it you could ease him off with you a little. He'd live longer."

The Old Man shifted his head on his cupped hands, took his sleepy eyes off Bauer, and looked into space.

"Goddamn it," he said musingly, "aside from my personal distress to hear this, it is going to put me and the Service in a very tight spot. We're shorthanded as it is—always have been. And with Tom Wilder out of it, or at least slowed, it's going to make things very close. More than that Tom's the one I had in mind to take over when I'm done."

"Christ, Amos," Bauer said, "you'll never be done. Why, you old bastard, you're indestructible. You'll be bellying up to the operating table when you're eighty and that's a hell of a long time away."

The Old Man smiled thinly. "Sometimes now it doesn't seem so. I'm sixty and I'm beginning to feel it."

"Sheer manure," Bauer said loyally. "Physically you're maybe forty-five. I'm a few years younger than you are and I wish I had your guts and your blood pressure. Every time I've examined you I've been amazed. No credit to you of course, just damned good protoplasm. Now about Tom Wilder. You will ease it up for him? I'm not asking that he quit entirely. Besides I hear you've got some good boys coming up like what's his name, Maines?"

"Maines is good—too young yet. Needs a lot more experience before he could run Wilder's division of the Service. He's got his surgical board to pass."

"That's the kid who beat the hell out of Santry isn't it?" Bauer said, chuckling.

"That's the one. He's still on probation for it. He's really the best young one I've got or I would have almost had to fire him for that. Had to make a special recommendation to the board to keep him because Santry made a direct complaint—"

"Sure. Santry would do that. I heard that he did."

"He did," the Old Man said.

"Can't Santry and Wortle between them cover Wilder's end of things for a while so that he gets a rest?"

"They're going to have to, I suppose, till I can figure out some kind of replacement for him. The trouble is, covering the Service is going to get more and more difficult. There won't be qualified personnel left in another year, they'll all be in the Army."

Bauer looked at the Old Man curiously. "Do you really think we're going to get into that European schweinerei, Amos?"

The Old Man grunted. "Get into it? We're up to our asses in it right now. Get out of that Goddamned ivory tower of yours, Otto, and read a newspaper once in a while or listen to the radio. One of these days something will happen to push us into a formal declaration—"

"Amos, by God, I believe you're an alarmist."

"Hah," the Old Man snorted, "and you're an academic ostrich. Another year or so and we'll be fighting in Europe and Christ knows where . . ."

The weeks went on for Roy in a long descent of rapid, work-ridden days. Occasionally something happened to jar the monotony of them and one of these was Dutch Ransahoff's abruptly resigning his residency in internal medicine and leaving the Charity for good.

Ransahoff announced his decision after a convivial session at the Asterion over an endless parade of bottles of Szabo's Bohemian Beer. He showed Roy the letter he had gotten from Blinn.

"And by God," Ransahoff went on, "it didn't take me very long to decide either. I called old Blinn and told him I'd be with him just as soon as I could wind things up here."

"But, Jesus," Roy said, "you've only got the same time I've got to go here and then you'll be eligible for your board in internal medicine. That's just another year, Dutch, till you're done. I think you ought to finish and then go out there with Blinn as a certified specialist."

"Hell, Roy," Dutch said, "I'm fed to the teeth with the hospital and what I'm doing in it, which is marking time. I've been sick of it for a long time. Sick of the Goddamn place, the work, the hours, and particularly of being poor. Jesus Christ, am I sick of that. I'm sicker of being poor than anything else. Besides this thing with Blinn is just too good to say no to and

Blinn says it won't wait. You know Blinn as well as I do, and you know he doesn't ever kid anybody. Ever since his old man died he's been down there with all of the practice killing himself with work. But Jesus, is he making money at it. The town and the practice are expanding to beat hell and he's simply got to have someone. Look what he's offering me—full partnership immediately for more dough guaranteed the first year than I ever heard of. Offices fully equipped, which we use together. And I don't have one cent of investment to make. For me it's all gravy. So, maybe I won't be a boarded specialist in internal medicine. But I'll be the best Goddamned country doc that ever came down the pike. And I'll be making that old dough, that beautiful long green dough—"

"You'd do that anyway, Dutch," Roy said, "with Blinn or anywhere else."

"I don't know," Ransahoff said. "But by God, old Blinn is giving me a bird-in-the-hand deal down there with him. And I'm taking it."

Ransahoff's farewell to the Charity was properly bacchanalian. The resident staff gave Dutch his valedictory at the Asterion. By subscription and a little concession from Chris, the Asterion was rented for the afternoon and night and closed to the general public. There was a gentleman's agreement between Chris and the sponsors that any breakage was to be covered exclusive of Chris's over-all price. What followed was a tombola. A tombola is allegedly a Sicilian term for which there is no exact translation, but the general connotation is one of a universal whooping, hell-bellering celebration to which everyone is invited and no holds barred. Enough personnel was left at the Charity to man the wards, operating and emergency room, and the rest turned out to the Asterion. Rybecki came over with a deputation from the Police Department. Intermittently the members of every service in the hospital turned out for it. The Asterion boiled with alcohol and good fellowship from five in the afternoon till two in the morning. Even the Old Man came in. Chris served an early and late round of buffet. There were periodic speeches and resounding applause. The men's room was intermittently busy with regurgitants. But the end came when Roy and a Charity delegation took Ransahoff, bag, baggage, loaded, and maudlin to his early morning train for Careysville.

Dutch said good-by to Roy in an impatient hissing of locomotive steam. "Jesus, Roy, you guys, all of you—I can't tell you—hell, I'm drunk. But everybody—everybody. The Old Man even came, didn't he? I love everybody. Ol' Roy, ol' Roy. I wish I wasn't going. I wish this wasn't it. Even the Goddamn Charity—I'm going to miss the old hole. Hell, look at this stuff you guys gave me. Look at it. It's wonderful. Just wonderful. I'll write you, Roy. Say Roy, man to man, friend to friend, Damon to Pythias, if I tell you something keep it quiet will you?"

"Sure, Dutch."

"Well, if it works out down there with Blinn, I'm going to get married—"

"Well, well," Roy said.

"Yeah, and just as soon as I can—to Ruth."

"Ruth?"

"Ruth Kinerem—you know."

"I thought things there were all off after she almost drank you to death at the Tokay."

Ransahoff shook his head.

"That just started it. Hell, if I had the money I'd have a ring on her right now. So do an old friend a favor will you, Roy, and keep the wolves away from her, till I can make it legal? And incidentally don't you, you Goddamn Casanova—"

"Not me," Roy said, chuckling. "Don't worry about me. I'm already married."

"What?"

"Yeah," Roy said, "to the Old Man's Surgical Service. Congratulations, Dutch, and good luck."

He handed Ransahoff to the waiting porter and watched him stumble aboard the train.

11

In the course of Capshaw's increasingly frequent meetings with Klaus Schneider, he and Schneider had acquired a good deal of respect for each other. And through their exchange of information their gradual rapport became casual and complete. These sessions were invariably at the Asterion at a time convenient to both. This was usually sometime between two and four in the morning, when the place was deserted except for a late drunk or a hamburger-eating intern from the Charity night shift. They invariably sat in the last booth, Schneider facing toward the entrance. And invariably Schneider bought and paid for the whiskey which he took with Capshaw drink for drink.

The hands on the big bald clock over the Asterion's bar had now come around to another 45-degree angle. It was three o'clock in the morning. It was Chris's night off and Gus, his relief man, was in his place at the cash register. Capshaw and Schneider had two drinks and some desultory conversation before Schneider came to the main business of their session.

"I want to talk to you about this Dr. Santry. I've just gotten a special directive on him."

"Oh yes," Capshaw said, "the good doctor. Well he's a special kind of nut. What about him?"

"Apparently he is," Schneider said. "It seems that the good doctor has got a good deal bigger piece of the German propaganda operation than the local *Bund* movement here. It looks like he's got some very interesting connections with some of the Fascist-oriented boys in Washington. We've got a pretty good idea who but no real proof. We'd like to get some. One of his contacts is in a sensitive position in the State Department. We know there's been some correspondence between them and it would be very helpful to have what there is as evidence when the time comes to use it. In fact"—Schneider sipped his bourbon thoughtfully—"it's very essential to get all we can of it—particularly from the doctor's side. So much so that I have a direct order to get it and not to spare the horses doing it either. *Carte blanche* is the word."

"Sounds easy," Capshaw said, "you know where he lives. Now all you need is a search warrant. When's the raid—so I can cover it?"

"No good," Schneider said. "The hooker here is that there must be no possibility of fingering the Bureau for any connection with it. This has got to be a strictly nonofficial caper. Otherwise our mitt is liable to be tipped before we blow the whistle. And that would be bad, very bad. It might job it for the final roundup of master-race enthusiasts when the time comes. See what I mean?"

"Certainly," Capshaw said, "all the *Bund* boys get the picture and start running out or holding up once they know the Bureau's got the fist on them."

"Exactly," Klaus Schneider said. "I'm glad to see you've got an aptitude for intelligence strategy."

"Oh, I have, I have, I have," Capshaw said. "Great gift for intrigue of any kind. Just don't get the opportunity to practice much in the newspaper business. But I'm a regular male Mata Hari—"

Schneider grunted.

"Well, that's the situation, Capshaw. And I'm on the dirty end of the stick. Now, I think you understand what has to be done. You have any suggestions?"

Capshaw finished his drink and looked back at Schneider's impassive, nondescript face. "Let's just see if I've got it all straight before I make any. One—you want anything Santry's got in the way of correspondence that will tie up with any Nazi smell in the State Department. Two—no matter how you get it, the Bureau must have no traceable connection with it. Three—you don't care how it's done as long as you get the stuff and the Bureau stays clean. That right?"

"Right," Klaus Schneider said.

"O.K.," Capshaw said, "that means somebody is going to have to make the try for whatever Santry's got—somebody who can't be traced to any connection with the Bureau, no matter what happens—say for instance getting caught. So?"

"So," Schneider said, "you have a good basic grasp of he problem."

"That means probably a breaking and entry job on Santry's residence and a rip and tear look through whatever personal files and papers Santry's got—by someone who can't be connected with the Bureau—"

"That's the logic," Schneider said.

"You suggesting that maybe I might be the boy for it?" Capshaw arched an eyebrow at him.

"Hell no," Schneider said, "you're a newspaperman. You're doing it would be almost as bad as if I did it, if things went wrong. What kind of Goddamned foolishness are you talking about anyway?"

Capshaw sat for a few minutes turning his glass in his fingers.

"O.K. Klaus, I think maybe we can get a right boy for it. You know Rybecki, chief of Homicide here in the Police Department?"

"Heard the name," Schneider said. "Apparently a smart, square cop. Ripstein said so."

"All of that," Capshaw said, "a real solid citizen too. I can vouch for him. Wait a minute . . ."

Capshaw went to the Asterion's phone booth, dialed central police, and asked for Homicide. Rybecki was still there but it was some time before his voice came on.

"Hello, Javert," Capshaw said, "Valjean, here, Jean Valjean. Just wanted you to know that I returned the bishop's candlesticks."

"Listen, Capshaw," Rybecki's voice came back at him savagely, "you son-of-a-bitch, you. I'm not in the mood for any drunken talk. I got a bad cold, real bad, and I'm going home to bed. I don't want no drink and I'm not going to listen to any Goddamn whiskey conversation."

Capshaw's voice, suddenly hard, curdled in Rybecki's ear. "Well, you better listen to this, Stanislaus. And you better do what I tell you, that's get over here to Chris's right away. And I'm not kidding. I've got a big-time federal dick with me and he wants to talk to you. And right now, Inspector, right now. It's urgent."

The phone went dead and Rybecki, cursing, hung up on his end and picked up his hat.

Inspector Rybecki's office at the Homicide Bureau was a stark box of a room with an arrangement of grim-looking metal furniture. There was a desk, mostly used by his secretary, a row of steel filing cabinets, and an oversized table, usually littered with papers and anything else the inspector happened to throw on it. At the moment Rybecki and a small impassive-faced man in a disheveled suit were sitting at it. They had been talking for some time. The man was Klaus Schneider.

Rybecki sucked his golden incisors thoughtfully. "This son-of-a-bitch they're going to bring in is a cheap hood by the name of Comalli, Iggy Comalli. He's the one by the way who fingered the Kite for us when I got shot up. Comalli's yellow as they come and when there is any kind of heat on him he's likely to rat. He's not stoop shouldered from carrying his brains around either. But there's one thing about him—the bastard is a real artist when it comes to breaking and entering and picking up whatever there is around. In my opinion he's the best second-story man and there aren't very many of them left any more. Considering everything you told me about this job I'd say Comalli was the best bet—if he'll go for it. I've got a hell of a lot on him and I know him, so maybe I'd better do the talking. Now you look him over and see what you think. And if you don't think he's right for it there's a couple of other possibilities. O.K.?"

"All right, Inspector." Schneider nodded.

Rybecki pressed a button on his desk. A uniformed sergeant opened the door, allowed a man to pass in, and then closed it. The sergeant did not come in. Comalli stood by the chair before the desk. Schneider's eyes went methodically over the deadpan face, the sullen slouch, and the sharp clothes.

"Hello, Comalli." The inspector's gold teeth flashed at Comalli genially. "How are you? Sit down."

Comalli gave the inspector and Schneider a look just short of a glower and slowly sat.

"You're looking pretty good, Iggy," the inspector said. "By the way this is a friend of mine, a real big-time type of cop. Just might be he could do you a lot of good."

Comalli shifted in his chair and stared back at them stonily. "Yeah?"

"Yeah," the inspector went on. "People like my friend here got ways, means, and angles that ordinary law like me don't have. They want to, they can square a lot of things for a lot of guys—who play ball right that is."

"Like what?" Comalli said sourly.

"Like getting the bad heat off of you—getting your nose clean with the books. You're a three-time loser Iggy boy and a two-shot parole breaker. And if you hadn't tipped us on the Kite you'd be on your ass right now in the big kitty doing a full stretch under the Baume's law for habituals."

Comalli's face showed the barest flicker of animation. "O.K. so you fixed it, but that was the deal and I done my end of it, didn't I?"

"Yes, you did, Comalli." The inspector nodded indulgently. "You certainly did. We got the Kite on your tip. Of course, I got the living Jesus shot out of me doing it."

Comalli sat up in his chair. "Well, Goddamn it, Inspector, that isn't my fault. You knew he'd be heeled when you went in to take him. He was never anything else."

"Why hell yes," Rybecki said soothingly. "Nobody's blaming you, least of all me because I caught one in the belly. Did I let you down? Hell no. On my recommendation your last parole violation was overlooked. And did I pass the word along to any of the Kite's friends that it was you who stooled on him? Hell no! You're still walking around on the outside, aren't you? Breathing in and out with no holes in you?"

"O.K. O.K.," Comalli said.

"O.K.," the inspector said, and then raised a thick forefinger and leveled it at Comalli. "But Iggy boy, you still got them two convictions and them two parole violations against you on the books. That's not changed, and one more Goddamned flap can still fix you. Right?"

The inspector made a rhetorical pause and a reflective sucking sound through his resplendent dentures. "Right. Of course, it's right Iggy. Nobody knows that better than you me. Now look, and I'm not going to give you any marmy manure when I say as sons-of-bitches go Comalli you ain't really so bad, at least I've never thought so, at least you're not a hophead yourself and you never pushed any dope. So far as I know, you've never killed or raped anybody or set fire to anything so you're not so bad with me personally. But you're part of the book, and so far as the law is concerned you stink like last week's mackerel, Comalli, and one more rap that sticks on you can fix you good. Now you know that as well as I do. Now"—the inspector's voice, Schneider noted, admiringly took on an almost paternal quality—"let's level with each other. How'd you like to have it that all of that stuff is whipped right off the book like it never happened? So that if you ever did get into trouble again and the D.A. made it stick, you wouldn't be sent up under the Sullivan Act till you came out in a box in one of Lopardi's hearses. How'd you like that Comalli? A real Mexican standoff with the law—nose clean, nothing on the books, and you start all over from scratch. How about that?"

Comalli sat slouched before them staring alternately at the floor and at Rybecki.

"Well, how about it?"

"Go on," Comalli said slowly, "what's the kicker? Lots of lip. It's gotta be something tough. What do you want out of me?"

Rybecki shot a glance at Schneider and caught his barely perceptible nod.

"You know you're pretty smart at that, Comalli," the inspector said, "pretty smart. O.K. Let's get down to it. This is kind of a queer caper. This is a special bust in and heist job. Very confidential. On a private residence. It'll have my blessing. It will be solo for you. All by yourself—just you. You'll get some help, but not a lot. You case it alone and you do it alone and you bring whatever you find back. The more you bring back that's of any use, the bigger the payoff. But just for trying Comalli you'd get a lot of points—like maybe clearing the book on you and I mean clearing just like you were a first-time offender."

Comalli looked at Rybecki and then took a longer one at Schneider. "That right, mister?"

"That's right, Comalli," Schneider said. "The inspector's been telling you right. Just one thing though—you're not going to get any help on this really. And you get into any real trouble with this caper you may not get any at all for a while."

Comalli looked at him. "What's this here kind of caper for anyway? Who's it for?"

"Never mind that, Comalli," the inspector said hurriedly. "That's an answer you don't need. The point is you'll go for it the way we said."

Comalli sat staring at his shoes for some seconds. The hostility, Schneider noted, was pretty well out of him.

"O.K.," Comalli said. "I'll go for it."

"Good," Rybecki said, "good. You've got a chance to be quite a guy here, Comalli, if you bring it off right."

The inspector looked at Schneider. "O.K.?"

"O.K.," Schneider said.

"Fine," Rybecki said. "Now, here's the pitch. The house is at 286 St. Vrain Street. It belongs to a Dr. Santry. He's got a private office on the second floor back." The inspector pushed a paper toward him. "Here's the floor plan and it's probably pretty accurate. We got it from someone who knows it pretty well. That's one of the maids. There's a desk and some files. There may be a safe. But when you get in there you clean it out—understand? We want to look at everything you can get your mitts on—everything including what's in the safe if there is one—understand?"

Rybecki turned toward Schneider. Schneider shook his head. "That's right. Bring anything and everything that's got any writing on it, particularly letters."

"And I get nailed doing it?"

"You better not do that," the inspector said. "A pushover caper like this shouldn't give a guy like you any trouble."

Whatever Comalli was going to say was stopped by the look which Schneider fixed on him. It was a high hard look, straight at him, and there was a good deal of bite in it. Schneider's voice came at him the same way.

"Get it straight, Comalli—you only do real well if you deliver on this case. Screw it up and you're right where you started. And God help you if you flap your jaw about it either way. If you do, you'll be taken care of—I promise you that. Now you don't like it that way you say, so now take it or leave it. But this is where you say so—one way or another."

Comalli's eyes stood under Schneider's only briefly. Then he shifted them to his shoes and began to rub one hand over the other. "O.K., like I said I'll go for it."

"Fine," Schneider said and sat back.

"Good, Comalli," Rybecki said briskly. "You're acting like a real bright guy. Now let's get down to some more details."

Rybecki pulled another sheet of paper from the disorder on his desk. "Here's a little more on the layout that it might be a help to know."

Rybecki had not overestimated Ignatio Comalli's talent for breaking and entering. For Comalli's penetration of Santry's house several nights later was a virtuoso example of cat thiefs' technique. Shortly after midnight Comalli left his watching position in the alley behind the place. And fifteen minutes later he was not only in the big dark house, but he had found the right room. This was Santry's study, the one marked X on the crudely drawn floor plan. He had arrived there quickly and soundlessly, using only three of his basic tools—a glass cutter, a jimmy, and a fountain-pen flashlight. The operation was entirely flawless except for one ominous error. And it was an understandable error. Comalli had assumed because there had been no signs of light or activity in the house for several hours that there was no one in it. He was wrong. Santry was there in his bedroom two doors away from the darkened silent room in which Comalli now stood. An hour before Comalli had arrived for his vigil in the back alley, Santry had returned home from a late case at the Charity. The two-hour tension of it had given Santry one of his infrequent but severe headaches. For this he had given himself the usual treatment. He had drunk a pint of milk, taken one quarter of a grain of morphine, and gone immediately to bed. Then, after the pounding had eased out of his brows, he had slept. Sometime before Comalli began to cut the window glass and use the jimmy on the sill, Santry had awakened. He lay in the black out of his bedroom, pain gone, and with full consciousness seeping back into him. As with most paranoics, Santry's hearing was extremely acute. And it caught the faint tinkle of the glass Comalli had cut from the window and pushed inward above the lock. Now, with the drug receding rapidly out of him, Santry raised himself on his elbow and listened. Not long after and not far away there was a succession of cracking noises such as metal makes on seasoned wood. At this point Santry knew intuitively that some one was making a stealthy entry into his house. Slowly he swung his feet over the side of the bed and rose into sitting position. Slowly he opened the drawer of the night table by his bed and took out the sleek well-oiled, well-loaded thing he always kept there. It was a beautiful piece, that white Luger—sighted in with trigger adjusted to target shooting. He had a flash memory of the time he had bought it in Erfurt when he was an exchange student in Germany. He pushed down the safety and levered back the ejector. There was now a bullet in the barrel and six more behind it to go at any touch on the trigger. He sat hefting the gun and smiling, in the darkness, but above all, listening. He felt a peculiar, pleasant tingle beginning low in his pelvis and spreading to his loins, the same feeling that he sometimes could get with a woman, or any whore if he could make her hurt a little. He continued to sit there listening. . . .

Comalli flashed his pen light around the blackness of the room. Yeah, this was it. This was it all right. Desk, files, pictures, lamps. Lamp on the desk. Comalli flashed a quick glance at the window. Venetian blinds turned right so nothing would show outside. He put the desk lamp on the floor and pressed the button at its base. The room was now fully apparent with unobtrusive light. Desk first.

Comalli tried the drawers. All locked. Effortlessly he jimmied them open and began turning them out. Letters, Rybecki had said, and that deadpanned little son-of-a-bitch with him. There were one hell of a lot of them here. O.K., he'd take them all. He began stuffing them into his pockets. He was about this when it happened.

The room was suddenly flooded with light. Comalli jumped instantly upright and away from the litter of the desk, his right hand moving toward the blackjack in his left hip pocket.

A man with the worst face he had ever seen and the whitest face he had ever seen stood by the main light switch of the open door. He was holding a strange-looking hand gun on him. Comalli, who never carried a gun himself, much less used one, was mortally afraid of them. And he was much afraid of the gun that this one held in his white and bony hand. But he was more afraid of that face, more particularly the mouth of that face, because of the smile on it. Comalli did not know what it reminded him of, but it was the grin of a death's-head.

The smiling mouth spoke to him. The voice that came out of it was distinct, toneless, and strangely casual. "Find anything interesting?"

"Listen, mister." Comalli began some kind of dry-mouthed answer without knowing in the least what he might have been going to say. He saw now that the gun was a Luger and that the man held it with the certain easy deftness of the expert.

"Put your hands on the top of your head and keep them there."

Comalli did this.

"Now sit down in that chair, there—the one against the wall."

Comalli did this also, noting that, as he moved to do it, the ugly round hole of the muzzle moved with him so that it never left the center of his chest. Comalli began to feel the sweat of stark terror breaking out on him—that face, that gun, that voice, and more than anything, that smile. He could almost feel the flat unblinking eyes moving systematically over him, his face, his black hat, dark suit, and kid-gloved hands. Curiously Comalli found himself wishing the man would hurry up and call the police. He could do it easily enough. There were two phones on the desk. The man made no move to do it. This one, Comalli knew, had to be the one, the doctor, named Santry, who owned the place.

"Name?" the voice came at him again.

"Coletti."

"A lie, naturally," Santry said, "but good enough to give me something to call you. How did you get in here, Coletti?"

"Back window, second story on the right."

Santry nodded.

"Then you had to stand on the ledge while you worked on

it. Quite a trick. That tells me you're a professional. Are you?"

"I ain't doing any more talking," Comalli said.

"I think you will," Santry said.

Horrified, Comalli saw him move the gun slightly upward and to the left and pull the trigger. Comalli heard the report, felt a stinging pain in his right ear and let out a yell. He grabbed the ear with both hands.

"Stay in that chair, Coletti. I've only pinked you."

Comalli could not have gotten out of it anyway. His legs were rubber under him and he felt like he wanted to vomit. He knew though that the slug had only grazed him. He also knew that he was only about six feet away from a deadly accurate marksman.

"Jesus Christ! Jesus Christ! I'm bleeding, I'm bleeding—"

"Not much," Santry said. "Just keep your hands on the top of your head and let it bleed. It will stop soon." Then incongruously, "I used to practice notching pigs' ears with this pistol. I see I'm still very good at it. Now, Coletti, let's get back to our conversation.

"Why this place? Why my house? Or are you still not talking?"

Santry moved the pistol ever so slightly.

Comalli's words spilled out of him frantically. "Please, Jesus Christ, yes. Sure I'll talk. Only, Jesus, don't let that piece you got go at me again."

Comalli now knew instinctively or otherwise that his life very probably depended on what he said to that queer mad bastard on the other end of the gun, who would just as soon shoot him as look at him.

"I'm listening," Santry said, "go on."

"Well, it looked like a good place to take. Nice house, no lights, no one around. So I made the try."

"What did you think you might find?"

"Anything around. Money maybe. Maybe rings, jewelry left around. Any kind of stuff you might get on a quick heist."

Santry's smile widened very slightly and his flat-looking eyes narrowed somewhat, as they frequently did when he was closely examining something momentarily unclear to him. Several seconds of silence, terrifying for Comalli.

"Two things, Coletti. One, why did you come to this room first before any of the others. Why, Coletti?"

"First one I come to."

"No, Coletti. An old professional like you would go through

all the rooms systematically, beginning with the first one he came to. There are three before this one. You didn't even bother with those did you? You came here to my study. Now, why?"

"Door was open," Comalli said desperately.

"No, Coletti. It's never open. I always keep it shut, like all the others. Your lying about it tells me half the answer. Now, let's see if you can do better with number two. If you were looking for money or jewelry, why take anything else, like papers from my desk you were sticking in your pockets? Why, Coletti?"

"Sometimes there's money or something in papers and letters and things and I—" Comalli began frantically.

Santry chuckled mirthlessly. "That gives me the rest of it. Now I understand. Some of it anyway. And you're going to tell me the rest. We are at this point, Coletti. I know that this was no chance job for you. You came here with something specific in mind. That was to clean out and take away my personal papers. And you knew exactly where to come to do that didn't you? Now what I want from you is who's on the other end? Who, Coletti?"

Comalli, who was now almost entirely terrified by the gun and the smile and the rest of it, made one last attempt to rally. It was an unfortunate decision for him. "Listen, mister, I may be a heist guy. And you nailed me cold. But I still got rights. I'll do the rest of my talking to the cops. Go ahead, call them."

"Oh, I wouldn't do that, Coletti. Not until you've answered me. And I'm going to give you a little more help with it."

Santry raised the Luger, sighted, and fired once—adjusted his sighting and instantly fired again.

Comalli felt the slam then the pain of the first one that entered his right hip joint and paralyzed his leg. But that hard hurt was lost in the burning flash of agony of the second shot, which tore through his right arm, high where it joined his body. Through it all he was conscious of Santry's voice when it came as he lay gasping in the chair. He was aware too, that the white face with the smile was looking down at him.

"Now, Coletti," he heard it say, "I'm going to give you a little while to think. I don't really think I've hit anything vital. I certainly didn't intend to. You can still make it. Now think about that Coletti. You still have a chance. But you're going to have to talk for it. So I'm going to let you think about it for a while. My advice to you is not to try to move—you won't be able to anyway, but it will only increase your bleeding if you try—"

Comalli was aware of the face moving away from him as he lay gasping and paralyzed in his chair. Santry moved the phones on their extension cords off the desk, setting them high on one of the filing cabinets. He then came back and stared down at Comalli.

"Don't try to get to the phones, Coletti. You won't be able to reach them. Just try to do some thinking because that's all you can do. I'll be back in a little while to listen to what you are going to tell me. That's who put you up to this. . . ." The casual voice went on. "And if you still don't, Coletti, I am going to shoot you in the belly."

Santry went out, leaving the door of the study open. He was feeling now the urgent thirst that was always an aftermath of his migraine episodes and morphine he took for them. He went down the hall to the back stairs and then to the kitchen. There he drank another two containers of milk. And then, his pressing thirst quenched and head now absolutely clear, he went back to the study again.

Comalli had slipped from his chair and was moving like a stricken fly on the floor beside it. Santry stood looking down at him for some moments, enjoying the warm tingle of lust in his loins as he listened to the animal-like whimpering.

"Recess is over, Coletti. Time for recitation. Now let's hear all about it. Try not to leave anything out. Give it all to me. If you don't you simply won't believe what I'll do to help you."

Through his pain and fear Comalli began babbling everything and anything that might be what that white-faced smiling horror standing above him was after. Rybecki, the other nameless cop, the set-up job with them, even his own previous arrests and convictions. He kept on with frantic desperate eagerness until words from the smiling mouth stopped him.

"Good. Very good, Coletti. I think you've given me the picture. Now . . ."

Santry took three quick steps backward. Then, in one swift movement he raised the gun, sighted it, and fired. The bullet tore into Comalli's right eye and straight back toward the base of his skull. All that Comalli felt was the sudden flash of light that put him beyond the law, the moment, and the pain.

Santry snapped on the safety and waited for what was left of Comalli to stop its agonal twitching.

"Like Spallanzani's decerebrate frog," Santry said to himself thoughtfully.

He looked at his wrist watch, went around the desk, and took the phones from the shelf. On one he dialed the operator for the police. When the bored voice of one of the sergeants at the Central Precinct switchboard came on, Santry spoke briefly and casually:

"This is Dr. Lothar Santry at 286 St. Vrain Street. I wish to report a shooting here . . ."

The official news coverage of Comalli's killing was personally handled by Capshaw. It was very inconspicuous and very brief. It appeared on page fourteen of the *Record* under a minimal lead line which said, PAROLE VIOLATOR SLAIN. The text under it was a model of terseness. It said that one, Ignatio Comalli, was dead on arrival at the Charity Hospital of fatal gunshot wounds. Police investigation of the shooting by Inspector Rybecki of the Homicide Bureau revealed that Comalli, a known criminal and parole violator, had been shot during attempted robbery of a private residence. The slaying had been ruled justifiable homicide. It had been established that Dr. Lothar Santry who surprised the culprit had shot in self-defense. Dr. Santry had been immediately exonerated. That is what the obscure official item in the *Record* said. That officially closed the incident for the public. But not for Messrs. Schneider, Rybecki, and Capshaw. They continued to reflect on it at some length. It was, in fact, the chief topic of conversation at one of their nocturnal seances at the Asterion.

"I guess the rap for this one belongs on me, Klaus," Inspector Rybecki said. "I was the one that sold you on Comalli for the job. But I was sure he was right for it. It looked like an easy enough caper and it was right up his alley."

"You can't call them all. I thought he looked right for it too. Trouble is, it's probably gotten the good doctor very edgy and guessing. He's certainly no fool," Schneider said.

"You bet he isn't," Capshaw said, "and it's just possible that he's got the whole pitch Comalli made figured for what it was."

"How the hell could he do that unless he was a mind reader?" Rybecki said.

"Comalli might have done some singing before the good doctor let him have it."

"Come on, Capshaw. Don't get carried away. How the Jesus could that happen? Santry hears a noise, gets his gun, catches Comalli in the act, and gives it to him before he gets it himself. He didn't give Comalli any time for any oratory."

"That's what he says. Maybe so. Maybe not. I kind of think maybe not. You looked Comalli over at the scene and I saw him in the morgue. What did you think about all those holes in him?"

"I immediately recognised them as bullet holes," Rybecki said. "What did you think about them, Mr. Holmes?"

"Depends on your guess as to the sequence in which they were fired. That and the fact that the *Herr Doktor* among other things is one hell of a good pistol shot. Got a lot of medals. And last year he won hands down in the sectional target matches of the National Association."

"So? What's your point? He didn't miss on that poor son-of-a-bitch Comalli either."

"That's right," Capshaw said, "that's the point. Anybody that good and that close can put a bullet anywhere he wants to. He could have fixed Comalli with one shot. Instead he took four to do it."

"Interesting though," Klaus Schneider said. "You've got quite a head, Capshaw. You mean the doctor may have shot some information out of Comalli before he gave him the big one in the eye. It's possible."

Capshaw nodded.

"And the more I find out about that queer evil son-of-a-bitch, the more I believe that's what happened with Comalli."

Rybecki sniffed deprecatingly. "Well, that ain't the way I got it figured. First place, shooting at a Goddamn hood you catch in your house and don't know whether he's carrying a piece on him or not is one hell of a lot different than standing up to a target that ain't going to shoot back. I think the doc, bastard or not, done exactly what anyone would have done with a lick of sense in the same—got nervous and let go till he was sure he wouldn't get shot back at. That's what I think. Anyhow it don't make any difference anyway. It's justifiable homicide. And Santry's in the clear."

The inspector finished what was left of his bourbon and

turned to Schneider. "And I'll say this, it's a Goddamn good thing we played it this way considering. Suppose it had been one of your guys in there instead of Comalli. Wouldn't that have been a pretty kettle of fish?"

"We're all agreed that it would have been, Inspector," Schneider said dryly. "That was why we tried Comalli. What actually happened is only academic. Let's waste no more time on it. I still have my problem, that is getting what the Bureau wants from Santry—the writing and the rest of it that Comalli didn't get, if the doctor hasn't already done away with it. Now there's two strikes against doing it."

Capshaw looked up suddenly from the glass he had been absently turning in his fingers. "Klaus, are you still willing to try another one of my ideas? I think I've got one."

"Let's have it," Schneider said.

"It's one of my less ethical inspirations," Capshaw said, "but it could work with a lot more luck than we had on this last one. I assume that we are still pursuing a no-holds-barred policy with regard to the eminent Dr. Santry—"

"Assumed," Schneider said, "if there's any chance of taking him for what we want. Let's have it, Cappy."

Capshaw thoughtfully poured three more drinks and set the bottle down. "This one is predicated on the fact that the good doctor has some rather baroque tastes in sexual play. In face he is a sadist. Not a Jack the Ripper type—but still a sadist. He likes to inflict minor injuries before copulation. In fact without this stimulation it is probable that he cannot copulate at all."

Rybecki gave him a surprised frown. "How the hell do you know that, Capshaw?"

"A good newspaperman never reveals his sources, Stanislaus," Capshaw said superiorly. "However, in this instance, I feel justified in violating our sacred code. You are acquainted with the establishment of Madame Anastasia Kondoleon, are you not, Inspector?"

"Come on, now, Goddamn it, Capshaw," the inspector said uneasily.

"I'm sure you are, Inspector," Capshaw said, "from the glowing testimonials about your patronage. The point is, Dr. Lothar Santry occasionally frequents her emporium, even as you and I, Inspector. Apparently he has a particular fancy for one of her bacchantes, name of Rita. Took her on call outside once and wanted her to let him burn her as a kind of antipasto. She ran, but he's been back to the main plant several times since, Stasia tells me, but more or less as a straight customer—"

Capshaw turned to Schneider. "See what I'm getting at, Klaus."

Schneider nodded slowly. "Yes, I think so. Go on."

"Well," Capshaw said, "if I can con Stasia into it, I was thinking in terms of a recorded rendezvous, starring the good doctor and his paramour, say Rita, complete with technicolor and sound tracks. These fancy upstairs cribs of Stasia's with all the drapes and decor have always seemed to me ideal for rigging. You could hide a microphone and camera in any one of them—along with a horse and buggy if you wanted to and nobody would know the difference—"

"Why you Goddamn creep, Capshaw." There was a shocked note in the inspector's voice.

"Shut up, Stanislaus," Capshaw said, again addressing himself to Schneider.

"Of course, it'll be a little like ice fishing. We may wait a long time with rig waiting for the star of the production to come in. But if he does and we get any kind of a performance, I am sure we'd be in a very powerful bargaining way with the good doctor. I know his kind of ego and I know he couldn't stand that kind of guff—"

Rybecki shook his head signifying disbelief. "Capshaw you unprincipled blackmailing son-of-a-bitch."

"Shut up, Stanislaus. Flattery will get you nowhere. How about it, Klaus? Sound like it's worth a try, you think?"

Klaus Schneider pondered this. "Anything that stands any chance of working is worth a try now," he said. "Of course you understand I can't have any direct connection with—"

"Look," Capshaw said, "I understand all that. It's my idea. I'll handle it, including any presentation of material to the good doctor. Besides I've got the able assistance of the inspector here, haven't I, Inspector?"

"I'll be Goddamned if I'll be a party to anything like that," Rybecki said vigorously. "What about my position? Besides, what the hell do you expect me to do?"

"Nothing, Stanislaus. Absolutely nothing. When have you ever done anything else? I'll preserve the sacred image of the law both federal and civil. Just don't raid the place when it's going on—" Capshaw chuckled.

"Remember, 'They also serve who only stand and wait.' Remember that. This may take a little time . . ."

Capshaw's delicate project involving Anastasia Kondoleon's establishment was begun the day after his meeting with Schneider and the inspector. His appointment with Anastasia was made for an off hour and on her premises. Anastasia, always punctual, did not keep him waiting more than five minutes in the small elegant room she used as an office. She sat across from Capshaw, her dark eyes on him expectantly. Capshaw began this sitting as he always did with her, by a flattering touch.

"Stasia," he said, "lovely as ever, I see. How are you, my Circassian queen?"

Anastasia's eyes flickered slightly with amusement. "Very well, Cappy, thank you. What's on your mind that wouldn't wait?"

"All right," Capshaw said, "since you won't let me sit here and drink in your beauty, I'll get right to it."

"Yes, do that, Cappy. It must be very important."

"It is, Stase," Capshaw's voice was now entirely serious, "I want some help and you're the only person who can give it to me."

"Yes?"

"Look, Stase, first I want some information. You remember that weirdo who called for a send-out trick and you sent Rita? And he wanted a special job like burning her with cigarettes before he made it? And Rita ran out?"

"I remember."

"He's a doctor."

"Yes."

"At the Charity."

"Yes, Rita told me."

"Well, look. He's been in here since hasn't he? You told me once he had."

"Yes. But as a straight trick. I won't have my girls hurt or—"

"Listen, Stase, I know that. But he has been in here since he propositioned Rita for that specialty job on a call out, hasn't he?"

"Yes. I told you he had when you asked me before."

"Often? You must have kept an eye on him?"

"I don't know how often Cappy. Several times. He never made any trouble here. What is all this about?"

"I'll get to that, Stase. Thing is he comes here, or has been coming here, hasn't he? Kind of regular? Now, how often?"

"I don't really know, Cappy. I can't say because I never kept count. I know who he is."

"Maybe once a week?"

"Maybe."

"Any particular preference with the girls?"

"Rita, if she's not busy. If she is, then Sue, Helen, or someone else. Now what is all this, Cappy?"

Capshaw rubbed a hand over the beginning stubble on his chin, took a cigarette out of his pocket, and lit it.

"Anastasia, you remember the first and only time the vice squad ever raided this place? And I got the story killed and almost got canned doing it?"

"Yes."

"And you told me, that no matter what, that if I ever needed a big favor to square it off, all I had to do was ask?"

Anastasia Kondoleon's oblique black eyes now narrowed considerably as they fixed on Capshaw. "Don't you think I've squared one off with you by this time, Cappy?"

Capshaw nodded. "Yes, I do, Anastasia. We've been even for a long time. But now I'm asking you to go on the line for me again. Do it and you can have anything I've got anywhere, anytime. That includes blood transfusions, fillings out of my teeth, and my job on the *Record*."

"Go on, Cappy. Let's hear about it."

"All right. I'll tell you. I want that weirdo we were talking about named Santry. I want to get it on him and I want to get it on him good. So good that he'll have to listen to anything I say. And not just listen either, but do what I say. It's very important that I do that Stase."

"It must be," Anastasia said. "Do you want to tell me why, Cappy?"

Capshaw shook his head. "No, I don't want to tell you that. And I won't. That you'll have to take on faith, if you're going to take it. I'll say this about it though, it's not for me or the *Record*. It's for a lot of other people. He's a dangerous, destructive son-of-a-bitch and he's got to be had, no matter how. One guy got killed trying to do it. I don't intend to be. But I intend to get him any way I can. I'm in the spot for it."

Anastasia Kondoleon leaned forward in her chair and put

one of her plump, beautifully manicured hands over one of Capshaw's. "Come on Cappy," she said, "you've given me quite a build-up. Just tell me what it is you want from me will you? I think we've gotten to it finally, haven't we?"

"Anastasia," Capshaw said, taking her plump white hand in his, "I think we have. Now look. This is the pitch. What I'm asking you to do is let me bug just one room of this place with a wide-angle lens camera synchronized with a microphone and recording tape, connected to a little button. So that when it's pressed the sights and sounds are recorded automatically for the next five minutes. And after it's all rigged, by a very able friend of mine, it will only be used once. That will be when that lousy smiling son-of-a-bitch comes in here and takes Rita, or whoever else is handy, to that room."

Anastasia Kondoleon slowly and negatively shook her head. "I won't do that Cappy. I won't do that even for you."

"Listen Stase," Capshaw said, "yes, you will. If you won't do it for me, you'll do it for your uncle, the one you see in cartoons with striped pants, stars on his coat, and gaiter shoes."

Anastasia looked at Capshaw a long time before saying anything. "Is it really that big, Cappy? Is it really a federal case?"

"Anastasia, have I ever put you in a spot by lying to you?"

"No."

"That's right. I haven't. Now, how about it?"

"All right, Cappy. I'll do what I can. The rest is up to you."

"Fine," Capshaw said, and looked at his watch. "Hell, I'm an hour late with my column copy. Now the next time the son-of-a-bitch comes in here, Rita or whoever he takes, see that he gets to the room."

"Meantime," Capshaw added thoughtfully to himself, "I'm going to keep right on twisting the good doctor's tail."

12

The first sign of Wild Will Wortle's illness was discovered by Wortle himself, and for Wortle it was a devastating surprise. It was the sudden loss of his enormous taste and tolerance for liquor. His awareness of it came as he sat in the Asterion with Roy.

He and Roy had just finished a very late case at the Charity. And as usual they had gone immediately to one of the Asterion's back booths for refreshment and meditation. It was an off-duty night for Roy and the drinks and dinner, also as usual, were on Wortle.

"We'll have a few belts over at Chris's," Wortle had said, "and then we'll go over to Sobrano's and eat our way right through the menu. Today's the day they've got chicken cacciatore—"

Chris, a long-time familiar of Wortle's postoperative self-medication routine, had nodded when they came into the Asterion and sat down. Then, without order, he had brought over a bottle of bourbon, water, and glasses. Wortle poured two staggering dollops of whiskey for Roy and himself and raised his glass.

"Let's drink this first one to Jesus Christ, Roy. He's a damned sweet guy even if he is a Jew. And He was right in there pitching with us today or we never would have gotten that poor son-of-a-bitch off the table alive."

"You looked pretty good in there yourself, Will," Roy said. "That was probably the best and fastest piece of dissection I've ever seen of the pulmonary artery."

"Matter of fact," Wortle said, "I was pretty good, I thought. But Christ deserves a lot of credit, particularly for helping us stop that one bad hemorrhage. When it comes to a tight squeak like that I really believe I'd just as soon have Christ around as the Old Man—"

"Don't ever say that to the Old Man." Roy grinned. "It might hurt his feelings."

"Oh, I wouldn't do that," Wortle said. "I know how sensitive the Old Man is about competition. The Old Man's always been a little piqued because Christ can still beat him at walking on water."

"I'm going to get the hell out of here and away from you, you blaspheming bastard, before a thunderbolt knocks us both off. God doesn't like this kind of talk about His only son."

Wortle chuckled. "Come on, drink up," he said.

Wortle put the half tumbler of whiskey to his mouth and downed it, licked his lips, and reached for the water. It was just at this point that he noted it, the strangely unfamiliar and nauseating taste the whiskey had. He grimaced and looked at Roy.

"What the hell's the matter with this booze?" Wortle said. "Doesn't it taste lousy?"

"I don't see anything wrong with it," Roy said.

"Well, there is. Trouble is you don't drink enough to know anything about good and bad whiskey. I do and there's something wrong with this stuff. It tastes funny."

Wortle picked up the bourbon bottle and looked at the label. There was nothing different about it. Old Wisenheimer Bourbon. His favorite brand.

"Hey, Chris." Wortle motioned Chris over from his station between the cash register and the bar.

Chris stood before them in his white apron. "Yes, Dr. Wortle?"

"What are you pulling on us, you Circassian poisoner? What's in this bottle?"

Chris glanced at the bottle and then at Wortle. "It's what you always drink, Dr. Wortle. Old Wisenheimer Bourbon."

"The hell it is, you fornicating myrmidon," Wortle said. "You've been saving old urine or something in that bottle. Here"—Wortle pushed the bottle and an empty water glass toward Chris—"taste it yourself."

Chris barely covered the bottom of the glass and downed it. "That's just what it says there on the label, Dr. Wortle. Good bourbon. The kind you always like, Old Wisenheimer," Chris said imperturbably.

"It is not, Goddamn it, you Levantine assassin. Are you going to stand there and tell me I can't tell about whiskey?"

Chris's dark eyes stared at Wortle for a moment. "Excuse me, Doctor."

Chris went to the bar and came back with three unopened bottles of Old Wisenheimer with revenue stamps intact over their caps. Expertly he opened them all and set them down before Wild Will.

"Same as these, Dr. Wortle."

Wortle did not bother with the conventionality of glass pouring. He put each of the opened bottles successively to his lips and drank briefly. He sat for a moment and contemplated them.

"Well, I'll be Goddamned. Same taste. They're all the same. Same taste. They're all lousy. What did you do, Chris, get a hold of a bad case of booze?"

"No, Dr. Wortle," Chris said, "I buy direct from the Old Wisenheimer Distillery in Lexington, Kentucky. They don't make any bad liquor. It's all the same, the best aged bourbon there is." Chris turned to Roy. "Does it seem all right to you, Dr. Maines?"

"It seems all right to me," Roy said.

Wortle reflected on this. His voice had suddenly become subdued and a little reflective. "All right, Chris, my apologies. Must be me. Losing my sense of taste I guess. They say it happens to all old booze fighters at one time or another. Sorry Chris—"

"It's all right, Dr. Wortle," Chris said, beginning to gather up the bottles.

Wortle pulled out his wallet, thumbed through a sheaf of bills, and pulled one out and laid it on the table.

"Will that cover it, Chris?" he said. "Will that cover my mistake and my Goddamn affront to your classic Athenian dignity?"

Chris's eyes flicked at the bill on the table with General Grant's picture on it and then back at Wortle.

"This is on the house and my pleasure, Dr. Wortle."

Wortle looked at Chris. "Listen, my Achaen friend," Wortle said slowly, "I've been drinking here for a long time. I made a mistake and I'm sorry. There's nothing wrong with your whiskey. The trouble is apparently with me. Now if you want my continued patronage, you will pick up that money. If you don't I'll tear it up like this, see?"

Wortle picked up the bill and tore it across its width. "And I'll keep on tearing it into little pieces so that it can't be redeemed. And I'll never come in here again. Now, will you take the money with my apology?"

Chris looked at Wild Will Wortle, swept the two halves of

the torn fifty into his hand, and said with a kind of dignity that Roy would long remember:

"Dr. Wortle, please, I am taking the money. Your apology I cannot accept. No matter what he does in my place, a man like you never has to apologize to a man like me."

Chris left then, taking the bottles with him.

Wild Will rubbed a hand over his eyes. "Come on, Roy," he said, "let's go to Sobrano's for some chicken cacciatore. Don't bother to open the door for me—I can crawl under it. There must be something wrong with me, Roy. I don't know what it is, but there's something wrong with me, when a drink of good bourbon makes me gag."

A week later Wild Will Wortle was in a private room of the Charity, his skin and eyeballs jaundiced to the color of strong tea. The Old Man's face was thoughtful when he examined Wortle and it got more and more grave as Wortle's X rays and laboratory reports began coming in. The more obvious Wortle's diagnosis become the less the Old Man was inclined to discuss it. Then, one morning before rounds, when he and Roy were sitting in the Old Man's office, the Old Man finally broke his silence about it. He had been staring out the window as he listened to Roy's morning report of the wards when he suddenly swiveled his chair around and looked at Roy.

"What do you think about Wortle?"

Roy stopped what he was saying in mid-sentence and looked back at the Old Man. The hated words came dryly out of his throat.

"Obstructive jaundice from cancer of the head of the pancreas," Roy said. "Typical picture—loss of taste for alcohol and all the rest of it."

The Old Man nodded absently. "Yes. Always the chance with Wortle's alcoholic history that it might be cirrhosis. But that's not very likely, is it?"

"No, sir."

"He's going to have to be opened up for a look. When do you think it ought to be done?"

Roy swallowed hard. "Anytime now, sir, I think. I don't see much point in waiting any longer."

The Old Man nodded slowly. "Neither do I. Right after ward rounds we'll go talk to him about it."

"Yes, sir," Roy said.

The Old Man got out of his chair and Roy followed with a sick and sinking sensation in his belly that he had felt before and would feel many times thereafter.

The color and stink of death had been increasing on Will Wortle ever since he had noted the first sign of his sickness at the Asterion. Lying there in the high narrow bed in his room at the Charity and looking out at the teeming action below him on Velle Street, he had recognized it and felt it growing. Between the sessions in X ray and the jabbing of his arms for blood specimens, he had thought about it, and, so far as he could had come to some kind of acceptance and then to resignation. With this he had arrived at ultimate awareness. He knew that he was going to die. And he knew that he would do his dying at the Charity—possibly in the room where he lay or perhaps in the high hot glare of the operating room, with the Old Man pawing competently and methodically over his guts. Just as he, William MacTavish Wortle, had done on many, so many, figures of dying protoplasm before. Then he had held the decisive knife and now it would probably—not probably—most certainly, be held on him. Held by the Old Man. Well, that was good enough. Certainly if he had to be split and to have what was probably cancer looked at, there wasn't anybody better for it than the Old Man. And it was cancer, too, that they would be going into him for. They would have to look, as he had had to look, and then see what could be done about it. The chances were, with himself now, that nothing much could be done about it. It certainly didn't look so from what he had found out from his chart. And he knew pretty well about that from his sneaking trips to the nursing station down the hall when everyone had gone for coffee except one sleepy attendant.

Well, so be it. He was going to die, here one way or another in the Charity, where he had helped or hindered so many others in this same stead. They weren't fooling him. He was "going for the bundle" now himself—he was going to "buy the farm." Pretty soon they would be coming in to tell him that they would have to open him. Just now with the morphine in him it didn't look like it was going to be as rough as he had thought. He had thought he would have a lot of regrets. And about those regrets about dying, what was there to regret? Not a lot really. He certainly did not regret the good honest sins of his body, his drunkenness, his fornications, and the rest of his high hard living. What he regretted now were his sins of omission—the times when he could have been more honest, more generous, and more brave. What he had not done, his sins of omission, were, he saw now with piercing clarity, what should make a dying man contrite about his life.

"Oh, Lord, we have done those things which we ought not to have done, and we have left undone those things which we ought to have done . . ." That was the significant part: ". . . left undone those things which we ought to have done."

At this point in Will Wortle's lonely soul searching there was a knock on the door and the Old Man and Roy came into the room.

"Well, well," Wortle said, "enter Aesculapius and a lesser god, staffed, robed, and with healing in their wings."

"Morning, Will," the Old Man said. "How do you feel?"

Wortle chuckled mirthlessly. "How do I look?"

"About the same."

"That's how I feel, too, Amos."

"How about the nausea? Had any more vomiting?"

"No. Not as long as I get that beautiful needle every four hours. By the way, how much of that Goddamn morphine am I taking now?"

"Quarter of a grain is all," the Old Man said.

"Great drug, morphine," Wortle said. "Faster than whiskey and a real nice effect. Now, what's the deal with me, Amos? I'm getting sick of lying around here dead ass with no information."

The Old Man stood by the bed looking down at Wortle absently and rubbing his chin. "Well, this business with you still isn't too clear cut. And the only way we're going to be positive about it is to take a look in there and make sure what's going on."

Wortle stared back at the Old Man for a few seconds. "Uh-huh. I figured that much. When?"

"You're scheduled for eight o'clock tomorrow morning, Will."

"Uh-huh. Who'll be assisting?"

"Wilder and Roy."

Wortle winked at Roy. "How about Jesus Christ? Won't he be there? Just to hold retractors, I mean."

The Old Man's thin mouth turned up in something of a smile. "He'll be there. All arranged."

"You better have the Holy Ghost, too. You may need them both for this one."

The Old Man slowly shook his head. "Wortle, you're an unregenerate. Now. Agreed about tomorrow?"

"Certainly," Wortle said. "When did I ever argue with the chief about scheduling a case?"

"All right, Will. Then that's it, I guess."

"Not quite, Amos." Wortle turned to Roy. "Roy, let me have a few words in private with the father confessor here for a minute, will you?"

"Sure, Will," Roy said. "See you later." He nodded to the Old Man and left the room. Outside in the hall he stopped immediately at the drinking fountain and stood there for a while trying to drink away the hard lump sticking in his throat.

They scrubbed in silence. The Old Man at the first sink, Wilder at the next, and Roy at the third. Inside under a blasting cone of concentrated light, Will Wortle lay snoring and insensible, his belly, chest, and thighs vermilion from two coatings of skin antiseptic. Roy looked from the panel window to the clock. Just ten minutes. They were beginning to lay the drapes on the scarlet-tinted belly. Roy let the jets of water hit his hands and forearms all over to get off the last of the soap. He looked over at the Old Man and Wilder.

"Ten minutes," Roy said.

"All right," Wilder said.

The Old Man nodded.

Roy let the jets hit his hands again for an instant, spreading his fingers wide apart under them. They were as clean as they would ever be, or had ever been. In one or two places they were raw, but they were steady as rock. . . . They went into the operating room Indian file, the Old Man first, and stood hands elevated and dripping, waiting to be gowned up. All of Wortle's supine figure had disappeared under the shroudlike folds of draping except a long slot of flaming skin.

Their gowns were on and the back strings laced. Roy felt the back strings being pulled tight.

Wilder and Roy took their places across from the Old Man, first and second instrument nurses below them at the table's foot. The light was right. The knife came into the Old Man's hand and his fingers closed upon it. There was a frozen instant, and then he brought the edge down exactly perpendicular to the flesh in a slow firm sweep. The unscarred skin opened into a ruddy arc. Wilder began his miraculous dexterity with the clamps and Roy kept up an elusive sponging. Side towels to the incision doubled to the margins and clipped on. The clean second knife. Deep fascia, muscles, peritoneum all cut, and the bleeding controlled by ties. They were now in Wortle's belly. And Wortle's trouble became almost immediately apparent. The tumor lay a sly, evil, bulging thing and glistening slightly out of the head of the pancreas. It looked like its name, cancer. Cancer—a crab. This one, a malignant parasitic, white, nestled obscurely gripping the gland and the biggest artery in the body in its visible part, and extending God knew where and clutching God knew what where it could not be seen. The Old Man began exploring it and its lumpy undeterminable extrusions with his hand. He took his hand out of Wortle's open belly.

"Feel," he said, nodding to Wilder and Roy.

Wilder's hand, then Roy's, went into the incision and repeated the exploratory motions of the Old Man's.

"Jesus," Wilder said, "what a Christ-crying shame. Not a chance. Not a prayer in hell."

For an instant the Old Man looked away from the table and stared at nothing. The first instrument nurse stood expectantly with suture for closing.

"We're going to swing on it," the Old Man said.

Roy saw Wilder's eyes widen above his mask. "Amos, for Christ's sake, that's inoperable."

The Old Man shot him a paralyzing look.

"I said we're going to swing on it, Tom."

"Jesus Christ," Wilder said.

"Dissecting forceps," the Old Man said, "and a knife with a number fifteen blade."

"Clean sponge and the suction," Roy said to the second nurse.

"Now, give me those Goddamn long-handled hemostats," the Old Man said, "and keep them coming."

One hour—two severe hemorrhages controlled and the blood loss replaced by transfusion, the duodenum sacrificed but the visible part of the tumor free with it.

One hour and a half—the growth entirely loose from the big vessels, with only an approximate third left clinging along the vertebral attachments of the diaphragm. A bad pressure drop stabilized, and a warning from the anesthetist that Wortle's heart action was intermittently irregular with a rising pulse.

Two hours and six minutes— "Can you get a ligature around from your side, Tom? We're at the end of it."

"Not and hold the clamp right where it is. I can't see."

"All right, I'll try on my side then. Get the suction over Roy, so I can see."

In the oozing treacherous tunnel of tissue with the beak of a long right-angle clamp at the end of it, Roy watched the Old Man's finger, with the ligature tight over the tip, go down, down, down. The end of the clamp, ligature off the finger and around the beak end, then over the rest of the clamp. Tie once . . .

"Loosen the clamp but leave it on, Tom. I've got it."

Down tight.

"Clamp it down again."

Tie twice. Tie three times. Tie four times.

"Loosen the clamp then take it off." Wilder's fingers loosened the clamp and then receded. No bleeding.

Roy let out his pent-up breath.

"O.K. Long scissors," the Old Man's voice cracked out again.

Cut ligature. Cut tissue. No bleeding. The Old Man withdrew his hand and the thing in it. The sly filthy deadly bloom of destruction with an awesome amount of normal flesh surrounding it was out—and so far as it looked then—cleanly out.

The sharp tableau of their looking at it was broken by the harried voice of the anesthetist:

"Pulse just cut out on a fade at 160—no pressure—"

They exploded frantically back into action in Wortle's belly again.

"Still no pulse and no pressure—"

Three hours and eighteen minutes:—"Still no pulse, no pressure—" Heart massage and intracardiac adrenalin. No vital signs. Wild Will Wortle was dead.

The Old Man was the first to break the stunned immobility that descended upon them. He stood with the rest of them for some moments, then turned abruptly from the table and the carnage upon it. Roy automatically followed him to a corner and undid the strings of his gown for him.

The Old Man began slipping off his gloves and pulled his mask down. Roy, still fumbling with the strings of his own gown now, was close enough to hear what the Old Man was saying to himself between his clenched teeth.

"Goddamn it. Goddamn it all anyway." And then just perceptibly, "We tried, though . . . we tried."

Later in the dressing room, all of them silent and shaken, the Old Man was methodically putting on his clothes, when Wilder, now dressed, came up to him.

"Amos," Wilder began, "I just want to say—"

The Old Man turned on him fiercely and instantly cut him off. "I know what you want to say. And I don't want to hear you say it. You want to do something for me—go home and get some rest. Do that, will you, Tom? This is a hard day."

"All right, Amos," Wilder said. "Just wanted you to know—"

"I know, Tom," the Old Man said.

Roy stood with the Old Man watching Wilder's slumped shoulders go out the door. Suddenly and unexpectedly he turned toward Roy.

"Well, Maines, you did pretty well in there. You and Wortle were good friends, weren't you?"

"Yes, sir," Roy said. "We were very good friends."

"Yes," the Old Man said, "now are you in doubt about anything that happened in there? I think you probably are."

Roy still sick and numb from it, blurted it out. "Yes, sir, I am. You knew it was inoperable. Dr. Wilder knew it was inoperable. Even I knew it was inoperable. You could tell that by seeing it and feeling it. I'm only trying to learn and after this I guess I don't know anything. But why did you go ahead and try, and kill him doing it?"

The Old Man put his hand on Roy's shoulder and looked at him. "You're a little young at this business yet to understand it, but remember what I say." He looked past Roy and then back at him. "Let's just say I did it as a matter of professional courtesy, Doctor. He would have done as much for me. . . ."

13

The Old Man sat ruminating at the habitual disorder of papers on his desk. At the moment he was occupied with the pressing problem of administration that Wortle's death and Wilder's illness had left for him to solve. These catastrophes had left his Surgical Service crippled, for the key personnel he had to have to keep up its efficiency and reputation. Now there was only Santry and himself left, with the limited help Wilder would be able to give. What he needed most was someone to fill, somehow, someway, the position left by irreplaceable Wild Will Wortle. There was a war on now and anyone with an ounce of perception knew that the country would soon be in it. Hospitals, medical schools, and communities were going to be depleted of doctors by the call to service. And all of them were going to fight to keep what they could of their best men with them as long as they could. His chances therefore of importing anyone adequate as replacements for Wortle and Wilder from any place else were then, now, and would be, getting thinner. The answer was promotion from the lower ranks of his own Service—his resident group. All of them were too green. There wasn't one of them who was really dry behind the ears surgically speaking. He didn't like doing it, but, like it or not, it was going to have to be done anyway and it might have to be done not once, but several times. He would have to have each one of them qualified by certifying examination in any case before they came on the Service in the hierarchy of attending surgeons. That was mandatory to maintain any kind of standard of his Service. No one without official specialty qualification could bear the title of attending surgeon on the Charity surgical staff. That he had insisted on and at his own insistence it had been incorporated into the Charity's by-laws. Now, since he had to pick one of those green ones, still wet behind the ears for replacement, he'd pick his best one.

The Old Man flipped up the switch of the intercom to his

secretary in the outer office. "Bertha, get hold of Dr. Maines. He'll probably be on Ward C. Tell him to come over here as soon as he can."

Twenty minutes later, conscious of his dirty white shoes and soiled white uniform, Roy was sitting expectantly before the Old Man.

The Old Man surveyed him briefly and then got to it. "Roy, how much time do you have to put in before you can take the surgery board?"

"I'd figured on another year, sir, before applying."

The Old Man nodded. "Yes, ordinarily that would be about right. Have you kept up on your reading?"

"Yes. I try to get in a couple of hours a day one way or another."

"That's good," the Old Man said. "Have you been able to do that consistently?"

"Well, more or less, sir. A lot of times I miss on weekdays, but I can usually catch up one way or another on the weekends off duty."

"Have you had a look at what's been asked on the written examinations in the last couple of years?"

"Yes, sir, I have. The questions on the written for the last five years are in the teaching file."

"Well, you've seen them. Do you think you could pass if you took the examination right now, say, or in the next month, or whenever it's going to be given next?"

Roy looked at the placid face of the Old Man and wondered what he was getting at. "Why yes, sir, I think I could. All of the questions I've seen don't seem to be too hard. Most of them seem to be on what I know. They're pretty fair—pretty practical."

"I'm glad to hear your opinion on that," the Old Man said, dryly. "A lot of them are on subjects I suggested. Now, you say you think you could do well enough to make at least a seventy-five if you had to answer them?"

"Yes, sir," Roy said without hesitation, "I think I could do that. I think I could do that right now."

"Good." The Old Man nodded. "There's nothing like youthful confidence. Well, you're going to get the chance. Make the application at once and give my name as your first endorsement."

"Jesus Christ," Roy thought on leaving the Old Man's office, "the residency a year early was a break. But the board this far ahead of time—what for anyway? That means every damned minute I can get on the books on top of everything else I have to do on the Service. If I had thought for one minute when he asked me if I thought I could pass them that he was going to beat me into doing it, I wouldn't have. But I did though, I bought it by shooting my mouth off. All right, then, Goddamn it, the king says 'Try,' so I'll try—what the hell's the line? 'Theirs not to make reply, Theirs not to reason why, Theirs but to do or die. Half a league, half a league, half a league, half a league onward.' Sometimes I wonder if his mind doesn't wander at times. . . ."

For the next long descent of days, Roy hardly left the hospital. His off time he went to the library and he kept a stack of the recent surgical literature by his bed. His absences from late off-night drinking sessions at the Asterion with the Charity staff, or Capshaw or Rybecki, were so complete that there was inevitable comment. He turned down innumerable invitations from all of them, and read relentlessly on.

"Jesus Christ," Capshaw said to Chris, "he can't stay holed up like that indefinitely. Not with that belly-killing hospital food. He's got to come out sometime. Doesn't he ever come around any more?"

"Oh yes, Mr. Capshaw," Chris said superiorly, regarding his fingernails, "he comes in sometimes real late after it's quiet for a sandwich and coffee, two, three, four o'clock in the morning. Reads while he's eating."

"Oh, he does, does he?" Capshaw said morosely. "Sneaks over here and drinks on the quiet—"

"No," Chris said, "he just reads and eats. Doesn't drink anything at all any more except coffee."

"Must be sick," Capshaw said. "Too much learning fevers the brain. Maybe we'd better look into it." Capshaw left the booth and called the Charity.

Roy, surfeited with another prolonged session of reading, was thankful for the interruption. He joined Capshaw shortly.

"Where the hell have you been, Doc?" Capshaw said as Roy sat down. "You've got me and the Greek pretty concerned. What is all this with you anyway?"

"I've been on the books," Roy said. "I'm taking the Goddamn surgical board. Special edict from the king."

"What's the hurry? I thought you told me once that came next year."

"I thought so. Ask the Old Man. He called me in and said take it now. So I'm taking it. I've got a beautiful chance of getting knocked on my ass doing it too."

"I doubt that, Doc," Capshaw said smiling. "The Old Man knows the boys in his chain gang pretty well. Particularly you. Way I hear it from the other boys you're his golden-haired lad."

"I'll tell the examining board that," Roy said. "It'll be a great help when the going gets tough, which it will be."

"When it gets too tough for the rest of the boys it'll be just about right for you. Remember that, Doc." Capshaw chuckled.

"Thanks. I'll tell them that, too. They like that kind of confidence. Always makes a big impression."

Capshaw regarded him with amusement. "You're really worried about it, huh?"

"That's one of your more outstanding understatements. Worried? Jesus, I practically go into Cheyne-Stokes respiration every time I think about it."

"I'm just an untutored layman, Doc. What's Cheyne-Stokes respiration?"

"Agonal breathing," Roy said. "The kind Lopardi the elite mortician lies awake nights listening for. Inevitably means another customer for him."

"Doc, I'm grieved to see that you've turned into a neurotic about this examination business. A smart young hot-shot surgeon like you."

"Look, Cappy, I'm not neurotic. I'm realistic. I'm really not prepared for it. Not really, and I won't be when I take it either. That's bad enough. But on top of that I've got something else to think about. Heard it the other day, and when I did I turned blue and started shaking. And I haven't stopped yet."

"What's that? Did you find out your examiners are going to be the Four Horsemen of the Apocalypse?"

"That's pretty close." Roy grinned mirthlessly. "Matter of fact, I'd rather take my chances with war, pestilence, famine, and death than with that son-of-a-bitch."

"Than with what son-of-a-bitch, Doc? You've lost me."

"Than with Dr. Lothar Santry. The Smiler. Smiler Santry. After Wortle died he was appointed specialty board examiner as Charity representative to take his place. You remember the one I belted in the mouth—senior surgeon and—"

"I remember real well, Doc." Capshaw's amused look had left his face. He slowly sat forward in the booth, his chin in his hand, and his eyes intent. "I remember the good doctor very well indeed. I now understand your concern."

"Well, I'm Goddamned glad somebody does," Roy said. "I mentioned this fact very coyly to the Old Man, who knew it anyway. Guess what he said, very casually. 'If you get him on your oral just give him the right answers.' Very sound advice. If I remember to do that, it will be a big help."

"Chance you might not get him, though, that right, Doc?"

"Yeah," Roy said, "but I'm not counting on it. Particularly with my kind of luck. The main thing is that I'm taking the whole Goddamned thing, written and oral, right here in town over at St. Marks Hospital. That's the regional exam center this year like the Charity was last time. There aren't many candidates this time either. I'm almost a dead cinch to get him at one point or another."

Capshaw rubbed his chin and squinted thoughtfully at his glass.

"Well, Doc, I think I see the basis for your anxiety. Seems well warranted. However, I'm going to make a little prognostication. You beat the bastard once and you'll beat him again. I'd like to put money on it. Come on, have just one good belt of bourbon with me."

"No, Cappy." Roy shook his head. "If I did that, the way I feel now, I'd sit right here and polish off a bottle with you. I can't do that. So to hell with it. I've got to get back and get at it. See you later."

Roy got out of the booth and started toward the door.

"*Vayo con dios*," Capshaw said as he walked away.

Roy stopped and turned around. "What Cappy?"

"*Vaya con dios*," Capshaw repeated.

"Oh," Roy said. "Well thanks, *vaya* you too, Cappy."

Five minutes later Roy was back in his room at the Charity and had picked up his opened book.

St. Marks Hospital and the Charity had identical functions —the care of the diseased. But, beyond that, any similarity between them was at least physically almost ridiculous. They bore the same architectural resemblance to each other that, say, a cathedral does to a waterfront warehouse.

St. Marks was an awesome, gracefully executed unity of glass and stone at the edge of the city's residential district. The grounds around it, a spacious stretch of river front, were as precisely planted as a park. St. Marks was the materialization of a special design by a world-famed American architect and unlimited funds. It had been recently built and endowed on tax deductable subscriptions from a long list of philanthropic millionaires, including several tycoons. St. Marks was actually a private nonprofit institution planned primarily for the housing of the highly solvent sick. And the place reflected this inside as well as out.

When Roy had received notification that he had passed Part I (written) of the board, a card had been enclosed with a day and hour for the oral (Part II) examination, also to be held at St. Marks. For this he was directed to report, with his card, to the St. Marks Hospital board room lounge one half hour in advance. Roy now sat there, heart pounding, waiting for his turn, trying to appear casual as he looked around him.

The room, extending some fifty by sixty feet, rose loftily to a gothically arched ceiling. Around its walls were the blazoned seals of American universities. Roy looked for, and found, with a queer satisfaction, that his own had been included. The place and the decor, he noted, gave off an aura of impersonal, taken for granted kind of luxury. This came from the fused impressions of its oak paneling, enormous Norman-styled fireplace, and plethora of leather sofas and chairs. A thin curtain of cigarette smoke swung hazily halfway to the ceiling. Beneath it one or two were pacing, but most of them were sitting like himself. There were eight other candidates—the straggling survivors of Part I. There were, Roy noted, frequent goings and comings between the room and door discreetly marked GENTLEMEN. This nervous reaction he recalled well from medical school examinations and it was very evident again now. He had already gone twice himself.

"Sheep for the slaughter," he thought, waiting there. The time wore on. He controlled his tendency to fidget and urinate again by smoking another cigarette. Then it finally came. One of the bright-looking girl secretaries who had been pouring in and out with cards and number-calling came back again.

"Number seven please. Number seven."

"Here," Roy said and got up. This was it.

He followed her out, and then down a long phalanx of paneled doors. She stopped at one, knocked, and opened the door. She nodded to Roy.

The room was not large, but seemed so because of the sparsity of its furnishings. It had been cleared except for a long table and three chairs. Two of these were behind the table and two men sat in them. There was one vacant. The first thing Roy noticed was the vacant chair. The phase "hot seat" flashed through his head. Then he looked at the two men. One of them he vaguely remembered as having seen once at the Charity on grand surgical rounds with the Old Man. The other one was Dr. Lothar Santry.

The secretary put his card on the table and said in a low confidential voice, as if some spy might hear it, "Candidate number seven."

She nodded her head brightly at them and went out.

"Goddamn," Roy heard himself saying to himself as he looked at Santry's impassive face and the upturned slot of a mouth. "I would. I was sure I'd get the Smiler for this. And I have."

Santry made no sign of recognition and neither did Roy. Roy stood there for a few moments before this tribunal while the other man checked his card with some papers in front of him. During it Roy could feel every primeval alarm system in his body beginning to burst out in an instant ringing. His throat, dry before, was now like blotting paper. The palms of his hands, a little damp with sweat, he could feel now were almost dripping. And he was aware that his heart was beating as if it were going to climb out of his chest.

"Sympathetic nervous system reaction," Roy thought as he stood there. "I always get it hard. But it will quiet down, if I just keep hold of its tail." And it did as he stood there.

Santry did not take his eyes or his smile off Roy. And Roy, with a hot reveille of his hate mounting in him, looked back at him. He looked at Santry's abnormally fine-cut face with its small head and narrow distinct features. He looked at the lean, coiled spring of Santry's body, now clothed richly and impeccably in dark, regally tailored cloth. He looked at the Phi Beta Kappa and Alpha Omega Alpha keys hanging on the watch chain across Santry's vest. He looked at the pale eyes and then forced himself to look at the mouth he had driven his fist into once. Still smiling. But not a smile at all—

simply an evil concave crease in the lips that left a glint of incisors showing. Not a smile but a travesty of one—a mirthless grimace—cold and colubrine.

"If cobras can smile," Roy thought, "they must smile like that. That's the way they must look when they're about to kill something—poised and hood spread. All right you son-of-a-bitch, I'm ready to try being your mongoose. Come on, let's go."

Roy was aware of the casual voice and gesture of the other man at the desk. "Please sit down, Doctor," the bland-faced man sitting by Santry said. "I'm Dr. Wallace. This is Dr. Santry."

Roy nodded and sat. By the side of Santry, Wallace was a considerable contrast. He looked friendly, impersonal, and nondescript, the way an examiner ought to look.

Roy sat down, never taking his eyes off Santry's until the little hard lights in them left his to look at some papers on the table.

Before it began, Roy sat there, very calm now, with some old forgotten phrases of lit school running in his head:

"The smiler with the knife beneath his cloak." Chaucer.

"He surest strikes that smiling gives the blow." Also Chaucer.

Then Wallace nodded at Santry and Roy's inquisition began. He stiffened as Santry's flat, cultured voice came at him.

"You have had some experience with injury cases, Doctor?"

"Some," Roy said.

"Very well. Let us consider that for a moment. A man is shot in the abdomen with a hand gun, let us say a .38 pistol at close range, let us say six or eight feet. The bullet enters two inches above and to the left of his navel and makes a straight traverse from before backward and lodges beneath the skin in the region of his left twelfth rib. Do you follow that?"

"Yes," Roy said. He thought oddly of an excerpt he had read from the *Record* about someone who had been hurt like that.

"Very well, then. Is there anything else besides the bullet itself that can cause injury to this man or increase the damage of the missile?"

"Yes. He is likely to be knocked down by the force of a .38 at that range. He may injure another part of his body in the force of his fall, maybe his head or an extremity. Besides this, since the bullet entered his abdomen and traversed it in the area named, it would hit bowel. If he had anything in his intestines at the time he was hit, say a heavy meal, whatever was there would be set in motion by the energy of the bullet. It would act as a secondary missile likely to accentuate the direct damage of the bullet itself."

The smile did not change, but there was a slight pause. "Cobra and mongoose," Roy thought.

"You seem very sure of your answer, Doctor. You have seen such cases?"

"A few," Roy said.

"I see." Santry's smile widened a little.

"Yes, you son-of-a-bitch," Roy thought.

"Very well. This same hypothetical gunshot wound, what would be the first thing you would do for him?"

"Treat his shock in the usual way. With compatible blood if I had it, failing that with plasma or a plasma expander, failing that with intravenous saline or glucose. Nothing by mouth. Shock position, and adequate dosage of morphine."

"When would you operate?"

"As soon as he was out of shock."

"Suppose he did not come out of shock?"

"I would wait for what I thought was the optimum time. Give him steady forced transfusion and proceed."

"And how do you tell the optimum time if he does not come out of shock?"

"That is a matter of judgment in the individual case. There are no set criteria that I know of. There's some indication of it by the vital signs. The blood pressure, pulse, and respiration tend to stabilize at some level."

Right or wrong, Roy got the impression that Santry's questions were designed not to test his knowledge but to ensnare him. This, his instinctive hatred, and the rest of it had an effect on his performance. As Santry's relentless interrogation went on, Roy's answers began coming with thinly veiled rancor. Finally they came with almost open truculence. Santry's smile widened. He turned to the man beside him.

"I believe the doctor is surfeited with me at the moment. I'll desist for a while." Santry made a deprecatory gesture with the white well-manicured hand.

Roy's other examiner, who had been following the exchange with close interest, took it up. Roy calmed down at once. The questions now were solid, standard legitimate queries which Roy immediately and gratefully answered. There was an approving nod at the end of it. He turned to Santry:

"All right," Wallace said. "Anything more?"

Santry, with his smile in an immobile grin, waved a hand. "Only one thing." He looked unblinkingly at Roy. "Why are you so hostile, Doctor?"

Roy looked straight into the pale unblinking eyes with the abnormally dilated pupils. "I don't like you. And we're both from the Charity."

There was a frozen instant between them. Santry's smile almost left his face.

"Would you like to say why? Not for the record—"

At that moment a strange thing came into Roy's head. It was his recollection of a stained-glass window in the chancel of the chapel at Amityville. The window was from Tiffany's and a memorial to some alumnus. The beautifully articulated polygons of its glass showed the Archangel Michael in combat with the devil. This curious thought went away almost at once and left Roy looking into Santry's dilated pulils.

"Your smile," Roy said.

Then another strange thing happened. Santry threw back his head and laughed. It was not a long laugh; it was short, brittle, and mirthless.

"All right, Doctor, that's all." Santry looked at Wallace and Wallace nodded.

Roy got out of his chair, mumbled, "Thank you," and went out the door.

"That boy was pretty good," Wallace said. "One of your Charity boys, isn't he?"

Santry nodded slightly.

"I'm giving him a straight ninety," Wallace said.

"By all means," Santry said. He looked at his own grade card, turned it over thoughtfully, and put down fifty—twenty-five points below passing.

This mark, calculated by Santry as certain to fail Roy for the whole examination, came perilously close to doing it. Close, but not quite. He had done well in the written and the rest of the oral, which gave him barely enough margin. A brief consideration by the review committee confirmed it and he was passed. He did not of course make the honors section as he otherwise might have. Still he passed, and the congratulatory form letter and the certificate arrived on schedule. He had done it, finally done it. He was now officially a member of the guild. He was a bona fide, 100 per cent, accept no substitute, certified surgical specialist as stated in the terse formal lines of the diploma. He had the usual reaction of the successful candidate. There was one wild night of celebration, most of it confined to the Asterion, where he was greatly assisted by Chris, Rybecki, and Capshaw. From this it took him another day to recover with a regime of black coffee, aspirin, and endless trips to the Charity drinking fountains. Through it the routine grind of the Surgical Service continued as before.

During the height of his postalcholic expiation, Roy thought, as he often had, "no matter what, this place never changes, never stops. It's like Jesus Christ—the same today, yesterday, tomorrow, and forever."

14

Dutch Ransahoff's return in splendor to the Charity had all the trappings of dramatic romance. It had a distinctly Dumasian flavor. In many ways it resembled the resplendent reappearance of Edmond Dantes in the Count of Monte Cristo. Dutch returned to the scene of his former penury and servitude in a high state of opulence. He was wearing a brand-new custom-made suit, hand-lasted shoes, and accessories to match. He was driving a brand-new convertible of a make commonly associated with the more discriminating tycoons. Not only were these items paid for, but Dutch's oversized, limp leather wallet was stuffed with bills of hair-raising denominations. Dutch had finally made it. He was not only solvent, but he positively reeked with the odor of success. There was no doubt that part of the motive of his triumphal revisitation of the Charity was for this display. But his main purpose was matrimony. He had come to bear away in lawful wedlock the long-time object of his passion, Miss Ruth Kinerem, the lissome supervisor of ward L. His reunion with Roy was raucous and heartfelt on both sides. It was cause for immediate celebration together at the Asterion.

None of the signs of Ransahoff's new-found affluence were

missed by Chris's appraising eye, after his greeting. This was an additional dividend of satisfaction to Ransahoff.

"I see you're weighing in my wrist watch and cuff links, you Hellenic usurer," Ransahoff said. "Green with envy, hey? Well, you ought to be. A Patek Philippe worth a king's ransom. For what I paid for the son-of-a-bitch I could have bought the whole Goddamn Acropolis. Solid gold case and facing. Want me to take it off so you can bite it and see?"

"No, Dr. Ransahoff. It's a beautiful watch."

"Maybe you'd like to try the cuff links, you invidious Peloponnesian shark. They're gold too. Antique gold at that. Made out of Sappho's breastplates as a matter of fact. They're the gift of a Greek shipping magnate to me for saving his life. I took them instead of the half interest in his financial holdings he was begging to give me."

"They are very handsome, Dr. Ransahoff," Chris said imperturbably. "You don't mind my admiring them?"

"Not at all," Ransahoff said. "I've always said that for a vulgarian your taste was surprisingly good."

"Thank you, Dr. Ransahoff," Chris said gravely. "What would you gentlemen be drinking?"

"The usual for me I suppose. That's the most expensive drink in the house. What would that be now? I've been away now so long I can't remember—"

"Anything you'd like Dr. Ransahoff. It's all on the house."

"The hell it is," Ransahoff said, taking out his Florentine tooled-leather wallet. "What Ransahoff drinks, Ransahoff pays for. The secret of my success can be summed up in a few very simple axioms. The most important one is 'Never take a favor from a Greek.'"

"Anyway you want it, Dr. Ransahoff."

"Good," Ransahoff said. He extracted a fifty dollar bill and put it on the table. "Now, Dr. Maines and I will drink on this. We are going to drink boilermakers. The whiskey will be Old Wisenheimer Bourbon and the beer will be Szabo's Bohemian, of course."

"Yes, Dr. Ransahoff." Chris bowed and started to move away toward the bar, straightening his apron.

"Just a minute," Ransahoff said.

Chris came back to the booth and stood.

"I want you to change this fifty, Christopher, right away, and get one hundred nickels. That's five dollars of it. And I want you to put every one of those nickels into that Goddamn juke box." Ransahoff waved his hand toward the magnificent mechanism of glass, bulbs, and plastic at the far end of the bar. "It says that that son-of-a-bitch has one hundred separate selections. I never believed it when I was here and I don't believe it now. Now Goddamn it, Dr. Maines and I, as conscientious scientists with an endowment fund, are going to test it. We're going to sit here and drink and do some counting."

"Yes, Dr. Ransahoff," Chris said seriously. "But it does do that, if you'll take my word for it. I'm here all the time. And I listen to it. It does it just like it's supposed to."

"That's what you say," Ransahoff said, "but you're a Goddamn unschooled Greeek bartender. Dr. Maines and I are scientists, schooled in the research method. We're going to sit and see."

Chris nodded.

"I'll put all the nickels in, Dr. Ransahoff."

"You better do that, you loose-living Levantine," Ransahoff said. "We're going to sit here and count."

"Yes, Dr. Ransahoff." Chris nodded. "But even with the drinks and the juke box you'll be getting a lot of change from this fifty. Maybe I should save it for you?"

"No, Goddamn it," Ransahoff said. "Whatever's left when we get through you bring it to me. Bring it to me in small money—fives. I need it to distribute as largesse to the poor."

"I'll do that, Dr. Ransahoff," Chris said, and moved off toward the bar.

"Goddamn it," Ransahoff said looking after him, "he's great, isn't he, Roy?"

"Yes he is, Dutch. He's the greatest bartender in the world."

Chris brought their boilermakers and discreetly departed to his position between the bar and the cash register.

Roy looked at the pleased expression on Ransahoff's face. "You came back here to marry Ruth, didn't you, Dutch?"

"That's right. She's just about the greatest dame I ever knew. After that night at the Tokay I knew she was. I knew she was for me."

"Well, good," Roy said. "She must have said yes. She did, didn't she?"

"Yeah. She did."

"I thought so," Roy said. "Now all that's left is the ceremony. If you're looking for a best man, well I'm—"

"I am not, Roy," Ransahoff said, smiling.

"Well, I kind of thought that maybe you were going to ask me to stand up with you and Ruth. I thought that—"

"Look, Roy, we were going to do just that. But we decided to do it as fast as we could. So we went to a county judge and did it. It was real easy, too, you know—that way. Ruth and I were married this morning."

Roy pushed his drink back. "Well, Jesus Christ," he said, "what are you doing here drinking with me then?"

"She's getting things squared away at the hospital and the nursing office. And when she does we're going to take off. Hell, she hasn't even resigned yet, given notice, or anything. Even her family doesn't know it yet."

"Dutch," Roy said, "you certainly move in fast when you start."

"That's me," Dutch said, "the Flying Dutchman. Rapid Ransahoff. What about that Ruth though? She didn't waste any time grabbing me either. That's one of the wonderful things about her—she knows a real prize when she sees one."

"Well, she's got one now." Roy grinned. "The flower of the flock, you might say. Now that I'm over the shock, congratulations and here's luck—" Roy raised his glass and drank.

"By the way," Dutch said, "what about you and Katy Winter? How is she?"

"I wouldn't know how Mrs. Preston Knox is. That's her name now."

Dutch looked at him quizzically. "Hah. Went and got married on you, did she? That's a surprise. I had it figured she'd stick with you no matter what, including being a Charity resident's unmarried widow."

"Well, she didn't," Roy said.

"Did you ask her?"

"Never really got the chance. I was going to—"

"Sure," Ransahoff said, "but you married the Old Man's Service first didn't you? Then you decided to get around to propositioning her? That's the way it was, wasn't it?"

"Why yes, councillor, you're right. That's exactly the way it was. She declined, so what the hell's the difference? She's Mrs. Preston Knox now, and good luck to both of them. I've got more important things to think about now."

"Didn't bother you a bit, huh? Just like that you wrote her off?"

"Look, Dutch," Roy said a little irritably, "let's knock off on this talk shall we? It makes me uncomfortable. It couldn't be less important now anyway."

"Why sure," Ransahoff said, "it's perfectly evident though that you're still nursing torch burns for her all the way up to your armpit. You're still in love with her aren't you?"

"Listen, for Christ's sake, Dutch, I'm a lot too busy to bother about things that are over and done with that I can't help. I don't know whether I loved her or not. If I did so what? Or if I didn't so what? It's a dead issue anyway. Let's quit talking about it."

"All right, we will, but you know something, you Quixotic bastard? You remind me of one of the most tragic figures of poetic literature, you really do."

"That so?" Roy said. "Before we get too drunk, who was that?"

"A character from a poem called 'Lochinvar' from *Marmion* by Sir Walter Scott. Ever hear of it?"

"Listen, you son-of-a-bitch, just married or not, don't try to patronize me with your familiarity with eighth-grade 'memory gem' literature. I know all about 'Lochinvar.' I got a prize once for reciting it.

Oh, young Lochinvar is come out of the west
Through all the wide border his steed was the best . . .

"That's it," Ransahoff said, "that's the one."

"Good," Roy said. "I'm at least as literate as you are, you bastard.

"Now just what do you think Lochinvar and I have in common?"

"You don't have one good Goddamn thing in common with Lochinvar. Your affinity is with the Goddamn bridegroom. The husband of the fair Ellen. You're the bridegroom.

a laggard in love and a dastard in war
was to wed the fair Ellen of brave Lochinvar.

"He was also the bastard who stood around while the fair Ellen got took off and carried away—remember, while Lochinvar is dancing with the broad?

While her mother did fret and her father did fume
And the bridegroom stood dangling his bonnet and plume.

"Yeah," Roy said, "and after that comes, 'So stately his form and so lovely her face,' etc."

"That's right, but you're the bridegroom in Lochinvar. How long are you going to sit around on the Old Man's Service dangling your Goddamned bonnet and plume while women like Katy are ridden off with by guys like Knox or whatever his name is?"

"Till I get off the Old Man's Surgical Service apparently. I'm not worried though. Friend of mine, great authority on women, tells me they're like streetcars—they'll always be another one along."

"Well," Ransahoff said, "if that's the way you really feel it's plain you don't think you need any advice to the lovelorn from kindly old Dr. Ransahoff, the marriage councillor."

"That's right, I don't."

"Good. Then we can move on to something that's a whole hell of a lot more important. That my lad, is your future—"

"What are you going to do, Dutch, read my palm or my horoscope?"

"About this, I'm serious. Incidentally I hear you passed the board in surgery. Congratulations. Ruth told me."

"How word does get around. Yeah. I passed it—mostly by the grace of God and the Old Man's endorsement."

"Very tough, huh?"

"Very. Particularly for me. Believe it or not I had that leering son-of-a-bitch Santry as one of my examiners on the oral part. How's that for an opener?"

"Jesus," Ransahoff said. "Tell me about it."

Roy gave him a vivid and more or less accurate description of his inquisition. When he had finished Dutch chuckled.

"You know, Roy, aside from being the Old Man's fair-haired boy, I, by God, believe you're a child of destiny. It's got to be that way or you never would have gotten by the Smiler, sitting there waiting for you with his knife out."

"I think the Old Man's fine Italian touch had more to do with it."

"Maybe. The thing is, though, you made it. It is official though, isn't it?"

"No doubt about that," Roy said. "I got my certificate in the mail three days ago."

Ransahoff shook his head happily. "Roy boy, you've got it made. And I mean made, son, made. Now don't interrupt me . . ." Dutch signaled Chris for more beer.

"Look, Roy, aside from coming up here to marry Ruth, the next most important thing was to talk to you. That's the truth. I've been down there with Blinn in that Goddamn town for less than two years, in that clinic his father left him, and we're cleaning up. The place is a gold mine. Just that short time, and I'm loaded. Look at me. Old Dutch didn't have a pot to piss in when he left here. Now everything high on the hog—big doctor, big car, big dough. This is a two hundred-dollar suit. I've got four more like it. All custom made. Twenty thousand bucks in the bank, besides the small change I carry around on me like two or three hundred. Why Christ, Roy, you talk about having a hog with both feet in the trough. Blinn and I are in it wallowing around up to our eyeballs. We're working like hell, but we're making it like hell. I'd hate to tell you what our take was last year because you wouldn't believe it. And that, Roy, my lad, is what we do just taking care of general practice cases—no surgery except the minor stuff, what Blinn and I can handle in the office, or with limited privileges in the hospital . . ." Ransahoff paused and drank thoughtfully. "That Goddamn town of ours is one of the fastest growing industrial areas in the state, too. It's a natural locality for industry and it's coming in too—"

"What the hell are you now, Dutch?" Roy said. "The mayor or the president of the Chamber of Commerce?"

"Shut up and listen will you?" Ransahoff said. "There isn't a surgeon down there. There are guys who do surgery, half-assed, half-baked, and self-taught. But there's not a real one with any kind of training, who's got his papers like you out of the Charity. And Christ, how we need one!"

Ransahoff paused and lifted his glass and put it back on the table. "And if you'll just come down there with us, Roy. My God, if you just will, you can write your own ticket—"

Ransahoff fumbled in his jacket and brought out an embossed leather check book. He opened it, scribbled his name on one of the blank checks, and passed it to Roy.

"Like that, see, Roy. Write in what you want. My balance is twenty-one thousand, five hundred and eighty-six dollars, and twenty-one cents. And if that's not enough write it for anything you want to. It will be covered out of the clinic or Blinn's account."

Ransahoff pushed the check toward Roy. Roy picked it up and looked at it and pushed it back toward Ransahoff.

"Dutch, you always were a dramatic son-of-a-bitch. No, I

mean a melodramatic son-of-a-bitch. Especially when you get your navel distended by a few drinks."

Ransahoff drew back. "What's the matter. Don't you believe me?"

Roy nodded. "Yes, Dutch, I believe you."

"Well, you'd better. It's all by God truth. You think I'm kidding? Don't you think I've got—we—Blinn and I've got that much dough in the bank?"

"Sure, I think you've got it," Roy said. "I'm Goddamn sure you have."

"Well, then, for Christ's sake, what's the matter with you? Here it is all laid out. We're guaranteeing you up to twenty thousand a year the first year, if you'll come with us. I know what you're making here. Room, board, laundry, and one fifty. What the hell is the matter with you, Roy?"

"Nothing. But the Old Man, he—"

"Screw the Old Man," Ransahoff said hotly, "screw him. Jesus Christ, you've been his slave for long enough, haven't you? You've given the old son-of-a-bitch value received, haven't you? You've worked your ass off doing his bidding, holding up his Service in its true tradition whatever the Christ that is. Don't you think you've been his itsy bitsy beautiful kid long enough now? Don't you think it's about time you got out from under his all-protective surgical umbrella into the rain on your own? Don't you think you ought to cut this Goddamn unnatural umbilical cord of piano wire between you and that domineering son-of-a-bitch?"

Roy shook his head slowly. "Dutch, you don't really know him. I do. Please don't talk that way about the Old Man. He stands for a lot to a lot of people. He stands for a lot to me. There's a war on, Dutch, aside from all of this or anything else. We're going to be in on it."

"Sure there is," Ransahoff said, "and sure, we're going to be in it. That's pretty obvious. But for Christ's sake, Roy, you don't have to worry about that. Come down with us and we'll get you declared essential. Be no problem about it. Christ, Blinn is the doctor on the draft selection board they just formed up—"

Roy drank the whiskey part of the boilermaker, then the beer, and looked at Ransahoff. "I'll still have to talk to the Old Man, Dutch."

"And that will be the worst Goddamn mistake you ever made too. He'll try to con you into staying on at the Charity.

Wait and see if he doesn't. Then you can screw around the rest of your life, around the Charity for glory and peanuts for dough when you could be making a million. To hell with that Roy. Can't you make up your own mind for Christ's sake?"

"Yes. I can still do that. And I will. But not without talking to the Old Man. And I really haven't had the chance to since I passed the board. We've been so damned busy."

"Trouble with you is," Dutch growled, "you've got such a bad case of hospitalitis you don't know what's going on outside of that lousy pesthouse. You ought—"

Dutch suddenly stopped, rose from the booth, and looked toward the door of the Asterion.

"Hey, baby. Here, over here. There she is, by God. Finished everything early. Just look at her, Roy," he said dotingly, "Mrs. Otto Ransahoff, Jr. Isn't she lovely?"

She was, too, Roy noted, as her arresting body swayed toward them. To Roy, who had seldom seen her out of her nurse's uniform, she was a radiant revelation. Ruth was wearing a dark-cloth traveling suit that fitted her flawlessly, and in it she looked more like a high-fashion model.

"Ah, my queen," Ransahoff said to her as she came to the booth. And then to Roy:

"Get up, you base-born son-of-a-bitch, and kiss the bride. Nothing sexy now." Roy got up and kissed Ruth.

Forty-five minutes and a lot of conversation later, Roy stood at the curb before the Charity watching Ransahoff's car merge into the disorderly congestion of vehicles on St. Marks Street. He stood for a while looking after it, feeling a peculiar hollow ache in his belly through the drinks they had had at Chris's.

"It could have been like that for me too," he thought, "for Katy and me, like it is now for them. That's the way it could have been. And that's the way it isn't ever going to be. Well . . ."

He turned from the curb toward the Charity's front entrance. Late afternoon visiting hours were over now, and the usual shabby stream of people who had lingered late over the diseased and dying on its wards, was flowing steadily outward.

Roy elbowed his way through them toward the entrance doors and he suddenly felt very lonely. Tonight was his night off and he had no plans for it. Well, he could stay in and read. He checked at the switchboard and went to his room.

15

The private office of J. Abbott Pelly on the seventh floor of the *Record* building was a place of imposing decor. Its dimensions were roughly those of a tennis court or perhaps a trifle larger. Its walls were completely paneled in smoked oak, and at precisely spaced intervals along them there were original Piranesi engravings of which Pelly was a collector. The furniture consisted of massive chairs and sofas made to Pelly's order and upholstered in hand-rubbed Spanish cordovan. There were some specially designed bookcases containing an awesome array of first editions of which Pelly was also a fancier. At the far end of the room was the enormous desk and chair (formerly the property of the Emperor Franz Ferdinand). These had been acquired by Pelly at great cost on one of his not infrequent yacht excursions to Europe. He spent a great deal of time at this desk ruling his journalistic empire of twenty-eight publications, including the *Record*. The office of J. Abbott Pelly was imposing, but so indeed was J. Abbott Pelly.

Pelly was a big man, physically as well as otherwise. His life had been one continued chronicle of success and good living and it had left him, besides a great deal of money, with a good deal of fat. The money was properly concealed in various banks and trust concerns, but the fat of his success was another matter. That he had not been able to conceal in spite of elaborate tailoring. He had enormous jowls and a truly remarkable paunch. Pelly had the appearance and the gut of one of the more decadent Renaissance popes. It was this feature of him that had struck Capshaw, who was accustomed to refer to him as "Pelly the Belly," or simply as "The Belly." Capshaw also referred to him as "The Big Mamoo." Almost everyone in the *Record's* employ had come to adopt Capshaw's designations of J. Abbott Pelly. But never in his hearing, of course. In his immediate and august presence he was addressed as Mr. Pelly.

And Capshaw so addressed him as he sat with him in closed audience, his feet ankle deep in the wall-to-wall carpeting of the room. Capshaw was not unfamiliar with this carpet. He had been on it several times before. His usual policy with Pelly at these times was to adopt a wholesome and unmitigated innocence. He did so this time.

"Got the word you wanted to see me, Mr. Pelly."

Pelly picked up a paper from his desk, glanced at it, and then at Capshaw. "Capshaw, thanks to you, the *Record* is involved in another defamation suit. This time for a half a million dollars. Do you ever write anything in that column of yours but libel?"

Capshaw gave Pelly his best blank look. "I don't write anything I can't substantiate, Mr. Pelly. Substantiated truth is not libel. I think we both agree."

"I am not going into the dialectics of that with you, Capshaw. We're concerned here with libel laws with which you're familiar. What you wrote in your October 5th column is a glaring violation. Even our legal department thinks so."

Capshaw gave a good performance of pretending to reflect on this.

"That would be what I said on *Bund* propaganda activities by the fascist elements around town."

"Yes, it would," Pelly's voice was heavy with sarcasm, "that's exactly right, Capshaw. And you knew what you were writing was actionable when you wrote it."

"I really don't see what's legally actionable about it, Mr. Pelly."

"You don't? Your generalizations in it may be true. It's the specific personal attack you made against that doctor."

"That the plaintiff, Mr. Pelly? Dr. Lothar Gamaliel Santry?"

"Of course, that's the plaintiff," Pelly snarled, "who else would it be? You singled him out by name for some of your most florid vilification. How the hell do you know he's a sadistic crackpot, dangerous paranoic, covert sex degenerate?"

"He is," Capshaw said almost serenely. It was Capshaw's refusal to be disturbed about any of it that goaded Pelly's irritation with him into full anger, with which he now spoke.

"Goddamn it, Capshaw. That's your personal opinion and you state it as a fact. That's what makes libel suits, stating personal opinions of individual character as facts which can't be substantiated before a court of law."

Capshaw smiled benignly back at Pelly's reddened face. "What I said about the good doctor is a fact, Mr. Pelly, that's why it's my opinion. I got the facts first. There won't be any libel suit against the *Record*—"

"There won't?" Pelly said, flipping two clipped sheets of paper across the desk toward Capshaw. "There's the letter from Rykina, Doane, and Cleate, the doctor's council. Probably the best in the state next to our own. With the injunction."

Capshaw did not bother to look at it, something that further irritated Pelly. Capshaw's nonchalance about the whole business remained complete. Pelly looked at the thin disheveled figure in the chair in front of the desk; at Capshaw's narrow face with the smoldering eyes, the hard lean jaw with the hair of yesterday's stubble on it; at the rumpled suit, pants bagging over the crossed knees; at the unshined leaky-looking shoes and the frayed cuffs of Capshaw's jacket sleeves. And as he did so, the ire began to die out of Pelly. Something incongruous had sudden erupted into his head. Something from a play he had read once in lit school at Princeton. It was a concatenation of lines of a play. What the hell was the name of it? Ah! He had it. Of course. Shakespeare, somewhere in Othello:

He who steals my purse, steals trash. . . . But he who taketh away my good name taketh that which doth not enrich him but maketh me poorer than the meanest bondsman.

Then there was Cyrano, Rostand's *Cyrano de Bergerac*. That was more like it. Capshaw was like Cyrano. Head bloody many times, but still unbowed and likely to have it smashed "some lacky with a log." From this unexpected advantage of his limited literary heritage Pelly suddenly and peculiarly began to look at Capshaw in that light. And the anger in Pelly's practical soul began to quiet. He listened now, even eagerly, to what Capshaw was saying.

"Mr. Pelly," Capshaw said, "I never have deliberately put the *Record* on any kind of hook, legal or otherwise. I write my column. And I write features. And I try to write as honestly as I can. And I am going to continue to do that. You don't like it, then maybe you'd better fire me."

"Nobody said a Goddamn word about firing you," Pelly said. "Nobody said a word about that."

Capshaw nodded his head. "Well, you might want to, Mr.

Pelly. And that would be all right too, you know. I understand your position as publisher. And I'm sorry about this threatened libel suit. But"—Capshaw paused, felt in his pocket for a cigarette, found one, and lit it—"I can promise you right here and now though, that there won't be any. Dr. Santry won't press it."

"No? What do you have in mind to stop it? A page-one retraction, signed by you, Coles as editor, and me as publisher?"

"No, Mr. Pelly. Before I'd put the *Record*, you, Coles, and myself to that kind of damage and humiliation I'd quit the paper, and let him make it a suit against me personally. That is what he would love to do. In fact, Mr. Pelly, if he insists on proceeding with it, that is exactly what I will do. But you see he won't. I knew that before I did that piece."

Pelly arched his thick eyebrows at Capshaw. "Let me hear why you think he won't, Capshaw."

The ash from Capshaw's cigarette fell on the beautiful carpet and Capshaw thoughtfully ground it into the piling with his foot.

"Because I am going to have a personal interview with the good doctor, Mr. Pelly. And after I do, he'll drop the suit. He will do that because he won't have any choice."

"Really?" Pelly said, looking with sharp interest at the set expression on Capshaw's face. "Tell me about that."

Capshaw shook his head. "No, Mr. Pelly, I am not going to do that. Afterward maybe. Right now I am not going to add to your present embarrassment or the *Record's*. I'll handle it."

Pelly continued to survey Capshaw silently for some moments. "All right, Capshaw, you handle it. And you'd better be right. Do you mind putting your cigarette ashes in the tray instead of on the floor?"

"Not at all," Capshaw said, and stubbed his cigarette out in the ashtray on Pelly's desk that looked like an elaborate hors d'oeuvre dish.

"When is this interview with Dr. Santry?"

Capshaw looked at his wrist, where his cheap watch clung like a metallic spider.

"In about an hour, Mr. Pelly. I'm talking to the good doctor at his residence at 286 St. Vrain Street. I've got a few things to do before that. So unless you have something else to consider with me I think I'd better be going."

Capshaw got out of the beautifully comfortable chair before

Pelly's desk, nodded, and started across the long expanse of carpeting toward the door.

Pelly watched his dilapidated figure in the ragged sacklike topcoat recede from him for an instant and felt something turn in his chest, his head, and his magnificent expanse of belly.

"Capshaw!"

Capshaw turned, his thin white face suddenly brought out in a curious relief against one of the smoked-oak panels of the room.

"Yes, Mr. Pelly?"

"Look, Capshaw, I want to know how this business comes out. Be here till four. At the club still seven. Then at home. I want you to call me no matter what time. Will you do that? You have the phone numbers."

"Yes, I have, Mr. Pelly. I'll do that."

Pelly watched the shabby form move past the door and the door close behind him. After he had gone, J. Abbott Pelly sat motionless at his desk looking at the opulence of the place, the walls, the Piranesi prints on them, the bookcases, the carpet, and finally at himself and the big magnificent belly that was so evidently a part of him. The big fat belly with the pearl-gray vest and the Phi Beta Kappa key on the massive gold chain that swung majestically across it. He patted his Homeric belly thoughtfully. "Guts," he said to himself. "Not this kind, but Capshaw's kind. Maybe that's the answer to everything in life."

In his locker just outside of the press room Capshaw paused long enough to pick up three items. One was a Burton and Cowles film projector (the compact model suitable, as advertised, for instant home-movie use complete with sound-track apparatus). The next was a carefully wrapped roll of film. The third was a fully loaded Smith and Wesson short-barreled .38. He checked the loading and the action of the revolver first, which he put into the right-hand pocket of his topcoat. Then he stuffed the small brown-paper-wrapped package of the .16-mm film into the left-hand pocket of his coat. Then he picked up the small case that held the film projector. With these he went to the men's room, tended to his wants, looked at himself in the mirror, and adjusted his tie. Outside, with just ten minutes to spare, he got a taxi to 286 St. Vrain Street.

Capshaw's confrontation of Santry took place precisely on time in Santry's library. An impersonal-looking uniformed maid showed Capshaw in and retired. Capshaw's immediate impression of the place was the quantity of books which lined it floor to ceiling and its austerity otherwise. This was relieved somewhat by a rather ornate marble fireplace and the large ormolu clock on its mantel. The only furniture was a long refectory table and three high-backed chairs, one at the end of the table, and the other two flanking it. Santry sat in the one at the end with a book open in front of him, which he may or may not have been reading. He rose as Capshaw came in carrying the projection case.

Santry inclined his head slightly. He did not extend his hand. Neither did Capshaw. Santry's eyes went over Capshaw briefly and the case he held. And in turn Capshaw looked at Santry and his smile.

"Mr. Capshaw, you are punctual."

"Thank you, Dr. Santry, so are you."

Santry's lean springlike body relaxed into the chair. He waved a hand at one of the others. "Sit down, Mr. Capshaw."

Capshaw sat down, putting his projector case beside him. Capshaw felt Santry's eyes crawling over him with a kind of assured insolence that made what was smoldering in Capshaw begin to flicker into flame.

"You're here at the instance of your paper, I suppose, Mr. Capshaw? That is to say, your publisher?"

"No," Capshaw said easily, "matter of fact, I'm not, Dr. Santry. I'm here on my own."

Santry's eyebrows raised slightly. "Ah, on your own. That's interesting."

"I think you'll find it that way, Doctor. When we get a little further with it. First though, so that we can cut any Goddamned ridiculous preliminary fencing exercise to a minimum, I'd like to say something."

Santry spread a condescending hand. "Splendid idea. Your floor, Mr. Capshaw."

"Good," Capshaw said. "Now understand this, Doctor. I am not here to negotiate any propitiatory deals with you because you have put a libel suit on the *Record* for what I wrote about you. I am not here to offer you either personal apology or a public retraction on my own part or the paper's. That was your assumption I think, Doctor, wasn't it?"

The smile on Santry's mouth, Capshaw noted with satisfaction, had tightened more than a little, enough that the white, sharp-looking incisors were beginning to glint through it.

"Hardly an unreasonable assumption."

"Maybe not, but based on incomplete knowledge of the character of my information concerning you, Doctor. You see, there is nothing I have written about you that I am not prepared to prove."

"Ah, so? For example?"

"I implied," Capshaw said, "among other things that you were a dangerous political subversive and a sex degenerate. How would either one of these do as an example, Dr. Santry?"

Capshaw saw the skin around Santry's mouth draw so tightly that it looked like the flayed hide on a drum head. The look now in the unblinking eyes was undisguisedly venomous. They continued to stare at Capshaw silently.

"Suppose we consider my deliberate use of the term sex degenerate. That is certainly the more offensive to you probably. Certainly the one of most interest to the prurient public. They simply dote on that abnormal sex stuff, you now, Doctor. Particularly when a preacher or a doctor is one of the principals."

"Swine," Santry's voice came out now with a kind of low hissing timbre to it, "unmitigated unprincipled swine."

Capshaw nodded. "That's the general impression I tried to give of you, Doctor. I see that you actually do indulge in self-analysis. But we were speaking specifically of your baroque sexual tastes just now. So, let's look at you in that department. I have here with me some pretty sensational documentary evidence on it. Eight minutes of .16-mm film with a synchronized sound track."

Capshaw pulled the paper-wrapped disk from his pocket and tossed it on the table before Santry.

"There it is in the unedited original and more or less complete. It records the more bestial moments of the evening of September 17 between you and a sad little strumpet by the name of Rita. Rita incidentally is recovering nicely from what she let you do to her in that room on the second floor of Madame Anastasia Kondoleon's establishment."

The ormolu clock on the mantel suddenly chimed and then gave off a final banging note marking the half hour. Capshaw waited till it subsided and then went on.

"For an extemporaneous and unrehearsed performance,

Doctor, I think what we have here"—he pointed at the paper-wrapped cylinder on the table before Santry—"is rather good. You show up well, very well. So does Rita. The close action I think is astonishingly clear, considering the automatic conditions of filming. Thought you'd like to look at it"—Capshaw kicked the carrying case at his feet—"so I brought along a projector all rigged for sound in case you don't happen to have one. Care to take a look at it?"

Except for the barely perceptible ticking of the ormolu clock, the room was absolutely silent as Capshaw and Santry continued to stare at each other.

"Then I guess you have your own projector," Capshaw said. "Run it off when you have the time." He nodded toward the wrapped parcel on the table.

"Don't bother to return that film, Doctor. There are several duplicates, the original, the one with the local police department, and the one just filed with the Federal Bureau of Security."

Santry was sitting forward now staring intently at Capshaw. The grimace of his mouth was still there, the lips as taut and colorless as his face.

"I see," he said. "Now just what is it you are actually after from me, Capshaw?"

Capshaw fought down the hatred and exultation that was rising in him.

"You concede the suit against the *Record* and myself is off? That's right, isn't it, Doctor?"

"That it?"

"Not quite," Capshaw said. "There's another thing—more important than how you spend your spare time committing paid mayhem on whores. And that's your Lonely Hearts Club correspondence with a guy in Washington in the State Department name of Henry Bader. Old friend of your as I understand it, from the dear dead days when you were exchange students in Erfurt and elsewhere in the Third Reich. I might say you don't have to bother with all of it. The Bureau has his half from you. They'd like yours—what you got from him. Just to round things out so everybody understands each other, when the war finally becomes official. I know about that you see, Doctor. That's why I knew that I was pretty safe calling you a political subversive. Just supporting the *Bund* propaganda here wouldn't have been enough. A lot of small-time subsidized idiots do that. But not a guy like you. See what I mean?"

Santry nodded slowly. "What that thug I shot was sent in here to get—"

"Why, yes," Capshaw said, "the one you gave a very patriotic death to. Habitual criminal. Stupid. Vain. And not very apt as it turned out. But still with something to recommend him in a negative sense. He never tried to sell out his being a United States citizen. Died pretty well I thought."

Capshaw paused and looked at Santry. Then, sure there was no reply, he went on.

"You shot the be-Jesus out of him didn't you, Doctor, before you finally killed him? You let him roll around for a while, didn't you, holding his poor Goddamned busted belly and the rest of it before you put one through his head? Wasn't that really the way it was, Doctor? Perfectly within your legal rights to have killed him then and there as an intruder, possibly armed. But you didn't, did you? You hit him and let him writhe around so you could enjoy it. Just like you lit matches and burned little Rita before you could get on with it. . . ."

"I asked you what you wanted," Santry said, "and if it's money—"

"I've told you what I want," Capshaw said. "Give me what Bader wrote to you."

Santry's voice and look at Capshaw had some timbre of truth in them.

"All of that is gone. What was left of it I destroyed after that hireling hoodlum of yours came in here for it."

Capshaw looked at the absolutely white face and the still present smile before he spoke. "That's too bad, Doctor. Too bad for you, I mean. You see that's what I really came here to get from you. But since you say you don't have it, well then, I won't waste any more of your time or mine."

Capshaw started to get out of his chair. But before he could Santry was on his feet, his hands moving about the table. Capshaw had the Smith and Wesson out and in his right hand instantly, its muzzle centered on Santry's chest, pointing directly at what he estimated as Santry's heart.

"Just stay like that, Doctor," Capshaw said in a quiet, almost frozen voice. "One cute play and I'll empty this Goddamned thing right into you. I have a legal permit for this gun, signed out of Homicide. Can't think of a better way to use it. So just sit down, will you, and everything will be all right."

Santry sat down. For a while Capshaw thoughtfully held the gun on him. Santry stayed in his chair staring at nothing, then Capshaw put the gun in his pocket and pointed at the paper-wrapped parcel on the table.

"Like I told you, Doctor, no need to return it."

Capshaw picked up his carrying case without a backward glance and walked out of the room.

For some time after Capshaw had left his house Santry sat on his chair looking at nothing. The ormolu clock behind him whirred, clicked, and pealed off another quarter of an hour. Santry roused himself, reached for the brown-papered parcel on the table where Capshaw had tossed it. He tore it open and pulled out the single flat spool of film it contained. He unfixed the slip of binding tape and, getting up, took it to the window where he began looking at the infinite number of small frames against the light. He ran the reel to the end of the spindle, wadded the film in his hands, and with a sudden gesture hurled it into the empty fireplace. Santry, being a nonsmoker, had no matches on him. In the drawer of the table he found one and, lighting it, threw it on the tangled skein in the fireplace. It flamed instantly and was gone, leaving only the blackened cylinder. He stared at it briefly, then, taking the unused pack of matches, he went out of the room.

Upstairs he stood hesitating a moment before going into his bedroom. When he did he went instantly to the night table beside his bed and opened the lower drawer. He reached in and took out the gun. He had meticulously cleaned and reloaded the Luger after the police had done with it and given it back. He stood now for a few moments looking at it absently and hefting it in his hand. He noted there was a thin streak left by the oil on its otherwise immaculate blue-steel barrel. He took out his breast-pocket handkerchief and wiped it away so that the hard clean shine of it was uniform. He pressed the magazine release and let the loaded clip fall out in his hand. Then he replaced it. He pulled back on the two small round disks of the ejector hinge and looked into the chamber. There was a bullet already in it. He let the ejector hinge down to close the chamber, pressed the set button, and snapped off the safety. Then with his gun in his hand, he walked across the hall to his study. He sat down behind his desk and laid the gun down in front of him. And for some time he sat there thinking.

For the first time in his life, Lothar Gamaliel Santry felt completely free—free of the formalities, lusts, and obsessions that had hag-ridden him for his fifty breathing years. And he felt free now of the necessity of maintaining a façade that would cover them and the loathing he had always had of the world and himself. The hatred of both he had felt first and been aware of as a rich only child, and of his monolithic mother twenty-five years dead. But to whom he was and always had been bound by an uncut umbilical cord of spiritual piano wire. He thought of that Brunhilde, massive of breast and buttock, when he had come running to her crying, as he frequently did. Specifically now he thought of the time he had done so after his classmates, boys and girls, in the Swiss school had pulled his pants down, and then by turn spit, with snorts of derision, on his underdeveloped genitals. Ten years old he had been then. More than forty years ago and he could recall all of it now, as he always could, with a perfect and torturing clarity.

"*Regardez ça. Regardez cette petite . . .*"

He had told his mother about that, all of it. And she had listened with a set and strong face.

"Never mind, my little good one. My little Siegfried. Remember that you are of great blood. Do not mind the *schweinerei* of the little pigs who are beneath you. Smile at them. Smile, no matter what. That is the way of good blood. And when the time comes for you, smite them for the vermin that they are. But smile, my son. As you walk and talk about the world, remember to smile at everyone and everything. That is the way to disarm and beguile the world until you are ready to take what you wish of it."

That was a very long time ago, Santry contemplated, thinking now of his father, a heavy-set abstracted man whom he could never remember because he had seen him so seldom. Santry cut his reflections to the present and its implications.

"Poor Heinie, poor Bader. Friend of my best days at Erfurt and the rest of it. I'm sure he'll understand . . ."

Santry made a sudden motion and picked up the Luger. He snapped off the safety and opened his mouth. He stuck the barrel into it, clamped his teeth on the barrel, and, feeling the sight scraping his tongue, pulled the trigger. What else flew out of Santry's head along with his brains would be difficult to say.

Roy was lying on his bed half asleep when the call came from emergency. He picked up the phone.

"Yeah?" Roy said.

"Dr. Maines," the excited voice of the intern came over to him, "we got something real urgent down here. Will you come down? A D.O.A. and—"

"Goddamn it," Roy said, "what's the matter with you? Why call me on a dead on arrival?"

"Well, you'd better come down and look at this one," the intern said. "The whole Goddamned police force is here, and—"

"Be down," Roy said, and hung up the phone.

In room number seven of the Charity emergency suite there was quite an aggregation. The small room was filled with Rybecki's homicide retinue and emergency-room duty staff.

Roy instantly saw the inspector. Rybecki was standing by the stretcher with the sheeted form on it, reflectively sucking his teeth.

"Hello, Inspector," Roy said as the swinging door of number seven fanned shut behind him.

"Hello, Doc," the inspector said, his gold teeth barely glinting. "We got something pretty special here. Take a look."

"That so?" Roy said. "What's that?"

The inspector waved a hand at the sheet-covered form on the stretcher. Roy went over and raised the sheet.

"Good God!"

The strange image of death that was Santry's face stared up at him from a welter of clot. The blood-suffused eyeballs starting from their sockets, the livid puffiness of the skin brought to Roy's mind the flash memory of an anomalous monster he had delivered once as intern on obstetrics. This similarity between Santry's dead visage and that of the monstrous child was accentuated by the fact that there was so little left of Santry's head above the brow line. The stillborn infant had had none at all. But through the spill and contortion of agonal tissue, Santry's features were recognizable enough. Only one characteristic was missing. The smile that Roy had never seen that face without was gone. The bloodless lips were slightly parted in a thin neutral line. Death had wiped away the smile and left something just as secret and noncommittal in its place.

Roy took a deep breath and drew the sheet back over the carnage.

"Medical examiner case," Roy said, aware of the idiocy of his statement and the fact that his throat was very dry.

"Yeah," Rybecki said, "already ruled suicide by us. Question of disposition of the body till claimed is why we brought it over here."

"O.K.," Roy said, "it can go downstairs till there's some disposition."

"Fine," the inspector said. He nodded to his attending sleuths. "Well, I guess that winds up our end of it. Got a minute, Doc?"

"Yes," Roy said, and followed Rybecki out into the hall where they stood for a moment.

"How about a drink together over at Chris's, Doc? Capshaw's over there."

"Anyone call the Old Man about this, Inspector?"

"I don't know, Doc. Maybe Capshaw did. Happened pretty fast."

"All right. I'll see. Join you later, unless the Old Man's got some special ideas of something about this."

On the phone Roy got the Old Man. He had had no word. Roy gave him all of it and then waited for the dead silent seconds before the Old Man said something definitive.

"Your night off isn't it, Roy?"

"Yes, sir, but I was going to be around anyway."

"I don't see that there's anything more to be done at the moment. We'll go into this further in the morning. Meet me a half hour early at the office."

"Yes, sir, I'll be there."

"Good," the Old Man said.

Roy hung up and went over to the Asterion.

Capshaw, Rybecki, and a swarthy little man Roy vaguely remembered having seen before were engrossed in what was apparently a deep discussion in a back booth when Roy came in. This instantly stopped, Roy noted, when he came up and sat down.

Roy's introduction to the stranger was perfunctory. Roy shook Schneider's hand and sat down.

"Thought you might be able to use a drink after that one, Doc," the inspector said.

"Yeah," Roy said, "I never expected to see him dead, let alone in that kind of shape."

Roy turned to Capshaw, who was moodily fingering his glass.

"I didn't see you there, Cappy."

"Paid my respects to the deceased earlier at his house," Capshaw said. "Courtesy of the inspector here. One look was enough."

"A .6-mm Luger does quite a job when a guy sticks it in his mouth and pulls the trigger. At least he had some head left though. Now if he'd done it with a shotgun, say a twelve-gauge full-choke double-barrel, like I seen once—"

Capshaw grimaced and turned on him irritably. "Let it go, will you, Inspector? I'm having enough trouble keeping this booze down as it is."

"First time I ever knew you had such a delicate stummick," Rybecki said, somewhat affronted. "What's the matter with you, sudden case of ulcers or something?"

"My stomach and my liver are probably in better shape than yours are, Stanislaus," Capshaw said. "It's just that I don't want any of your layman's descriptions of traumatic blood and guts. I've seen enough of it for today. I've had a Goddamn gory gothic afternoon."

"Well, fine, you temperamental son-of-a-bitch," Rybecki said.

He turned to Roy. "You get a hold of the Old Man and tell him?"

"Yes," Roy said.

The inspector nodded sympathetically. "I'll bet that shook him didn't it, Doc? One of the top guys under him doing that to himself. Belt out of the blue, so to speak—"

"I don't know," Roy said, thinking suddenly of the chaos in the operating room and afterward when Wild Will Wortle died. And now Santry.

"Maybe it did shake him. I wouldn't know. Didn't seem to much when I talked with him about it over the phone. I've never seen him get shaken about anything really, in the operating room or out of it. The Old Man just doesn't shake, or doesn't show it anyway about anything."

"That's the reason he runs the show, eh, Doc?"

"That's one reason certainly," Roy said.

Schneider, who had been covertly evaluating Roy, spoke. "How well did you know this Santry, Doctor?"

Roy grinned wryly. "Well enough to have hit him once. The Old Man put me on probabtion for it, instead of firing me."

"I gather you didn't like him."

"I didn't," Roy said. "I hated his guts. Can't say that I really knew him though. I don't think anybody did, even the Old Man. I can say one thing for him, he was one hell of a good surgeon. This is going to leave a big hole in the surgical service."

"Had an office over there at the hospital, didn't he?"

"Yes," Roy said, "every senior surgeon on the Service does."

Schneider turned to Capshaw and Rybecki. "Might be worth a look there. Just to complete things."

Capshaw noted the confused look on Roy's face. "Mr. Schneider is a federal-type dick, Doc. That's just between us. Santry was part of his job here."

"I see," Roy said.

"Do you think your chief, the Old Man, whatever you call him, would object to an unofficial look around at whatever there is over there in Santry's office? Before anything is moved out of it, that is?"

Roy's eyes went over Schneider, now with some comprehension in them. "You could ask him, Mr. Schneider. His home number is Dorchester 8-4451. He's at home now and will be in his office tomorrow morning. It you want to make it early he's always there at seven unless he's operating. He won't be tomorrow morning."

"Thanks, Doctor." Schneider nodded.

Roy knew that he had interrupted their close talk. And he could feel the restriction his presence was putting on them. In spite of his itching curiosity he finished his drink and stood up.

"Better be getting back," Roy said. "I told the Old Man I'd stay available. Nice to have met you, Mr. Schneider. See you Cappy. Thanks for the drink, Inspector."

They watched him stop for a moment and speak to Chris before he went out.

"A real nice young guy." Rybecki nodded approvingly. "And a real surgeon-type doctor, Doc Maines. You know, Cappy, he reminds me a hell of a lot of his boss, Doc Hand.

This kid talks and even walks like him, doesn't he, Cappy?"

Capshaw nodded slowly. It was his seventh bourbon and water and he was feeling something of it. "Yes, he does, Stanislaus. You're very observing, It's the Great Stone Face phenomenon. I've been watching it for sometime now."

"The what?" the inspector said, winking at Schneider. "What's the Great Stone Face phenomenon?"

"I'd hardly expect a crass untutored son-of-a-bitch like you to understand any obscure literary references beyond the *Police Gazette*," Capshaw said, dreamily lifting his refilled glass. "I'm talking about a short story by Hawthorne called *The Great Stone Face*. It's about a guy who looked at something so long and so hard and with so much reverence that he began to look like it himself."

"Well," Rybecki said defensively, "I didn't expect to be made a horse's ass on account of my lack of education simply because I said Doc Maines reminds me of Dr. Hand. They've both taken care of me."

"Stanislaus," Capshaw said almost gently, "you're perfectly right. Young Maines does look like and act like him—he's becoming the symbol by worship of it."

"You know, Capshaw," Rybecki said seriously, "if you weren't a writer, I'd say that you were a real crazy son-of-a-bitch. At times nobody can say nothing to you without coming out looking like a Goddamn fool for saying it."

Rybecki turned toward Schneider. "Ain't that right, Klaus? Ain't that the way you feel about it? You understand him?" Rybecki jerked his head toward Capshaw.

"Why, I think so," Schneider said, "some idea anyway. Let's go back to what we were talking about before Dr. Maines came in."

"Good idea," Rybecki said. He looked at Capshaw severely. "I thought when the call came to Homicide that maybe you'd done the job on him all by yourself, Cappy."

Capshaw sniffed.

"Well, I gave you the Smith and Wesson all intact. You've done a paraffin test on me. For Christ's sake, you know he blew his head off all by himself with that Goddamned Luger he killed Comalli with. What the Jesus are we sitting around mooning about it for? You're not looking for a murderer are you, Inspector?"

"No, I'm not," Rybecki said. "What are you going to write about it, Capshaw?"

"Not any more than I wrote about Comalli," Capshaw said. "That was on page three. This will be the same way."

The inspector shook his head sorrowfully. "Homicide never gets any good publicity."

Capshaw looked at him. "You think you ought to have some on this one?"

The inspector sucked at his gold incisors. "Well, no, I guess not."

"That's a good guess," Capshaw said. "All I'm going to say is that Inspector Rybecki, the famous nemesis of crime, solved this complicated case with his usual dispatch."

Rybecki looked at Capshaw speculatively. "Just what the hell is the matter with you, Capshaw? Guy can't say a word to you today without you coming around and snapping at his ass. Hell, you twist my tail plenty, but do I get nasty with you?"

Capshaw grunted. "O.K. I guess you're right. You've got a point. Killing anyone or anything is inclined to make me morose. Sorry."

"Aw, come off it, Cappy," Rybecki said. "I'm surprised you'd let it get to you. Can you help it if that queer mad son-of-a-bitch decides to blow his own head off? Better that way all around for everybody. Simplifies things a lot, don't it, Klaus?"

"Some ways." Schneider nodded.

"Well, thanks, gentlemen, for your commiseration," Capshaw said. "The fact remains, though, that I flipped the switch on him. Morally speaking, I killed him, because I left him with no way out but that. All he did was jam that Luger between his teeth and pull the trigger."

Capshaw poured himself a fast double shot of bourbon, downed it, and started getting out of the booth. "Well, I promised Pelly the Belly I'd let him know how I made out squaring the good doctor's libel suit against the *Record*. Haven't called him yet, so I guess I'd better go do that. Be a nice surprise for the Belly. See you, gentlemen."

The inspector and Klaus watched Capshaw's silent perfunctory thumbing of his nose at Chris as he went out the door.

16

It would have given Roy a great deal of mean satisfaction to know of Katy Winter's difficulties in adjusting to her rebound marriage with Preston Knox. Roy, of course, did not know this. And neither did anyone else, including Preston Knox, for quite some time. It could be said for Katy that she worked hard at concealing it, particularly from herself. But a common seed of matrimonial turmoil was there, and little by little it began to grow. This was the fact that Katy had married Knox out of hurt pride and the old feminine yearning for security. Her pride was assuaged and she got the security with the ring. But these, she began to see with a sickening realization, were not enough. The trouble was she did not love Preston. Nor was she going to be able to learn to. And no amount of security, she was gradually being forced to admit to herself, would compensate that unfortunate fact for her. This admission is very hard for a woman like Katy to make. And Katy took some time making it. It was particularly hard, because Preston Knox was, as husbands went, quite a catch for any woman on many counts.

Knox was a fair product of moneyed family background and sophisticated eastern schooling. He had the esoteric advantages of four years of preparatory at St. Paul's and another four at Princeton, where he had had his choice of undergraduate clubs. (He had taken Cannon—the best one, all things considered, at the time.) The years at St. Paul's and Princeton had more or less made him into what he was—a good, sound, Ivy League specimen. A gentleman, worldly, literate, impeccable of taste, and easy in any company. Those years, too, along with the family connections, had also given him an assured future. He had become in a remarkably short time vice president of the agency Katy worked for. There he was generally regarded as the man to watch as its ultimate chief. Preston Knox, however, was not without weakness.

One of them, acquired at college, was for the bottle. The other, acquired much later, was for the full-breasted, shapely legged brunette named Katy Winter who was his secretary.

When Pres Knox had suddenly married Katy, there had been a surprised arching of eyebrows over the announcement in some quarters. And in at least one, there had been some private, well-bred weeping. This was on the part of a post-debutante graduate of Bryn Mawr by the name of Isobel Leighton. It was a matter of common knowledge that Miss Leighton had been waiting for Pres Knox to make up his mind about her. And she had waited an inordinately long time. It took Isobel awhile, but she finally accepted the fact of the marriage.

And this was more than Katy herself was ever able to do. It was not that Katy did not try. She did. But her real feelings occasionally came out in spite of her determined suppression of them. The first time this happened was after she had been married less than a year. It was a signal event, particularly for Preston Knox. He was neither stupid nor insensitive, and, after it, he began an examination of Katy's attitude toward their marriage and himself. From this episode he got an ego-crumbling answer to something that had puzzled him considerably. This was Katy's unexpected lack of ardor for him. Katy gave him the explanation for this without even knowing it. And that is what made it one of the most damaging experiences of Preston Knox's well-assured, well-regulated life.

It happened in bed after they had closed the door on the last lingering guest of a farewell party for a friend. All evening long Knox had been watching Katy as she drank and milled through the separated knots of people that filled their apartment. She was pretty good at doing it too. Not the smooth hostess yet that she would be. But good enough. And as he watched her he was aware of sudden desire. He wanted her and he wished they all would go. And they finally did. By that time Knox was comfortably drunk, reasonably drunk, as drunk as a gentleman should ever get, but certainly no drunker, *le juste milieu* to use the French phrase for it. His wits and his charm were unimpaired, and so was his perception. He perceived that Katy was drunk too, drunker in fact than he had ever seen her, but certainly not showing it. It looked like she, too, had hit it exactly right—*le juste milieu*.

"Come on, Katy," he had said, after they all had gone, "to hell with this mess." He swept a hand around to include the shamble of glasses, plates, and coffee cups littered over everything, "Eulie's the best party maid in the business. She'll clean it up. Come on, let's go to bed."

"All right." Katy gave him a glazed smile. "That's a good idea. Let's do that."

Knox put his arm around her and they swayed out of the living room down the hall to the bedroom. At this point he realized that Katy was more drunk that he had thought—a good deal drunker. He would have preferred her just a little more sober for the lovemaking he had in mind.

Preston Knox as a lover was admirably restrained. He had learned the niceties of the ritual in a succession of affairs long before he ever married Katy, and his theory and practice of it were considerably beyond those of the usual spouse. He was, in fact, what could be called accomplished. And in this particular instance he took particular pains with his performance. Despite the intensity of his urge, he took an inordinate amount of time with it. The result was gratifying, for the peculiar reticence that he always sensed in Katy had, for once, apparently disappeared. She began to respond with an abandon that surprised and delighted him.

The moment of brutal truth for Preston Knox was at their precise acme of orgiastic action as Katy moved and moaned witlessly beneath him.

"Oh, Roy," her panting, half-smothered voice came up to him. "Roy! Roy . . ."

That was all. But it was enough. For Knox the revelation was almost instantaneous and crushingly complete—in *vino, veritas.*

The next morning across the breakfast table, Katy caught the serious, abstracted expression on Knox's face.

"What's the matter, Pres darling, is your head killing you?"

"No, my head's all right, Katy. How's yours?"

"Simply marvelous, considering. My, but it was drunk out last night, wasn't it? God, I've never been that way before in my life. Tell me, was I nice enough with the people?"

"You were very nice, Katy."

"And I didn't make any *faux pas* or do anything awful to embarrass you?"

Knox looked at her for a searching instant. "Now Katy, you weren't that drunk were you, that you don't remember?"

"Honestly, Pres, I spent the last two hours of our little whoop-to-do in a cloud. The last thing I remember was when everyone began leaving. After that, I don't remember anything. Now you've got me worried."

Knox looked at her and tried to make his smile convincing. "It was a damned nice party, Katy. Everybody said so. You took care of your end of things beautifully."

"I'm so glad, Pres," Katy said. "Good God though, Pres, I don't ever want to get that drunk again at any of our parties or anywhere else. I don't even remember going to bed . . ."

"I know you don't," Preston said, and picked up his coffee cup. Even with sugar the taste of it was somehow very bitter.

That revelatory party night put the relationship between Katy and Preston Knox beyond the point of any chance of return. The culmination was rapid and violent. On the day that it happened, Knox had awakened with the presaging discomfort of one of his sinus headaches. As the day wore on, the pain in his forehead and around his eyes became worse. By lunchtime it was a savage intensity. And at two o'clock Knox had thrown in the sponge and gone home to nurse it. The nagging hurt of it persisted in spite of the pills he had taken, so he had turned to some less specific medication. This was several drinks of Scotch whiskey. That had not helped much either. In fact the pain, the pills, and the liquor had only increased his general irritability.

Around five o'clock, when Katy got back from her appointment with the hairdresser, she found her husband still on the living-room sofa and still with a drink in his hand. She found, too, by a quick, almost automatic look at the bottle on the bar, that it was three quarters gone. She also found that the soup and sandwiches she had left for him had been left untouched. For some moments Katy stood over him looking down at his sprawling figure on the living-room sofa.

"Damn it, Pres," she said, "you said you were going to have a drink, one drink, eat something, and then go to bed. Why didn't you? Instead you're sitting around sucking on that Scotch bottle. Really, Pres! You drink too much anyhow."

"Look, Kate," Knox said, arching a brow at her, "let's just skip it, shall we? The one thing I don't need right now with this headache is a temperance lecture from you."

"You could do with one though, you know. A full course of them. You think your trouble is sinusitis. It's really not, Preston. It's too much Old Fairbairn Scotch."

That one stung him on the quick because there was more than a little truth in it. Ordinarily he would have probably let it pass. But he did not this time. The state of tension that had been quietly building between them since the night of Katy's unconscious revelation had been smoldering long within him. Now it had been sharpened considerably by over a half bottle of Old Fairbairn Scotch. Caught in the raw, Knox did pretty well.

"Listen, Kate," he said, taking away the heating pad he was holding to his forehead, "for some time now I've been fighting down the idea that I married a bitch. So stop trying to convince me that I have, will you?"

Katy's eyes narrowed as she looked at him. "I see. I'm a bitch now for trying to tell you the truth. Well at least I'm making progress in one direction or another—secretary to wife to bitch."

"Look, Kate"—Knox felt like a bull already pinked by the picador and now having to move against the barbs of a banderillo—"cut it out will you? I'm in no mood for any cuteness. Leave me alone, will you? I'll be just fine. Just go somewhere and be quiet. I hurt."

"I'm sure you do," Katy said mercilessly. "Truth has a way of hurting."

Knox suddenly reared up off the sofa. "Listen, Kate, are you going to shut up and leave me alone, or not?"

Katy regarded him coldly. "I'll be delighted to do that, Pres, when you've heard me out. It's high time that we—"

Knox got off the sofa and stumbled toward the chair where he had hung his coat. "Yeah. Maybe it is high time. But I'm certainly in no mood to do any listening to you or do any talking to you right now."

Katy watched Preston slowly and carefully take his coat off the chair and put it on.

"You're pretty drunk, you know, Pres," she said. "Wait a minute, I'll get my coat and come with you."

Knox, swaying a little, turned and looked at her.

"No, you won't, Kate. Get dressed up and go somewhere else with your pretty hairdo will you? Like the Charity Hospital maybe. Why don't you do that? But stay the hell away from me, will you? Just do that as a personal favor to me?"

Katy watched him adjust his tie and his pocket handkerchief and move toward the door.

"Where are you going, Pres?"

"Out," Knox said with his hand on the knob.

"Don't be childish, Pres," Katy said. "Where are you going?"

"Just out." He stood for an instant and looked at her and then closed the door behind him.

Among the many concrete symbols of Preston Knox's success was a Superna-Solari sports car. This one, the F-82, was a comparative rarity even among the fairly large fraternity of foreign-car enthusiasts. It was, as Knox was prone to casually point out to the curious, "a queer kind of job—three-fifty-horse Superna engine with a Solari custom body." It was like most similar prohibitively priced Italian imports made with the hand-tooled precision of a watch. And it looked it. Even standing still it gave the impression of being in motion. Its low-slung sleekness and streamlining made it look that way. And there was about it that almost evil impression of speed and power that all such cars have. Preston Knox's F-82 Superna was painted a beautiful lacquered black. It had a minimum of chrome fittings. It really belonged on a race track. Knox kept it perfectly tuned and adjusted and drove it constantly. Over the two years he had owned it he had gradually become familiar with it. Learning to drive it, and he had very sensibly taken not a little instruction in this, had been like his learning to ride a fast, soft-mouthed thoroughbred. That was not a bad analogy, as Knox was often to point out. There was the same difference between his Superna-Solari and any American standard car that exists between a spirited hunter and a docile saddle horse. Driving the Superna gave him a good deal of pleasure. And he had come to do it pretty well for a nonprofessional. He would never allow Katy behind the wheel of it in spite of her constant importuning.

"Goddamn it, Kate, I am not going to let you drive that automobile. You could get yourself killed in it. Later on, all right, when I can get time to go out with you in it and show you about it. I will when I get the time. But meanwhile just use the other car, will you please?"

After his acrimonious exchange with Katy, Knox took the elevator to the ground floor and left the building. Outside it was quite dark now. A light mist was gathering about the street lights and the sidewalks and asphalt were wet with the light, fitful fall of autumn rain.

Knox went to the garage and spoke to the night attendant. Five minutes later he was behind the wheel of his sinister black beauty.

"Bad night, ain't it, Mr. Knox?" Fred, the night attendant's face shone up at him as he stood on the ramp beside the car waiting for Knox to move out.

"Lousy, Fred."

"Guess you won't be able to rev it much—too slick on wet asphalt."

Knox was aware that Fred had caught the liquor on his breath and was politely cautioning him. "That's right, Fred. Have to take it easy."

"Yes, sir. You'll have to do that. This wet makes everything slicker'n glass. You got them heavy treads on though, that's good."

"Sure, Fred. Well, I'll be back pretty soon."

There was a break in the traffic outside the asphalt ramp and Knox slid into it. He had nowhere to go in particular. The mainstream of traffic was toward town and he fell in with it. Over the wetness of the street he had the pleasing sensation of floating on oil that the Superna always gave him. Most of the lights he caught and passed just as they were turning green. It was almost as if the innominate faces and vehicles in the sluggish welter of it were consciously moving aside for him. Knox enjoyed this. It gave him what he had certainly not been getting at home from Katy. As the traffic began to thin out on Grand Boulevard this feeling was interrupted by a car that suddenly cut in front of him two hundred yards before the next light. The light turned and, Knox, cursing, had to brake hard to avoid slamming into the back of it. He felt the rear wheels of the Superna lose traction on the wet pavement and slide a little before they took hold. Car in the right lane behind him narrowly missed his own back end. The car ahead, Knox noted, was a fire-engine red. "Standard make, juiced up with a smart aleck behind the wheel," he said to himself.

"That one needs a lesson," he thought, "and not having anything better to do, maybe I'll give it to him."

When the light turned the red car started to shoot into the half left turn that began the river road out of the city limits. Knox bore down on the accelerator. The Superna's wheels spun, caught, and he felt it almost leap out from under him. He shot around the red car on the left inside as if it were standing still. In the flash of the headlights he got a bare glimpse of the driver—a thin-faced adolescent wearing a beret. They were out of the main line of traffic and in another two minutes the traffic around them had thinned out to nothing. The two-lane stretch of the road with the white line down the center was now clear ahead of them. The red car was keeping dangerously close on his rear. Apparently he wanted to contest things. Knox eased on the accelerator. When it tried to pass on the left Knox gunned the engine just enough to keep ahead of it. Then there was another try on the right.

"Crazy bastard," Knox thought. He moved over just enough to keep it behind. The road ahead was now unreeling very fast. Gently Knox began weaving the Superna back and forth to prevent any further attempts at passing on either side. With this maneuver he began braking down. The speedometer and tachometer hovered on their dials and then began dropping back toward zero. Knox, aware that he was feeling a mean puerile kind of satisfaction, then proceeded to slow the Superna and the car behind to a humiliating fifty, then forty, and finally thirty miles an hour. And he kept it there for two or three minutes.

"Now you smart aleck little son-of-a-bitch in that red goat's nest of yours," Knox said to himself, "let's see who's got the juice."

His foot went down on the accelerator and the Superna left the crawling headlights behind as if they had been lamps on a horse-drawn buggy. A moment later he was around the first of the three curves of the River Road before it terminated at the state highway. On the short straightaway between that and the highway he was doing eighty.

"Made my point," he thought, "time to ease down."

He had started to do this for the second curve, which was now almost on him, when a small feeble light close to the ground came whizzing toward him on the left. The glare of the headlights swept over the figure of a boy on a bicycle. He got the impression of the young face turned toward him as he bulleted past. Almost instantly he was upon more lights like it ahead.

"Jesus Christ," Knox thought, "Boy Scouts on bicycles. What the hell are they doing out on a night like this? They ought to know better than to—"

Preston Knox never finished that thought. Directly ahead

of him, his lights caught another small figure, furiously peddling, crossing the road directly in his path less than sixty
yards ahead.

"Good God! I'm going to hit him. No! No! Hit anything—
do anything. But not that kid—not that kid—"

That was almost the last thing Preston Knox would remember for quite a while, for he slammed into his brake and
wrenched the wheel to the right. There was a hissing screech
as the heavy treads of the Superna missed, caught, missed
and caught, then missed again on the wet glaze of the road.
Knox would remember hearing this, and then the sensation
of the long looping skid the car made as it went by and slid
beyond the terrified little face on the bicycle. The ultimate
succession of sensations for Knox was of being for an instant
in space and turning over and over. Then there was a flat
crush of absolute darkness as the Superna hit the berm of
the road and rolled once, end over end, upside down to a
stop. Fortunately the Superna did not catch on fire.

Roy had spent many of his nights off duty as he was spending this one. That was alone in his room in a half-hearted attempt at desultory reading of the current surgical literature.
He had gotten through one or two recent periodicals, none
of which had given him much, and then had taken off his
uniform and gone to bed. For a while he had lain in the darkness thinking about Ransahoff and Ruth and how good things
were going to be for them. Then he had thought about Katy,
as he almost always did, and wondered what was going on
with her. Then he had thought about the wards and the next
day's operating schedule. Awhile before going to sleep he
had lain in the darkness listening to the noise outside. Then
he had gone to sleep. The persistent sound of the telephone
awakened him. The switchboard operator's voice came over
it.

"Dr. Maines, sorry to disturb you. But can you tell
me where I can reach Dr. Hand?"

"He's at a meeting or something at the Plaza Hotel. Why
don't you try there?"

"I have, Dr. Maines. He's not there and not at home
either. I know it's your night off, but seeing that you were in
anyway—"

"All right," Roy said, "I'll take the call for him. What's so
important anyway?"

"Emergency room," the operator said. "Just a moment, I'll connect you."

The harried voice of one of the emergency interns presently came on.

"Hello, sir, Dr. Hand?"

"This is Maines," Roy said. "Dr. Hand isn't available at the moment. I'll take it. What's the big problem?"

"Single car smash on the River Road just brought in, kind of bad—"

"How many?" Roy said levering himself up out of bed.

"Just one, but he doesn't look very good. And they told me I was supposed to call—"

"Never mind that," Roy said. "What the hell is the matter with him?"

"He's got some ribs on the left side and a real tight belly, and maybe a head injury."

"Is he in shock?"

"Well, maybe he's borderline—he doesn't look so good."

"All right," Roy said, "get him typed and cross-matched and start an intravenous on him."

"I've already done that, Dr. Maines."

"Well, good for you," Roy said. "I'll be around in a minute for a look at him."

Down in Room 8 of the emergency suite, Roy, with the intern at his elbow, looked and poked at the dirty mud-spattered form on the stretcher. By this time all of the filthy clothes had been cut from him and the man lay bare under a sheet. Roy went over him and stood away, with the intern still hovering at his side.

"Yeah," Roy said, "I think you're right. He does have something ruptured in his belly. We'll have to take him upstairs and see what's going on in there."

Roy skimmed through the sparse pages of the emergency-room record, mainly the time of injury and the laboratory report on the blood bank. The name, if he even glanced at it, did not register with him. Names made no difference anyway in the emergency room and he rarely bothered to look at them. It was what had to be done that counted. Knox's name, if he saw it at all, had not registered in his mind.

Two hours later he had done the necessary work on Preston Knox without knowing who he was and was on his way back to bed. In that two hours Roy had opened Knox's belly, sewn up his lacerated liver, repaired two perforations in his small intestine, and taken out his ruptured spleen. There had been, too, a split in the left diaphragm which Roy had had some difficulty in closing.

"Not bad," Roy thought as they were moving the inert but still living lump off the operating table. "Not as good or as fast as the Old Man or Wild Will Wortle would have done it. But not bad. He's big enough and tough enough to make it. He will."

In the dressing room he peeled out of his scrub clothes, took a shower, and went back to his room. When he got there the phone was ringing. Roy picked it up.

"Outside call, Dr. Maines."

An instant later a familiar voice came on—it was Capshaw's.

"Hello, Doc. Tried to get you before but you were still in the Goddamn abattoir."

"Just finished," Roy said. "How are you Cappy?"

"I want a little favor from you, Doc."

"Sure, Cappy, if I can. What?"

"I don't like to talk across open switchboards, Doc. I'm at Chris's. Come on over and we'll go into it along with a drink."

Ten minutes later Roy fanned through the door of the Asterion and sat down across from Capshaw, who had the drink waiting for him.

"Hello, Cappy," Roy said, "what's on your mind?"

"An official statement from you and your latest mission of mercy. This for the *Record*."

"Oh," Roy said, "that accident case I just finished. Why, he'll make it all right I think. Banged up to beat hell. Lacerations of the liver and spleen and a possible head injury. But I think he's going to do all right. That all? I could have told you that over the phone. I thought it was something very confidential like treating a dose of clap for you."

"Never had it and don't want it again." Capshaw chuckled and then looked at Roy quizzically.

"Roy, you son-of-a-bitch, I'm just beginning to realize what umplumbed depths there are in you. Next to your boss, the great Amos Abelard Hand, you've got the greatest damned talent for underplaying dramatic situations I've ever seen or heard of. Jesus, you're beautiful at it. You and the Old Man could both make a fortune doing *Hamlet*."

Roy looked at Capshaw in honest puzzlement. "Cappy, you

don't look drunk. And you don't sound drunk. But you sure as hell must be. I'm not. I'm stone sober. I'm listening intently and I can't follow you. What the hell are you talking about? You've lost me."

"Maines"—Capshaw looked at him intently, and Roy could almost see the beautifully meshed mechanism of Capshaw's mind working—"didn't doing that operation bother your psyche a bit—not even one little bit?"

"Why hell no," Roy said, "why should it bother me? That's my business. Why should it bother my psyche? The Old Man was at a meeting. They couldn't get him. I'm his senior surgical resident. So I took the call. I've done it before. That's routine." Roy put his glass down and looked at Capshaw. "What's so unusual about that?"

"Maines," Capshaw said, looking at him intently, "if I had a hat on I'd take it off to you like I take it off when the flag is passing. You son-of-a-bitch I believe you stand for something. Something real great like Mother, the Supreme Court, or the National Anthem. Come on now, Roy boy, didn't the fact that you were operating on Preston Knox bother you at all?"

"What?" Roy said. "Knox? Preston Knox? Sure. That's the guy who married Katy. What's that got to do with it?" Roy stopped and reflected. He recalled his superficial thumbing of the chart only to catch the essentials. And he had caught them well enough. At least he had gotten that muddy gasping piece of banged-up protoplasm off the table with a good chance of staying alive. And he had done it automatically almost. He had not looked at the first thing on the emergency sheet. That was the patient's name.

"You mean that poor banged-up son-of-a-bitch was Knox —Katy's husband?"

Capshaw looked at him intently.

"You thought it was just another unidentified John Doe, police accident case, huh?"

"That's right." Roy nodded his head. "I thought it was just another John Doe. I spent the time looking at him, not his chart. Half the time on those emergencies I don't know the patient's name till the next day on the ward."

"But didn't you recognize him? Didn't you know him? Hadn't you met him before?"

"Hell no," Roy said, "never saw him before in my life. I think I remember seeing his picture once on the society page.

But I wouldn't know him from Adam's off ox. But I never saw him before he married Katy or since."

"Well, you have now." Capshaw chuckled sardonically. "Makes you bosom buddies. Quite a story. Great human-interest angle. May get me the Pulitzer Prize if I do it right. Let's see what'll I use for a headline—*Doctor Cuts Rival's Guts.* Tell me something, Doc. Would it have made any difference to you if you'd known who he was?"

"Like what?"

"Like being nervous about doing the operating?"

Roy reflected briefly. "I don't think so. Why should it? The poor bastard had to be cut as soon as possible. They couldn't reach the Old Man. I was around so I did it. When somebody's belly has to have the steel stuck in it, and you're there, what difference does it make whose belly it is, as long as you can help him by doing it?"

Capshaw sat back regarding him with the first smile of its kind Roy had ever seen on his face. Most of Capshaw's smiles were like his words and his writing, tinged with a certain cynicism and bitterness. There was nothing of either in this one. It was a surprising expression for Capshaw, with something akin to tenderness in it.

"That your personal surgical philosophy, Doc?"

"Sure," Roy said, "what's wrong with it?"

"Nothing," Capshaw said. "It's a nice one for a guy who cuts people for a living to have. Did you figure it out all by yourself, Doc?"

"I don't know," Roy said, "probably not. I guess it's like everything else I ever learned about the theory and practice of the trade. I'm damned sure that's the way the Old Man feels about it. So I probably picked up the idea from him."

Capshaw nodded. "Well, Doc, it's a nice idea no matter where you got it. It's a real nice idea for a guy like you to have. I hope to Jesus you keep it. One good idea like that can make up for a lot of bad ones."

Roy put down his glass and looked at Capshaw. "Cappy what the hell is this? You didn't get me over here for any thin-ice philosophical discussion. That's certain. Now what—"

"That's right," Capshaw said, "I wanted your end of what turns out to be a pretty damned good story on what happened with a guy called Preston Knox. I've got your end and I pretty much know what went on with him before that—courtesy of the Police Department."

"Well," Roy said, "I just got him off the operating table. He married my girl right under my nose. So naturally I'm interested. How did he wind up as a police case at the Charity?"

Capshaw rubbed a hand over the twenty-four hour stubble on his thin jowls. "Before you got him, Doc, he turned over four times in his car on the river Road. He made junk out of fifteen thousand dollars' worth of that Italian sports bomb he owns and was driving. He might have been a little drunk—"

"Well," Roy said, "he's not the first rich drunk who—"

Capshaw held up his hand. "Wait a minute, Doc. Let me finish so you'll get all the picture. He wasn't just a rich drunk in a souped-up sports job. Matter of fact, from the way the boys over at headquarters in the Traffic Division put it together, he comes off looking real good. A gang of kids on bicycles were on the road and he deliberately piled up to keep from killing one of them. It's apparently true from at least one eyewitness account. That was from some young jerk who had been trying to pass him."

Roy's hand lingered over his glass. He raised it and put it down.

"Well, good," Roy said, "I'm glad Katy married a hero. From what you say he must be one. First hero I ever operated on. And isn't it nice that Katy got herself one?"

"Come on, Doc," Capshaw said, "don't try to be cynical, will you? Doesn't become you. You did a real good job. So did he, it looks like. Leaving your girl Katy out of it, wouldn't this make you think he was a pretty nice guy?"

"You make him sound like one," Roy said. "Tell me, Cappy, are you related to him in any way? You're not his half brother or cousin or anything?"

"No," Capshaw said, "nobody in our family ever had his kind of dough or pedigree. We're strickly bums you know. Particularly me, the last of the line. Always have been from way back. How about a hamburger and some coffee, Doc?"

Roy sat back in the booth and looked at Capshaw. "Sure. Let's have the hamburgers and the coffee, Cappy. What the hell did you get me over here for? On the phone it sounded pretty Goddamned important."

"For Christ's sake it is or was," Capshaw said. "It's a great story. I wanted to know all of it. Now I do."

"What the hell are you going to do, Cappy? Splatter the whole Goddamn maudlin business over page two of the *Record*? Is that it? With pictures at the scene?"

Capshaw looked at Roy, finished his drink, and looked at him again.

"Roy, boy, your trade is the knife. Mine is the pen. Too bad you're not a general, then you'd have a sword and we could fulfill the old maxim 'The pen is mightier than the sword.' But you do your good or your mischief with a stinking little bit of a blade, don't you? A little bit of steel no longer than my pencil point, or maybe just as long. You can carve all day with it on some poor unconscious son-of-a-bitch and do him great good. Like your friend Knox for instance. And I, with my pen, which is a hell of a lot duller and less learned than your instrument, can ruin you and everything you've done or tried to do with a word—or maybe several words. The thing is people don't see what you do. But they usually look at what I write. See what I mean? The *Record* has three hundred and fifty thousand circulation."

"Sure," Roy said, "now about this thing with Knox. You're not going to make anything big out of it are you, Cappy? Jesus, I'll tell you if you do, I'll have to quit. The Old Man won't have any publicity about himself and/or anyone under him—"

"Don't tell me anything about the Old Man," Capshaw said. "I know Amos Abelard Hand very well and his aversion to any kind of publicity. I know how he hates it. And I know what he'll do to avoid it. So just don't worry about it will you? I'm old at the game, Doc. It's more important to know about anything than to write about it. This Goddamn business with Knox's accident will be discreet, Doc. I'll see that it gets in there that way. The thing is that I know what happened. I may not write about it, but I could, because I know."

Chris stood at the booth with their sandwiches and coffee. "Let's have it, Chris boy," Capshaw said.

Capshaw ate ravenously and between bites looked up at Roy.

"Look, Doc, don't you ever worry about anything I write—nothing I write will ever hurt you."

Roy's first postoperative visit to Preston Knox was made in company with the Old Man. Roy stood by with the chart while the Old Man completed the meticulous ritual of examination he always went through with all cases just operated. Knox had the usual washed-out look of brittle waxiness that comes from blood loss and severe injury. Otherwise he seemed to be doing relatively well. He lay, eyes closed, head and torso in semielevated position, an intravenous needle in one arm and a blood-pressure cuff on the other. The Old Man finished listening to his chest and gently feeling his belly, and turned to Roy.

"Good enough," the Old Man said. "Watch him for ileus. If he starts to distend get a tube down him right away. He's got a little congestion in the base of his left lung. Go easy on the morphine."

"Yes, sir," Roy said.

At this point Knox opened his eyes.

"Gentlemen," he said thickly, looking first at the Old Man and then at Roy.

"Well," the Old Man said, "you're awake, are you? How do you feel?"

"Like I'd been through a Goddamned cement mixer," Knox said. "How am I doing?"

"Pretty well, Mr. Knox," the Old Man said. "I'm Dr. Hand. This is Dr. Maines."

"You're my doctors," Knox's head slowly nodded. He considered something very far away for a moment and then turned his gaze slowly on Roy.

"You must be Dr. Maines."

"That's right, Mr. Knox."

Knox, from his cloud of morphine, continued to look at Roy. "I remember you from somewhere, Dr. Maines. Just give me a minute and I'll have it."

"I saw you last night when they brought you in, Mr. Knox."

Knox kept on looking at Roy out of the placid distance of his morphine.

"Yes, yes. Now I remember. You were trying to do something for me I think, when all those people were around, where the bright lights were. You're a nice guy, Dr. Maines."

Knox continued to look at Roy and nod slowly. "Dr. Maines. So you're Dr. Maines."

"Just take it easy, Mr. Knox," Roy said. "Why don't you lie back now and get a little sleep?" Roy turned to the Old Man:

"Ready to go, sir? We've still got the ward cases to look at."

They were turning from the bed when the door opened and the floor supervisor came into the room.

"Dr. Hand. Mrs. Knox is outside in the waiting room. She'd like to know about her husband."

"You talk to her, Roy," the Old Man said. "I'll meet you down on the ward."

"Sir," Roy said, feeling a nameless kind of panic beginning to stir in him, "if you don't mind I think she probably would want to talk to you. I'll go on down to the ward and wait for you."

The Old Man's half-lidded eyes cut into him for a fraction of a second, a little dark with displeasure. "This is your case, isn't it, Maines? You operated him, didn't you?"

"Yes, sir, but I thought—"

"Never mind what you thought. Did you do anything in that operating room that you might be ashamed to talk about to anybody?"

"No, sir," Roy said.

"All right," the Old Man said, "it looks like you did pretty well. Go out there and talk to this man's wife. What's the matter with you?"

The Old Man gave him a slashing glance and left the room. Roy turned to follow him. What stopped him was a feeble voice from the supine figure in the bed.

"Dr. Maines, Dr. Maines."

Roy turned and went back to the stand at the bedside.

"You're the one who did the job on me—the operation?"

"That's right, Mr. Knox," Roy said.

He stared at Roy with his morphine-fixed pupils for some time with Roy feeling strangely uncomfortable looking back at him. Knox slowly nodded his head. "Yes. It would have to be that way. You know this world is the Goddamnedest place I've ever lived in."

Knox's eyes crinkled a little and his bloodless lips came up in a faint smile. Roy felt himself smiling too.

"Often felt that way myself, Mr. Knox."

"Name's Pres, Doctor."

"All right, Pres."

"I suppose I'm going to make it. Am I?"

"You're going to make it. Take a little while. But you're going to make it just fine, Pres."

Knox closed his eyes briefly and opened them again. "That's good. I'll count on it."

"You do that, Pres. You're going to be all right."

Knox slowly brought his waxen right hand from under the sheets and held it out toward Roy. Roy took it.

"Thanks, Dr. Maines, for all of it—for everything. Appreciate it. Appreciate it. Try to show you that sometime. Right now I . . ."

"Right now is a good time for you to get some more sleep," Roy said, slowly disengaging his hand from Knox's.

"That's easy, that's very easy," Knox's voice tailed off with his closing eyes.

Roy stood looking down on him for several seconds before he went out and shut the door behind him.

In the waiting room Katy Winter Knox had been sitting spastically smoking one cigarette after another for almost an hour. She was in the act of lighting another one when Roy came in.

The months of separation and silence between them was concentrated in the first sharp instance in which they stood there silently appraising each other. In the flash of it Roy saw that Katy was thinner, surprisingly older, and her thin body more tense. But still the same Katy. And Roy felt the old familiar churning at the pit of his ribs as he looked at her.

"Hello, Katy," he said self-consciously, and put out his hand. "How are you?"

The damp grip of her hand had some tremor in it. "Hello, Roy," she said. "How is he? May I see him?"

"Sure," Roy said, "sit down a minute and let me tell you how things are with him."

Roy steered her to a chair and took another across from her.

"He is going to be all right isn't he, Roy?" Her face strained anxiously at him through its careless makeup. "He's not going to die or anything? Or be crippled for the rest of his life or anything like that?"

Roy felt his self-possession rapidly dwindling and with it the tendency to make everything with Katy as casual as possible.

"He's going to be all right, Katy," he said. "That's the Old Man's opinion as well as mine. He's going to have to stay around in the hospital awhile and he might keep a little limp for sometime because of those fractures. I doubt that it will ever be permanent."

Roy gave the supplementary details on Knox's injuries and

what had been done about them. Katy listened to him abstractedly and without interruption.

"And I guess that about covers it, Katy," he concluded.

"Roy"—he saw her eyes tear suddenly—"are they, the police I mean, are they going to hold him or prosecute him, when he's well enough—when he's out of this?"

"Hold him on charge for the accident, you mean? Why no. Why should they?"

"Well, you see—this is all confidential isn't it Roy—what we're saying?"

"Of course, Katy—all privileged communication—patient to physician, and all that. Why, what's the matter?"

"Well, you see, I know Pres had been drinking just before it happened and he could have been—well—I don't know how much, but he could have been drunk and, well, it was all my fault that he had been, and I've been thinking what they do to drunken drivers if they don't happen to kill themselves."

"Wait a minute, Katy," Roy said, looking at her quizzically, "didn't they tell you how this happened?"

"No. Just that an accident happened and that he's down here in critical condition. So I came right down without knowing anything else, you see—"

"I see," Roy said. "Well, I don't know anything about his drinking and neither do the police. That I can tell you. I can also tell you what the official report of the accident is according to several witnesses. And that is that he was doing about eighty miles an hour on a wet road when a kid on a bicycle pulled out in front of him and he deliberately threw the car into a spin and off the road to avoid hitting him and Goldamned near got killed doing it."

The tears were running freely down Katy's cheeks now, making rivulets through the rouge and powder and streaking the mascara. She began groping in her small ineffectual handbag and got out a handkerchief.

"They didn't tell me any of that. All they said was . . ." Katy began dabbing her eyes. Roy had a cleanly laundered handkerchief in the pocket of his white tunic, which was rare. He longed to pull it out and give it to her to use instead of the pitiful lace doily she was using but he didn't.

"Well," he said, "don't worry about any legal complications, Katy. There aren't going to be any. As a matter of fact, aside from being pretty well busted up, he looks real good, particularly for what he did."

Katy turned her tear-smeared face up at him. "He's a really very nice guy, you know, Roy. He really is. And I've been such a bitch with him."

"Yes," Roy said, "I think you've got yourself a real nice guy there, Katy. Now look. Why don't you go on in there and see him? Don't stay too long. Right now he needs his rest, and remember, anything he says, he's saying through a cloud of morphine about two feet thick. Go ahead in and see him."

Katy stood there with her smeared face looking at him for a second or two. "He is really quite a guy, isn't he Roy, don't you think?"

Roy looked at her and suddenly understood the question and what was behind it very well. "Yes, he is, Katy. You married quite a guy. Go on in there and see him. Room 815, three doors down on the right."

He watched her sexy, hip-swinging walk to the door. Before she went out of it, she stood in its aperture looking at him.

"Thank you, Roy. You're a real nice guy yourself. I guess I never knew that."

"Why hell, Katy," Roy said, smiling mirthlessly, "I can't help it, I'm an honor Boy Scout, thrifty, brave, clean, reverent. And helpful at all times. Why don't you get on down there and see him?"

She closed the door behind her as she left the room. For a little while after she had left Roy stood at the window looking down at the entering congestion of traffic on the corner of Velle and St. Marks. The night subdued street, honk and traffic of it, rafted to him through the filtered silence of the room. He still had evening rounds to make and then his final report about them to the Old Man. He turned from the window. Katy's lipstick-stained cigarette, almost burned out, was smoldering in one of the ashtrays. He picked it up, puffed at it, and held it till it began burning his fingers.

"Goddamn it," he thought, still feeling the knot in his belly lessening a little, "she's not the most beautiful one I ever saw. She's not the smartest. And she is certainly not the most sympathetic. She's married now, and as it turns out, to a pretty nice kind of guy. Why the hell does it have to be this way? Why can't I stop feeling this way? All I have to do is look at her and I turn into pure aching mush inside."

He stood at the window a little longer looking out across the frantic intercourse of evening traffic twisting and honking along St. Marks Street. He looked at it and the grim and graying façade of the Criminal Courts building with its brooding seated figure of Justice, blindfolded, with sword and scales.

"Justice and love," Roy thought, "both of them blinder than Goddamn bats. The Greeks had it about right."

He ground the cigarette out in the ashtray and went down to make evening rounds on the wards.

Preston Knox's well-fleshed, well-cared-for body had done extremely well through his convalescence. His recovery was a good deal more rapid than either the Old Man or Roy had thought possible. He healed solidly and Roy took out his stitches two days ahead of the normal time and sent him to physiotherapy. In the descent of days he progressed from bed to a wheel chair and finally graduated to crutches and finally full ambulation with a cane. In this time, Knox had had a good deal of time to think about himself, and for the first time in his life, about those who were in one way or another concerned with it. This thinking, largely done in the long hours that he lay or sat in bed, between the visits of the Old Man and Roy, or Katy's faithful sojurns with him, had become more introspected. It was a good deal more analytical about himself than it had ever been. So much so, that by the time Knox was almost ready to leave the Charity and continue his recovery on his own, he could look at himself and at his own personal reality as something other than a nicely growing cultivated creature in an ordained hot house of assured success and security. Once he felt and understood this, Knox began not only to push but to explore his new found identity. This was noted when Katy came to see him on the day when he had first been allowed to walk unaided with a cane.

Katy had come, as she commendably did during his illness, at regular visiting hours and sat by him.

"You walked by yourself with your cane today, Pres, and they say you are going to be out of here maybe in a week."

"That's right, Kate," Knox said. "Dr. Hand said that and so did Roy Maines. So I guess it must be right. I will be getting out—"

"Well, I've been planning on it. We got a good private-duty nurse for you when you come home, I've got things all ready for that."

Knox lay for some moments without saying anything, and looked out of the window that was ten stories up from the mass and swarm that was the corner of St. Marks and Velle streets. The words that he spoke scalded his throat.

"Kate," he said, "I don't know whether this is the time to say it. You've been pretty good, you know, through all of this. And you know, Kate, that I'd like to be pretty good, or at least back like it was, pretty good myself."

"You are pretty good, Pres. And not just pretty good either. Very good."

Katy began an ineffectual groping in her bag for a handkerchief.

"Well, I'm glad you think so, Kate. You've asked me a lot of times if there were anything that you could do for me. Well, there is now. And I'd like you to do it. Not just one, but a couple of things. The first thing is, I want you to divorce me as soon as you can."

"Pres—"

"I mean it," Knox said. "Just do that for both of us will you? Granted I'm not any Freud or any Jung. But I don't have to be to figure out what our trouble is."

"Pres—"

"Now wait a minute, Katy. I know that you haven't been cheating on me with him. And that thought used to concern me—it doesn't any more. I know that you haven't seen him since we've been married or even since I've been hurt. But still Katy, I'm a cuckcold. The worst kind, too, a spiritual cuckold because he's always in your mind no matter what. Do you think I don't know that every time we get in bed together what's happening? That he's right in there with us, and between us? And the only thing probably that makes our consummation durable for you is that you're thinking about him as we squirm and pant? Don't you think I know that? And—"

"Pres"—Katy made an only partially successful effort to control her rising agitation—"that's the most bitter, most unfair thing you've ever said to me. I've—"

Knox continued to regard her steadily. "Also one of the truest, Katy."

The tears that had been imminent in Katy's eyes began welling out of them and she sat head down, unable to contain them. Knox pulled a handkerchief from his robe pocket and handed it to her.

"Here, use this, and listen to me Kate, will you? I didn't know it and neither did you when we stood up together for better or worse. I think we both got married in good faith. I know you did and I'm damned certain I did. But, Kate, it didn't work out and it never will because of one big fundamental trouble which neither one of us knew at the time. And it's something neither one of us could do very much about, you see. Things like that take awhile to learn—"

"Things like what, Pres?" Katy said in a stifled voice.

"I was talking about the trouble with our marriage—with us, Kate."

"I know, go on—"

"The trouble was and is, Kate, that I'm not Roy Maines. That's the plain bald Goddamned truth of it . . ."

Knox looked at her bowed head and shaking shoulders as she sat before him, and then went on. "And now that we both understand that, well, Kate, let's quit wasting each other's lives over conscience and conventionality, shall we? Let's do that, and get ourselves untangled real fast so that we can get back to some kind of honest living again. Don't you think that's right for us, Kate?"

There was no answer.

"Well, I do," Knox went on. "And let's start out right here with this, whatever you want to call it, moment of truth. Let's do that, Kate, shall we?"

No answer.

"Now look, there's a war on. We're not actually in it, but we're certainly going to be. And when we are, it's going to tear a lot of things up the front and down the middle. And some people are going to have a lot less time and choice than they think. I'm sure that Roy Maines is going to be one of them. And I believe you ought to think about that, Kate. You love this guy. I think you ought to have some time with him. So if you'll just listen to me and cooperate I'm going to try to arrange that for you."

Katy got out of her chair and stood for a moment, and with the handkerchief to her nose, looking out of the window.

"Is that the way you want things, Pres?"

"That's the way I want them," he said. "Now as to the actual legal mechanics, I guess it's simple enough—immediate separation first, and then divorce, and you get it anyway you like. I'll go along with whatever it is. I've already spoken to my legal eagles. You know, Rybund, Sloane, and Kleet—call them tomorrow, Kate. Now, why don't you go on home and get some sleep. I'd like to. I'm pretty tired."

Katy suddenly turned from the window, and wordlessly moved to Knox where he lay on the bed and kissed him full on the mouth. He lay back savoring the full honesty of it as he watched her go out of the door.

As Knox continued to mend, surgical rounds for him became more or less a routine formality. During them, except for brief examination and inquiries, the talk was general and irrelevant, most of it about the incessant war reports coming in over the radio. Knox who had nothing to do now except read or listen to them, spent a good deal of his time monitoring these and reflecting on them. The Old Man and Roy, neither of whom had time for anything but an occasional evening news broadcast, listened to his comments about them whenever they came. Not infrequently the Old Man addressed Knox jocularly:

"Well, Mr. Heater, what's the news now? You agree with Mr. Kaltenborn and Mr. Thomas that things look pretty dim generally? We haven't made any formal declaration yet, have we? Yesterday you said it would be anytime now—"

"Not yet, chief," Knox said, "but the supermen have just put another strike over on the home team. Won't be anytime now till we'll have to get off of the bench and save the bacon."

"There's no doubt about that," the Old Man said. "I heard the tail end of the broadcast last night saying all units of the regular Reserves have been alerted and some with assembly and movement orders—"

"That's right. I caught that one too. Incidentally"—Knox looked at Roy and the Old Man—"I'm not going to be so busted up when I get out of here that I can't pass a service physical, am I? I'm in the Reserves myself."

"That so?" the Old Man said. "Which of its many incompetent and undertrained branches?"

"Navy. I don't know what the hell branch. I signed up when I graduated from college. I'm quite a sailor—held the wheel a couple of times on a forty-foot sloop race around the Block Island light—"

"Ah yes," the Old Man said, "Naval Reserves are you? Well, that's the gentlemen's service—the Navy, so I don't know anything about it. Being a peasant, I was a foot soldier in the last one. Right through the Soissons offensive, we were armed with rakes and bats. But I can tell you one thing, Knox. You won't have to worry about passing a service physical even if we send you there with crutches and a bedpan. When the time comes they'll take you in the Navy just like they do in the Army. All you have to be is warm and breathing. You'll be that all right."

"You make the service sound like a real pleasure, chief," Knox said, grinning. "Gives me a lot of assurance, too—knowing that there will be a lot of guys like me in it."

The Old Man grunted and would have said something else. A knock on the door and the appearance of the floor nurse interrupted whatever it was.

"Urgent personal phone call for you, Dr. Hand."

"See you on the ward, Roy," the Old Man said, following her out.

"See you, Pres," Roy said, turning to go.

"Can you give me another couple of minutes, Doc?"

"Why sure," Roy said. "What's on your mind?"

"You and the Old Man are always in such a hell of a rush all the time. Sit down a minute. I won't keep you long."

Roy took the chair by the bed.

Up until then Knox had not been sure just how to say it. But in that moment he decided on a direct approach.

"Have you seen Kate at all, Doc?"

Roy looked at him sharply. "We run into each other in the hall once in awhile when she comes in to see you. Why?"

"I mean to talk to?"

"We say hello. That's about it."

"Then she probably hasn't told you—Kate and I are getting a divorce, Doc. As of today we're legally separated."

Knox, smiling faintly, took a legal-looking envelope from the bed table and held it up. "This dispatch from Messrs. Rykund, Sloane, and Kleet, attorneys at law, came in my mail yesterday making it official."

For several seconds Roy returned Knox's steady half-quizzical gaze.

"Thought you might like to know that, Doc."

"Did you?" Roy said stiffly. "It's hardly any of my business, is it?"

"Yes, Doc. I think it is. You and Kate—"

Roy suddenly got out of his chair. His voice was tense and with an edge to it that made Knox wince inwardly.

"Look, Knox, I guess I get it. And if you think that Katy and

I have been together while you've been laid up here in the hospital or any other time—if you think—"

"Goddamn it, Doc," Knox said, "no, you don't get it. I don't think anything of the sort and I didn't mean to imply it. I know Kate has always been straight with me. So have you. Now I'm trying to be straight with you and Kate. So give me half a chance will you? Sit down, you oversensitive bastard, and just listen to me. This is quite an event for me. It's one of the two or three times in my life out of all the chances I've had that I'm trying to think of somebody else instead of myself. I've got a pretty late start, but just this once, anyway, I'd like to be a nice guy. Sit down, Doc—"

Roy sat down again.

"Now look. Kate and I are getting this divorce strictly on grounds of mutual incompatibility. That and no other reason. There's no question of infidelity, see? Nor any implication of it. Nobody's cuckold before the law. Kate and I are just plain incompatible—are now and always have been. I hope I've got that through to you—"

"Go on," Roy said.

"Well, like any two sensible people should under the circumstances, we decided to stop making each other unhappy and call it quits. Now we have it"—Knox waved a hand toward the legal envelope on the bed table—"all wrapped up. All legal. Kate can do what she wants to. So can I. As of right now."

Roy, sitting there listening, still tense, but a lot less so, waited for him to go on. He did presently.

"I'm telling you this, Doc, because people waste a lot of good living time suckling their pride. And false pride at that. Christ, that's the story of my life. I've been one of the all time champions at it. Kate's another one—she's a pride-feeling time waster like me—I guess all women are.

"The point is she'd never tell you about what's with us. So I thought I'd better just do that to save us all some time—"

Knox stopped again and grinned wryly at him.

Roy, relaxed now, and looking at Knox with something akin to admiration, said, "Who are you doing this for, Knox? Katy? Me? You?"

Pres's grin spread wider. "Why Goddamn it Doc, as I said, I'm doing it for everybody. Katy, you, and me." Knox threw his head back and laughed. "Mostly for me, though, I guess. It's taken a ruptured spleen, some busted guts, and a lot of reflection in this trap to find out that I can be a pretty good guy. Or anyway try to—"

"I think you've made it," Roy said, "on a couple of counts. Now about Katy—"

"Free as a bird, Doc. Just like me. But she won't start anything with you. You'll have to come up with the first pass. If I were you I'd do that pretty quick. We've got a war coming up and—"

The phone on the bedside table began an almost steady ringing. Knox picked it up.

"Yep, he's here," Knox pushed the phone toward Roy.

The Old Man's voice twanged through irritably into Roy's ear. "Where the hell are you Maines? I've been down here on the ward waiting for you for ten minutes."

"Be right down, sir. Right away."

Roy cradled the phone. "The Old Man," Roy said. "Look, Pres, I—"

"Never mind that," Knox said. "I guess now we understand each other don't we?"

"Yes," Roy said, "talk to you later. Can't keep the king waiting though."

"No," Knox said, "for Christ's sake don't do that. But talk to Kate, will you?"

Knox put out his hand and Roy took it.

"I will," Roy said. "Thanks, Pres."

Knox watched Roy's lean white-clad figure out of the room and the door closed behind it. Then for a while he lay back in his bed looking out and down at the swarm and moil of pedestrians and vehicles on St. Marks Street.

17

That Sunday Roy slept in a good deal later than usual. His Saturday night on call in emergency and in the operating room had been one sustained madhouse stretch of frantic activity. One of those sudden unaccountable deluges of drunk, diseased, and demolished protoplasm had hit the Charity's doors beginning at about seven o'clock in the evening and had kept bulging against them until three in the morning.

Some of it could be attributed to the weather. A fine wind-driven snow turning to sleet had converted the city streets to a glare of ice. On it the old, the drunken, and the pedestrians had slipped and fallen. And drivers slid through lights and intersections and crashed into each other. Then, too, there were some disastrous conventions in town which were notoriously traumatic. One of these was the National Legionaires, which met in solemn and sodden assembly to elect another commander in their usual violent drunken democratic style. Most of the Charity's emergency-room customers had come from them. But there had been some formidable additions from a local convening of the Federated Ethical Morticians of America and the Brotherhood of National Janitors who were passing resolutions or electing somebody. In any case the Charity emergency was swamped and overflowing with the hurt, vomiting, puking lot of them.

One of the high points of it for Roy was when he had been specially summoned by an intern to Room 7 of the emergency suite.

"We got a son-of-a-bitch claims you're his doctor," the intern said. "Got a nice one right over his eye. It will take about ten stitches, but he won't let us touch him till he sees you or his lawyer. Want to look at him, Doc? He's not too drunk—"

Roy followed the intern into Room 7 to a stretcher on which a thin little man lay restrained by the canvas belt about his hands and feet.

Roy looked at his bleeding face and his indignity and recognized him at once.

"For Christ's sake," Roy said, so pleased that he could hardly contain himself, "Lopardi! Well, well, the maestro of Elite Funerals. What the hell happened to you? Drunk on your own embalming fluid?"

"Please, Dr. Maines," Lopardi said with admirable dignity under the circumstances, "I am not drunk. I was at the Hotel Lewellens, where our convention is, in a discussion with some delegates from out of town. We were minding our own business when a group of Legionaires came into the bar and started making insulting remarks about our profession and—"

Roy chuckled evilly. "O.K., Lopardi. I get the picture. You got wounded defending the honor of the Federated Morticians of America. You'll probably get cited for this, Lopardi, for gallantry above and beyond the call of money. Get the

order of the Golden Chisel—maybe with Crossed Coffins.
Incidentally, did the guy have brass knuckles? That's a pretty
nice slice you've got there. Now lie still while I suture it up."

Lopardi's face took on an expression of even greater anxiety. "Dr. Maines please could you do a real nice job so it
won't look bad and have a scar? And so I can cover it up with
some Maskex or something? I got a real big funeral tomorrow—"

"Why, you little bastard," Roy said. "Are you insinuating
that I ever do anything else but the most artistic work? Even
on drunken undertakers?"

"Dr. Maines, I didn't mean—"

"I know what you meant," Roy said, eyeing the situation
briefly. "Now shut up and lie still while I restore your famed
beauty for your big death dance tomorrow. I'm going to lay
a shot of novocaine in there so you won't feel anything."

Lopardi's large dark eyes continued to regard Roy plead-
ingly. "And please, Dr. Maines, would you please use real fine
dermal suture and a subcuticular stitch, so it won't show, I
mean."

"Why you vain little son-of-a-bitch," Roy snarled at him
gleefully, "are you going to lie there and try to tell me how
to fix your skimpy skull? Is that it?"

"Dr. Maines, I was just suggesting—"

"Telling grandmother how to knit socks, eh, Lopardi?" Roy
said happily. "Well one more word out of you and I'll let
one of the interns do it. They all need experience, particularly
Bill Shambauger. He's an ex-hockey player. Should have
stayed with the game—handles all instruments like they
were hockey sticks."

"Dr. Maines." Lopardi said in a stricken voice, "I didn't
mean nothing. Aren't you please going to do it yourself, Dr.
Maines, please? I asked for you Dr. Maines because you're
the best there is here at the Charity and—"

"All right, Lopardi," Roy said, pleased in spite of himself.
"I will on one condition. And that is the next time or any other
time there's a doubtful consent on an autopsy you'll cooperate instead of—"

"I will, Dr. Maines. I honest to God will, I promise. I'll do
everything I can to get—"

"O.K.," Roy said. "Now just lie still and shut up."

Roy turned to the open suture tray on the Mayo stand
and began putting on the gloves. That had been at two-

thirty that Sunday morning and Roy had had three calls after
he had watched Lopardi move unsteadily out to a waiting
taxi. He had finally fallen into bed at five and slept till two
in the afternoon. Then he went to the Asterion to eat.

At that hour on Sundays, the Asterion was invariably
empty and it was now except for one lone customer. This was
Capshaw. Capshaw was not in his usual place in the back
booth, but standing beside Chris at the bar. Chris had put his
portable radio on the counter between them. And Roy came
up in time to catch the peculiarly tense voice coming out of it.

"And that concludes for the moment the official news re-
leases. For further developments as they occur stay tuned to
this station." There was an immediate transition to the soft
sounds of a string quartet. Both Capshaw and Chris looked
at Roy with curiously serious expressions and their greeting
was singularly subdued.

Roy looked from one to the other of them. "Well," Roy
said, "what am I interrupting, some kind of a radio church
service? Chris, how about a fast double order of bacon and
eggs and some coffee right away?"

Chris looked at him somewhat blankly and nodded and
kept standing there. Capshaw frowned.

"Doc, you're a facetious bastard," Capshaw said.

"No, just hungry," Roy said. "Boy, last night was one to
take the rag off the bush. We had everything over there in
the Goddamn flesh pot, even Lopardi. I took twelve stitches
through his sconce. Sit down with me Cappy while I eat
and I'll tell you about it—"

Capshaw continued to survey him critically. "Doesn't anything get through to you, Doc, except what happens in your
own little personal world over there in the lazar house? Don't
you know what this means?"

"Don't I know what what means?" Roy said, looking at Capshaw confusedly. "Just what the hell is the matter with you
and Chris anyway?"

"Where have you been, Doc—anesthetized?"

"Not quite," Roy said. "I got to bed at five this morning
after wading around emergency in mud and blood for twelve
hours. Slept for another nine. I woke up hungry and came
over here. Why?"

Capshaw arched a look at Chris. "Hasn't heard I guess.
That explains it."

Chris nodded solemnly. "I'll go get your order ready, Doc."

"Yeah," Capshaw said, "let's sit right here at the bar, Doc. I'll have a little more bourbon while you have breakfast. And I'll tell you how the world's exploded while you've been over there in the pesthouse dead-ass asleep—Chris, have that God-damn radio turned up."

Chris went back to the Asterion's kitchen. The little box radio between them went on with the sweet monotonous sounds of Haydn chamber music. Chris almost immediately brought two cups of scalding hot coffee and set them down before Roy and Capshaw.

"Eggs and the rest in a minute," Chris said.

Capshaw turned to Roy. "War, Doctor, we're finally in it. Not that we haven't been right along, but now we've got to admit it."

"What?"

"That's right. Early this morning the Japanese bombed the hell out of our Pacific fleet at Pearl Harbor in a sneak attack. So it's on now. Really on."

"Jesus," Roy said, "I guess even you wouldn't kid about something like this."

"Hardly," Capshaw said. "Intermittent reports have been coming in on the *Record* newstape and all the radio hook-ups beginning around nine this morning."

"Well, Goddamn," Roy said, "now we're actually at war with Japan, huh?"

"And Germany and Italy. Actually but not formally till the President makes the formal declaration before the Senate and the House tomorrow. But this is it, Doc, no doubt about that."

Chris emerged from the kitchen with Roy's food and set it on the bar.

"Try another station, Chris." Capshaw jerked his head toward the radio.

The voice of an announcer broke out of it in an excited staccato, "No accurate estimation as yet of the Pearl Harbor casualties. This station will be on constant stand-by. Stay tuned—"

Capshaw finished his bourbon while Roy ate his eggs and bacon.

"There'll be more stuff on the newstape than the radio," Capshaw said. "Want to come over to the *Record* with me, Doc, and watch it as it comes in?"

"I'd like to, Cappy, but I'm still on call till the Old Man phones in."

Roy had intended to tell Capshaw and Chris about his ridiculous interlude with Lopardi. But he did not. Somehow, it no longer seemed worth mentioning.

Capshaw nodded absently. They left the Asterion together, Roy for the Charity and Capshaw for the *Record* building. A light snow had begun falling. St. Marks Street, ordinarily quiet on Sundays, was now absolutely deserted of either pedestrians or vehicles, Roy noted as he walked toward the Charity entrance.

The next day, Monday, December 8, the schedule in the Charity operating room, as it often did, ran late. The Old Man Roy, and Wilder were in the dressing room a couple of hours behind time waiting for their next cases. The small tinnysounding radio that had been blaring music and inconsequential communiques suddenly stopped. There was an interval of silence and then a properly awed voice came on:

"Ladies and Gentlemen, the President of the United States."

The voice, restrained for what it had to say, was completely calm, completely possessed, and compelling as it should have been:

"Mr. Vice President, Mr. Speaker, members of the Senate and House of Representatives . . .

"Yesterday, December 7th, 1941, a date that will live in infamy, the United States of America was suddenly and deliberately attacked by naval and air forces of the empire of Japan. The United States was at peace with that nation . . ."

The Old Man, Wilder, and Roy, sitting there in their sweatsagged scrub suits did not move as the forced calm of the voice went on.

"The attack yesterday on the Hawaiian Islands—action against Midway—attacked Hong Kong—attacked Guam—the Philippine Islands—Wake—since the unprovoked attack by Japan—a state of war has existed between the United States and the Japanese Empire. . . ."

18

The Old Man was sitting at his desk with his chair swiveled toward the window when Roy entered. He turned slowly as Roy stood expectantly before him.

"Morning, Roy. Sit down."

The Old Man's sleepy, half-lidded eyes regarded him abstractedly.

"As of now, you are attending surgeon on the Surgical Service." The Old Man pushed a paper toward him. "This is your notification of appointment."

Roy took it in stunned silence and looked at it without really reading the one terse paragraph over the Old Man's scrawling signature.

"I have arranged," the Old Man's voice went on casually, "with the board to have your chief resident's salary continued plus a six thousand dollar annual increase to remunerate you for the additional work and responsibility. At my suggestion, the board has also agreed as a special concession to extend your present living arrangements indefinitely at the hospital without charge: quarters, board, and laundry."

The Old Man paused and cocked his head slowly at Roy. "Does that seem like a fair proposition to you?"

Roy sat numbly holding the letter. Jesus, God. Just like that. Attending surgeon, full attending surgeon. Attending surgeon on the surgical staff of Amos Abelard Hand at the Charity Hospital.

"Sir," Roy's voice began an answer out of his dry throat. He had no idea whatever of what to say. But at the moment it made no difference, for the Old Man went on:

"You will, of course, be exempted as essential civilian personnel from any and all military service on hospital recommendation to the Draft Board."

The Old Man sat back and ruminated briefly. "Now—before you actually come on as attending surgeon I think it would be a good idea for you to take a little time off. Say a week or ten days so that you're not going right into it out of the white suit. Do what you like during it, see your people, tend to any business whatever. Then come back and start in. That sound all right to you?"

Roy sat, still not quite believing it, but now beginning to feel an enormous elation. It was true though. It was true. He was sitting right there listening to the Old Man say it, handing it to him on a platter—something a lot of men worked and waited for years to get. All his and right now. Greatest break in the world, and probably the greatest one he would ever be given by anyone, anywhere, or anytime. And yet as he sat there feeling the exultation, something uneasy and insistent was stirring in his head against the Old Man's words. At the moment it was only stirring faintly, but it was there. It was there and Roy in a vague way realized that it was the formless figure of his conscience slowly staring at him and shaking a monitory finger. He was suddenly aware that the Old Man was looking at him expectantly.

"Well, sir," he began lamely, "I never expected anything like this. It sounds like I was sitting here dreaming it. You see, now that there's a war on and we're in it, well, I was figuring that naturally I'd be going. And it didn't occur to me that anything like this was going to happen to me. So when that notice about volunteers for the Medical Corps went up on the hospital bulletin board, I thought I'd put my name down for an application and I did."

The Old Man suddenly pulled his chair up to the desk, leaned his elbows on it; his gaze on Roy became very sharp.

"I know you did," the Old Man said. He pulled two mimeographed papers off his desk and tapped at them with his spatulate forefinger. "Here they are for my endorsement. And that's one of the reasons I've told you what I have right now."

The Old Man passed a hand over the lean jut of his chin. "Now, I want you to listen to me. And I want you to remember what I say. I appreciate your impulse in volunteering. It is a sound gesture and one that every able-bodied man ought to make at a time like this. No man, woman, or child should be exempt from service of his country during wartime, not if his country is going to win. And we had better win this one. Not better do it, we have to do it. It can be done better and faster if every man, jack, woman, and child serves in his best capacity—doing the thing he is best fitted for. That unfortunately is not easy to determine for most people—so they serve in whatever capacity they can. That usually is where-ever they are put by the big, impersonal, hateful, slow-moving slab of official mobilized military command. It makes horrible errors doing this because wars, at least American wars, are always fought by civilians in uniform. Good riflemen become engineers and fight that way. Bad engineers become worse riflemen and they fight that way. Ribbon clerks become company commanders. And professional soldiers sit at desks signing papers a hundred miles from the line. That's the way it is usually. But not entirely. There are some exceptions. And one of them is the Medical Corps."

The Old Man grunted mirthlessly, wiped his hands over his chin and proceeded. "In actual combat, the doctor is pretty much a morale factor. But always there if he's any Goddamn good at all. Can't do much, but does what he can. His main function is to be around when he's needed. That's his main function. Strangely enough, just that, just his being around up there and unarmed and ready to take care of anybody hurt doing the fighting means a great deal to those who are doing it. You see what I mean?"

"Yes, sir," Roy said, with the formless figure at the back of his head nodding slowly in assent. "I see what you mean."

The Old Man looked at him, his heavy upper lids open now and all of his pale blue eyes fully visible.

"But that," the Old Man said, "is a position of a line doctor in combat. God help him. The fact of the matter is he would probably be a hell of a lot more use taking care of people who keep up the fighting at home." The Old Man extended his elbow further across his desk and leaned on it, still keeping his pale eyes on Roy's. "What I am trying to say, my boy, is this. It is more important for you to stay here at the Charity doing the job you're best fitted for. That's taking care of those who are supporting the ones who are going to do the line fighting." The Old Man stopped and chewed his upper lip with his lower teeth.

"Sir," Roy said, with the nameless figure of his conscience nodding slowly behind him, "I saw it in your biographical sketch in 'Who's Who,' weren't you cited at Soissons?"

"Well, well," the Old Man said, "that what it says?"

"That's what it says, sir," Roy said.

The Old Man sat silent for an instant. "Well," he said, "actually I did very little in my length of service but dive in the mud. Soissons or anywhere else, I could have been of far more value to the country if I had done what you're going to do and that's stay where you're most needed to give your most effective help.

"Now about your leave of absence from here. I want you to begin that soon, now, if you like. Take at least two weeks, an extra week if you like. Get away. Forget things for a while, get some outside perspective—before you start in on the new routine."

This Roy recognized was tantamount to a direct order. Any positive suggestion from the Old Man always was.

"All right, sir."

"Haven't seen your folks back in Tusculum for quite a while now, have you?"

"No," Roy said. "It's been awhile."

"Then I suppose you'll want to do that."

"Yes, sir," Roy said, "I ought to do that."

"Good," the Old Man said. "I've been through Tusculum once or twice. Nice quiet little town. Good place to get some rest . . ."

There is a certain climate of nostalgia about decaying rural towns that is as much a part of them as their unhurried streets or the granite memorials on their public squares. It is more than anything a sensation of the forsakenness of the place, of the time, and of the people. This forsaken feeling is particularly sensed about the town's railroad station, for the railroad station is almost always typical. It is invariably an old and dejected landmark of the town. There is almost always a sad air of neglect about it, an atmosphere of pathetic expectation, of hopeless waiting for some great arrivals or departures that have never happened and never will. This climate of futility and loneliness is always there. And only from time to time is it momentarily dispelled by the sharp brief clamor of the infrequent trains.

Roy felt this forlorn familiar climate of the station and the town of Tusculum as he swung down from the day-coach steps at 7:15 in the morning. There was a short hurried exchange of mail sacks and baggage in the car ahead before the train got under way again. In the watery December dawn a light sift of snow had begun to fall. Under it the town was still dormant. There were as yet no signs of movement about the gradually whitening streets or the houses along them. All of it, the station and the whitening roofs and buildings, had the vacant look of abandonment they always had on Sundays, holidays, or very early on any morning. There was a brisk spit of wind now out of the lightening sky that caught and swirled the flecks of snow. The full day, when it came, would be cold and overcast. The train pulled rapidly out of the station and began almost immediately to whistle for one of its closer crossings.

Roy picked up his battered suitcase and walked down the deserted platform toward the taxi stand and the solitary car. A stooped figure moved arthritically away from it.

"Taxi, mister?"

"Yes," Roy said. "230 Grant Avenue."

"That's Orry Maines place, ain't it?"

"That's right," Roy said. "How are you, Jud?"

The man's eyes moved over Roy for a moment.

"Well, I guess I don't recognize—why it's young Roy Maines, ain't it?"

"Right. How are you, Jud?"

"Well, well. Young Roy Maines. Here, leave me take your grip there. Didn't recognize you there at first. Face is older and thinner. My eyesight ain't so good neither. Been away quite a while this time ain't you, Roy?"

"Quite a while, Jud. How are things with you?"

"Been fair, Roy, outside of my arthritis." Jud let out the clutch and they lurched away from the platform. "Seen a little squib in the paper while back about how you was a doctor now, working at the big city hospital."

"That's right," Roy said.

Jud turned out of the station into Market Street toward the square.

"Back to see the folks, I reckon."

"For a few days."

"Ain't going to stay?"

"No," Roy said, "just a visit."

"Be in the Army one of these days likely. Some of the boys here's in uniform already. Seen them around the armory quite a bit. National Guard's been called for duty. Some of them's already gone out. Looks like it's going to be another long fight."

"It looks like it," Roy said.

"Been a lot of other changes in town since you was here last too," Jud ruminated. "Lots of people gone lately. Old Judge Rugchild died this morning. Jim Freer died the week before that"—Jud paused—"Carrie's gone too, you know."

Roy suddenly remembered Jud's fat and constantly ailing wife.

"Yep. Carrie's gone. Be six months now day after tomorrow—"

"Sorry to hear it Jud. Very sorry. I hadn't heard about it."

"Yep, she's gone," Jud said. "Married to her for almost forty years. Big loss to me. Missed by a lot of people too. Come real sudden. Stroke, Doc Mandeville said. Well, that's a merciful way to go for a person up in years. That way they don't suffer none. She just kind of went off like she was sleeping. Her father went that way too—he was eighty-two when he went, kept his faculties too, just like she did right up to the last. Carrie said to me just before, 'Jud I'm real tired. I think I'll go lay down on the couch for a while.' Never got up again. Happened in her sleep. Best way to go there is for anybody when the time comes. Comes to everybody, though, don't it? Good, bad, rich, and poor. 'The young may die and the old must,' as the book says . . ."

Roy looked at the slowly passing landmarks of Tusculum as he listened. The town of Tusculum, for the past fifty years, had waged a static struggle against slow extinction. For the last half of that time the population, except for the increase of a few hundred, had remained stationary. Birth and death rates in Tusculum approximately equaled each other. When Roy was born there had been a sign on the state road about two miles before it merged with the Main Street of the town. This sign said, "City of Tusculum, Population 10,000. On the way to fifteen thousandville. Welcome. Tusculum Chamber of Commerce." The sign was long since gone, but Tusculum was still a long way from fifteen thousand. The day Roy got off the train this time, Tusculum's total aggregation of souls was 10,857. The truth was that the world and growth had passed Tusculum by, just as it had passed many other of the state's towns of which Tusculum was a prototype and a contemporary. Bucephalus, Ulysses, Telemachus, Rome, and many others. All of these were founded in the late eighteenth or early nineteenth century and given classical names by the men who had come to the territory and torn enough clear land from the wilderness to live, propagate, and congregate upon. Some of them like Iberia, Macedonia, Albion, and Lutice had risen, thrived briefly, and sunk back into their original crossroads oblivion. Some, like the state capital, had picked up a tempo of commerce, transport, and communication and ascended to the status of cities. Others, like Tusculum, grew for a while as far as their economies and locations would permit, and then began a gradual withering because there was nothing to sustain a further growth. They were essentially agricultural communities, places of exchange and congregation for adjacent outlying farmers. They had no material or power for industry, and no strategic location for transport. They gradually became static, romantically named points on the Midwestern map, way stations on an increasing flux of railroad lines.

The axis of Tusculum's activity was the square, where Main and Market streets intersected. In its center was an heroic lead statue, surrounded by drinking troughs, of the locally famous hero, Colonel Amasa Hosford. In 1820, the colonel and his small command had been surrounded by a war party of Delawares under Chief High Knife. The colonel was subsequently burned at the stake. The statue commemorated this with an idealized figure of the colonel, bareheaded, erect, and bound to the stake. On the plinth beneath were inscribed the colonel's last words—an exhortation to his captive men: "Fate has led us into the hands of our enemies. Let us be strong and die as men." The statue and the inscription were perennially whitened with pigeon droppings; these, however, did not detract from the statue's basic nobility.

Around the square was a periphery of boxlike, high-windowed brick buildings of three or four stories which housed Tusculum's principal businesses and professions: A. J. Solter, Wholesale Grain and Feed, Gideon Sloane, Hardware and Cutlery, Jason Labat, Farm Machinery, the Tusculum National Bank, Capital Assets $2,000,000, the Hub Clothiers, the United States Post Office, Spandell Howes, Insurance and Notary Public, the Hackedorn Pharmacy, Luke Mandeville, M.D., Physician and Surgeon, Klopp's Economy shop, the Tusculum House, American and European plan, the Chief High Knife Saloon, Druid Brothers Jewelry and Watch Repair—Opticians, Waldeman Kissel, Livestock Trade and Assay, the Western Union Telegraph, the Tusculum *Daily Globe-Courier*, the Augustus Lieberkrantz Funeral Home (since 1898), Orion T. Maines, Attorney at Law.

These familiar landmarks of the town stood silent and shuttered in the emptiness of early morning. They clanked across the square and pulled up before the square's only traffic light.

The light changed and they churned down Grant Street through its arcade of elms to the big frame house near its end.

Roy got out with his valise and stood for an instant watching Jud turn his cab around and rumble away again toward the square. He went up the steps to the shadow of the porch and tried the door. It was locked. He pushed the bell. The door opened and his Aunt Madge stood there, in a quilted dressing gown, her hair in curlers, and her eyes sleep-swollen in her wrinkled face.

"Roy," she said, "come in, dear boy. We got your telegram. I thought sure I'd hear the 7:15 come in, but I went to sleep again, I guess. Your uncle didn't hear it either."

She held Roy in a brittle hug, and he felt her thin lips on his forehead. They moved into the dark house.

"Your uncle will be down directly. You look thin, Roy. Just put your satchel anywhere. I've got your breakfast already to get." She took his arm and steered him past the parlor. "You must be hungry, you'd best eat." They went to the dining room.

"All I want is some coffee, Aunt Madge."

He sat down at the table next to his uncle's place at the head of it and listened to Aunt Madge in the kitchen as she rattled on.

"My, my, but it's real good to have you home again, Roy. So many people've asked about you."

He caught the sound of his uncle's solid tread on the stairs. A moment later Orion Maines lumbered into the light of the dining room blinking and disheveled. Roy got out of his chair for his uncle's heavy handshake and heavy hug. He pushed Roy away and looked at him.

"Well, well, boy. How's the doctor? How are you, Roy, my boy?"

"I'm fine, Uncle Orry," Roy said. "You're looking well."

"I feel good," Uncle Orry said. "Good for an old man. Sit down, boy, sit down and we'll eat. Madge, how long for the victuals? Roy you look thin. Don't they feed you there at that hospital? I was going to get down to the train for you. Both of us overslept I guess."

Uncle Orry levered himself into his chair. Roy noted, with something of a pang, that Uncle Orry was an old man now, old, more ponderous, and beginning to fumble a little, as he was fumbling now with his napkin ring. So much older than he had been when he and Aunt Madge had watched Roy come up to the commencement stage for his doctor's diploma.

"Madge, you've got two hungry men out here. What's going on out there? Where's the coffee? Let's have the coffee and the eggs . . ."

Uncle Orry's voice, too, Roy noted, now had the querulous note of age in it.

"It's coming, Orry," Aunt Madge's protest rose above the sounds of cookery in the kitchen. "Now you just wait a minute . . ."

Uncle Orry's appetite adequately supported his considerable bulk. He was an astonishing feeder. Eating was a serious business with him and one of his few remaining pleasures. Roy watched him finish the platter of bacon and eggs and his fourth cup of coffee.

"What's the matter with you, Roy?" His uncle wiped his lips and poured some more. "You're not eating anything. That's damned good bacon and eggs, boy. What's the matter with you?"

"Don't the eggs suit you Roy?" Aunt Madge looked at him anxiously. "They're done just like you used to like them. Real fresh, and that's Harad's bacon—"

"I got hungry and had a sandwich and coffee on the train," Roy lied. The truth was that he wasn't hungry at all. This homecoming, the town, and the incredible aging of Uncle Orry and his aunt had depressed him beyond any appetite. It did not seem possible that he could have been away that long.

"You oughtn't to piece between meals on bad food like that, Roy," Aunt Madge said. Like all good cooks she was sensitive about any spurned cooking. "No wonder you look peaked."

Uncle Orry wiped his mouth on his egg-stained napkin and pushed back from the table. He looked at Roy with affectionate satisfaction.

"We'll fatten him up. He's got some time for that now. Have you gotten your certificate yet from that big specialist examination?"

"It came a while back," Roy said.

"Was it a pretty stiff going over, Roy? I can still remember how my law board was. I guess one of those special medical kind is as bad or worse."

"It wasn't too bad," Roy said. "It was a pretty fair examination."

Uncle Orry chuckled. "Well, you don't have to be so modest about it, boy. Anybody who can pass one is entitled to crow a little. I was talking to Doc Mandeville the other day about it. And he told me that it was one of the stiffest examinations a man could take—even a graduate doctor. That's what he said. And he said something else, too, that I got a lot of pleasure out of hearing him say. He said that it didn't surprise him any. When he heard that you'd done it. Tell you exactly what he said, 'Roy's a smart boy, Orry. Always been a smart boy. Done well in school right straight along. And he's going to make a hell of a fine doctor. Just like Rex was.' That's what he said, Roy. And you know Luke Mandeville. It's Goddamned seldom he says anything good about Tusculum or anybody in it! And how long has he been in practice here? Let's see. Luke started here as a doctor just about the time that I did in law. Doesn't seem possible, but it's almost forty years. Yes, it is that, almost. Next year it will be . . ."

Uncle Orry stared off into space briefly before he turned back to Roy. "You're going to be staying for a while now aren't you Roy? or a little rest? Till you make up your mind about what you're going to do?"

"That's pretty well settled, Uncle Orry. Didn't I write you that I was going to stay on with Dr. Hand at the Charity? About being offered the job?"

"Well, yes," Uncle Orry said, "but you didn't sound like you were real certain about it. And I hope you aren't. You stay there and the first thing you know you'll be in the Army wasting your time and all you've learned when you could be—"

"No, Uncle Orry. I'm draft exempt as essential personnel. The Old Man—Dr. Hand—the chief, is making me full attending surgeon on the Service."

"And what's he going to be paying you for it Roy?"

Roy told him.

"Hah! He is, is he?" Uncle Orry said triumphantly, "Very generous isn't he? Well, now you just listen to me for a minute—"

"Orry," Aunt Madge said, "that can wait. Let him eat his food—"

"He can listen and eat. Now's as good a time as any to tell him. Now look here, Roy. I want to tell you some things that you probably haven't even really thought about.

"First place, your chief at the hospital, what's his name,

isn't the only one who can get you exempted from military service. Fact is that it can be done right here, too—right in Tusculum. Draft Board's just been appointed and I'm on it and so is Luke Mandeville. So there's no difficulty about that if you're here in Tusculum."

"Uncle Orry," Roy said uneasily. "I'm not taking the job at the Charity to get exempted from any military service. I'm taking it because—"

"I know you're not, Roy. Nobody said you were. I'm not implying that. No, you just let me go on here a minute—"

Uncle Orry, knowing that he had precipitated this moment with Roy, warmed enthusiastically, almost desperately to the subject.

"Why, Roy, boy, with your background, experience, surgical specialist now and all, and education, you could be the biggest doctor in Tusculum in no time, in the county even. Everybody in this town knows you and what you've done— an honor student in one of the biggest medical schools in the country, internship and the rest of it at the Charity Hospital everyone reads about. Why, Roy, if you'd just settle right down here with your own people right now, right here in Tusculum, you'd be the biggest doctor in Hosford County. You'd be rich in five years, Roy. My, the practice you'd have! Why, the day doesn't pass that somebody uptown doesn't ask me about it. Now you take the other day, Doc Mandeville came over to the office and sat awhile. 'Well, Luke,' I said, 'I don't know. Says he still wants to stay there in the city at the Charity Hospital.' 'Is that boy crazy?' Luke says. 'Stay there? What does he mean? There he's just another doctor—another surgeon. You tell him to get back here to Tusculum and get busy. That boy could be the biggest thing around here. He'd be rich in five years. Hell, less than that, in two years he'd have it all his own way. You tell him to get back down here and get started, Orry, and quit his nonsense and fooling around of being a little frog in a big puddle.' That's what Luke Mandeville said, Roy, and he's dead right too. Why, you'd just stay right here with your Aunt Madge and me, like always, till you got married and wanted a place of your own. You'd have your office right up there on the square in my building or anywhere else up there you wanted it. You know where Lester Howe has his office right next to Hackerdorn's Drugstore? Well, you can have that for an office if you want it. I was talking to Lester at the Lodge the other night. He's going to retire any time now. Know what he said? He said, 'When Roy gets back here to practice he can have my place, Orry. I'll move out the day he wants to move in or before.' That's what he said, Roy. Why, that's the best office for a doctor in town. Right there on the ground floor of the McFarquar Building and next to the drugstore and all. Think of that now. You could have it tomorrow if you'd take it, Roy. And then you could fix it up just the way you wanted it. There's a lot of space in that office of Lester's, Roy—a lot of space. You could have any kind of fancy X rays or machines for treatment or anything else you wanted in there and room to spare. Just the way you'd like it. And this is it, Roy. I'd get it all for you, every smidgeon of it—every stick of furniture, lock, stock, and barrel—everything you wanted, just the way you wanted it. It'd be all yours, all paid for cash over the barrelhead. That'd be my little contribution to your practice. Not much considering what you'd do, and then . . ."

And as Roy listened to this from Uncle Orry the lump in his throat felt like an egg. But as he listened to it there was listening within him the figure he had in his mind of the Old Man, gowned, gloved, and moving with authority in the hot haste of the operating room. And there was something else, too, in his head now that was just as disconcerting. This was an image of the increasing aggregate of men in uniform that he saw now anywhere he went. Most of them like himself, and not a few, kids, who looked like they were playing hookey from school somewhere.

Aunt Madge, Roy noted, was still the same obsessive housekeeper. Roy put his suitcase down on the floor and stood for a moment in the center of the room looking around at the orderliness of it. His old familiar room was neat as a pin and smelling slightly of mothballs, the way it always did whenever he came back to it. Aunt Madge, who was extremely sentimental about such things, had never moved or stored any of his adolescent or student accumulations of junk. She simply dusted and neatly arranged the disorder of it. It was all there, every bit of it, the pictures, the books, his desk and chair. All of it was there even down to the lacrosse stick and baseball bat in the corner and his boxing gloves and track shoes hanging from their pegs on the closet door. Roy looked at all of it and at the old carpet, the faded curtains, and the massive golden-oak furniture, all of it there, and just as they were now, ever since he could remember. There were, though, a couple of minor changes. Aunt Madge had rehung the pictures on the wall side of his window desk around three of his diplomas—the ones from prep school, undergraduate college, and medical school. She had had the mountings changed too, apparently so that now they were all similarly matted and framed. Roy crossed the room and looked at the new framings and the arrangement of pictures about them. Roy's usual images of his mother and father were derived largely from two of these pictures. They were both formal photographs that had been hanging there as long as he could remember.

The one of his father, the likeness of a slender, intent-looking young man in an ill-fitting officers field uniform of the American Expeditionary Force of 1917-18, had been posed so that the high stiff collar of the tunic with the insignia of the Medical Corps and the first lieutenant's bar would be sufficiently prominent. Roy did not know it, but his father's body had been shipped back home to Tusculum in that same uniform. Lieutenant Rex Andrew Maines, United States Army Medical (Reserves) had died in the influenza epidemic of 1917-18 that decimated Camp Foster. At the time Lieutenant Maines was stricken he was in the embarkation area and awaiting final orders for overseas duty. That is what the official communication from the War Department said when it came to the stunned next of kin. These were Lieutenant Rex Maines's wife, his brother and sister-in-law, Mr. and Mrs. Orian Maines.

The picture of Roy's mother, next to his father's, was of a slight, ethereal-looking girl taken in three-quarter-face view. She was wearing a pleated shirtwaist and a black boater hat. Neither of these distracted from or accentuated the fine-cut sensitive beauty of her face. It could not be in any way deduced from the picture, but at the time that it was taken Mrs. Rex (nee Helen Holmes) Maines was six months pregnant with Roy's stillborn younger brother. Helen Maines died trying to bear him—in forced childbirth just three months after the death of her husband. Roy was four when this happened, and his only memory of either of these familial tragedies were the long dark boxes with people slowly filing past them in a flower-decked room. He had never missed his father and mother because he had never known them. It was also because Aunt Madge and Uncle Orry, childless themselves, had immediately and lovingly taken him to rear as their own. And that had not been easy for them either.

They were, not without cause, continually concerned about Roy's health. His early years were anything but robust. Roy had been a sickly infant and he was a sickly child. By the time he was eight he had miraculously survived every childhood disease in the pediatric decalogue. He had also survived the heroic treatment prescribed by Dr. Luke Mandeville, who, as an omniscient country practitioner was occasionally called in consultation on a sick cow or horse. Mandeville was prone to regard his human and animal patients in much the same category.

But measles, mumps, whooping cough, scarlet fever, and diphtheria, and intervals of infantile dysentery, had not killed Roy. Nor had Mandeville's frequently heavy handed therapeutics. They had, though, apparently in terms of the time "stunted his growth." Roy at twelve was a thin, pale, underweight adolescent about whom Aunt Madge and Uncle Orry perpetually fretted. It was at this point, after a good deal of gruff assurance from Luke Mandeville, that they decided to send Roy to Amityville Preparatory School.

"Now, Orry, Madge," Luke Mandeville had said, "I'm not saying this just because I went there, but I think you ought to send that kid to Amityville just about now. I'm saying it because it will do him a lot of good. He's developed into a smart, sensitive kid. But he's frail from all his sickness and he's like an only chick in a barnyard with too much protection from the rooster and the hen. He's gotten over every Goddamn disease I can recognize and a few that I don't. Chances are he won't be sick much more because he's had them all. Thing is now he needs to get out from your protective umbrella. Needs to get out more with other kids and get himself built up and more on his own. They'll do that for him at Amity. Scholastically it's one of the best places in the country. And a big athletic program. Physically and mentally they'll work the be-Jesus out of him. Six hours of class every day and the rest of the time in the gym or on the field. That's what he needs now."

Roy went to Amityville that fall, the youngest, weakest and, as it turned out, judging from his subsequent report cards, the most studious boy in his class. Now looking at the succession of Amityville photographs, Roy remembered with sudden clarity intervals of the long-gone and difficult first year of it.

Particularly the fights he had had as all "new boys" did behind the "rock pile" after the three-thirty afternoon roll call. In one of them, particularly etched on his memory, a squat, broad-faced Amity "old boy," also from Tusculum, named Carnes had knocked Roy down four times.

"Don't get up Maines," Carnes had said, "just stay there, till I get out of here."

Roy had gotten to his feet mainly by the blind rage that was upon him and Carnes had promptly and easily knocked him down again with an indifferent blow to Roy's left eye.

"I'll learn how to fight," Roy remembered thinking as he lay there. "I have to learn how to fight with my fists since that's the way it is here."

And after that there were the long hours in the gymnasium, working on the pulley weights and chinning of himself on the high bar to build up his skinny arms and torso so that he would have something to put into a punch if he ever landed a good one. And he remembered his hard and secret training with the light and heavy punching bags, the heavy one particularly, which swung only a few inches either way no matter how hard it was hit. Then there were the special boxing sessions he had appealed to Uncle Orry for and Uncle Orry's immediate and interested acquiescence. And then, over a year later, he had pushed Carnes, who was a senior now, out of line in the assembly hall and insolently invited him over to the rock pile or the gym if he wanted to make anything of it. And Carnes had instantly accepted, along with Roy's suggestion that they fight with real professional gloves, the eight-ounce ones designed only to protect the hands of those who wear them and nothing else. And then how he had been able, and without too much effort, to dodge and evade Carnes's heavy-handed swings and counterpunch him in the belly and in the face until his brows, nose, and mouth were gratifyingly bloody. And then seeing Carnes, who had once knocked him down four times, strictly through courtesy he let him get up, stagger around, swinging blindly and hitting nothing because of his bloodied eyes. And then the inordinate satisfaction of seeing the fight stopped because of what he had done to Carnes.

It was probably just there that Roy began to appreciate the inherent goodness of some people. Tip Carnes was certainly one of them. Showered and dressed and on his way back to the dormitory, he waited for Roy outside the gymnasium.

"Say, Maines."

"Yes?" Roy said looking at Carnes's assortedly bandaged face.

"Mind if I talk to you?"

"No," Roy said.

"Well," Carnes said, "just wanted to say that you've gotten to be a damned good boxer. Doesn't seem like all of them hit so hard. But, boy, how you can keep them coming."

"You knocked me down four times once," Roy said ignobly. Carnes's bandaged face nodded at him. "Well, I had to do that. I didn't hit you as hard as I could've though. You were a new boy and all, even if we are both from Tusculum."

After that Carnes and he became good friends.

Where was Carnes now he wondered, and where were the rest of them whose young intent faces stared back at him from the group photographs of the track team, the swimming and the gym squads, and the graduating class?

Looking at them he felt probably for the first time a mordant pang of real nostalgia about Amityville Preparatory School. And this he found was extended to the now fairly distant past of his undergraduate and medical school years. Aunt Madge had arranged the oddment of photographs of these with an astonishing chronological accuracy. In all of them Roy saw himself gradually changing from a callow, skinny, everserious adolescent into what he looked like in the last picture of the lot. This was one Ransahoff had casually snapped of him standing by the Charity's rear entrance. That one Roy recalled was taken at just about the time he had gone on as an intern in surgery. Aunt Madge had had an enlargement made of it. It showed a gaunt, wiry young man nonchalantly slouched against the sliding door of the Charity ambulance ramp. He was dressed in a white hospital uniform, the tunic unbuttoned at the neck, and the pants bagging, neither of them any too clean. The enlargement of the snapshot had been of sufficient dimension to catch his hair badly needing a haircut. The enlargement had also been sufficiently ample to indicate some other unflattering features of Roy's face, the bags under his wide-set eyes, the too prominent nose and chin, and the stretch of his full-lipped mouth. Taken altogether, he had the visage of an old and tired-looking young man frozen for the moment in an attitude of indifference. Roy continued to examine it with a curious and amused detachment.

"I guess that's about what I look like now too," he thought, "plus being a couple of years older and maybe a little wiser—well . . ."

He turned away from Aunt Madge's personally arranged pictorial gallery of his life feeling suddenly and unaccountably depressed. He went to the bed where he had put his suitcase and began to unpack the little he had brought.

The depression that began with Roy on the first day of his return to Tusculum continued to deepen during the few days of his stay. This time he knew and felt that it was a stranger's sojourn. He had somehow or in some way grown irrevocably away from the people and the place. As he rightly surmised, he had been doing this for some time without the realization. But this time home he knew and understood with a kind of reluctant intuition that he had become a stranger to what had always been the most familiar to him. He was back to what had always been home, but he saw now with an increasing clarity that he was no longer at home. And why wasn't he? It was not just because in long intervals of absence, the times, circumstances, and persons of Tusculum had gone down its own lonesome road toward oblivion. As he had gone on his. The simple fact of the matter was that he no longer had a home in the sense that he had always known it. Home now for him had become the place where he could best function in terms of his idea of himself. That, at least currently, was at the Charity, where he had learned, where he could exercise whatever he had learned or might learn, in his obsessive preoccupation with diagnosis and technique. It could be anywhere else, too. The Charity was certainly not the only place. It could be anywhere, any other place at all as long as he could hold or add to the slowly accumulating image he had of himself. That he knew was derivative of his hero worship of the Old Man.

The Old Man, who had a ghostly authority that seemed supremely invested from within himself. The Old Man, who could stand with a sharp-hooked piece of steel in his big, bony, clumsy-looking right hand and spit, if only for an instant, into the dirty yellow face of death. And sometimes win, too, win at least for long enough to call it winning. The Old Man's place to do this was the Charity.

"And maybe it's mine too," Roy thought, "but one thing is sure, it's not here in Tusculum, not here. I don't think . . ."

Roy was ready to leave Tusculum within forty-eight hours

after his coming. But a nagging sense of duty toward Aunt Madge and Uncle Orry kept him there for a bored oppressive succession of days. Nothing that happened in them did anything but intensify the sense of dejection the place and people precipitated in him. One or two of these incidents, trivial in themselves, left him with an almost desperate impulse to board the next outgoing train. Particularly dismal was the funeral of Judge Loomis Christian Rugchild, long-time judge of the circuit court, long-time prominent citizen of Tusculum, long-time friend of Aunt Madge and Uncle Orry. Roy, fully conversant with Tusculum funerals, valiantly strove to escape this ordeal.

"Look, Aunt Madge, why don't you and Uncle Orry just go ahead and go on without me? I've gotten kind of funny about funerals, you know. I'd rather not go. Suppose I drive you and Uncle Orry down and pick you up afterward?"

Aunt Madge looked at him with pursed lips in shocked silence. "Why, Roy Maines," she said, "do you mean to say that you can stand there and tell me that you don't want to go? You don't want to be present when the judge is laid to rest? Why, Roy, I can't believe I'm hearing you right. You don't want to come and pay your last respects to one of the finest men that God ever let breathe? A man whose been such a friend to us over all these years? A man who was a great admirer of your father and mother? Why he used to take you on his lap when you were a little baby, Roy, and say how cute you were, right here in this house . . ."

Aunt Madge paused, compressed her faded lips, and tears began forming in the wrinkled lids. "Why, Roy, *you were almost named after him!* Why, he was your Uncle Loomis. Do you mean to tell me that you don't want to come and see him on his way to everlasting peace?"

"All right, Aunt Madge," Roy said wearily, "just thought I'd like to remember him the way he was when he was alive. That's why—never mind that though. I'll come—"

"Well, I should think so," Aunt Madge said, somewhat mollified. "Besides you've hardly been out of this house at all. Just sitting around moping with your books. Now you get upstairs and get your best suit on with that beautiful dark silk tie I sent you. You look so handsome in that suit." Aunt Madge paused and then called up the stairs, "Orry, are you ready?"

"Be right down," Uncle Orry's voice faintly responded.

"Now hurry, Roy," Aunt Madge said, "get into your clothes.

Everybody in town will be there—we don't want to miss anything."

Funerals in Tusculum, as anywhere else, were held for the vanity of the living rather than for honor of the dead. In Tusculum, as in any other small insular town, they were highly regarded forms of entertainment—definite social events in the same elite category as church bazaars, weddings, the firemen's block party, and open-house functions of the local chapters of the Macabbees, Eastern Star, and the Veterans of Foreign Wars. In fact, funerals, as diversions, were generally superior even to these. They provided unexcelled opportunities for audience participation, public exhibition of emotion, actual or assumed, and displays of elegance in dress and conduct that was otherwise out of place. Funerals in Tusculum were events of enjoyable communal psychiatric catharsis. They were, and always had been, highly regarded forms of divertisement—spiritual barbecues, so to speak, in which the corpse supplanted the roasted carcass of the traditional ox as the focal point for the conviviality. Tusculum funerals, no matter whose, were invariably well attended.

The obsequies for the late Judge Loomis Christian Rugchild were exceptionally assisted. Practically the entire town turned out for it. And small wonder. In the mortuary annals of Tusculum it was a classic. Not since the ceremonies, twenty years before, for Martin Van Buren Stump, native son of Tusculum and United States Senator, had there been a comparable panoply. And as some of Tusculum's very elder citizens said afterward, the final rites for Judge Rugchild were almost the equal of that peerless occasion. The old judge, providentially, had died after a long and lingering terminal cancer of the prostate. Thus Tusculum had had ample time to anticipate and plan a fittingly elaborate valedictory. And those responsible had done this in high and magnificent style right down to the last detail.

It was, as one authoritative septuagenarian said, several times afterward, "One hell of a fine funeral. By God, it was just beautiful. Everything just right. Aren't many like that one or going to be, here or anywhere else, even in the whole state."

It was Roy's privilege to attend it, all of it, with Aunt Madge and Uncle Orry. They arrived in good time at the Lieberkrantz Funeral Home (Since 1898) and were given preferential seating. Preferential seating meant chairs up front, close to the speaker's podium and close to the flower-decked catafalque and corpse.

The judge lay in a magnificent, three-quarters-open, carved-mahogany casket (item 804 in the morticians catalogue: "The Lord Altamont model, truly our finest. A distinguished repository for any distinguished deceased. . . . Suggested when circumstances make cost of no concern," etc.). The judge's age and his ailment had left his face and his frame a grotesque shell of wrinkled skin over bony prominences. August Lieberkrantz, considering what he had to work with, had performed an Homeric task in restoring this grim image to a likeness of life. Even the most sophisticated metropolitan undertaker might have been justly proud of it. The judge, as he now lay, was Lieberkrantz's masterpiece—a veritable jewel, a Kohinoor, a Hope diamond of embalming art. By deft use of the paraffin syringe and cosmetics, Lieberkrantz had filled out the judge's emaciated features into plumpness and rosy vitality. He had also by skillful distribution of padding over the stiff, almost skeletalized frame, conferred upon the judge a synthetic body that was just short of being gladiatorial. All in all, with the impeccable morning clothes in which he had finally decked out his subject, Lieberkrantz had done an amazing job. Roy looked at this crimped, curled, painted effigy of what he had remembered as a vigorous kindly old man, and his inherent hatred of all undertakers flamed afresh.

"Lopardi ought to see this," he thought to himself sardonically. "It would give him something to shoot at."

Following Aunt Madge and Uncle Orry, Roy filed by the bier toward the rapidly filling rows of chairs and sat down. Almost immediately there was a spontaneous hush, and then it began.

The subdued sob of the organ, which had been just perceptible up until then, began to swell into a volume sufficient for attention. The strains of it undulated up and down, around and about for some moments. Then they fell into the theme of one of the great Tusculum funeral favorites—"Beautiful Isle of Somewhere." This faded into diminuendo. It was almost immediately followed by another Tusculum crowd-pleaser—"The Last Link Is Broken." Here the organ interlude was exquisitely assisted *viva voce*, Roy recognized, by Carrie Sponhauer, who had once studied for opera in New

York. Carrie was still held in perennial esteem as the leading soprano of the Tusculum Grace Episcopal Church. Madame Sponhauer's voice on this occasion was in full-tone classic diction, and, as always, quite clear.

> The lah-last lah-hink is bro-ho-hoken,
> Earth's bah-bondage na-how is oer-a
> And na-how in fah-harwella token-nn
> We ga-hather at the sha-hore.

A translation of this Tusculum tour de force for anyone who had never heard Carrie Sponhauer sing it would be:

> The last link is broken
> Earth's bondage now is oer
> And now in farewell token
> We gather at the shore.

Roy did not need any translation. He had heard it before as rendered by Madame Sponhauer. There were other cantos of it, which she finished presently to the organ's tremolo accompaniment. When Madame Sponhauer and the organ had subsided there was an interval of hushed silence before the Reverend Pythias Carrington Chubb advanced to the podium for the first of the several oratorical tributes. During the interlude Roy examined the audience. Not a few of the expectant, upturned faces Roy recognized and instantly associated. Others had a certain familiarity that he could only vaguely recall.

One of those he immediately identified was Beulah Timmons. Ah, Beulah Timmons, the buxom belle of the ball and the object of his panting adolescent libido for one whole summer after his graduation from Amityville. Looking at her he suddenly remembered with a sudden piercing clarity the insufferably hot August night that he had made an all-out attempt to eliminate Beulah's virginal status, and incidentally his own. He had taken her to the show at the Mystic Theatre and to Rubley's Drugstore afterward for refreshment. Then in Uncle Orry's antediluvian Buick, he had driven her to one of the secluded side roads outside of Tusculum and parked. There in the smother of summer darkness he made an inept and fumbling attempt to gratify his dark desires. They had clung to each other stickily with much lingual searching between the gluey fusion of their mouths. There had been too much mutual palpation of ordinarily prohibited parts. In spite of the promising preliminaries, virtue had triumphed. They had finally left the trysting, both virginally intact. This was not of Roy's restraint but Beulah's, who had never forgotten her mother's ringing injunction to "save yourself for the man you marry." On this occasion at least, Beulah had succeeded in preserving her most prized female commodity. The victory was to Beulah and the angels of rectitude. But not entirely. Roy had succeeded in thoroughly exploring Beulah before she sat up suddenly, slapped his face, and demanded to be taken home instantly. That had been quite a few years ago, Roy thought now with something of a pang as he looked at her. She had long since been lawfully wed and fruitful with offspring by one of Roy's Tusculum contemporaries. What was her married name now? He ought to remember. Aunt Madge had sent him a clipping from the Tusculum *Globe-Courier's* society page showing Beulah in bridal trappings with a lengthy lah-de-dah description of her wedding. Roy looked at her again. Still Beulah all right. Recognize her anywhere, but now her finely formed face and lissome body were beginning to be obscured by a soft curtain of early middle-age fat.

Another face that caught and held Roy's attention was one that he first noted because of the metallic glint of metal on the neck under it. This was the collar insignia of the blue uniform of the Royal Air Force. The features above were gaunt, bony, and pale under the close-cropped hair. But to Roy they were recognizable enough. They should have been, for he had spent three years at Amityville looking intermittently at that face. It was the face of Tip Carnes of Tusculum and of Roy's vintage at the Academy. Tip Carnes, who had licked him and whom he had licked. Aunt Madge had sent him a *Globe-Courier* clipping about Carnes. That one was about how Carnes had been an R.A.F. volunteer in the reformed Lafayette Escadrille before Pearl Harbor. He had returned to the United States to continue in the Air Force after all volunteer service had been canceled, etc., etc.

Roy looked at Carnes's face again. It was an old, young face now, a gaunt and hard-lined caricature of its youthfulness. . . .

Roy's contemplation of it was interrupted by the bulbous voice of Reverend Chubb standing at the podium. Chubb, who had had ample time to prepare, had done so. He rose to the summit of his florid oratory. In spite of a slight sinusitis, he expatiated richly and at length on the virtues of the deceased. He had never been, in spite of his nasal infirmity, in better voice.

"Dearly beloved," he bulbously began to intone, "we are gathered together in this sorrowful time to pay our ultimate tribute to one who . . ."

And at this point, Roy, who was pretty familiar with his sermons, continued to muse on other things. From time to time, though, it was impossible not to assimilate something of what that unctuous voice was maundering on about.

The theme of it was that the late Judge Rugchild was one of the apogees of human evolution. He was apparently, in the opinion of the Reverend Chubb, a departed saint and an Episcopalian saint at that. Loomis Christian Rugchild was, the Reverend Chubb intimated, an unbelievable amalgam of Solomon as a judge, of Chevalier Bayard with respect to his courage, and very possibly of Jesus Christ in matters of ghostly devotion. Roy listened off and on to the Reverend Chubb's sonorous twaddle as he did to the rest of the protracted rites.

The judge was a popular and communal figure. He had been a chronic joiner of all organizations that might and did advance him politically. And now that he was dead, all of them came flapping in for a piece of his glory.

When the Reverend Chubb had finished, the Masonic funeral squad of the local Tusculum chapter came on with their esoteric mummery. They were followed by the Odd Fellows. After that came the International Woodmen of the World. Then the Redmen of America. And just before the lid was closed over the judge's clay, a delegation from the Tusculum Chamber of Commerce mumbled something over him.

Roy sat through it all, perishing for a smoke and a drink. He thought he would be out of it when the casket was closed and there was a postlude in which the assemblage filed out to the strains of Handel's "Dead March from Saul." But it was not over. There was the interment at the cemetery and Roy did not escape that either. He stood with Aunt Madge and Uncle Orry, not far from the open hole, while the judge's beautiful mahogany box was lowered into the steel casing long ready for it. The Reverend Chubb came forward for the final gesture. He picked up, with some difficulty, a handful of the frozen dirt, and spoke the final words in Latin, as high-church Episcopalians are prone to do:

"*Ex argilla, ad argillam . . .*"

Roy looked at Aunt Madge and Uncle Orry. "I guess we can go now, can't we, Aunt Madge?"

Aunt Madge looked at him severely. "There's the reception at the judge's," she said, "and we don't want to be the first ones there. Now, Roy, you just wait a minute. Amy Rugchild specially invited us . . ."

That was fully in keeping, Roy thought, the inevitable baked meats following one of Tusculum's burial parties. Weddings and funerals always necessitated the elaborate consumption of food. This was expected and traditional in Tusculum. Joy, grief, and food were inextricably associated. Following any considerable occasion there had to be a post facto session of eating.

Roy drove Aunt Madge and Uncle Ory over the silent winding road and through the main gates of the cemetery back to the town. Judge Rugchild's big frame house at the corner of Market and Bank streets was ablaze with lights. Around it was an increasing crowd of cars carrying those who, after having sorrowed sufficiently for the judge, were now gathering at his house to be victualed. Roy made his obsequies to Amy Rugchild, the judge's waiting widow, along with his uncle and aunt, and moved into the general line of congestion. This was centered on a long trestle table that extended the length of the living room. At the near end of it, Roy noted gladly, was a bar where drinks were being busily poured. And stretching away from it a long line of heaped and steaming dishes. After sighting the bar, Roy promptly lost Aunt Madge and Uncle Orry.

"Double bourbon and water," Roy said to the boy in the white coat who was ineptly doing the pouring.

"Why it's Roy Maines isn't it?" The voice came from a woman at his elbow, "It is Roy, isn't it?"

Roy, drink in hand, looked at her. The face turned up at him was that of Beulah Timmons.

"Why, hello, Beulah," Roy said awkwardly. "Hello. How are you, Beulah?"

"Well, Roy"—Beulah pursed her lips which made her fattening cheeks seem fatter—"goodness, but it's good to see you."

Beulah's eyes, which had always been large and inviting,

were still that way. But, he noted, there were bags, not big ones but still bags, beginning to pull down the lower lids of them. The young face that he remembered best from the sickly moonlight of that hot August darkness in Uncle Orry's car had considerably wrinkled and considerably coarsened.

"Nice to see you, Beulah. How are you, Beulah?"

"Well, it's certainly nice to see you, Roy," Beulah said. "It certainly is. I was sure I recognized you at the funeral. I said to Mama while we were sitting there, you know, looking around while Carrie was singing, I said, 'Why that's Roy Maines, I believe,' and Mama looked over at where you were and said, 'Why, yes it is, it's Roy Maines. He's a doctor now.' But I knew that anyway."

Roy found himself being steered by Beulah out of the general congestion around the bar. They walked across the hall into the relatively free space of what had been the judge's library. There were at the moment vacant chairs there around the solid walls of books.

"You look wonderful, Roy," she said, batting her eyes at him. "I suppose you know I'm divorced."

"No," Roy said uncomfortably, "hadn't heard."

"Well, I am." Beulah peered into the depths of her glass and turned to him. "It was a big mistake you know. Ed and me getting married. But everything is settled now. And I'm free as a bird, except for the kids of course."

"Well," Roy said gropingly, "I'm glad to hear that things are coming well with—"

At this point Roy was stopped by a heavy hand on his shoulder. He looked up. Looking down at him was a man in a baggy tweed suit. The man had a broad face and a beard grayer now than Roy recalled it. The man was Dr. Luke Mandeville.

"Well, well," Mandeville's voice boomed at Roy hoarsely, "hello, Doctor. Been looking for you, and here you are."

Mandeville shot a paralyzing glance at Beulah. "Don't mind do you, Beulah? The doctor here and I have got some important things to talk about."

Mandeville's grip on Roy's shoulder tightened and brought him out of his chair."

"Well, Beulah," Roy started to say.

"Never mind," Luke Mandeville said. "Excuse us, will you, Beulah? We've got some important talking to do."

Mandeville, still keeping his crushing grip on Roy's shoulder piloted him across the room to a couple of vacant chairs. Mandeville took one after he had sat Roy down in the other.

"Just got you rescued in time, Roy." Luke Mandeville winked at him broadly. "Since Beulah divorced Ed Volk, she's been on the loose with her claws out for whoever's available. You'd make a great runner-up. I could see her figuring that, while she was standing over there talking to you, switching her bait around. So just look out, Doctor, unless you want to be hit number two. Could do worse I suppose"—Mandeville gave Roy another broad wink—"but that's not what I want to talk about"—Mandeville rattled the ice in his glass—"how's your drink?"

Roy held up his glass.

"Good. We'll have a couple more in a minute. Now, laddy bucks, I want you to listen to me."

Mandeville leaned forward and poked Roy's chest with a gnarled forefinger. "I don't know whether you realize it or not, but your future's right back here in your own backyard. Right here in Tusculum, my boy. And it's going to be a great one. Can't help but be. All you've got to do is just use your head and do like I tell you, and quit this nonsense about being a big-time city surgeon. That's what your Uncle Orry says you've got in your head. Why hell, Roy, you get back here and open up shop and in no time, not even a year, you'll be making dollars where those smart-aleck city bastards are making peanuts. In less than a year you'll be doing it. You think I'm just talking? Well, I'm not. Let me tell you why. Things are all lined up here for you. The surgery I can't do myself I send down to the city like every other God-damned general practitioner around here does. And how much do you think that amounts to? Well, it amounts to one hell of a lot."

Luke Mandeville leaned forward and stabbed Roy's chest again with his forefinger. "What would you say if I told you that I send about thirty thousand dollars' worth of surgery down there every year and have been for quite a while, just out of my own general practice—my own practice, that's all, what would you say to that?"

Luke Mandeville stared at Roy, waiting for him to be properly impressed. Roy tried to give a proper impression of being so.

"Seems like quite a lot," he said.

"Hah!" Mandeville said, "quite a lot, you're damned right it's quite a lot. But it's nothing Roy, it's nothing. Because it's only part of what you're going to get. Now listen to this. There are five other general practitioners, just like me, all good friends of mine, all lined up and waiting to send their stuff the moment you're available for it."

Luke Mandeville began a precise enumeration of them, numbering the thick fingers of his left hand with the thumb and index of his right.

"One, there's Prax Bates. Praxiteles Bates, out there in Ilion in that Goddamned little doghouse of an office of his just treating dirt farmers, has a paid practice that's Goddamned near as big as my own. Two, there's Shep Howard, doctor for the whole Cox Brass plant plus his private practice on the side. Three, Bill Whymiler, whose got everything in the town of Waverly sewed up and has had for ten years. Four, that conniving little Italian son-of-a-bitch De Martino, who's got every Italian in the county. Five, that Goddamned Lipsky, who's got all the Jews cornered into thinking he's the greatest thing since Moses—why, Christ knows, but he has—probably because he speaks Yid like De Martino speaks Italian.

"Point is I've got them all primed and set to send you their stuff—minute you open here in Tusculum. And they see one hell of a lot of surgical stuff that they send out because they can't handle it themselves. Just like I do."

Roy thought of Tusculum's antediluvian Good Samaritan Hospital—a converted private residence with abortive, hastily added additions of white brick.

"The hospital—there's not the facilities for—"

"Wait a minute now," Mandeville held up an inhibitory hand, "wait a minute, Roy, boy. I know what you're going to say. You're going to say that the old Samaritan hasn't got the equipment and the rest of it to handle a big volume of big surgical stuff, right? Isn't that what you were going to say?"

"Well," Roy said, "that's right, isn't it?"

Mandeville chuckled and looked at him. Then suddenly he took Roy by his coat lapel and pulled his face down level with his bearded jowls.

"I'm going to tell you something." Luke Mandeville's voice came at him in a coarse bourbon-tainted whisper. "I'm going to tell you something that Goddamned few people know. I'm going to tell you because, by Jesus, I want you to know it."

Mandeville's steely eyes peered into Roy's from under their

frosty brows, and his bourbon breath came heavily in Roy's face.

"We've just buried the judge haven't we?"

"Yes," Roy said feelingly, "we certainly have."

"I pronounced him dead right up here at the hospital. Loo's been a patient of mine for forty years, ever since he got his first dose of clap."

"Yes—"

"I'm an executor of the will, Loo's will, have been ever since your Uncle Orry made it out. So I know what's in it."

"Well . . ." Roy said, groping for something acceptable to say.

Luke Mandeville looked carefully around him, and then stuck Roy's chest again with his formidable forefinger. "Roy, this is doctor to doctor. Tell it and I'll kill you."

"Maybe you'd better not."

"No, by God, I am going to tell you," Mandeville said. "Loo Rugchild's estate is worth a million and a quarter dollars. A million of it is going to the hospital here. And the rest to Amy—for her natural life. Then she'll probably leave whatever's left like Loo did. See what that means?"

"Well," Roy said, without having the chance to finish.

"It means we can have a hell of a fine little community hospital here and whatever you might happen to want for it you could have—anything they've got down there at the Charity. I'd see to that, Roy . . ."

There was a time when this kind of talk from old Luke Mandeville would have flattered and pleased him enormously. But now he found somehow that the prospect Mandeville was painting for him of spending the rest of his life in Tusculum almost as depressing as the funeral. He was secretly much relieved when the white-coated boy at the bar interrupted it by coming over with the message that there was an urgent call for Dr. Mandeville.

"Stay right there, Roy," Mandeville said, "I don't think this is anything much. Be right back. I'm not finished yet."

Roy watched him disappearing into the general milling of the crowd. Then he went to the bar for another double bourbon. The whiskey now was the only thing that could make the whole depressing assemblage endurable till he could escape. He downed the whiskey neat and got another one. He felt a sudden firm pressure on his arm from behind.

"Hello, Maines."

Roy turned around. Tip Carnes, in his foreign-looking blue uniform with a pair of silver wings and spray of ribbons on the tunic of it, was smiling at him quizzically.

"Well, hello, Tip," Roy said, transferring his drink clumsily so that he could shake hands. The first glance that Roy got of Carnes's eyes told him that Tip was probably in the bourbon equilibrium that Roy was trying to acquire. Carnes looked, and was, comfortably drunk—not stoned, just obviously at ease.

"Come on," Carnes said, "bring your drink and let's get out of this *cochonnerie*. I'm up to my arse with it, aren't you?" They found some space near the stairs in the foyer.

"Christ," Carnes said, "it's good to find a launceman in this shamozzle. How are you anyway? It's been a long time."

"Pretty good, Tip," Roy said. "You look good. How are you bearing up under celebrity?"

"Oh, I'm in great shape," Carnes said. "You saw the old judge over there at Augie Lieberkrantz'. Well, the dear old son-of-a-bitch died feeling better than I do now."

Carnes held out the hand without the glass in it. The tremor in it was not exaggerated. "Look at that. Steady as a rock—that's the way I am all over. Don't tell it around town though. On account of since Pearl Harbor I'm the local hero. Might detract from my reputation."

"That seems pretty secure," Roy said, grinning. "Judging from your press notices in the *Globe-Courier*."

"Weren't they great though?" Carnes snorted mirthlessly. "My mother's got them all cut and pasted in a limp leather scrap book already. I understand she and Pop damned near bought up a whole edition of the *Globe-Courier* to send out to friends and relatives. I'm the greatest thing in Tusculum since Colonel Amasa Hosford and his statue in the square. Tell me something, Roy, is that Goddamned statue made out of pigeon shit? It always looked like it was."

For the first time since he had come back to Tusculum this time, Roy felt like laughing. And he did.

"No," he said, "I always thought it was myself. Looks like it. Fact is though, it's lead underneath."

"That so?" Carnes said, grinning. "Well, I'm glad to hear that it's that substantial. Now if they want to put one up of me, and I think they'll have to after what the *Globe-Courier* printed, I want it made out of pure chicken shit in keeping with its subject."

"Come on now, Tip," Roy said, liking him more every minute, "that's no Goddamn way for a hero to talk."

Carnes's eyes glazed a little more now, looked at him.

"Say that again and I'll belt you one, Maines. Look, let's get out of this Goddamned *schweinerei* and go somewhere and get drunk, shall we? Come on, we'll get our coats and duck out the back."

Ten minutes later they were seated in an unobtrusive booth of the Chief High Knife Saloon.

"Just bring the bottle, Gib," Carnes said to the bartender, "and save yourself some exercise. The doc and I are going to be here for a while."

When it came Carnes poured two drinks, either of which would have anesthetized a horse.

"Jesus, I can't drink them like that, Tip," Roy said.

"Sure you can," Carnes said. "Take a swallow of water with it. Straight transfusion. We both need it after that Goddamned shabackle for the judge. Boy, I want to tell you that's the last Tusculum funeral I ever get sucked into, family or no family."

"That makes two of us," Roy said, and raised his glass. How long have you been back now, Tip?"

"In the country a month. Here in town two weeks, seems like two years, the two weeks here in town I mean. Christ, Roy, I can't take this place any more. It gives me the bull horrors. Thank God I'm due to report at Ordman Air Force Base in another week for reorientation and reclassification. And I can hardly wait. My assignment's probably going to be as instructor in fighter combat tactics. That's what everybody else back out of the group has drawn."

"You mean you're out of the Royal Air Force?"

"Oh, hell yes. Actually, but not officially. Not until I'm recommissioned with ours—that ought to be through anytime now. That's what they're doing with all the repatriated American and Canadian R.A.F. volunteers since Pearl Harbor. Procedure is to send us home for six weeks rest and recuperation, and discharge us with the same rank and grade right back into some combat group here in the States or Canada."

"How long were you over, Tip?"

"Two years, two months, and four days," Carnes said, fingering his glass.

"You must have gotten one hell of a good first-hand look at it." Roy felt a strong kind of envy stirring in him.

"Yeah." Carnes nodded thoughtfully. "I guess you can say that. Enough anyway to change some of my ideas about myself and give me a tail-wind start to a drunkard's grave."

"You've done all right, apparently," Roy said, "from the look of these ribbons on your front."

"Hah," Carnes snorted. "Just window dressing, strictly crap, all routine awards. American Volunteers' ribbon, British service ribbon, and the fogey award—missions completed patch—hell, anybody who was around long enough got them as a matter of routine. Only one I've got that's worth a damn I haven't got the guts to wear . . ." Carnes's voice suddenly trailed off as he put his glass to his mouth.

"No?" Roy said, looking at him with interest, "why not, Tip?"

"Because," Carnes said staring at him, "the guy who really deserved it in the operation I got it for is dead. Didn't get anything except his name on the K.I.A. posting."

"What's that?" Roy said.

"The killed in action list," Carnes said moodily. "The scratch off. He made that all right. Say, how in the hell did we get into this anyway? Christ I must be getting loaded. What the hell are you, Roy? You listen like a lousy psychiatrist. I thought you were supposed to be a surgeon?"

"I am allegedly," Roy said, "got a paper to prove it. But you know, Tip, it's not often anyone gets to talk to somebody who really has been there—right now particularly with all that's going on in the papers, radio, rest of it. But if you don't want to talk about it—"

"Oh hell"—Carnes waved an unsteady hand—"sure I do. I don't know what I'm being so Goddamned coy about. Come on, let's talk about it. Reason I don't is that with a little of the old booze in me I get blabbing off like I was out of Hemingway. *Hell's Angels, War Birds,* or some other corn from World War I. Pretty maudlin, pretty disgusting, and makes me want to puke when I think about it sober. You know, though, secretly I guess that I want to talk about it. I haven't though up to now. So come on, let's get at it. I'll give you a junior birdman's opinion of the great world foul-up till now as seen from the air—"

"Tip," Roy said feelingly with an enormous interest now, "you're quite a guy."

"Yeah," Carnes said dryly, "it would seem so. The teeming metropolis of Tusculum, the town of our nativity, thinks so anyway. I'm supposed to shine my ass around at a Bond rally day after tomorrow. That's courtesy of my ever-loving family, who fixed it all up with the local committee. May do it, too, if I'm not too hung over. Nothing like the plaudits of the grateful crowd to balm the wounds of a soldier home at last. Jesus, aren't you getting drunk, Roy? I am—"

"Yeah, I know you are," Roy said, "and I'm right in there with you. But before we both pass out tell me something, will you, Tip, man to man, Amity man to Amity man—"

"Why, hell yes."

"You've been up to your ass in it. And I guess you're going to stay in it. Now tell me, are you glad you did? Is it worth it? Would you do it again? If you didn't have to?"

Carnes put his elbows on the table, rested his chin in one hand, and lifted his glass with the other, drank, and put it down again. He slowly shook his head.

"Yeah." He nodded solemnly. "I would."

"You would? Why?"

"Well, Roy, I'll give it to you as straight as I can. As straight as I now see it, that is. Yes, I would. All the patriotic bull aside, I would. I'd do it again. Never mind would I do it for my country—I'd do it for that anytime anywhere, I like to think and hope. But the real reason that I'd do it again is probably strictly for me. I'd do it again and will do it again for that reason alone."

"Why, Tip?" Roy was hanging on his words now.

"Well," Carnes said, "it may sound a little nutty or abstract or something, but it's because of what you learn about yourself when the chips are down—by that I mean, I don't think you ever get to know that except in not one or two but a series of critical situations, where you have to make a lot of decisions, good or bad, and then live with them or maybe die with them afterward. I don't think you ever know till you've had that. An average guy like me I don't think ever learns about himself unless he's had it in a war or something like that. And there isn't much like it except maybe what you do —or bullfighters do, and soldiers of any kind—that's stick the old steel in, or try to, and then live along with yourself after doing it." Carnes grinned mirthlessly and almost sheepishly. "Pretty vague stuff, I'm talking, huh, Roy?"

"The hell it is," Roy said. "I know exactly what you mean, Tip."

Carnes looked at him fixedly through the blur of the bourbon.

"Yeah, I guess maybe you do. I'm not saying it so well, though."

"You're doing pretty good," Roy said. "Go on."

"You get a different idea about time that's kind of hard to get used to. You start off thinking that time is going to be forever for you. And you live that way—not for the right now, but far ahead, for the future. Say next year, next month, next week, next day. But when the heat gets really on, like when you personally can be knocked off like a lot of guys are getting, who are better men than you are, or anyway as good, you begin to live more for the present, in the good old right now. And that can be, depending on the particular jam you're in, for the next hour, the next minute, and sometimes maybe for the next few seconds. And when you get down to that last few seconds point a few times, you begin to learn what clocks are really made for. They're really made for people who don't know a Goddamned thing about time and have plenty of it to waste looking at them. Einstein had it right, time's entirely relative. A guy can live a hundred years in one lousy minute and less, or he can be around, breathing in and out, without ever having lived for a minute at all. That's what I think now, anyway."

Carnes sagely shook his head. And Roy stared at him.

"I've been on one side of it enough to know what you're saying. Now tell me—what we were getting to, Tip, what did you learn about yourself after being in rehearsal for what we're in now for two years? That's what we were getting at, wasn't it?"

"Yeah, I guess that was it." Carnes nodded. "By the way, how do you feel after you've come out of the operating room after having cut some poor son-of-a-bitch from hell to breakfast?"

Roy looked at Carnes with a considerable and now almost absolute respect.

"I'll try to tell you about that if we don't pass out first. Right now we're on you and we're talking about how you learn about yourself during the war—you personally that is. Come on, Tip, let's have it."

Carnes licked his lips. "Well, yeah, all right. You're talking now about 'Cognosce Te Ipsum,' that's the old Amityville slogan isn't it? 'Know Thyself.' That's it. I'm beginning to know that. Matter of fact I know about 'Cognosce Te Ipsum.' "

"You do?" Roy said, "let's hear about that."

"Well, in my case, it's not too flattering. It's what you might call a Mexican stand-off with my alter ego, way I see it. I was early in for the show and one of the last out of it—scared piss-less—in between, but I stuck till the bloody end. That counts for something."

"Plus the fact that you're an American Air Ace. Twelve planes, wasn't it, the Globe-Courier said?"

"Actually eight enemy aircraft, and excuse me for count-ing modestly," Carnes said, and coughed appropriately. "Time was a hell of a long time betwixt and between. Let's get back to 'Cognosce Te Ipsum.' "

"Yes, let's do that," Roy said, "let's consider 'Cognisce Te Ipsum.' You said you knew now what it meant. But, do you know yourself, Tip?"

"Yeah," Carnes said, "pretty well. Not entirely. Nobody, I think, gets too close to 'Cognosce Te Ipsum.' "

"But being in it you found out about it—about yourself, I mean."

"Yeah, I found out about it. At least, I think so." Carnes's eyes now were very far away.

"Come on, Tip," Roy said, "what did you find out—about the war, about anything, about yourself—"

"About the war"—Carnes looked past him sightlessly now —"we Goddamned well have to get off our asses and win it. About me personally—well I could be a better guy than I am."

"You're a real good guy right now," Roy said. "How do you figure to be better?"

Carnes's eyes were now a long way past Roy's. They finally came back to his.

"I can answer that real easy, if I ever get the chance. That'll be doing for somebody what a guy who was a hell of a lot better man than I am did for me."

"Jesus," Roy said, "you didn't come out of it liking yourself very well, did you?"

"No, I didn't. And no, I don't," Carnes said.

"You don't want to talk about this any more?"

"No, I don't. Let's quit, shall we, Roy, and just get drunk. We've got a pretty good start."

"Fine, let's do that!" And between them they finished the bottle and closed the Chief High Knife Saloon.

Roy delivered Carnes to his house, where there were still a few lights on by Jud's asthmatic taxi, and went back to the Rugchild funeral feast. The house was ominously silent and ominously dark. The congestion of cars was gone, including his Uncle Orry's. Jud drove him home.

Roy's foggily planned design of surreptitious entry and a fast silent transit to bed without waking anyone was aborted at the outset. Aunt Madge had been waiting up. She opened the door for him when he was ineptly fumbling with his keys.

"Oh, Aunt Madge—sorry. Thought you'd be in bed," Roy said sucking his breath in in a ridiculous attempt to keep her from smelling the whiskey on it.

"Come in, Roy, and be real quiet. Your uncle's asleep. My, I've been so worried about you. . . ." The gentle recrimination in her voice made Roy wince even through the protective miasma of the bourbon. She closed the door and started to help him with his coat.

"Oh, never mind, Aunt Madge. Thanks. I'm fine, I can do it." Roy made a valiant attempt at the tone and posture of sobriety. Aunt Madge insisted on helping him anyway as he fumbled out of it.

"Come out to the kitchen, Roy. I've got some coffee ready for you."

"Look, Aunt Madge, I don't need anything. I'm fine. Just fine. Sorry I missed you and Uncle Orry. You see—"

"Come out to the kitchen, Roy, and have some coffee," Aunt Madge said gently and inexorably. "It's all ready. You'd best have some."

Roy resentfully and guiltily followed her out, knowing she wasn't fooled a bit. Back in the kitchen he sat down at the big, square, oilcloth-covered table while she puttered briefly at the stove, brought him the steaming cup with the cream and sugar for it, and then sat down with him.

"Are you hungry, Roy? I think maybe I'd better get you something—"

"Aunt Madge, I'm not hungry. Just let me have this coffee since you've fixed it."

"You're sure now, Roy?" Aunt Madge peered at him critically.

"Of course, I'm sure. Say what is all this? What's the matter anyway?"

"Well, drinking and all—leaving the judge's to go off there to the Chief Saloon with that drunken Carnes boy—"

"Jesus Christ," Roy thought, "the Goddamned Tusculum grapevine. I'd forgotten about that. How could she possibly know this fast. Who was the fink? There wasn't anybody at the bar or in the place, I don't think, when Tip and I went in. She knows though. No use trying to deny it."

Roy threw in the sponge. "All right, Aunt Madge. Yes, Carnes and I went over to the Chief. How did you find out so quickly."

Aunt Madge pursed her lips in a grim, satisfied smile. "Be sure your sins will find you out."

She saw that Roy's cup was empty and filled it instantly. Roy gratefully noted that with the first cup he had scalded his throat and his belly, and he was sobering rapidly.

"Come on, Aunt Madge, tell me. How did you find that out this fast?"

"Roy, in a town this size, you don't keep things concealed. You know that—"

"You bet I do," Roy said fervently. "I'd just forgotten. Now tell me—"

"Well," Aunt Madge said, "Beulah Timmons, Beulah Volk, that is, that's her name now since she's divorced Ed Volk and not taken her maiden name again, wanted to talk to you and was waiting till you got through speaking with that Carnes boy. Lieutenant Carnes now I guess it is. She saw you leave with him. Saw you get your coats. And then with all those people there at the judge's, drinking and all, which I think and so do a lot of other people, is a shame and a disgrace, to serve all that liquor at a funeral reception. They always do. But that doesn't make it right even if Amy Rugchild, poor bereaved woman, let them do it. And I told Amy in a nice way that I didn't think that it was a good thing to do. I said, 'Amy, I think it would be best just to have the food and never mind having any drinks—you know how the men get—'" Aunt Madge would have gone on.

"Come on, Aunt Madge," Roy said incisively, "Beulah Timmons, that is Beulah Volk, saw Tip and me leave. Now let's get to how you found out we went over to the Chief."

"Well, it stood to reason, where you would be going. Young Carnes has done nothing but spend his time there drinking since he got back. Everybody knows that, hero or not, and it's a shame that he's done that since he's come home. So—"

"So, you put two and two together," Roy said.

"Well, besides that, they apparently didn't know how much people would be drinking there at the judge's and they ran out of liquor and sent over to the Chief for more, and Gib, the bartender over there, was going to send it over with you and the Carnes boy. Then he called back and said that you and the Carnes boy were in no shape to bring it. So he got someone else and—"

"Very clear," Roy said, "I get the picture. I'd forgotten what a Goddamned goldfish bowl Tusculum is."

"Roy, please don't curse. Tusculum is your home, Roy, and—"

"Not any more," Roy said.

"What?"

"Nothing."

"And," Aunt Madge went on, "it's as nice and pretty a town as there is in the state. And the people are as fine and nice as you'll find anywhere . . . and a lot friendlier than most. And Roy, you've got so many friends here yourself. It's such a shame you didn't stay at the judge's instead of running off like that. Why, practically everybody there was just bursting to see you and say hello and like that. Why everyone your uncle and I saw asked about you, wanted to know where you were, looking forward to seeing you and all. It's such a shame you went off over there. And Luke Mandeville was hurt that you didn't even wait for him to finish what he was saying to you—very important Luke said it was—and well, whatever possessed you to do a thing like that, Roy? Why . . ."

There was more of this, with Roy listening wearily, every fiber of him aching to tell Aunt Madge to shut up. Finally he had to.

"Look, Aunt Madge, let's get off the subject now, shall we? I don't want to listen to any more of it. I'm not a kid in knee pants. You don't have to spell everything out for me. Right now, I'm tired . . ."

Aunt Madge peered at him in silence for a moment and her eyes suddenly filled with tears. "Land sakes, Roy, well, I was only trying to make you see—"

Roy felt an instant stab of remorse. "I know. I'm sorry, Aunt Madge. Look, let's forget it for tonight. I'd like to go to bed."

"Do you feel all right, Roy? Are you sick?"
"I'm all right. Just want to get some sleep."

But he did not sleep. He lay, wakeful with the coffee and liquor churning restlessly in his belly, and feeling with it a sly insistent nausea. His head, though, was entirely clear, his thoughts feverishly sharp. The sense of oppression that came with them was almost intolerable. He could not recall ever having been so depressed. Nothing since his arrival in Tusculum had happened to relieve it. Everything in his review of his homecoming had only intensified it. The sad, surprising decay of the old surroundings and the people in it, the brittle senility of his uncle and aunt, of Luke Mandeville's, the forlorn coyness of Beulah Timmons, the almost desperate preoccupation of the others he had met with trivialities of the town's restricted life. The funeral and the *totentanz* later. And now that he thought on it, more than anything his fortuitous and drunken reunion with Tip Carnes. And what was it about that that now aggravated his despondency? Was it seeing Carnes in uniform and listening to his honest confession of self-disillusionment that gave Roy some fingering sense of guilt, that heightened his depression? Or was it something else? What was it that he had sensed about Carnes that he communicated to Roy to further sadden and oppress him? Whatever it was, Roy knew that he had felt this before and not infrequently. He should be able to identify it, for it emanated from Carnes almost like an aura or an odor of some kind. What was it? For some time he lay in the darkness thinking on this. And as he did so, out of the half-formed images in the back of his mind there rose the grimy façade of the Charity with its rows of boatlike beds in its wards peopled by those drifting inevitably toward death. Then there came the jaundiced face and body of Wild Will Wortle supine in one of them. And as this hung for an instant in his head, Roy recognized what it was about Tip Carnes that intensified his own melancholy. It was the subtle, specific, and unmistakable aroma of death. That was it. Roy considered this for some time before his mind gradually turned from it.

"One thing is certain, the way I feel now I've had about all of Tusculum and home I can take right now. And still another week to go. I'll never be able to stick it. I've either got to get out of here or stay drunk for the rest of the time. But how, without lacerating Aunt Madge and Uncle Orry's feelings beyond repair? How in the hell can I possibly do that?"

And then as he lay there fretting in the darkness the escape from his Tusculum entrapment suddenly came. He looked at the luminous dial of his watch. Now three o'clock. Aunt Madge and Uncle Orry now were long asleep. He got out of bed, threw on his bathrobe, and moved silently down the stairs to the telephone in the back hall.

The rural telephone service in Tusculum, never at the peak of efficiency at anytime, was considerably less than that on long-distance calls after midnight. But, Roy, cursing and fuming at the delay, persisted. Luck was finally with him. He got through to Capshaw.

"Well, well, Doc," Capshaw's voice crackled back at him on a clear connection. "What's up out there in the hay and Bible belt? Operator said you're calling from Tusculum— must be important."

"I am, Cappy, and it is. Listen, you've got to do me a favor. I've got to get the hell out of here as fast as I can and you're the guy who can help me, so listen."

"Why, Doc"—he caught Capshaw's chuckle distinctly— "only been there a couple of days and got one of those bumpkin broads up the stump already?"

"No, Goddamn it, now listen—"

"O.K. Listening, Doc."

"Now here's what I want you to do—"

There was an interval of several minutes in which Roy did most of the talking.

"All right, Doc, you bucolic Machiavelli," Capshaw said. "I get the picture. It'll be easy. I'll handle the production just right from this end. Now, you want it at ten o'clock, right? So, you can get the next train out?"

"Right. And don't mess up on it for God's sake, Cappy."

"I won't mess up. See you at the Greek's when you get in. Now forget about it and go on back to bed."

They were still sitting over the breakfast coffee when the phone rang.

"Probably Alton Salter, calling about his insurance contract," Uncle Orry said as Aunt Madge got up to answer it.

Roy, still in his bathrobe and slippers, looked at the clock and took the spoon out of his cup. Precisely ten o'clock. Good old Capshaw. Right on the button.

"Hell? . . . Who?" Aunt Madge's voice came clearly to them from the back hall. "Yes, this is the Orion Maines residence. Who? . . . Oh yes, the hospital is it? . . . Long distance? . . . Urgent, you say? . . . Why yes, Dr. Roy Maines is here . . . Why yes . . . Who'd you say was calling? . . . Doctor who? . . . Oh yes, yes, Doctor. Well, yes, I'll get him for you right away. Just hold on please, Doctor."

Aunt Madge came bustling into the kitchen properly excited.

"What's all that?" Roy said, looking at her casually.

"It's for you, Roy. Long distance from the hospital. A Dr. something-or-other—couldn't quite catch his name—calling. Very urgent he said. Wants to talk to you right away."

He got up, crossed the kitchen into the back hall to the phone.

"Hello, yes, Maines speaking . . . Oh, hello, Doctor, didn't recognize your voice for a moment—"

"Hello, you perfidious son-of-a-bitch," Capshaw's amused voice came back at him. "Right on time see? Just like I said. Now, let's hear you go, boy. I'm the best straight man in the business—"

"Yes, Doctor," Roy said, keeping his voice up so that Aunt Madge and Uncle Orry would miss none of it, "yes, I see . . . Well no, I wasn't planning to leave here for at least another week . . . Well, I'm sorry to hear that . . . Yes, I understand how important it is . . . Well, in that case I couldn't possibly refuse . . . Of course. Yes, I will. I'll get back there as soon as I can . . . Yes, you can—you can count on it. There's a noon train out of here. I'll meet you at the hospital. . . ."

Roy hung up and came back into the kitchen for the critical part of his performance—the Act II curtain so to speak. The expression on his face was, he hoped, a proper compound of surprise, preoccupation, and disappointment, at the news. Aunt Madge and Uncle Orry looked up expectantly at him as he sat down.

"What's wrong? What's the matter, Roy?" Aunt Madge's eyes went over him uneasily.

"Well," Roy said, launching into his cover story, "it looks like I'll have to get back just as soon as I can, damn it all, something's come up that won't wait."

It seemed that his presence was immediately and absolutely required because of the sudden illness of Roy's alternate on the

Service. It was most urgent because his alternate had a particularly delicate operation scheduled that would not wait, and he, Roy, was the only other available man to do it, etc., etc.

Aunt Madge and Uncle Orry listened raptly and Roy was sure, gullibly, to his plausible lying. And Roy was silently thoughtful. He had, he thought, done it about right.

Uncle Orry shook his head understandingly, and said, "Well, I guess there's no help for it. That's the way it is when you get to be a specialist, I guess. Always some unexpected demand on your time because no one else can take care of things the way you can—"

"Oh, Roy," his Aunt Madge said worshipfully, "I know you have to go back right now. But it does seem like such a shame. I had a big surprise party and all planned for you—"

"I'm only the lousiest, most deceitful son-of-a-bitch in the world," Roy thought as he went upstairs to get ready to catch the noon train. "But thank Christ they went for it. Another couple of days here and I'd be ready to do a Santry . . ."

He caught the noon train back to the city. At the station he felt one of his keenest stabs of guilt about his petty conspiracy with Capshaw against Tusculum, Aunt Madge, and Uncle Orry. It came after he had boarded the whistling train and stood looking out at them from the coach window—at the farewell tableau of their aging loneliness—at both of them standing together on the vacant station platform waving to him as the train pulled out.

19

Back in the city, the reaction to Pearl Harbor and the war was a good deal more in evidence than it had been in Tusculum. The platforms and the waiting rooms of the station were plastered with recruiting posters stuck in every available space. Among them:

A grim, resolute Uncle Sam pointed directly with a hard, accusing finger. "I Need You" the caption under it said.

A comic-strip character, noted for his physical prowess and

consumption of spinach, was shown smashing both fists simultaneously into the swastika and a rising sun. "Hit Them Japanazis Hard."

Four clean and formidable-looking young men in uniforms of the Army, Navy, Air Force, and Marines stand out with expressions of determined devotion. "Which is You?"

The heel of a booted foot with a swastika on it was shown crushing into the center of an idealized map of Europe. "U.S. Next?"

Besides these, Roy was aware of the number of confused-looking men in uniform in transit.

Roy got a cab, instead of going to the Charity he had it drop him at the Asterion. Chris, at his usual station, did something unusual. When he saw Roy come in he instantly left his place between the cash register and the bar and came forward and put out his hand.

"Well, well, Doc. Welcome back. Welcome, Doc." Chris put Roy's suitcase behind the counter. "I take this, Doc. You get it when you want it. Mr. Capshaw called about fifteen minutes ago—"

"He did?" Roy sad, "well, I'll call him. Where is he?"

"Don't you bother, Doc. I got his number. I'll tend to it. You have a nice drink, Doc, eh? And maybe something to eat?"

Before Roy had a chance to answer, Chris was away at the phone booth. He came out of it presently.

"Cappy'll be here pretty quick. Now what's for you to drink, Doc?"

"Beer," Roy said.

"Right, Doc," Chris said, "right away."

"Where's Capshaw, Chris?"

"He's talking to the big man of his newspaper," Chris said.

"What's that?" Roy said.

"Don't know, Doc." Chris shrugged. "But they're holding the call till Mr. Capshaw can take it. He's with his publisher or something—"

"Well, good," Roy said, "he was supposed to meet me here."

"I'm sure he'll do that, Doc," Chris said earnestly.

Roy sat waiting and sipping his beer.

J. Abbott Pelly adjusted his magnificent paunch to the front of his desk and eyed Capshaw expectantly. Capshaw, slouched in the official audience chair, pulled out a battered pack of cigarettes from his coat and lit one.

"Sorry to bother you with this now, Mr. Pelly," Capshaw said, "but I think it's about time for it. Don't like to intrude, knowing how busy you are—"

"Never mind the amenities, Capshaw," Pelly said, "get to the point. And before you do, would you mind putting your ashes in that ashtray instead of all over the carpet?"

"Why, yes sir," Capshaw said, flicking his cigarette ash in the general direction of the ceramic platter on Pelly's desk, with half of it on the carpet anyway.

"Thank you," Pelly said. "Now what's on your mind?"

Capshaw crossed one baggy trouser leg over the other, surveyed his leaky-looking shoes abstractedly, and then looked at Pelly.

"Well, sir, now that we're officially in the war, I figure there's going to be an almost immediate overseas troop movement. In fact, I know there is, from a contact in the Security Bureau. I want to go along and cover it."

Pelly made one of his stalling gestures, long familiar to Capshaw. He pulled the impeccable handkerchief out of his breast pocket, slowly wiped his fleshy jut of nose, and replaced the handkerchief precisely.

"You would? What's the matter with going right along as you are now? You're just fine where you are. Let the regular A.P. and U.P. foreign-service boys take care of that end of things—"

"Mr. Pelly, this is going to be a very long, very tough, and very interesting war. It's going to be the main axis of operation in the world for as long as it lasts. I don't want to be sitting around at home covering stuff that is penny ante by comparison. I want to see as much as I can of the big action. I want to be in right from scratch. I want to write about it, or my part of it as I see it and feel it, and as it develops. A chance to do that doesn't come to very many even in a lifetime. I don't want to miss it—"

"Uh huh," Pelly said, "I understand your feeling, Capshaw. But as a matter of fact you've already done just that haven't you? In the Spanish Revolution and damned near got your tail shot off doing it?"

Capshaw, who had been staring thoughtfully at his shoes, looked up at him suddenly. "That was quite a lot different,

Mr. Pelly. I didn't come in right at the start and I left before it was over. I only got part of the picture, not all of it. I was a hell of a lot younger then and one whole hell of a lot less well informed. What I wrote then, I wrote looking through a keyhole. Now the door is open where I can see everything right from scratch. I want to do that, Mr. Pelly, and one way or another I'm going to do it. This is the time. This is my second chance. The fight in Spain was only a rehearsal for this one. I got there late. I left early. I had some idea of what it was all about, but not enough to say really what I thought about it. I know what this one's about. I'm thoroughly oriented now. What I wrote about the Spanish Revolution was pretty callow stuff, Mr. Pelly. I can really write about this one. And I'm going to—first hand—"

Pelly's eye was now intently on Capshaw. "You wrote some pretty good stuff, Capshaw," Pelly said. "You said, as I recall, that the Communists' infiltration of the Loyalists would alienate any aid to them. And it did."

"It alienated me anyway," Capshaw said thoughtfully. "That's why I got out."

Pelly shook his head. His manner became judicial. "Capshaw," he said, "I believe you've had enough of that kind of experience and whatever writing goes with it. Now look. Why don't you just simmer down and look at this business objectively? Why don't you just do that? I am not unmindful of your value to the *Record* or to our organization. It's considerable. Very considerable—" Pelly took out his handkerchief again needlessly, and, needlessly, wiped his nose. "Now suppose, as an alternative to what you are suggesting, Capshaw, we make you an associate editor on the *Record*, with a syndicated editorial column? That means all of the Pelly publications and its affiliates, which is quite extensive. Suppose we did that and—"

Capshaw stopped dangling his right foot. "I don't want it, Mr. Pelly," Capshaw said, flicking the last ashes of his cigarette on the beautiful ankle-deep carpet. "I don't want that at all. I want to go to this war right from scratch and I want to see and write about it as much as I can and as long as I can. You don't want to send me, that's all right. A.P. will send me, so will U.P., so will I.N.S. But I'm going, Mr. Pelly." Capshaw paused and looked at the leaky shoe on his motionless right foot.

"Capshaw," Pelly said, "I've been listening to you. Do you think for a moment you could possibly listen to me enough to hear me out?"

"I'm listening, Mr. Pelly."

"Good," Pelly said, "just listen well." Pelly fell silent and adjusted his belly to his desk and went on. "Capshaw, we have enough money and enough prestige that we must, or want to, or have to cover this war. We can do this through our wire service with U.P., A.P., or I.N.S., and I suppose do it fairly well. That's obvious. Now—if we want something more than that there are about a dozen young men I can send out on any war assignment that you want to do. Now you, Capshaw, you can do a great, a wonderful job, just being what you are. That's the best inside man this newspaper has ever had."

Capshaw looked at J. Abbot Pelly fixedly and for some moments of silence. "Mr. Pelly," Capshaw said, "you either send me, or I'll make my own arrangements."

"Capshaw," Pelly said, adjusting his belly and his P.B.K. key and chain to the desk, "just what in the name of hell is it you want?"

"To go to war," Capshaw said.

"Capshaw," he said, as seriously as anything he had ever said in his whole successful life, "I don't want to send you. There are a dozen eager, fairly talented, much younger bastards I can cite for that. But not you, Capshaw. You're too Goddamned valuable to the *Record* and to me just where you are. You're our inside man, Capshaw, that's what you are, and that's where you're going to stay."

Capshaw nodded. "I see, Mr. Pelly. That's quite a tribute. Matter of fact it's about the nicest one I've ever had. Now"—

Capshaw ground out the stub of his cigarette in the enormous ceramic tray before him on Pelly's desk.—"are you and the *Record* going to send me to cover this war or not? Because if you're not, A.P., U.P., or I.N.S. will. Right up to now there haven't been too many qualified."

Pelly's shrewd wide-spread eyes looked for a long time in silence into Capshaw's. "All right, Capshaw, we'll send you. I'd rather send someone else. Somebody without your guts and talent. We've got quite a few of those. And they are better able to have their heads blown off than you are. But that's the way you want it, that's the way you want to live, that's the way you want to die, that's the way you feel about life, war, death, the rest of it. Well, fine, fine . . ."

"Well, yes, Mr. Pelly," Capshaw said, "I guess we understand each other. I write pretty good and if the *Record* doesn't want me—"

Pelly's eyes flashed up at Capshaw. "All right, Capshaw," he said, "go to the Goddamn war. And do what I think you will. Get your Goddamned head blown off for no reason at all except risking it where you don't have to. Do that, Capshaw. Anyone who knows you wouldn't expect much else. Just don't go running to A.P., U.P., or I.N.S. to get yourself killed. We can do that right here at the *Record*."

"Thank you, Mr. Pelly," Capshaw said with a considerable dignity.

"No thanks at all," Pelly said, looking about at his smoked-oak, book-filled gymnasium of a room.

"We'll pay you better than the rest of those bastards can, Capshaw."

"Thank you very much, Mr. Pelly."

"You feel you have to do this, Capshaw?"

"Yes, I feel that I have to."

"Well, then," Pelly said, "go on, Capshaw. You don't have to do it with A.P., U.P., or I.N.S. You can go as an independent correspondent with the *Record*."

"I'd like to do that. That would be my idea of having the world's best assignment. Thank you, Mr. Pelly. There aren't many publishers with the understanding and foresight, the deep knowledge of human motivation that you have shown in this . . ."

Pelly's belly contracted suddenly in an expiratory snort that made the P.B.K. key scrape angrily on the desk edge. "Come off it, Capshaw. Don't give me any of that gratitude flap-doodle. This is Pelly you're talking to and you can omit the Goddamn salve you always lard me with when you've gotten what you want. Save that for when you're wheedling something out of somebody who doesn't know you. Not me. I can read you like page one, Capshaw. I always could, your opinion to the contrary and not withstanding. Christ knows, I ought to be able to at this point. After twenty years of putting up with your Goddamned gyrations, whims, and foibles, and the embarrassment and money they've cost me and the news-paper—"

"I'm sorry you feel—" Capshaw began.

"Shut up, Goddamn it, I'm not done yet," Pelly said.

"Yes, Mr. Pelly," Capshaw said almost demurely, noting with satisfaction the rise he had gotten.

"Yes, Mr. Pelly," Pelly creditably mimicked Capshaw's thoughtfully restrained voice. "One thing I can't tolerate is being underestimated. And you, by God, have always done that haven't you, with me, haven't you?"

"Why, Mr. Pelly, I've never—"

"Yes, you have, too. Big fat slob, sitting up there with his Gargantuan gut handing down encomiums like God. 'Pelly the Belly,' 'The Belly,' 'The Big Mamoo.' Don't you think that I know about that?"

Pelly ruminated for a moment. At this point Capshaw felt something stirring in him that was akin to genuine affection for J. Abbott Pelly.

"Look, Mr. Pelly—"

Pelly ignored Capshaw's attempted intrusion. "And another thing, Capshaw. Just to show you that I'm not quite the over-fed, fairly literate jackass you think I am, I'm going to tell you something else. I know the basic reason why you want to get in there as a war correspondent. I know very well. And I'm going to tell you whether you want to admit it or not. It's pretty simple.

"The fact is you're dying to get your jaw in the glory trough and you're afraid you'll miss doing it. Correct me if I'm wrong, but I think you've never forgiven yourself for missing it in the Spanish Revolution. You've never really squared it with your-self for pulling out of that one early, have you? Instead of stay-ing in there when you could have, and being known as the guy who wrote the whole bitter chronicle of it, right down to the bitter end? And maybe died trying to do it? Now isn't that right, Capshaw? Tell me now, isn't that right? And now you're going to make Goddamned sure you do it, win lose or draw in this one?"

For once Hugh Martin Capshaw had nothing to say. He simply stared at Pelly like a man who has seen first-hand a barnyard rooster suddenly metamorphosed into a high-flying hawk. Slowly, almost dreamily, Capshaw got out his crumpled package of cigarettes and lit one. He leaned forward and dropped his match in the elipse of the tray on the desk.

"Go on, please, Mr. Pelly."

"That's about it," Pelly said. "I'm telling you this, you frustrated, death-loving, quixotic bastard, for two reasons. One of them is that I think it's time that you know that someone has an idea of what makes you tick. That's the lesser. And the other and more important reason is that you quit underestimating and patronizing me as the big obese oaf who tolerates your genius, pays you your salary, and lets you get away with being the fourteen-karat-gold son-of-a-bitch you are and always have been—at least since you've been with me and the *Record*." Pelly momentarily stopped speaking, got out his handkerchief once more, wiped his nose, looked at his fat hands, and then at Capshaw. Then he went on. "I'm a good deal more than that, Capshaw. Believe it or not. Among other things, and you better remember it, I'm one of the few, and the pitifully few, friends you've got.

"Now, go to the Goddamn war, Capshaw. Do what you think you have to do. And, if you don't get your guts blown out, which is what I think you're really looking for, come back here and do what you can do best. Now"—Pelly looked at the gold Patek-Phillip on his wrist—"I'm fifteen minutes late for this next appointment."

Capshaw levered himself out of the chair slowly and thoughtfully, and stretched his hand across the vast expanse of Pelly's desk. Pelly took it briefly.

"Thanks, Mr. Pelly."

At this moment, one of the phones on the desk rang. Pelly picked it up.

"Yes," Pelly said, "he's here." He handed the phone to Capshaw.

"Be there right away," Capshaw said.

Pelly watched Capshaw's shabby shambling figure recede across the long expanse of carpet toward the door. When it had closed behind Capshaw, Pelly sat, elbows on the desk, examining the scattered ashes on the top of it, then the vast elegance of the room, and then the liver spots on the back of his pudgy hands.

"The Belly, Pelly the Belly, the Big Mamoo." He chuckled mirthlessly. "Falstaff, a fat, successful, rich Falstaff. Falstaff's body, anyway, hiding the yearnings or spirit of Byron the poet. George Gordon Byron as I recall—"

He flipped the switch of the bleak efficient-looking intercom.

"Next appointment, Miss Frame," he said.

Roy and Capshaw sat for some time at the Asterion, with Roy doing most of the talking about his sojourn in Tusculum. Capshaw gave him, as always, an interested and sympathetic ear and enough prompting comment for Roy to make a detailed account of it.

"I felt like hell asking you to do what you did, you know, Cappy. I still feel guilty about it, but another day in Tusculum and I would have been talking to myself. The place, the people, that Goddamn funeral, all of it, even my uncle and aunt, really put me down. Just couldn't take any more of it. I don't know why—never been like that before. What do you suppose is the matter with me?"

Capshaw looked at him and gave him a slow serious wink. "Growing pains, Doc, growing pains. Your growing pains, that is, not Tusculum's."

"That it?"

"Yeah, that's it. Had them myself one time or another. Tell me, have you ever read any of Thomas Wolfe, the old master of nostalgia, particularly this kind? Ever read *You Can't Go Home Again?*"

"No," Roy said.

"Well, read it. Sitting here listening to you is like reading a page out of it. Wolfe had it right—about you can't go home again. After a certain point of absence and experience you can't. And it's true about some other places besides home. Read it, Doc. You'll see what I mean."

"I will," Roy said. "Meantime what's been happening around here? I feel like I'd been away a year instead of a week."

"Well, let's see now. The big thing is that there are some encouraging indications that the Goddamn citizens around and about have finally gotten it through their skulls that we're going to have to fight a war."

"Yeah," Roy said, "I deduced that. Things are a good deal more frantic here than in Tusculum. A lot of soldiers and posters in the station when I got in today, more than when I left."

"Good sign though, Doc. Pearl Harbor caught us with our pants down. Like every other war we ever fought, we've stewed around too long. Now, we're going to have to get up off the floor and try to lick them."

"Nothing new in the local situation though is there? I mean around our own particular little microcosm."

"Well, yes," Capshaw said, chuckling and running a grubby finger around his glass. "Let's see now, how long have you been gone, Doc?"

"Nine days exactly," Roy said.

"Yes. Well in the last week there really have been some surprising developments. Lopardi," he said, "you won't believe this about Lopardi."

"I'll believe anything about Lopardi."

"Don't sell Lopardi so short," Capshaw said. "Lopardi's in uniform."

"What? Lopardi?"

"Yeah." Capshaw grinned. "Lopardi is now an officer and a gentleman—second lieutenant in Quartermaster—Graves Registration Division. Seems the little bastard has had a reserve commission right along. You ought to see him in his soldier suit, looks like a mouse in a gunny sack. Very proud of it though. I think he sleeps in it. All his funerals now, they tell me, have a distinctly military cast. Rybecki went to one the other day and gave me a full report. Said it was like something out of the 'Army Training Manual.'"

"How is the inspector?"

"You mean the major?" Capshaw chuckled.

"My God," Roy said, "don't tell me Inspector Rybecki joined up too?"

"Oh yes. Yes, indeed. Major Stanislaus Rybecki, very much so. He's taking it bigger than Lopardi even. Major Rybecki is with the Military Police—not in uniform yet, but because of age and experience commissioned with a majority right off the bat. Apparently they need guys like Rybecki right now and real badly. The major is frothing at the mouth waiting to get into the suit and get his assignment orders. Meantime he's continuing with his regular duties on what I believe is called detached service. He's still in civilian clothes at the moment. But be sure you address him as major though when you see him. He's very particular about that."

"Oh, I will, I will," Roy said, shaking his head incredulously. "I'll certainly do that."

Capshaw regarded Roy's surprise with amusement. "That's not the pay-off though, Doc. The present patriotic fervor goes even further than it—"

"It does?" Roy said. "How the hell can it? What's the pay-off?"

Capshaw shook his head in mock dejection. "It's sad, Doc. It's a great blow. Devotion to country far above and beyond the call of ordinary duty. A terrible blow to many of us. But it has to be faced. Anastasia Kondoleon—"

"Anastasia Kondoleon!" Roy said aghast. "Jesus Christ don't tell me that Stase has joined up? What the hell as, dean of women in the Women's Auxiliary Corps?"

"No," Capshaw said, "Madame Kondoleon has as yet no official status with the Armed Forces. She is, however, closing her establishment in the interests of the war effort—"

"Holy hell," Roy said.

"Yes, my boy"—Capshaw gave an exaggerated sigh—"we must all try to bear it. We must face it the best we can."

"Seriously?" Roy said. "What for?"

"Yeah," Capshaw said, "seriously. She is. The U.S.O. decided they'd like to have the place for a canteen."

"U.S.O.? What's that?"

"The United Services Organization. Newly formed. Every town's going to have one—for the respectable entertainment and recreation of our soldier boys. Anastasia's going to let them have the place for the duration. That, of course, won't be for a while yet. She told me the other day. Naturally I tried to dissuade her. No use though. Stase had already completed the arrangements. Stase takes her obligations of citizenship pretty seriously, you know, always has."

"What's she going to do?" Roy said, amazed and interested.

"Oh, I think Stase will continue to function somewhere else when she folds it. I believe she has some idea of moving her personnel and equipment to sunnier precincts where the demand will be just as great and the service more appreciated. Fort Tragg in Carolina I believe she mentioned as a likely spot. As I understand it, that's to be a training center for the parachute troops. No hurry though—"

Capshaw looked at him with an amused grunt. "We'll all have plenty of time to say good-by to Anastasia."

"That's good. At least I've got that to cling to. Tell me, is there, for Christ's sake, anybody going to be left around here? I suppose Chris has joined up too?"

"As a matter of fact, no," Capshaw said. "He tried though. Both at the induction center and then at the Red Cross. Neither one of them would take him. Seems that old Chris, aside from being fifty-eight years old, has got a mild diabetes. Old Chris tried though."

Capshaw, pretty well along now with the bourbon, yelled over at Chris, standing with his newspaper at the bar:

"Didn't you try, Chris?"

"Didn't I try what, Mr. Capshaw?"

"Didn't you try for the Greek Olympic sex team in 1940?"

"Oh yes," Chris said gravely, "yes, I did. The Greeks were eliminated early by the Americans of course." Chris went back to reading his newspaper.

"That Chris," Capshaw said, turning back to Roy. "Every American ought to be like him."

There was an interval now in which Roy and Capshaw drank reflectively.

"Cappy, let me ask you something."

"Sure, Doc."

"You're going too, aren't you?"

Capshaw looked at him for a moment and slowly nodded. "Yeah. But not in any Goddamned soldier suit. And when the right time comes."

"Why, Cappy? Why are you going? When?"

"It's a long story, Doc, about why, for me. About when I can tell you better. I'll go when the wagon comes. I don't know when that will be. But we all go when the wagon comes, my personal wagon that is. I'm hoping that it will be pretty quick. I've got things fixed for that just in case."

They finished another drink in silence.

"Cappy—"

"Yeah, Doc?"

"Do you think I ought to go? The way I've got it, I don't have to. I can stay out of it a lot of ways if I want to . . ."

Capshaw looked at Roy very hard for several moments. "You sure you want to talk about this? Right now, I mean, Doc? You're going to have a lot of time to think and talk about it."

"I've been thinking about it," Roy said. "Now I want to talk about it. And right now."

"All right, Doc. Let's talk about it right now."

"You think I ought to throw everything up with the Old Man here at the Charity and go?" Roy looked at Capshaw now and quite anxiously.

Capshaw sruveyed him seriously and then shook his head. "Doc, dear and good one, I can't answer that one for you.

That you'll have to answer yourself. Depends on how you feel. Like giving your consent to have your belly cut. I suppose, when you're awake, conscious, and maybe needing it, and can make the decision. That close enough? Understand me?"

"Yeah, I understand you," Roy said. "Pretty good analogy for me and I understand you."

"Fine," Capshaw said, "I think you do. You've got a choice in this Goddamned scheme. Just like I had. Now Roy, boy, whether you go or stay is strictly up to you. And you ought to think about it awhile before you make any move . . ." Capshaw paused and finished his drink.

"You've got plenty of time, Doc. You've got nothing but time. This is going to be a long war—a long, long war, just remember that. . . . Now"—Capshaw squared himself around in his seat and looked at Chris approaching with two cups of coffee—"that you'll have to determine with your private self, Doc. No hurry at all you know. It's got to be and it's going to be a very long war. . . . Another drink, Doc?"

Roy had another drink. And when the phone rang and Chris answered it and it was for Capshaw, Roy found himself a little glad. He was tired.

"Got something I'll have to tend to, Doc," Capshaw said.

"Get with it, Cappy," Roy said. "I'm exhausted from Tusculum. I'm going over to the Charity and go to bed."

"Call you later, Doc," Capshaw said, now intent on that last phone call.

"Do that, Cappy," Roy said.

He finished his beer, got his bag from Chris, and none too steadily carried it across Velle Street into the hospital and up to his room.

The Old Man's eyes went over Roy quizzically.

"Back way ahead of time aren't you, Roy? Didn't expect you for at least another week or so—"

"Yes, sir," Roy said, "I stayed as long as I could. But I found out this trip that my tolerance for the old home town has gotten pretty limited. Things aren't the same for me there any more."

"I know what you mean," the Old Man said. "It's happened to me at one time or another. Happens with places and persons too. You find that your attachments to them aren't there any more. You've lost something. Depressing isn't it?"

"Certainly is," Roy said feelingly.

"Well," the Old Man said, "I counted on giving you some more time and arranged for it. So what would you like to do with it?"

"Well, sir, if it's all right with you, I'd just as soon start working right now. In fact I'd like to."

The Old Man shook his head slowly. "That's easy. If you're sure to want to do that. There's plenty to be done."

"I'm sure," Roy said.

"All right. We'll remember you've still got some time coming and when you want it you can take it. Meantime the beds on K Ward are all yours, along with twenty beds on J. In other wards you'll be handling all of what was Wortle's end of the Service plus twenty beds of what was Santry's. Wilder and I will take the rest of what was his between us. The emergency-room call schedule will be the same as it was when you left—you'll be on for that every third night and every third weekend. Now, when do you want to start?"

"Now. Anytime," Roy said.

"Tomorrow morning?"

"Be fine, sir."

"All right. Tomorrow morning."

Roy got up to go.

"Incidentally," the Old Man said.

"Yes, sir?"

"Knox is still in the hospital. Be discharged in another day or two. Been asking when you'll be back. He's really your patient. Why don't you look in on him?"

"I'll do that, sir."

"Good," the Old Man said, "you do that. I was going to let him out in the next day or two—"

Probably Roy would not have gone to see Knox at that moment if he had known that Katy was there. But he did not know this and the floor nurse neglected to tell him. When he opened the door of 815 in response to Knox's reply to his knock, he found Knox and Katy seated across from each other with a hospital bed table between them. There were papers on it and Roy knew that he was interrupting something. Roy stood in the doorway embarrassedly.

"Hello, Pres, Katy—sorry—didn't know you were busy. Come back later."

"Hey, Doc," Knox said, waving him in, "come in, come in. We're all finished."

Roy stood hesitantly. He saw that Katy had her handkerchief in her hand and from the look of things had been crying into it.

"I'll make it later," Roy said.

"The hell you will," Knox said. "Goddamn it. Come on in, will you, Doc? We're all through here. Come, in, come in."

Knox's tone was genuinely friendly. Roy paused and then shut the door behind him.

"Kate and I were just winding up some mutual business," Knox said a little too brightly. "We're all done now, though, aren't we, Kate? Good to see you, Doc. The Old Man says he's discharging me pretty quick. Afraid I'd be gone without seeing you. How are things in the provinces—Tusculum's where you went, wasn't it? Your home town?"

"That's right," Roy said. "It's still Tusculum. Tusculum's always Tusculum."

Roy looked at Katy. She had evidently been doing no small amount of crying. Her thin face was now turned up at him, the eyes puffed and watery still through their dark lids.

"Well," Roy said self-consciously, "just got back and thought I'd drop in and say hello."

"Well sure," Knox said heartily, "you'd damned well better. And, boy, how I want to talk to you—about my Navy application, that is. My commission I've got, but I'll need a doctor's certificate saying when I can get on active service."

Knox looked at Katy, who was now quite composed. "Kate, why don't you excuse us for a while? I'd like to talk to the doc, man to man, about my disability."

"All right, Pres," Katy said stonily.

"Would you wait around though, please, Kate? And we can talk about things later? When the Doc and I get through here—"

"Of course, Pres," Katy said. She got out of her chair, went to the door and went out of it, closing it behind her.

"Now, Doc," Knox said when they were alone, "I tried to do this before. I'm going to try again, admitted that it's none of my business. But do everybody a favor will you, and go have a talk with Kate? Right now would be a good time. She's feeling like hell. Go buy her a drink or something, will you?"

The first few minutes between them were as awkward as any Roy had ever spent. They sat facing each other in a back booth of the Asterion, deserted at the moment except for Chris and two loungers at the bar. Katy's face, Roy noted, looked more thin and drawn than he had ever seen it. He saw, too, that that thin bacchante body of hers was slender now to the point of emaciation. . . . Chris came with the drinks.

"Just keep them coming, Chris," Roy said.

Chris nodded and returned to the bar.

"Well, Katy," Roy said, raising his glass, "here's to it—"

"Whatever that is," Katy said, picking up her own.

"Pres told me it would be all right with him if I bought you a drink," Roy said.

Katy gave him a brittle, tremulous smile. "He told you a good deal more than that, Roy."

"He's really a hell of a fellow. He really is."

"That's just the trouble. You don't have to tell me. I've never felt like such a bitch—"

"He's looked damned good all the way along through this thing. He's—"

Katy's mouth tightened and she set her glass down. "Now look, Roy, just stop it will you? Just stop all this John Alden, Miles Standish, Priscilla business. I feel bad enough as it is. And if you don't I'm going to get out of here right now—"

"Damn it, Katy—get off the muscle with me will you? I'm only trying to—"

"I know what you're trying to do"—she looked at him with suddenly tear-filled eyes—"and just quit that too, will you? Quit being noble with me, will you please?"

"I'm not trying to be noble, Kate."

"The hell you aren't. And so is Pres. And I must say you're both doing a great job of it. You're so Goddamned noble. I admit it. So just lay off now. And to begin with you can stop calling me Kate. I'm Katy to you and I always have been. So you either call me Katy, which is what you've always called me, or I'm going to get out of here."

Katy pushed her drink aside and started getting out of the booth. Roy reached across and grabbed the wrist of one of her frail, groping hands and held it. He turned to the bar, where Chris, with his two bar customers gone now, was ostensibly reading a newspaper.

"Chris, give me a check."

Chris was there almost at once. "I've got it on the book, Dr. Maines," Chris said distantly. "Want I should get you a taxi?"

"Yeah. Do that will you, Chris?" Roy said.

Outside of the Asterion in the cut of the January wind that

had begun to whistle down St. Marks Street, they waited, with Roy feeling the frailness of her against him. The cab came presently.

"I suppose you're going to come up with me," Katy said when it stopped at the entrance of the looming face of the apartment building.

"Well . . ." Roy said.

Katy suddenly disengaged the hand he had been holding.

"Suit yourself," she said, fumbling at the back-seat door handle, "but you and Pres should have decided who was going to be Chevalier du Bayard by this time."

Roy paid the cab and followed her into the marquee-lit frontage of the place. Then through the ornate lobby, up the elevator, to apartment 6D.

Outside the bedroom the late afternoon light was drawing rapidly away into the winter dusk. For sometime after the first wild ultimate of reunion they had lain together, spent, silent, and a little ashamed. Sated for the moment and suddenly conscious of their nakedness, Roy pulled the coverlet over them. Roy lay supine, arms crossed beneath his head, looking toward the window where the cleft of light between the drawn curtains was rapidly fading. Katy had not spoken since her sharp outcrying of incoherent words some time before. And Roy, conscious of the press of her body and breathing against him, thought she might be asleep. But Katy was not asleep. She was only in the short, half-somnolent limbo of the passion spent. Presently she stirred, kissed Roy on the neck, and raised herself on an elbow.

"Roy . . ."

"Yes, Katy."

"Nothing's changed has it? Nothing's really changed at all—"

"Not this way it hasn't, Kate."

"But"—Roy was aware of her face close to his—"but," she went on and there was a peculiar note of insistence in her voice, "I mean in any way. Nothing's changed for me at all. Has it for you? Has it, Roy?"

"Not this way. I just said that, Katy."

"But I mean in any way, Roy. Not just this."

"I don't know, Katy. Haven't been thinking about it. I haven't been thinking about much of anything except what we've been doing while we've been lying here."

"Well, think about it, about us, I mean, when we're not like this."

"All right, Katy," Roy said. "I'll think about that."

There was a pause in which Roy felt her lips fully on his neck, then on his ear, and then on his cheek.

"I mean think about it now," she said, continuing to nibble at him, "and tell me about it now."

"Katy, for Christ's sake, tell you what?"

Katy desisted from kissing him on his face and neck.

"You haven't told me that you love me. We've done all this and you haven't said that. I let you and you didn't say it."

"All right, I love you, Katy."

Roy was conscious that now with her head on her raised elbow she was peering intently at him through the complete gloom.

"You mean this way?"

"Certainly, I mean this way," Roy said.

"I want to know about the other way."

"What other way is that, Katy?"

"I mean about us when we aren't this way—about our living together and being together and having things together that haven't got anything to do with sex. What about that?"

"I don't know about that," Roy said, "never having had it. I can't say. I can only imagine it."

"Well, imagine it then." Katy's voice took on a certain tone of feminine petulance. "Can't you imagine it with me?"

"Yes," Roy said, "I can imagine it with you."

"Well then, tell me about it." She began nibbling at his ear again. "We'll have to get married for that, won't we? And we can now, can't we, now that everything's settled between Pres and me? You don't have to go to any stupid war. You can stay right here like you told me and we could—"

It was just at this point that what had been fomenting in Roy's head came to the surface and in sufficient concentration that he said precisely what was in his mind.

"Get up, Katy," he said. "Get up and turn on the lights."

"But what on earth for, Roy?"

"Because I tell you to."

"Well, all right, Roy." She moved about in the darkness and presently the bedside light came on.

"Whatever is the matter, Roy?" she sat now, naked, on the bed beside him.

"Listen to me, Katy," Roy said, and his tone almost froze her as she sat looking at him.

"I'm going to this war. Any way, anyhow I can. But I'm going. Why, you wouldn't give a damn about. Neither will anyone else probably. Because it's something that couldn't possibly make any difference to anyone except to me.

"And I'm not going to marry you now or before I go, Katy. I'm not going to do that. And I'll tell you exactly why. You just divorced a real good guy, Katy. By any standards he's a good one. Better you should have stayed with him. But you haven't, or we wouldn't be here like this." Roy's throat was now very dry. "Now you just listen to this about me," he went on inexorably. "It is my misfortune to happen to love you. But not enough, under these circumstances, to marry you—in view of you and a guy like Pres Knox." Roy paused.

"Right now he's a better man than you're a woman. I'm not going to marry you, Katy—until I get back from whatever it is I'll be getting into. Just understand that, Katy. That could be a very long time or not at all."

Roy started to get out of bed. Katy's arms around him stopped it. And then like a man at a chance fountain he drank and drank until he had no more thirst for her at all.

20

Roy, to his surprise and satisfaction, assumed the exotic trappings of full attending surgeon with a good deal more ease than he had anticipated. The additional paper work as a chief of section and the rest of it were not as difficult as he had imagined, but it all took time. And for a while he was almost completely preoccupied. His frequenting of the Asterion was cut down considerably. During one of his hurried impromptu excursions there he suddenly realized that he had not seen Capshaw for some time.

"Chris, just happened to think—where's Cappy? Haven't seen him around—"

"Went to Washington, Doc, for a week. Some kind of special assignment. Ought to be back anytime now—"

"Good," Roy said, "be just like him to take off without saying good-bye."

Chris shook his head with slow emphasis. "He wouldn't do anything like that, Doc. Said he was going down for some kind of papers and would be back. He wouldn't leave here for good without saying good-by to you and me."

Chris was right. Two days later, Roy got a call and found him as usual in the back booth of the Asterion.

"Well," Roy said, "what do you mean running out on everybody like that Cappy?"

"Official business," Capshaw said. "These days I'm official as all hell. I am now an official, accredited, 100 per cent, accept no substitute, war correspondent for that great organ of democracy the *Record*. Had to stick around in Washington getting what is known in the language of the drama as 'the papers.' But now I've got them by the grace of God, and J. Abbott Pelly's central connections."

Capshaw raised his glass.

"Hugh Martin Capshaw, at your service, general—cleared, booed, screwed, and tattooed by the bureaucracy for instant action, wherever the national crisis may require, as stated in my letters of marque to all and sundry. Got everything but my uniform."

"I didn't know correspondents wore uniforms," Roy said. "What's it like?"

"Ah," Capshaw said, "that's one of the beauties of being a war correspondent—there isn't any official uniform. What you wear is up to you, as long as your papers are in order. I've got some ideas about mine. At the moment I'm torn between adopting as my personal garb, an ensemble of a bolero jacket, gilt jock strap, and purple sneakers, or something more exotic like lace pants and a chromium-plated hat. I need something like that to distinguish me at the forefront of the coming battles. Big morale factor for the troops."

"How are things in Washington?" Roy said.

"Turmoil is the word for it," Capshaw said. "The mountain is laboring and bringing forth one Goddamned mouse after another. One good thing though, it looks like we've finally come to the fact that we've got a war to fight. Those sons-of-bitches down there are riding off in all directions about it just now, but at least they're doing some trying."

Capshaw gave him a baroque account of it that kept Roy chuckling. Then suddenly Capshaw became serious.

"I found out something down there while I was drunk at the Press Club with Milt Purline that might interest you though, Doc. Milt's public relations with the Army. Might interest you, it's about the Army Medical Corps."

"That so?" Roy gave him a long look. "What was that Cappy?"

"Well," Capshaw said, "it's strictly a volunteer proposition for carefully screened medical personnel. They're going to form up small, well-trained medical units to work very close up where the shooting is going on. Called Auxiliary Surgical Units. Idea is to give definitive medical care to the combat boys as soon as possible after they get hit, and not have them die waiting till they can be taken back to a base hospital like they did in '16, '17 and '18. Sounds as if it might be a good idea."

"Sounds like it, Cappy," Roy said.

"Yeah," Capshaw said, "sounded like that to me. Hard for me to judge about it, just being a layman, of course. But I thought about you, Doc, though, when I heard about it. Kind of sounded like something that would be right up your alley. Just about your dish, if you were interested."

"Look, Cappy," Roy said, "I'm all set war or no war. Right here at the Charity with the Old Man."

"Why sure," Cappy said, "I know that. And as attending surgeon too. Reason I mention it is for kid doctors, interns, who might want to see some action right away instead of sitting around in an M.D.R.P."

"What's that?" Roy said.

"M.D.R.P. means Medical Doctors' Replacement Pool where service-inducted doctors sit around waiting till they're wanted after they've been inducted."

"Who the hell would want that?" Roy said feelingly.

"Nobody," Capshaw said, "but there are a lot of you docs who are going to have to do that."

"Look, Cappy," Roy said guiltily, but accurately, "as of right now and even a month back I'm exempt from any kind of service. I'm essential, understand? Just like the Old Man."

"Sure you are." Capshaw nodded. "I'm not talking necessarily about you. You're all set. I'm talking about guys who have got to go or feel that they have to. I can save them a hell of a lot of red tape."

"You can?" Roy said, "how's that?"

"Well," Capshaw said, "this would be for the Auxiliary Surgical Unit thing that I was telling you about. Guys, docs that is, who were interested in that—"

Capshaw pulled a card from his battered wallet and passed it to Roy.

"This is the guy to contact direct—Colonel John A. Mercio, suite 818 at the Pentagon."

Roy looked at the card and passed it back.

"That's all right," Capshaw said, "go ahead and keep it."

Roy held the card in his hand, stared at it, and then at Capshaw. "You're really giving me this because you think I might be using it myself. Isn't that right, Cappy?"

Capshaw smiled slowly and slightly. "Just a hunch, Doc."

"What makes you think so? You know I'm all set here with the Old Man."

"For the moment maybe."

"Hell," Roy said, "for the duration."

"No, Doc. No, you're not."

"No? Why not?"

"Because you'll never be able to stand it. A lot of other guys could, can, and no doubt will. But not you, Doctor. You're not built that way."

"How's that Cappy?"

"You're fundamentally a ball carrier, Doc, and not a bleacher spectator. It's almost impossible for you to stand by and watch any action without sweating to get in it. That's one thing. Another thing, you're hag-ridden by a sense of responsibility, and like all guys who are, you've also got one hell of a guilt sense that you've got to keep square with your ego, no matter what. That's because you've a big solid chunk of ego —a hell of a chunk of it. The kind that won't let you alone unless you're in there holding it up the way it thinks you ought to be. And that's by looking as good or better than the next guy—at least to yourself—"

"I can do that by staying right here and doing the job with the Old Man."

"Sure you can, but you won't, Doc. And another reason why you won't is because like most guys with that kind of ego—you've got a lot of self-curiosity—always probing around to see what makes yourself tick and wondering how you'll react or if you'll react right in the critical corners with the old steel or without it—"

"I know pretty well about the steel end of things," Roy said.

"Sure you do," Capshaw said, "about one end of it. That's the end you've got in your hand, the handle of the knife. You know exactly how you react with that. But what worries you,

Doc, is how you might act when you're on the other end, under the blade yourself so to speak. You haven't ever really had that experience yet, have you, Doc? And not having had it, you really would give a lot to know about that —if the steel you hope you've got inside you is as good as the steel in your knife hand. That right, Doc?"

"*Cognosce Te Ipsum*," Roy said.

"Yeah," Capshaw said, "*Cognosce Te Ipsum*. Know thyself. The Aurelian imperative. You want to know about that. Marcus Aurelius learned about it fighting a war. And so, I think, will you. That's something that's going to put you in the soldier suit if nothing else."

Roy looked at Capshaw intently. "Capshaw, how the hell is it you know so Goddamned much?"

"About what? About you, you mean?"

"Yes, among other things, about me?"

Capshaw chuckled. "It won't do your ego any good to hear it, Doc. May be a great blow, in fact."

"Let's hear it."

"All right, I'll tell you. The answer's real easy. We were not born out of the same womb, Doctor. But we could have been —we are one hell of a lot alike."

Roy looked at Capshaw and said slowly and seriously, "I consider that a damned fine compliment Cappy—a really good one."

"I'm glad you do, Doc. It's about the best thing I've ever said about myself. . . . Come on we'll drink to that."

Aunt Madge's letters were always lengthy and filled with Tusculum trivia. This one, written in her precise and slightly tremulous hand, was no exception. But this one, because of the enclosure, left Roy saddened and not a little shaken. The enclosure was an item cut from the Tusculum *Globe-Courier* dated three days prior to the letter's postmark. The excerpt, taken apparently from an official communication, was under one of the *Globe's* larger headlines, DEAD IN TRAINING FLIGHT MISHAP.

First Lieutenant Tipton A. Carnes, recently returned to active duty with the Air Force at Ordman Air Force Base, has been reported as a fatality in a training flight crash. Lieutenant Carnes, formerly a volunteer pilot officer with the famed Lafayette Escadrille of the R.A.F., was instantly killed during a routine instruction flight. . . . Funeral arrangements and burial with full military honors are pending on further notification from A.A.F. sources.

Roy read the *Globe's* padded version of the official release. The actual details of the accident were, in accordance with Armed Services press policy, not given. Instead there was a somewhat panegyric exposition of Lieutenant Carnes past glory as a volunteer with the R.A.F. with emphasis on the lieutenant's participation in the Battle of Britain.

Roy read the clipping again. And, as he did, his whole interim with Tip at the Chief High Knife Saloon during the judge's post-mortem reception came fully back to him.

"Old Tip," he thought, remembering the sad honesty, the sad kind of gallantry, and particularly the sad aura and aroma of death about him, as they had sat there talking and drinking, drinking and talking. "I wonder how he knew it was coming? That business about '*Cognosce Te Ipsum.*' I wonder if he ever got that settled with himself? I wonder if he ever squared off what the hell it was that was gnawing his good honest guts? I wonder if he ever got to do that before he got chopped out? And I wonder how that happened and how he felt about it when it did? Too bad you can't speak with the dead. I'd like to be drunk with him right now, *post factum,* and hear how he felt when it happened and what he did. But I won't know that from Tip. If I ever find out about it, it will have to be when I'm in the same spot. I know what it is for other people from cutting them, but what would it be like for me? Tip was someone who could have told me. But Tip's gone. I wonder how the hell it was with Tip though when it came."

Roy was right about this. Nobody would know how Tip Carnes died except Tip himself. And it had come upon him, as death usually does, unexpectedly, suddenly, while he was doing something utterly familiar. And Combat Tactics Instructor Lieutenant Carnes, ex-R.A.F. and Lafayette Escadrille, was performing the familiar at Ordman Field, and had been doing so for several weeks. But what had happened in the matter of his exodus was relatively simple. It was due to mechanical failure in a badly, better to say, a hastily serviced training ship. If Lieutenant Carnes had survived to say how it happened, his account of it would have had a particular and searching interest for Roy. This was because Lieutenant Tipton Carnes finally learned all there was to know about "*Cognosce Te Ipsum.*" And he learned it flying an airplane with Dr. Thomas Wilder's son.

"All right, hot shot," Cadet Wilder's instructor had said as they walked toward their plane, "we've drawn that God-damned No. T-24 again. And I hope to Christ they've serviced her into better shape than she was a couple of days ago. If they haven't we can start bailing out before we ever get off the ground. Personally, I'd rather have us go up in a box kite. Now, this baby's got a real tricky stick so don't lean on it in any direction very hard. Let your feet mostly do the work when you're flying her level or bringing her out of anything. Don't feed in on the throttle too fast climbing or turning because if you do she'll cut out. She's a nose-heavy bitch, and if she does stall she'll drop like a lead kite. Now, you checked your chute? Here, let's see—O.K. Fine. Let's see—your name's"—the lieutenant looked at the stenciled name tag on the chest pocket of the cadet's jumper—"Wilder. O.K. Allen Wilder. Mine's Carnes."

"Yes, sir, Lieutenant," Cadet Wilder said.

"Carnes will be all right, or Tip if you want to. I'll call you Al. Allen Wilder it says there."

"Yes, sir, Tip."

"Good. Let's go Al boy. Now just take her up real easy to six thousand, level off, and then start doing what I tell you. I hear you're a pretty hot kid. That's the word around. Are you?"

"Well"—Cadet Wilder was so pleased to get this and a first-name basis from a senior combat instructor that he was almost inarticulate—"well, thank you, sir—Tip, I mean. I know who you are, everyone around here does. I'm sure glad to get the chance—"

"Come on, eagle," Carnes said, very pleased himself. "Let's get in there and show them how a couple of men can handle things. Now just remember, buster, do what I say and only what I say. Don't do it and I'll cut you off like Delilah cut Samson."

They crossed the strip and climbed up into the idling plane, Cadet Wilder in front and Carnes in the rear instructor's seat. The cowling slid over them.

"What a Goddamned tub," Carnes thought as he automatically checked out the instrument panel before him. "O.K., say when," he said into his intercom. He threw the controls into neutral.

The voice came back to him.

"Take her, boy," Carnes said.

There was the right full pull and then the lift. Seconds later they were air-borne.

Some minutes later they were at 20,000 feet with the oxygen on. Below them Ordman Field was now a minute, precise-looking rectangle no larger than a postage stamp.

Carnes flipped on the out button of the transmitter.

"Training flight twelve, ship T-twenty-four to field."

"Field to training flight twelve," the acknowledgment crackled back at him, "reading you."

"Checking out for individual maneuvers general direction and bearing due east, altitude variation 5000 to 25,000 feet. Clear?"

"Clear, flight twelve. Signal approach when finished."

"Will signal." Carnes flipped down the switch and spoke into the intercom to Cadet Wilder:

"All right, buster, we're clear. Take her to twenty thousand and then level off and start doing what I tell you to. Nothing smart now. Just what I say and nice and easy, O.K.?"

"O.K."

For the next thirty minutes Carnes sat monitoring Cadet Wilder's execution of some increasingly elaborate ordered maneuvers. During these Carnes hardly had to touch the stick or the rudder pedals. This kid was good, Carnes noted—had instinctively gotten the feel of things and was doing them about right. They finished the prescribed routine with a little time to spare.

"O.K., buster, pretty fair. Now give me a ride. Take her for anything you want to for a couple of minutes. Let's see what you think you can do."

"Yes, sir," the voice came back to him.

The ship shuddered with the vibration of full throttle and went into a high climbing power turn, up, up.

"He's going to spin her on the prop and bring her out with a full power dive and a tree-top pull-out," Carnes thought. "We're a little low for that. Well . . ." Carnes levered in his own controls just in case.

The ship shuddered again. The engine began the typical moaning sound of an impending stall, then almost immediately misfired several times and went dead. Carnes felt her wing over and drop off and begin the stonelike drop. Down, down. Carnes let it go on for several seconds. The kid got her nose down all right and they started an almost vertical descent. The vague, distant patchwork of the ground was becoming rapidly and progressively larger. Carnes felt the familiar pressure crack in his ears and with this a certain peculiar uneasiness. The kid was probably going to hold her down too long.

"O.K., buster, power on about now and then start easing her out."

No reaction.

"Power on, ease her out, Goddamn it."

"I'm trying to, sir." There was a note of consternation in the voice coming back.

"O.K. Neutral position. Hands and feet off everything. I'll take her."

"Yes, sir, all neutral."

Carnes threw in the power switch on his own panel and advanced the throttle. Nothing happened, the expected cut in roar of the engine did not come. Carnes tried again. Nothing. They had begun a series of wing overs. The horizon was now whirling from one dimension to another and the momentary flash of the earth was becoming plainer too fast. More than this, the ship was not responding to Carnes corrective motions with the stick.

"Trouble," flashed into Carnes's head. Then a split second later, "Real trouble. Goddamn it. Why can't I bring that right wing up?"

Down. Down. Now with the muffled whine of the descent increasing to a continuous snuffling moan, the altimeter was inexorably dropping, passing 12,000 feet.

"Christ," Carnes thought, "what's the matter with the fornicating tub? A couple of more minutes of this and . . ."

But the descent came faster than that. Carnes saw in the next few split seconds that he probably wasn't going to be able to pull her out.

"Check your chute, buster. We may have to bail out of this one . . ."

A moment later there was no doubt about it.

"Yes, sir."

"Impossible unless she's steadier than she is now." Carnes's thinking now was automatic. "I can't level her out enough."

Altimeter now at 6000 feet.

"Cowling coming back. When it's open enough jump, buster."

Carnes pressed the button for the power drawback of the cowling over them. Nothing. He began a frantic turning of the emergency hand crank. The cowling began to slide back, and with it the roar of air was instantly upon them.

"Out," Carnes screamed, "out."

He saw the figure of Wilder ahead struggling against the air, in his bulky harness, to get over the side of the cockpit, and then stop in some kind of frantic fumbling with his straps to free himself. In this frozen instant, with every bell of his body's alarm system ringing, Carnes heard the age-old primordial voice that every man hears when the time comes:

"Out. Out yourself. Now—now. It's you now, you. Forget anything else."

Carnes knew that voice well. He had heard it before and heeded it at least on one occasion on August 8 in what was now being called "The Battle of Britain," "The Blitz." He had run when he should have stayed, leaving a sad Irishman by the name of Finucane alone to face those murderous cross-marked things—Finucane alone in a Spitfire with a missing engine.

"You or him," the voice said inexorably, in that flash of time that was no time at all. "You or this kid. Now you've got approximately ten seconds. You are now at thirty-five hundred feet. You can keep it level as you can for him to get out. Or you can go now yourself and maybe make it. Not both though, Lieutenant Carnes. Not both. He makes it or you do. Which is it? Which is it to be, Lieutenant Carnes? This kid or you? You and your eighty completed missions and your George Flying Cross?"

Carnes made his last decision in that moment. He wrenched the stick as far to the left as he could and held it long enough to see Wilder finally free himself and fall out over the side into the lessening space left between the falling plane and the earth, where the landmarks were now extremely plain, as they always were at fifteen hundred feet.

"Good," the voice said a little more softly, as Carnes saw Cadet Wilder's parachute billow, "he's going to make it. Just barely, but he will. Now you can wear your George Medal if you want to. Isn't that nice? It doesn't belong to Finucane any more—it belongs to you personally, to you Lieutenant Carnes."

Altimeter now less than five hundred feet with the ship's nose down at an angle of forty-five degrees and at probably four hundred miles an hour.

"Now, Lieutenant Carnes," the voice in Carnes's head said hurriedly, "about 'Cognosce Te Ipsum,' 'Know thyself.' Do you think you know now?"

There was an instant in which Carnes possibly may have pondered this. But it was gone in the crash and flash that Pilot Training Plane No. T-24 made as it struck with incredible force, ploughed up a great spout of earth, instantly exploded, and began to burn.

There was in the same mail as Aunt Madge's letter another communique from Tusculum. That was one from Luke Mandeville. The tone of it was querulous and insistent.

". . . that you did not at least take the time to call me before you left Tusculum, in view of our unfinished conversation.

"However, I hope you will have the good sense to give the proposition you have got all set for you here in your own home town, your immediate and earnest consideration. If you will do that, Roy, you cannot help but realize that your future cannot be better assured . . . and please write or call me at once, as I have already told the Hospital Board that it is only a question of time until you would be coming on the staff . . ."

Roy put the letters from Aunt Madge and Luke Mandeville in the top drawer of the battered desk of his room at the Charity. He honestly intended to answer both of them immediately. He did not. In the press of his subsequent circumstances, neither of them got any answer at all.

The Old Man listened to Roy's words with a set and stony face.

". . . and I thought I could, sir, at the time when you offered me the job and I took it. I thought it was the greatest thing that ever happened to me, and I still do. Because it is. But I know now that I'm not ready for it—"

"I'm the judge of that," the Old Man's voice rasped at him. "You're ready for it or I wouldn't have put you where you are."

"I meant it in the sense, Dr. Hand, that I thought that I had it pretty well squared with myself, rationalized that is, about not going into the service. I meant ready in that way."

"I was including that aspect of things when I made your appointment, Doctor. I thought our understanding—your understanding particularly, was sufficient for that. Apparently I could not have been more wrong."

The Old Man's eyes were now regarding him icily. And Roy felt himself quailing under them. The Old Man he saw at this moment was disappointed, frustrated, and not a little irate. And not without reason either, Roy thought despairingly. But there was no other way and Roy went on with it in quiet desperation.

"I'm sorry, sir," he said lamely. "I wish—"

"We can dispense with your wishes, Maines." The Old Man's voice was even more harsh than before. "What is of importance to me, and what is left of the Surgical Service of the Charity Hospital, are your firm intentions. The ones you intend to act on now. That is if you have any. Not the kind you have led me to believe you have to date . . ."

Roy had always known that the Old Man was capable of this kind of cruelty, particularly when he was thwarted. He had seen it exercised against others with devastating effect. It had seldom, if ever, been directed against Roy himself. But now it was, and Roy, wincing under it and with his own anger beginning to stir in him, met it and went doggedly on.

"I don't think that's quite fair, sir. About my intentions. I thought I knew what they were then, when I took the job, or I wouldn't have accepted it."

"You weren't sure," the Old Man's voice was almost a snarl. "Why did you take it? Do you realize how this has disrupted things on the Service? Now, just what are your intentions as of right now—your real ones I mean. Do you think you can give them to me now?"

Roy strangely and suddenly felt himself become very calm. "Yes, sir. I can now. I am going to enlist as soon as I can. That's what I intend to do."

"They'll probably have you in a Goddamned dispensary somewhere Stateside," the Old Man growled almost to himself, "peddling out pills for colds and clap. If that's what you want when you could be here doing a right job—that's what happens to would-be heroes—in the Medical Corps anyway."

Roy, angry himsef now, even if it were the Old Man, could

not resist the implication. "Is that what happened to you, sir, in the first one?"

The Old Man who was about to say something, paused, and looked at Roy with something like surprise.

"No, it didn't. But it was only by chance that it didn't. There were plenty of men around as good or better than I was in the Medical Corps that it did happen to who would have been a hell of a lot better off and the country would have been a hell of a lot better off, if they'd just done their jobs at home," the Old Man said a little uneasily.

"But you didn't do that did you, sir? You took your chances didn't you?" Roy knew now that he had hold of something that few men had ever gotten their hands on. He had a hold of the Old Man's secret emotional tail, probably one of his several secret emotional tails that he always sat on or kept otherwise carefully hidden. And knowing that he had hold of it, Roy proceeded to give it some twisting.

"You got overseas didn't you, sir? It says in 'Who's Who' you went through three campaigns, Argonne, Chateau Thierry, and Soissons, and were decorated for—"

"That hasn't got one good Goddamned thing to do with what we're talking about, Maines." The Old Man's voice had an irritable and almost childsh tremor to it. "Nothing whatever, circumstances were different then. Everything was different. Now so far as you are concerned"—the Old Man's eyes flashed around the room and back at him—"you'd better do a lot of thinking before you do anything stupid like volunteering for the service when you don't know anything about it."

"I'm going to have to, sir," Roy said.

"You don't have to do anything," the Old Man said irritably. "You've got a choice. Now you think it over and try to make it a wise one."

"Yes, sir," Roy said. "But, as I said, I've already made it."

Roy left the Old Man at his desk, as disgruntled as he had ever seen him.

For a while after Roy had left, the Old Man sat at his desk, quietly fuming and looking out of the window as he fumed. After some minutes of it he turned abruptly and flipped on the intercom on his desk.

"Bertha, get Tom Wilder on the phone and tell him to get over here as soon as he can. It's important that I talk to him."

"Yes, Dr. Hand," Bertha said.

By the time Wilder got there the Old Man had recovered most of his iron-clad composure, enough of it anyway to present to Wilder his usual front of the calm that was naturally expected of him.

"Tom," the Old Man said after Wilder was seated before him, "I've just gotten some unfortunate news from Roy Maines. He's decided that he's going into the service."

Wilder looked at him thoughtfully for a moment before he spoke. "Well, Amos, I suppose it's natural that he should perhaps want to join up eventually and—"

"It is not, Goddamn it," the Old Man's voice came out of him hotly. "I made that young son-of-a-bitch attending surgeon on the Charity Hospital staff with an assumption on his part and his consent that he would have the good sense to stay with it, instead of acting like a Goddamned fool and running off and—"

"Going into the service," Wilder said. "That's it, isn't it, Amos?"

"That's it," the Old Man growled, "that's precisely it. Wortle gone. Santry gone. And now with Maines going, that leaves you and me to hold things up here. And that's physically impossible. And you know it. Two men can't cover it. Three yes, maybe and badly, but not two. Particularly—" the Old Man's voice broke off significantly.

"Particularly," Wilder finished for him, "when you've got somebody like me with angina holding up a big end of it."

"I wasn't saying that, Tom."

Wilder smiled at him faintly.

"Oh yes, you were, Amos. If you weren't saying it, that's what you meant. What you're saying is that now the Surgical Service of the Charity Hospital is going to have to be between you and me. And you don't like to have to say that. But you have to. Isn't that about the way things stand now?"

The Old Man looked at Wilder reflectively. "You know how things stand now with the Surgical Service as well as I do, Tom. The point is what can we do about it?"

"Every other hospital is having, or going to have, the personnel shortage, that we've got now."

"That doesn't help us any, does it?"

"No, but there is a solution to it. I mean of course taking doctors on the staff who are average or otherwise unfit for the Army—"

"And unfit for the Surgical Service here," the Old Man said. "I'll be damned if I'm going to compromise with the standard I've set for that—"

"Look, Amos. I know how you feel about that. But there are some good surgeons in this town who aren't going to war. They may not be board certified but they're still good surgeons. Good enough to do an adequate job if they got the chance. You know that as well as I do. And I can't think of one of them who wouldn't jump at the chance of coming on the staff part time, if only for the prestige—several of them have applied at one time or another—"

"And I rejected them because this is a closed staff and in my opinion they weren't qualified."

"I know." Wilder nodded. "But there wasn't a war on then. And there is now. And like it or not, Amos, just like anyone else, we're going to have to get help however and wherever we can get it. Besides, with you and me to oversee it, while it might not be ideal, I think we could get by."

There was no doubt about the reason in Wilder's words and the Old Man knew it. And after some further querulous protestations, the Old Man came around to a grudging acquiescence.

"All right, all right, Tom. I suppose there's no other way out —I guess we'll have to do it."

"I think so, Amos. There just isn't any other way."

"We wouldn't be in this bind if Roy Maines had any Goddamned gumption and would stay where he belongs—resigning and running off like this—"

"Now, Amos," Wilder said gently, "you can't be too hard on young Maines for doing that. You above all people can't censure a man for going into the service and doing his part in the war the way he thinks he has to do it. I seem to remember pretty well what you did in the first one when the circumstances were similar. Didn't old Charlie Horsely, who was superintendent here, tell you that if you quit your internship here at the Charity to join the Army he'd see that you didn't get any credit for the time you'd already put in? And didn't you say, 'You can go to hell, Horsely,' and leave a week later for Camp Willis? And then—"

"All right, all right"—the Old Man stirred in his chair irritably—"but things were a lot different then."

Wilder looked at the Old Man with amusement. "Yes,

Amos, it was longer ago than either of us likes to remember now and you weren't chief of the Surgical Service then."

After Wilder had left his office the Old Man sat for a while with his chair swiveled toward the window ruminating on the swarm and crawl of the Velle Street traffic below.

"Your own chickens always come home to roost," he chuckled mirthlessly to himself. "History is repetitious. Tom Wilder is right. I can't blame Roy Maines for throwing things away here and going to war. I did the same thing. I suppose I ought to be grateful that he didn't tell me in so many words to go to hell, like I did with old Doc Horsely."

21

The Old Man was sitting at his desk looking out of the window, and as Roy came in he swung around to face him. Roy, never anything but self-conscious in his new uniform, felt even more so as the Old Man's pale eyes went over him.

"Well, well, Captain," the Old Man's voice twanged at him, "sit down, sit down." Roy pulled a chair up in front of the desk.

"I got my stand-by orders this morning, Dr. Hand, with a no-further-communications after 1 P.M. I didn't expect them this soon. I wanted to see you—"

The Old Man chuckled dryly. "Got your embarkation orders, did you? They're sending you out pretty fast."

"This movement is supposed to be highly secret," Roy said, "but I haven't found anyone yet who doesn't know about it."

"That's standard operative procedure with the military. Never changes. Same in 1917 when I did my stretch in it."

"Well, sir," Roy said, "it looks like I'm on my way. And I wanted to see you before I got on it."

"Glad you did, Roy," the Old Man said.

"I wanted to tell you, sir," Roy went on self-consciously, "a couple of things that I couldn't say before now—before this, that is. I've wanted to a lot of times, but you see, if I had, it would have sounded like I was trying to kiss in with you or something. Like I was trying to—"

The Old Man grunted and moved his elbows on his desk. "I don't think anyone would ever accuse you of being a kiss in, Roy. Any more than they accuse me of being susceptible to it."

"I guess that's true. But anyway, now I guess I can say whatever I want to——"

"I think that you could have done that anyhow, Roy."

"Yes, sir. And I mostly did, at least about the Service, the patients I mean, and the rest of it. But I never felt that I could thank you right for what you've done for me. At least up until now, when it doesn't make much difference what I say. I guess what I'm trying to say, I'm saying badly."

The Old Man rubbed his hand over his chin. "I think you're saying it pretty well, Roy. I don't think you have to go on with it. I know what you want to say."

"But I'd like to say it anyway. I'd just like to say it to you. It sounds queer, but I kind of feel somehow that, one way or another, wherever I'm going or going to do, it's going to be important to know that I told you."

"Well, all right, Roy." The Old Man's voice was gentler now than Roy had ever heard it.

"What I wanted to say first was to thank you for everything you've taught me in the operating room and out of it."

The Old Man nodded. "I think you've learned well, Roy. I don't think that I've taught you anything that you'll have to unlearn. I don't think that I've done that with anybody, much less you, my boy."

There was a high hard lump now in Roy's throat that he had to speak beyond. "No, sir," Roy said, "that was one thing I was trying to say. So I don't have to say it now. And I also wanted to tell you that I know that I've let you down. I know that I could do a better job here with you at the Charity—just doing what has to be done—for the war effort or whatever you want to call it—than I'll be doing in this Goddamned soldier suit. The trouble is that I haven't got enough guts for it. I haven't got enough to stay out of the suit, the war, and the rest of it when everybody else is in. I tried to, but I couldn't."

"Roy," the Old Man's eyes were a long way past his, "I understand that. I did about the same thing myself one time in 1917. I was hoping you'd have more perception than I had. Well, you don't. And I can hardly blame you for that, can I?" The Old Man pulled at his nose reflectively.

"Well, sir," Roy said, "I'd like also to say this, mostly because I always planned to, if the time ever came. And I guess this is it. So I guess I can say it. No matter what happens with me, I'll do what you said. I'll do the best I can as long as I can."

"That's good enough," the Old Man said. "You remember that and it will be all right with you no matter what happens."

The time now, Roy saw by his wrist watch, was ten minutes late for his leaving.

"I've got to go now, sir," Roy said. "My A.P.O. number is 98104, whatever that is."

The Old Man jotted it quickly on a pad. "I'll expect to hear from you, Roy."

Roy got up. "You will, sir, anywhere and anytime I can write."

The Old Man got out of his chair and came around the desk and put out his right hand. Roy took it. And then the Old Man put his left hand on Roy's shoulder and patted it.

"Good luck, my boy," the Old Man said. "You know where to come when you get back."

"Yes, sir, I do," Roy said. "Right back here."

"That's right, Roy, right back here. All of it is waiting for you. I don't think it'll change much."

For some seconds after Roy had gone out the door the Old Man sat in his chair, swiveled to the window, looking down on the teeming mass of St. Marks Street below. He was waiting he knew, for Roy's khaki-clad figure to come out of the main entrance. And as he waited, the Old Man, in the seconds of waiting, gradually became aware of an atmosphere that had been there in the room from the time that Roy had entered it. Alone now, the Old Man, first gradually, and now suddenly, realized it with a complete and overwhelming acuity. What the Old Man was feeling was a something that he had felt many times before over the long rows of bedded sick in the Charity. The sensation that the Old Man felt was more akin to odor than to either sight or sound. It is something beyond ordinary perception, except to those who are long familiar with death. It is the odor of death. It is an aura that can come at anytime before, during, or after the event. The Old Man felt or rather smelled it very, very strongly as he looked down into the street. It was the same odor that he had noted with Wild Will Wortle, and Wortle had recognized as emanating from himself. And the Old Man now knew why he did. Roy had brought it in with him. And it was still lingering there in the silence of the room.

The sad stench of it filled the Old Man's nostrils as he stood impassively watching for Roy's khaki-clad figure to emerge from the Charity's entrance. Presently it did. He watched the car turn into the sluggish traffic of Velle Street. And he thought of explosions that burst witlessly and kill good and sentient men. And he wondered where it would be for Roy. He turned from the window. . . .

And far below in his cab, Roy looked up at the hard grimy façade of the Charity Hospital as they pulled away.

"No matter what happens to me in this uniform, I'll try to remember everything that's ever happened to me in my life. Particularly the most important part. And that may be what happened here."